CW00971551

Edward Frederic Benson was b... Berkshire in 1867. He was one of an extraordinary family. His father Edward White Benson – first headmaster of Wellington – later became Bishop at Lincoln, at Truro, and Archbishop of Canterbury. His mother, Mary Sidgwick, was described by Gladstone as 'the cleverest woman in Europe'. Two children died young but the other four, bachelors all, achieved distinction: Arthur Christopher as Master of Magdalene College, Cambridge and a prolific author; Maggie as an amateur egyptologist; Robert Hugh as a Catholic priest and a propagandist novelist; and Fred.

Like his brothers and sisters, Fred was a precocious scribbler. He was still a student at Cambridge when he published his first book, *Sketches from Marlborough*. While he was working as an archaeologist in Athens, his first novel *Dodo* was published (1893) to great success. Thereafter Benson devoted himself to writing, playing sports, watching birds, and gadding about. He mixed with the best and brightest of his day: Margot Asquith, Marie Corelli, his mother's friend Ethel Smyth and many other notables found their eccentricities exposed in the shrewd, hilarious world of his fiction.

Around 1918, E.F. Benson moved to Rye, Sussex. He was inaugurated mayor of the town in 1934. There in his secret garden, his collie Taffy beside him, Benson wrote many of his comic novels, his sentimental fiction, ghost stories, informal biographies and reminiscences like *As We Were* (1930) – over one hundred books in all. Ten days before his death on 29 February 1940, E.F. Benson delivered to his publisher a last autobiography, *Final Edition*.

The Hogarth Press also publishes *Mrs Ames*, *Paying Guests*, *Secret Lives*, *As We Are*, *As We Were*, *Dodo – An Omnibus*, *The Freaks of Mayfair*, *The Luck of the Vails*, *The Blotting Book* and *An Autumn Sowing*.

DAVID BLAIZE

E.F. Benson

New Introduction by
Peter Burton

THE HOGARTH PRESS

LONDON

Published in 1989 by
The Hogarth Press
30 Bedford Square
London WC1B 3SG

First published in Great Britain by Hodder & Stoughton 1916
Copyright © The Executors of the Estate of the Revd K.S.P. McDowall
Introduction copyright © Peter Burton 1989

A CIP catalogue record for this book is available from the British Library

ISBN 0 7012 0796 5

Printed in Finland by
Werner Söderström Oy

INTRODUCTION

Although it is usually a mistake to describe any given work of fiction as being no more than thinly disguised autobiography, E. F. Benson's seductively entertaining public school romance *David Blaize* is actually enhanced by a comparison with the author's own experiences. However, Benson didn't simply transmute life into art: the evolution of fiction is rarely that straightforward.

Benson's close friend Somerset Maugham admitted in *The Summing Up* that he was 'almost inclined to say' that he 'could not spend an hour in anyone's company without getting the material to write at least a readable story about him'. Yet clearly Maugham was cunningly drawing the magician's veil over the imaginative processes that transform an anecdote from life into the stuff of fiction, in which the original impulse becomes an almost indistinguishable thread. Few novelists could honestly claim they had derived no inspiration from their own life, and Benson was no exception.

Edward Frederic Benson ('Fred' to family and friends) published *David Blaize* in 1916; *David Blaize and the Blue Door* (a whimsical tale for children with little connection to the earlier work except the hero's name) appeared in 1918; *David of King's*, a chronological sequel to the first book, followed in 1924. It is not too fanciful to compare characters and incidents from the first and third book with characters and incidents from Benson's own life.

Benson was born in 1867, a younger son in a curiously ambiguous family whose head eventually became Archbishop of Canterbury. Their mother was acknowledged by her children to have sapphic inclinations and, indeed, the archbishop himself had taken part during his university days in one of those nineteenth-century close emotional male friendships. A strain of at least intellectual homosexuality was intensely evident in all the surviving children – notably Arthur Christopher, an Eton housemaster and latterly Master of Magdalene College, Cambridge and author of a diary running to some five million words; and Robert Hugh, a convert to Catholicism (subsequently a priest), an historical novelist and sometime associate of Frederick Rolfe, Baron Corvo. Both brothers were of distinctly 'Uranian' bent and both suffered from the crippling depression which ultimately incapacitated their sister Maggie.

Benson was educated at Marlborough and King's College, Cambridge, and it is safe to assume that many of the experiences of these formative years went into *David Blaize* and *David of King's*. Public school romances have a long and fairly honourable tradition and Benson's David Blaize books followed in the wake of Thomas Hughes' *Tom Brown's Schooldays* (1857), his own brother A. C. Benson's *Memoirs of Arthur Hamilton, BA, of Trinity College, Cambridge* (published under the pseudonym 'Christopher Carr') and Horace Annesley Vachell's *The Hill*, and were succeeded by other well-known evocations of 'the hothouse world' of the public school such as Alec Waugh's *The Loom of Youth* and, more recently, Michael Campbell's *Lord Dismiss Us*, Simon Raven's *Fielding Gray* and Christopher Dilke's *The Rotten Apple*. *Maurice*, which E. M. Forster completed in 1914, although it was not published until 1971, fits easily into this category.

David Blaize opens at Helmsworth Preparatory School, probably loosely based on 'a private school presided over by Mr Ottiwell Waterfield, at Temple Grove, East Sheen', at which, Benson tells us in *Our Family Affairs*, he spent three years from 1878. As the book opens, the blond and seemingly angelic David is thirteen. The physical appearance assigned to the young hero suggests that he might be what in Eton parlance is known as a 'tart' – but his beauty is married to a native wit (entirely without malice) which allows him to get the better of his masters, and to an athletic prowess which adroitly removes any hint of softness. David's prep school days are briskly covered in the first third of the book, which introduces other characters who figure prominently both here and in *David of King's* – notably

Crabtree, known as 'Bags' because of 'the somewhat voluminous appearance of his new pair of trousers', a half-Jewish boy whose initial enmity is but a mask for adoration; and Hughes, object of David's hero worship, subsequently under a cloud because of behaviour categorised as 'filthy' and only redeemed after his entry into Sandhurst.

When sitting his entrance examinations for Marchester, David encounters Frank Maddox, three years his senior and already a hero. 'Oh, go on, tell me about Maddox,' David asks Hughes, who has preceded him to Marchester. 'I dare say you'll see him. Sure to, in fact. He's not very tall, but he's damned good-looking. He's far the finest bat in the eleven, and the funny thing is he says cricket's rather a waste of time, and hardly ever goes up to a net. He's editor of the school-paper, and played racquets for us at Queen's last year. But what he likes best of all is reading.' Clearly, an intellectual athlete was an alluring figure to Benson.

Though Helmsworth can easily be matched to Temple Grove and Marchester to Marlborough, it is less easy to determine the models for David and Maddox, the pivotal characters of *David Blaize* and *David of King's*, whose at first unequal relationship eventually turns into a passionate and adoring but almost entirely platonic romance. Maddox, who suffers a brief moment of carnal temptation, is cast as a knowing protector of a David who is but dimly aware of the kind of schoolboy sexuality which will be familiar to readers of more explicit novels and memoirs of the past two decades (T. C. Worsley's *Flannelled Fool*, for example).

As the fiftieth anniversary of Benson's death takes place in 1990, we can anticipate a spate of celebratory biographies, and doubtless even now scholars, critics and admirers are furiously researching the materials of his life in the hopes of proving this, disproving that and providing the models from life who made their way so memorably into fiction. That David's embarrassingly clerical father is based upon Benson's own father need not be questioned. That David himself is based upon his creator seems clear – and indicates that Benson was not without a strong measure of self-knowledge; like Benson, David applies himself only fitfully and is ever eager to escape the rigours of intellectual application for the pleasures of a sporting pursuit. But what of Maddox?

It is my contention that while David represents Benson's innocence, Maddox represents Benson's awareness; that, in effect, Benson used the duality of his own nature to create *both* his central characters – giving to either David or Maddox the components from his own personality which most suited them. Thus David's horror at his father's appearance and behaviour at the cricket match coincides with something similar from Benson's schooldays, while Maddox's time at the archaeological school in Athens neatly coincides with Benson's own Athens experiences.

That Benson moved in homosexual circles is well attested. In 1894 he was travelling in Egypt with Reggie Turner and Robert Hichens and encountered Lord Alfred Douglas. Before the First World War, Benson shared a holiday villa in Capri with Somerset Maugham, seven years his junior, and John Ellingham Brooks (probably Maugham's first male lover).

The long shadow of the Wilde scandal clearly affected the lives of both Benson and Maugham. Maugham, a cosmopolitan wishing to act upon his inclinations, exiled himself to a more tolerant France; Benson, quintessentially English, stayed put in his native land, behaved with circumspection and later served in public office, as Mayor of Rye. There is no evidence that he ever fulfilled his emotional leanings; in fact the number of spinsters of both sexes in his many books suggests that he was without carnal knowledge, a knowing innocent.

David Blaize is set somewhere between 1878 (if we take Benson's arrival at Temple Grove as a direct parallel) and the mid-1880s. Written at the height of the First World War, this novel (unlike the later *David of King's*) contains no echoes of contemporary events, though it may well have been influenced by them. In 1916 Benson was approaching fifty; not old age, certainly, but well into middle age and a time for reflection. The events of the 'war to end all wars' were propitious: almost certainly the slaughter of thousand upon thousand of young men triggered in him the impulse to write an elegiac reflection on more tranquil days – a time when beautiful young men bathed naked in rivers and streams, played cricket under clear blue skies and planned brilliant futures as yet unblemished by hideous conflicts and mutilations.

That he should set such a book in his own past and most especially during his own schooldays seems inevitable. Once he had decided to mine his adolescent experience for the novel, it would have become clear that he must use incidents and characters from his past as the skeleton and flesh of his story. As the Bensons were almost pathological chroniclers of their family's life – Fred obsessively so – it is possible to trace in the later autobiographical books many of the incidents which were transmuted into his fiction. Anyone with access to a copy of *Our Family Affairs* can derive much harmless pleasure from the comparison of the factual and the fictional versions of events.

Yet the question remains: how well has *David Blaize* stood the test of time? Perhaps the sentiment might not be quite to modern tastes, perhaps the humour may seem quaint – but here is Benson at his most readable, effortlessly spinning an enchanted and enchanting web. To my mind – to use an appropriately Blaizian adjective – *David Blaize* is a very *jolly* read.

Peter Burton, Brighton 1988

CHAPTER I

THERE was a new class-room in course of construction
for the first form at Helmsworth Preparatory School,
and the ten senior boys, whose united ages amounted to
some hundred and thirty years, were taken for the time
being in the school museum. This was a big boarded
room, covered with corrugated iron and built out somewhat separate from the other class-rooms at the corner
of the cricket-field. The arrangement had many advantages from the point of view of the boys, for the room
was full of agreeably distracting and interesting objects,
and Cicero almost ceased to be tedious, even when he
wrote about friendship, if, when you were construing,
you could meditate on the skeleton of a kangaroo which
stood immediately in front of you, and refresh yourself
with the sight of the stuffed seal on whose nose the
short-sighted Ferrers Major had balanced his spectacles
before Mr. Dutton came in. Or, again, it was agreeable
to speculate on the number of buns a mammoth might
be able to put simultaneously into his mouth, seeing
that a huge yellowish object that stood on the top of
one of the cases was just one of his teeth. . . .

Of course it depended on how many teeth a mammoth
had, but the number of a boy's teeth might be some
guide, and David, in the throes of grinding out the
weekly letter to his father, passed his tongue round his
own teeth, trying to count them by the sensory quality
of it. But, losing count, he put an inky forefinger

into his mouth instead. There seemed to be fourteen in his lower jaw and thirteen and a half in the upper, for half of a front tooth had been missing ever since, a few weeks ago, he had fallen out of a tree on to his face, and the most industrious scrutiny of that fatal spot had never resulted in his finding it. In any case, then, he had twenty-seven and a half teeth, and it was reasonable to suppose that a mammoth, therefore, unless he had fallen out of a tree (if there were such in the glacial age) had at least twenty-eight. That huge yellow lump of a thing, then, as big as David's whole head, was only one twenty-eighth of his chewing apparatus. Why, an entire bun could stick to it and be unobserved. A mammoth could have twenty-eight buns in his mouth and really remain unaware of the fact. Fancy having a bun on every tooth and not knowing! How much ought a mammoth's pocket-money to be if you had to provide on this scale? And when would its mouth be really full? And how . . . David was growing a little sleepy.

" Blaize ! " said Mr. Dutton's voice.

David sucked his finger.

" Yes, sir ! " he said.

" Have you finished your letter home ? "

" No, sir," said David, with engaging candour.

" Then I would suggest that you ceased trying to clean your finger and get on with it."

" Rather, sir ! " said David.

The boys' desks, transferred from their old class-room, stood in a three-sided square in the centre of the museum, while Mr. Dutton's table, with his desk on it, was in the window. The door of the museum was open, so too was the window by the master's seat, for the hour was between four and five of the afternoon and the afternoon that of a sweltering July Sunday. Mr. Dutton himself was a tall and ineffective young man, entirely undistinguished for either physical or mental powers, who had taken a somewhat moderate degree at Cambridge, and had played lacrosse. By virtue of the mediocrity of his attainments, his scholastic career had not risen to the heights of a public school, and he had been obliged to be content with a mastership at this preparatory establishment. He bullied in a rather feeble manner the boys under his charge, and drew in his horns if they showed signs of not being afraid of him. But in these cases he took it out of them by sending in the gloomiest reports of their conduct and progress at the end of term, to the fierce and tremendous clergyman who was the head of the place. The Head inspired universal terror both among his assistant masters and his pupils, but he inspired also a whole-hearted admiration. He did not take more than half a dozen classes during the week, but he was liable to descend on any form without a moment's notice like a bolt from the blue. He used the cane with remarkable energy, and preached lamb-like sermons in the school chapel on Sunday. The boys, who were experienced augurs on such subjects, knew all about this, and dreaded a notably lamb-like sermon as presaging trouble on Monday. In fact, Mr. Acland had his notions about discipline, and completely lived up to them in his conduct.

Having told Blaize to get on with his home-letter, Mr. Dutton resumed his employment, which was not what it seemed. On his desk, it is true, was a large Prayer-book, for he had been hearing the boys their Catechism, in the matter of which Blaize had proved himself wonderfully ignorant, and had been condemned to write out his duty towards his neighbour (who had very agreeably attempted to prompt him) three times,

and show it up before morning school on Monday.
There was a Bible there also, out of which, when the
Sunday letters home were finished, Mr. Dutton would
read a chapter about the second missionary journey of
St. Paul, and then ask questions. But while these
letters were being written Mr. Dutton was not Sabbati-
cally employed, for nestling between his books was a
yellow-backed volume of stories by Guy de Maupassant.
. . . Mr. Dutton found him most entertaining: he
skated on such very thin ice, and never quite went
through.

Mr. Dutton turned the page. . . . Yes, how clever
not to go through, for there was certainly mud underneath. He gave a faint chuckle of interest, and dexter-
ously turned the chuckle into a cough. At that sound
a small sigh of relief, a sense of relaxation went round
the class, for it was clear that old Dutton (Dubs was
his more general nomenclature) was deep in his yellow
book. When that consummation, so devoutly wished,
was arrived at, any diversion of a moderately quiet
nature might be indulged in.

Crabtree began: he was a boy of goat-like face, and
had been known as Nanny, till the somewhat voluminous appearance of his new pair of trousers had caused
him to be re-christened Bags. He had finished his letter
to his mother with remarkable speed, and had, by writing
small, conveyed quite sufficient information to her on a
half-sheet. There was thus the other half-sheet, noise-
lessly torn off, to be framed into munitions of aerial
warfare. He folded it neatly into the form of a dart,
he inked the point of it by dipping it into the china
receptacle at the top of his desk, and launched it with
unerring aim, enfilading the cross-bench where David
sat. It hit him just exactly where the other half of his
missing tooth should have been, for his lip was drawn

back and his tongue slightly protruded in the agonies of composing a suitable letter to his father. The soft wet point struck it full, and spattered ink over his lip.

" Oh, damn," said David very softly.

Then he paused, stricken to stone, and quite ready to deny that he had spoken at all. His eyes apprehensively sought Mr. Dutton, and he saw that he had not heard, being deep in the misfortunes that happened to Mademoiselle Fifi.

" I'll lick you afterwards, Bags," he said gently.

" Better lick yourself now," whispered Bags.

A faint giggle at Bags's repartee went round the class, like the sound of a breaking ripple. This penetrated into Mr. Dutton's consciousness, and, shifting his attitude a little without looking up, he leaned his forehead on his open hand, so that he could observe the boys through the chinks of his fingers. David, of course, was far too old a hand to be caught by this paltry subterfuge, for " playing chinks " was a manœuvre of the enemy which had got quite stale through repetition, and he therefore gently laid down on the sloping top of his locker the dart which he had just dipped again in his inkpot to throw back at Bags, and with an industrious air turned to his letter again.

The twenty minutes allotted on Sunday afternoon school for writing home to parents was already more than half spent, but the date which he had copied off his neighbour and " My dear Papa " was as far as the first fine careless rapture of composition had carried him. It was really difficult to know what to say to his dear papa, for all the events of the past week were completely thrown into shadow by the one sunlit fact that he had got his school-colours for cricket, and had made twenty-four runs in the last match. But, as he knew perfectly well, his father cared as little for cricket as he did for football;

indeed, David ironically doubted if he knew the difference
between them, and that deplorable fact restricted the
zone of interests common to them.   And really the only
other event of true importance was that his aunt had
sent him a postal order for five shillings. It would not be
politic to tell his father about that, in case of inquiries
being made as to what he had done with it, when he
got home in a fortnight's time for the summer holidays.

He would have eaten it all long before then, for it was
strawberry-time.   David bit heavily into his wooden
pen-holder in his efforts to think of something innocuous
to say, and found his mouth full of fragments of chewed
wood.   These he proceeded to masticate rather ostentatiously while he still sucked his inky lip, the joy of
this being that old Dubs was still playing chinks, and
would certainly, as a surprise, ask him before long what
he was eating.   This was stimulating to the mind, and
he plunged into his letter.

" We are being taken in the museum, because they are
building a new first-form class-room.   There was dry-
rot, too, in the wanescotting of the old one.   We have
been doing Cicero this week, as well as Virgil, and Xeno-
phon in Greek, and Medea, and Holland in geography
and James 2.   I have got to division of decimals which
is very interesting, and square-root which is most difficult, because some have it and others don't——"

David gave one fleeting blue-eyed glance at Mr
Dutton, and saw that the blessed moment was approaching.   The chink had widened, and there was no doubt
whatever that it was he who was being observed.   Then
he bent his yellow head over his letter again, and chewed
the fragments of penholder with renewed vigour.

" It was very hot all this week, and I and two other

chaps were taken to bathe at the Richmond bathing-place day before yesterday by——"

"Blaize, what are you eating?" said Mr. Dutton suddenly.

David looked up in bland and innocent surprise.

"Eating, sir?" he asked. "My penholder, sir."

A slight titter went round the class, for David had the enviable reputation of "drawing" his pastors and masters (always excepting the Head) by the geniality and unexpectedness of his replies. But on this occasion the blandness was a little overdone, and instead of "taking a back seat" Mr. Dutton put down his yellow novel on his desk, back upwards, and came across the room to where David was sitting. The dart, with its wet, inky point lay there, and it was too late to draw his blotting-paper over it. But a more dramatic *dénouement* than the mere discovery of an inky dart, which might be assessed at fifty lies—or perhaps a hundred, since it was Sunday—hung in the air.

"Open your mouth," said Mr. Dutton, not yet seeing the dart.

David had a good large useful mouth, and he opened it very suddenly to its extremest extent, putting out his tongue a little, which might or might not have been an accident. That unruly member was undoubtedly covered with splinters of common penholder, and nothing else at all.

"Sir-may-I-shut-it-again?" said David all in one breath, opening it, the moment he had spoken, to its widest.

Mr. Dutton's eye fell on the inky dart.

"What is that?" he said.

David gave a prodigious gulp, and swallowed as much wood-fibre as was convenient.

"That, sir?" he said politely. "A paper dart, sir, inked."

"Did you make it?" asked Dubs.

David's face assumed an expression of horror.

"Sir? no, sir," he said in a tone of wounded and innocent indignation.

Suddenly David became conscious that his impeccable scene with Mr. Dutton was arousing no interest or amusement among the audience, and his artistic feelings were hurt, for he hated playing to apathetic benches. He looked earnestly and soulfully at Mr. Dutton, but missed appreciative giggles. Nobody appeared to be taking the smallest interest in the dialogue, and all round were bent heads and pens industriously scratching. Then he saw what the rest of the class had already seen. Standing just outside the open window, his foot noiseless on the grass, was the Head, austere and enormous, and fierce and frowning. He had picked up from Mr. Dutton's desk the yellow-backed novel that lay there, and was looking at it with a portentous face.

"Then who made it, if—I say, 'if'—you did not?" said Mr. Dutton, still unconscious of the presence of his superior.

"I suppose another fellow," said David, in very different tones from those in which his moral indignation had found dramatic utterance.

Mr. Dutton took up the dart, and inked his shirt-cuff, but David did not smile.

"Who made——" he began, and turned and saw.

"Oh, jam!" said David under his breath.

The Head left the window with the yellow book in his hand, took two steps to the door, and entered the classroom. He was a tall, grizzle-bearded man, lean and wiry, with cold grey eyes. To the boys he appeared of gigantic height, and was tragedy and fate personified. Terror encompassed him : he scintillated with it, as radium scintillates and is unconsumed. But he scintillated also with splendour : he was probably omniscient, and of his omnipotence there was no doubt whatever. He had rewed for Oxford against Cambridge, and the boys wondered that Cambridge had dared to put a boat on the river at all that year. He had also got a double-first, which in itself was less impressive, and he was believed to be fabulously wealthy. How any woman had ever ventured to marry him no one knew; but, after all, if he had expressed a wish that way, it was equally inconceivable that it should not be grati-fied. Though there was not a boy in the school who did not dread his displeasure above everything else in the world, there was none who would not have taken an infinity of trouble to be sure of winning his approbation. One of his legs was slightly shorter than the other, which gave him a swaying or rocking motion when he walked, which David could imitate admirably. But he would nearly have died of astonish-ment if he had known that more than once the Head had seen him do it, and had laughed in his beard with twinkling eyes.

There was no twinkle or laughter there to-day. Still with the yellow volume in his hand, he came and stood before the skeleton of the kangaroo, and a silence fell that will perhaps be equalled for breathlessness on the day that the judgment books are opened, but probably not before. Then he spoke :

" Silence ! " he said.

(There was not any more silence possible, so he had to be content with that.)

He addressed his lieutenant, who stood abjectly twirling a small moustache and trying to look tall. But what was the use of trying to look tall beside that

Matterhorn, or to twirl an adolescent moustache when
the Head's hand clawed his beard ? It was simply silly.

" Mr. Dutton," said the Head, when the silence had
begun to sing in the ears of the listeners. " By some
strange mischance—I repeat, by some strange mischance
—I have found this disgusting and licentious book on your
desk. How it got there, how it happened to be opened
at—at page 56, I do not wish to inquire. It is more
than enough for me to have found it there. I am willing
to believe, and to tell you so publicly, Mr. Dutton,
before the boys whom you are superintending on this
Sunday afternoon, I am willing to believe that some ob-
scene bird passed over the museum and dropped from its
claws this stinking—yes, sir, stinking—carrion. Dropped
it, sir, while your back was turned, on the very table
where I see the Book of books, and also the Book of
Common Prayer. With your leave, with your leave,
Mr. Dutton, I will do thus and thus to this unholy
carrion."

Then ensued a slight anticlimax, for the Head, though
a very strong man in hand and arm, found it impossible to do as he had designed, and tear three hundred
pages across and across. But the form generally, and
Mr. Dutton in particular, were too stiff with horror to
notice it. So, instead, the Head tore off section after
section of the lightly sewn leaves, instead of tearing
the pages, laid the dismembered carrion on the floor, and
stamped on it, and then, with an indescribable ejaculation
of disgust, threw the mutilated remains into the fireplace.

" You are excused, Mr. Dutton," he said, " from
the rest of this lesson, which I will take myself ; but
you will do me the honour to call on me immediately
after evensong this afternoon."

His fierce eye wandered from Mr. Dutton's stricken
face to David's desk, where lay the inky dart.

" You are engaged now, I see, in some inquiry," he said. " A paper dart, I perceive, on Blaize's desk. I will conduct the inquiry myself, and wish you a good afternoon."

He waited in tense silence till Mr. Dutton had taken his hat and left the room. Then he turned to David.

" Blaize, did you make that dart, or did you throw it ? " he asked.

An expression of despairing determination had come into David's face. He was conscious also of a large ink-stain on his lips.

" Neither, sir," he said.

" Then who made it ? " said the Head. " And also, for I perceive the point is blunted, who threw it ? "

Dead silence on David's part.

" Do you know ? " asked the Head.

" Yes, sir," said David.

" And do you refuse to tell me ? I am not here to be bullied, I may remind you."

David felt slightly sick, but he had swallowed a good deal of chewed pen-handle.

" Do you refuse to tell me ? " repeated the Head.

" Yes, sir," said David.

Then came one of those strange calms in the middle of cyclones, which sometimes puzzled the boys. But their conjecture, a perfectly right one, was that the Head, in spite of questions like these, did not like " sneaking." Anyhow, for a moment his fierceness faded, and he nodded at David, just as one pal might nod to another in sympathetic assent.

" Quite right, my boy," he said.

Then he turned to the rest of the class, holding up the bedraggled weapon.

" Name," he said.

The miserable Bags stood up, without speech.

" Oh you, Crabtree," said the awful voice. " And so Master Crabtree thinks that the calm and quiet of Sunday afternoon is made to give him leisure to forge these filthy weapons : that the paper you are given to write home on is designed to be desecrated to these foul usages, and the ink to supply filth to them. You will write out with the ink you have so strangely misused two hundred lines of Virgil in copper-plate hand, and eat your dinner at the pig-table, apart from your companions, for the next week."

The pig-table, it may be mentioned, was a separate table in the dining-room without chairs, where boys detected in swinish habits had to take their meals standing for the period of their sentence. But poor Bags's cup was not full yet, for the Head's eagle eye fell on David's inky mouth.

" I infer that the ink on Blaize's lips was made by this weapon," he said. " That is so ? Then you will now beg Blaize's pardon, and as soon as the Catechism and Bible-class is over, you will fetch a basin of water and bathe Blaize's mouth with your own sponge, until it is pronounced clean by your matron. The hour for writing home is up. Sign your names, and direct your envelopes. Catechism ! "

Now the Catechism-class had already been held, and the marks for it had been put down in the mottled-covered book which lay on Mr. Dutton's desk. But to suggest or hint this was not less inconceivable than to propose playing leap-frog. The more imaginative saw that there might be fresh trouble when Catechism marks were put down, and it was found that Mr. Dutton had already entered them in his neat small handwriting, but the idea of venturing to correct the Head when he was in this brimstone-mood was merely unthinkable. David, indeed, the boldest of them all, and, at the moment, with something of the halo of martyrdom about him, wondered what would happen if he did so, but quailed before the possible result.

So Catechism began again, and for a little all went smoothly. The Head, of course, knew that among small boys at school Christian names are held to be effeminate and disgraceful things, and so, omitting the first question, asked Stone, the head-boy, who had given him his name, and Stone knew. Ferrars also knew what his godfathers and godmothers then did for him, and David expressed himself accurately as bound to believe and to do what they had promised for him. The Commandments went smoothly, but trouble began when the boys had to explain what they chiefly learned from those Commandments. Any meaning that they might have possessed, any effort to attach rational ideas to them, was overshadowed by the fact that, primarily, this was a lesson that should have been acquired by heart in order to recite it faultlessly to that awe-inspiring presence that frowned at Mr. Dutton's desk. His duty towards his neighbour had already baffled David that afternoon, but for the moment, having recited the eighth Commandment, his turn was passed, and, troubles never coming singly, Bags was faced with this abstruse question. The first sentences went rightly enough, but then he began to falter.

" To honour and obey the King and all that are put in authority under her——"

" Her ? " asked the Head.

Bags's Prayer-book, a comparatively ancient one, given him at his christening by a godmother, was a Queen's Prayer-book.

" Queen, and all that are put in authority under her," he quavered, getting confused.

" Next," said the Head.

"King and all that are put in authority under him," said Sharpe Major in a shrill treble. "To submit myself to all my governors, teachers, spiritual pastors and masters; to order myself lowly and reverently to all my betters; to—to honour and obey the King——"

"Next," said the Head, with ominous calm.

The dreary tale of failure went on : with that portentous figure sitting in the chair of the innocuous Mr. Dutton, consecutive thought became impossible, and memory took wings and fled. Boys who had got full marks earlier in the afternoon found themselves unable, when facing this grim mood of the Head's, to repeat their duty towards anything. The ground already covered was taken again, in order to give them a fresh start, and now the Creed itself presented pitfalls and stumbling-blocks. Already the normal hour for the class had been exceeded, and from other and happier class-rooms the boys poured out into the field in front of the windows, or lay on rugs under the shade of the big still elms, and with linked arms and treble intercourse wandered across the sunny grass. And even when the Catechism was done, there was the Bible-lesson to follow, and before the Bible-lesson there was certain to be the discovery that the Catechism had already been put down. All this was that ass Dubs's fault for leaving his rotten French novel on his desk.

Worse than anything, the Bible-lesson, when it came, was that most inexplicable second voyage of St. Paul. Thyatira . . . or was it Laodicea ? . . . or were they the seven churches of Asia . . . and what exactly did underpinning the ship mean, or was that manœuvre executed on the other voyage ? Mr. Dutton always consulted the New Testament Maclear over this elusive cruise, whereas the boys had to shut up that useful volume when they were questioned. It seemed scarcely fair. And even the Bible-lesson had not been arrived at yet; they were still sticking and bogged in the quagmires of the Catechism.

At last they stuck altogether : there was no more progression possible. It only remained to hear the sentence on their condemned heads. Everybody without exception was condemned. One had to write out the Creed, another the Commandments, and all their duty towards their neighbours.

" And I shall myself take the same lesson to-day week," said the Head, " and if the form generally does not show a far better knowledge of the Catechism, I shall be unable to adopt the leniency with which I have treated their shortcomings to-day. Next Sunday, then, I shall hold the class in my study."

The significance of this was not lost upon anybody. The study was a room of awful import, and the comfort of the low red morocco settee, the interest of the photographs of Oxford crews on the wall, in which the Head appeared with side-whiskers and no beard could not compensate for the uneasy knowledge that in the middle drawer of the knee-hole table at which he sat were a couple of canes. It was no rare thing for the Head to take a bunch of rattling keys from his pocket, which was the first step, and to fit one of them into the centre drawer. Sometimes, with rising voice, he turned it and opened the drawer, and if things still went badly the trembling victim was put through the farce of choosing which cane he preferred and then advancing the palms of his hands. . . .

The Head paused after this prodigious announcement about the venue for the Catechism-class next Sunday and opened the mark-book. Mr. Dutton was scrupulously neat in his methods, and there in the first column

of the marks for the new week was his list, headed
" Catechism." The Head scrutinised these in silence.

" The marks for to-day's Catechism are already
entered," he said. " Stone, you are the head-boy of the
class, why did you not tell me that Mr. Dutton had
already heard you your Catechism ? I will tell you why.
You wanted me to waste my time and yours, so that
we should not have so long for the Bible-lesson. Was
that it ? "

" N-no, sir," said Stone.

" What was your reason, then, for not telling me ? "
Stone looked at him in a sort of stunned despair.

" I don't know sir," he said.

It was indeed a black afternoon. The Head, probably owing to his discovery on Mr. Dutton's desk,
was in his sternest and most awful mood. Already
five o'clock had struck, whereas the lesson should have
been over by half-past four, and outside the boys were
beginning to gather up their rugs and books, and were
strolling over the grass of the cricket-field to the school-
buildings from which the warning bell for tea was in-
vitingly clanging. It was maddening to think that all
this time might have been saved, and all the impositions
and the hour next Sunday in the dreaded study avoided
if only, as it now turned out, Stone had had the courage
to say that Mr. Dutton had already heard them their
Catechism. But courage was not a quality that blos-
somed when the Head was in a poor temper, and every
boy in the class knew that if he had been in Stone's
place he would have held his tongue. He might easily
have been told not to " bully " the Head (a somewhat
favourite expression) or have been witheringly requested
to give him permission to conduct the class in the manner
he preferred. Chapel was held at six, and when tea

was to come in was difficult of conjecture. Yet even a tea-less chapel would be something of a relief, if only the three-quarters of an hour that intervened could be got through without storms. But before then they would have to embark on this missionary enterprise, which, if it was as dangerous for St. Paul as it was likely to prove for the students of it, must have required a bold heart. And what added sting to it was that Stone had received a hamper from home only the day before, on which to-night his friends would have gorged sumptuously.

The minutes went by with paralysed slowness, for, if the Catechism had been trying, this was infinitely worse. The Head, who very likely wanted his tea too, but for the sake of discipline and education mortified his appetite as well as those of the boys, took a gloomier and gloomier view of them and their attainments. Collateral ignorance of the position of Iconium was seen to be a moral crime of the deepest dye, and the dictionary was beggared of wounding epithets in order adequately to convey the enormity of not knowing its position as regards Lystra. If Ferrers Major had committed parricide under circumstances of unique horror he could not have been held up to blacker obloquy than was volleyed on him for his remarks about Thessalonica. None escaped the task of making a map with the names of the principal towns and the track of the journey itself in red ink ; the less fortunate had to produce two maps by this time next week, and the only thing it was possible to be thankful for was that this nightmare of an hour had not been taken in the study. Else, it was felt, the function of the keys would not have been limited to mere rattling.

Already the field was beginning to be dotted over again with groups of boys who had come out of tea

and were waiting for chapel-bell to ring.   How earnestly
it was possible to desire chapel-time to come David
had never known before, but anything, even the Litany,
or, as would happen to-day, the psalm for the fifteenth
evening of the month, which had seventy-two verses, was
better than this sulphurous divinity-lesson. The whole
class was limp with heat and hunger and terror. Then
the merciful relief of the querulous bell came, and the
Head closed his Bible.

" The lesson has been disgraceful," he said. " I hope
for all your sakes—I say, I hope—that next Sunday
will not be a repetition of to-day. I am more particularly distressed when I think that some of you, like
Blaize, are the sons of clergymen, and have therefore
greater opportunities of studying sacred history."

He got up huge and towering, in his rustling silk gown,
and immediately, as was the amazing manner of him,
who never nagged however severe he might be, his mood
completely changed, and his eyes twinkled as he observed
the depressed class.

" There, my boys, that's over," he said; " and, like
good fellows, try not to make me angry with you again.
I hate finding fault : you may not believe it, but I do.
And neither you nor I have had any tea, so, when
chapel is over, you will all go to the housekeeper's room
and ask her, with my compliments, to give you a real
good tea."

He stalked out, rocking slightly as he went; and
instantly, the oppression of his anger being gone, the
spirits of the class rose sky-high.

" Jolly decent of him," said Ferrers. " Gosh, I'm
glad he didn't take us in the study."

" I say, Blazes, I wouldn't have my mouth washed
with Bags's sponge. It'll be fit to poison you. Why,
do you know what he does with his sponge ? "

Loathsome details, invented on the spur of the moment, followed.

" Fancy being washed by Bags at all," said Stone. " He don't know how to wash himself yet ! "

" Stone, you fool, why the devil couldn't you tell the Head that Dubs had taken the Catechism ? " This from Bags.

" Anyhow, I'm glad my father isn't a clergyman, like Blaize's. Do you do divinity with him in the study on Sunday afternoon in the holidays ? Whack, whack. ' There, my boy ! ' ' Oh, papa, don't hit me ! ' Whack, whack ! ' Oh, papa ! ' squeaked Sharpe Major.

David, by a dexterous movement, got Sharpe's head in Chancery, rubbed his nose on his desk, pulled his hair, and hit him over the biceps.

" Any more remarks about papa ? " he asked cheerfully. " Come on, out with them."

CHAPTER II

THE others poured out into the sunshine, but David
lingered behind with Bags and Ferrers Major, and
began burrowing in his locker to find the box belonging
to his two stag-beetles. They were male and female,
as the lady's absence of long horns testified, and it was
hoped that even in confinement she might some day
be confined. Indeed, there were several bets on, as to
which form the babies would take—whether they would
be eggs, or some sort of caterpillar, or minute but fully
developed stag-beetles. The box in question was a
small cardboard oblong, of cramped dimensions; but
really it was no more than their saloon travelling-
carriage, for they lived in David's washing-basin at
night, since it had been ascertained that the sides of
it were too steep and slippery to allow their escape,
and at other times had the run of his desk in school-
hours, and were allowed quantities of healthy exercise
when their owner was unoccupied and could look after
their wayward steps. But now, since after chapel
David would not come back to the class-room, it was
necessary to put them in their travelling-carriage,
which was pierced with holes, so that such air as there
might happen to be in David's pocket should penetrate
to them. A few slips of grass and leaves would be
sufficient to sustain them until they were regaled with
bits of cake and a strawberry or two from the tea which
was to be provided for the first form after chapel.

The lady was lying on her back, as good as gold, waving her legs slowly in the air, having probably fallen down on some climbing expedition about the roof of the locker, but the stag himself (called "The Monarch of the Glen") could not at once be found. But a little careful rummaging disclosed him sitting morosely in a crevice between a grammar and a geography book.

"I say, I don't believe the Monarch's well," said David.

"Shouldn't think so, living in your fuggy desk," said Bags, strolling out of the room.

Suddenly David perceived, as by a special revelation, that he must kick Bags. Bags had thrown an inky dart at him, and though, in the depression of the Bible-lesson, that had been forgotten, it started into prominence again in his mind. Further, Bags had added insult to injury by saying that his desk was fuggy. Certainly he must kick Bags, just once, juicily, and call it all square.

David gingerly took the Monarch by the waist, so that his pincers nipped the empty air, and put him and his spouse into their travelling-carriage.

"Come on, Ferrers," he said.

On their way across to chapel he paused a moment to pick a few leaves from the bright squibs of root-growth on the elm just outside the class-room, and took Ferrers's arm.

"Don't let's go too quick," he said. "I want to catch Bags up just as we get to chapel-door, and if I was alone he might suspect. Then you'll see: I'll give him one kick, just one, but a beauty. Let's seem to be talking."

Diabolically diplomatic, David managed his manœuvre well, gradually gaining on his unsuspecting victim, and stalking him with infinite stealth and relish. There

was no question of honour in coming behind him **thus**
unawares, for Bags had launched a dart at him without
provocation, and had also gone jauntily across to chapel
after making that ill-advised remark about David's
fuggy desk.   Should Bags resent a good sound kick,
which was a pretty just payment of the score, David
would be perfectly happy to fight him afterwards if he
desired it.   It was quite all right.

David, sometimes lounging, sometimes hurrying, and
all the time talking in a foolish, interested manner to
Ferrers, came up close to the rear of the enemy just two
steps outside chapel-door.   They were the last of the
boys to go in, and David had space to swing his leg.
For the moment Bags was too much astonished to be
hurt, and David passed him with a slight smile on his
hopelessly seraphic face, went up the gangway to his
seat in the choir just opposite the organ, knelt down, and
covered a gratified face with his hands.   He loved doing
things neatly, and to kick Bags, just once, quite correctly
like that, was as good as cutting a ball just out of reach
of point.

The evening service began, psalms and canticles and
hymns all to be sung.   It was that terrible fifteenth
evening of the month, and page after page of psalm
must be gone through.   Only that morning David and
Ferrers had had an impassioned argument as to whether
the Old or the New Testament was " the beastliest,"
Ferrers maintaining that there was nothing in the New
Testament that could compare with the Kings of Israel
and Judah, while David (and his argument was strength-
ened after the last hour) affirmed that nothing B.C.
could beat the missionary journeys, not if it tried with
both hands.   But as the psalm for the fifteenth evening
(to a single chant too) went on, he felt that it was difficult
to feel honestly that there could be anything beastlier,

especially if you had not had tea. He hoped Ferrers would not adduce that as a crushing argument for the supremacy of the Old Testament. On it went, and, as an antidote to its interminableness, David began to think of other and more pleasant things. There was his eleven-cap and his twenty-four runs in the last match to muse upon as a resisting topic to the tedium of the children of Israel, and in especial one gorgeous pull for four he had made. Also he could feel on the side of his leg the slight vibration from the travelling-carriage of the Monarch and his wife, which showed they were moving about, enjoying, it was to be hoped, the fresh elm-leaves he had nipped off for them. It was in his left-hand trousers pocket that these were confined, a place to be felt stealthily and exteriorly, since hands-in-pockets was a forbidden attitude in chapel. Just below the box were the two half-crowns, the yet unchanged splendour of Aunt Eleanor's gift. Also in anticipation was the thought of the tea that should succeed chapel, and in retrospect the remembrance of the beautiful kick he had given Bags. But the seventy-eighth psalm was a corker for all that, and if Ferrers Major brought it up, he would have to admit it.

The psalm began to show promise of ending, and it was already possible to count the remaining verses. Then suddenly there was something so delightful in it as a topical allusion, that Ferrers could no longer advance it as being beastlier than anything in the New Testament. And David's contribution to the music swelled out at once more lustily, and he looked and beamed towards Bags as he sang, " He smote his enemies in the hinder part, and put them to a perpetual shame."

Ferrers caught his eye and understood, but Bags did not, which was a pity. David felt he must have seen the appositeness of that verse, but he did not look up. Poor

old Bags ! perhaps he was much hurt. David had not
meant to hurt him much ; he had only wanted to kick
him neatly and squarely and peacefully, ready to fight
afterwards, if desired.

The senior boys of the first form read the lessons at
these services, and it was the turn of Stone and Ferrers
to " make asses of themselves " in the school phrase.
The rest of the congregation, masters and boys, followed
the reading in their Bibles, or at any rate found the
place and meditated.   Among the masters there was
Mr. Dutton, looking peculiarly depressed, with whom,
in spite of his general beastliness, David felt a certain
sympathy, as he was commanded to honour the Head
immediately afterwards on the subject of the yellow-
backed novel.   At the organ were seated the two Misses
Acland, daughters of the Head, one to play, the other
to turn over leaves for her sister and to pull out stops
or put them in.   She also poked away at the pedals and
occasionally dropped books on the keys, producing the
most Wagnerian effects. These two female figures,
with plump backs turned to him, afforded David plenty
of rather acid reflection.   Goggles (so called for obvious
reasons, but addressed as Miss Mabel) was the elder,
and wasn't so bad, though she had a woeful tendency to
improve and console the occasion when any of the boys
got into trouble, and was a kind of official dove with an
olive-branch after the deluge.   But Carrots (this concerned her hair, which otherwise belonged to Miss Edith)
had lately shown herself altogether too beastly.   It was
a moral certainty that it was she who had " sneaked "
to her father, when, last week, Ferrers had gone out of
bounds, because he had seen her in Richmond, and so of
course she had seen him and told the Head.   It had been
a whole-school day and all the other masters had been
in their class-rooms, and it *must* have been Carrots.

Ferrers had had the toothache, and was excused after-noon school, and, feeling better, had gone to Richmond. It wasn't fair of the family to spy for the Head; he, of course, and the rest of the masters, were your natural enemies, and if you were caught by them that was the fortune of war. But if Carrots or Goggles and all the crew were enemies also, they ought to be declared enemies. Instead they pretended to be friends, with their sisterly advice and their olive-branches and their treacherous smiles. . . . Oh, the Magnificat.

That was soon over, and again David's disapproving eye glanced up at Goggles and Carrots during the second lesson. This time they had turned round on their organ-bench and spread their Bibles on their knees, ostentatiously following the lesson as an example to the school. David was afraid they were hypocrites, and, having found his place, continued to meditate on them. Yes: there had been a first-form conference on the subject of Goggles and Carrots when Ferrers returned that afternoon from a short and extremely painful interview with the Head, and it had been settled that Goggles and Carrots must be cut. David had, at the time, been opposed to cutting Goggles as well as her sneaking sister, because Goggles wasn't such a bad chap, and there was nothing against her personally. But he and a small minority had been overruled; if Carrots had sneaked, Goggles might sneak next, and it was wiser to have no truck at all with the enemy's family. Though Goggles at this moment looked innocent enough, with the low sun shining through a stained-glass window on to her spectacles and protuberant eyes, David felt that, after all, it was wiser to err on the side of prudence than to be led into a course of mistaken kindness. But it was rather difficult: only yesterday she had con-gratulated him, with apparent sincerity, on his innings

of twenty-four, and had offered him a visit to the
strawberry-beds in the garden. He had been compelled, by the resolution passed by the sixth-form conference, to decline this temptation, and to say with a
stony face, "Thank you, Miss Mabel, but I can't."
Even that was not strictly in accordance with the
vow : he ought really to have icily raised his cap, and
said nothing whatever.

It was part of the career of Goggles and Carrots to
make the service what is called " bright," which meant
there was a good deal of singing. This presupposed, in
order to ensure a proper performance, a certain amount
of choir-practice. These practices were not allowed
to take the place of other school-work, but were held
in the less useful hours of play-time. In compensa-
tion, the members of the choir were rewarded with
an extra half-holiday towards the end of term, if they
had missed no practices, and before now Goggles had
been known, when a boy had missed, say, only one
practice, to falsify the register, and send up his name
to her father as an unremitting attendant, which did
not look as if she was a bad chap; but, on the other
hand, she was sister to her sister, about whom there
could be no doubt whatever. She *must* have sneaked ;
Ferrers had seen her in Richmond, and immediately
on his return he had been summoned and dealt with.
Probably all girls were dishonourable, and so it was
best to cut Goggles too. And it was not as if Carrots
was only a kid, who must be taught the proper ways
of school-life ; she was quite grown up, and, very
likely, would never see fifteen again. Besides . . . . oh,
the Nunc Dimittis, though they were a long way off
being dismissed yet.

A slight alleviation happened here, for the wind of
the organ suddenly ran out with a wail and a wheeze,

and was started again by the blower in so feverish a
haste that the notes shook and trembled as he pumped.
Soon after, in privacy of kneeling, David was able to
peep into the stag-beetles' travelling-carriage, and
observe with delight that the Monarch was browsing
on elm-leaves. He appeared to have an excellent
appetite, and was swiftly put away again as they rose
for the hymn. Instead, "Anthem" was announced by
the Head, without further particularisation, since there
was but one. But it seemed scarcely credible that
any one could have been so mean as to couple an
Anthem to that unending seventy-eighth psalm. No
doubt this was reprisal on the part of Goggles and
Carrots. It must be duly considered afterwards.

David's mind had been pretty busy with these
trains of thought, and his attention to the service, from
a devotional point of view, intermittent and frag-
mentary. More than once he stole a glance at Bags
as a general reconnoitring measure. It appeared from
a certain gingerliness in Bags's movements, when he sat
down or stood, that he was not quite comfortable, and,
since accounts had been squared between them, David
hoped he had not hurt him much ; the kick in the main
was meant to be symbolical, and he determined that
unless Bags actually wanted to be nasty, he would
make it up directly after chapel. David's cheerful and
eager soul hated prolonged or nagging warfare, and,
since Bags had been paid for his injudicious behaviour
during school that afternoon, David was quite ready
to proclaim or assent to a cordial *pax*. Naturally,
if Bags did not want *pax*, he should have as much
bellum as he wished for, and during the prayer for
Parliament, in which it was frankly impossible for a
proper boy of thirteen to take any interest, David
planned a raid or two. Bags was like a girl in some

ways : he couldn't stand creeping things, so if he didn't
want *pax*, he should find black-beetles in his bed
without any more ado about the matter. These were
easily procured ; they lived in the water-pipes of a
disused lavatory, and, by turning on a tap, horrible
half-drowned specimens descended wriggling into the
basin. He had put two in Bags's bed once before, with
the splendid effect that Bags spent the night on the
floor in his dressing-gown, rather than encounter them,
whereas, when he had tried the same trick on David,
David had smashed the intruders to death with his
slipper, and slept soundly amid the mutilated corpses.
Yes, they should be about Bags's path, and about his
bed—particularly his bed—he should find them in his
pockets and his boots, until he abandoned nagging
warfare, and either came to blows and had done with it,
or made peace like a gentleman. David had fought
Bags once before, and Bags did not want any more on
that occasion, and said so. David, as a matter of fact,
did not want any more either, and his face for the
next few days had been notably more lumpy than
Bags's, but, by virtue of an extra ounce of grit, he had
not said so. Therefore——

"Amen" sang David fervently, looking as if he had
just come down from an Italian picture of singing
angels. But he forgot that the last "Amen" went
down, instead of remaining on the same note.

Sermon-time afforded more opportunities for meditation, for he swiftly decided that he could not understand what the Head was driving at. . . . There was
another and most important cricket-match at the end
of this week, and until that was over he would not
be able to smoke at all, because he had made a vow
that if he made more than ten runs in the last match,
he would not smoke for ten days. This vow he had

written out on a piece of paper, and buried it in a match-box below a certain tree. On the whole that had been rather a clever vow, since, to begin with, he did not like smoking at all, and only did it because just now it was the smart thing to do. But a vow of this importance, which he would have to tell the smoking club about when they met on Tuesday, would certainly be held sacred even by Stone, who was the dashing president of the club, and often smoked a cigarette right through without minding, though it was only incumbent on members to smoke half a cigarette at these meetings. But they had to do that without being sick, and if you were sick three times you were turned out of the club. Furthermore, as an additional cleverness in the vow, he had been told by a fellow at a public school that smoking was bad for the eyes, and even when people were quite old, as at Oxford or Cambridge, they never smoked when they were in training. Again, if his vow was not accepted as a reason for abstention, he would have to resign, but that he really did not mind about, for it was stupid to put smoking before cricket. Also the secret of the smoking club had somehow leaked out, and now that the badge was no longer a mystery to those who did not belong, half the fun was gone. This badge was a piece of copper-wire bent into the shape of S.C., for Smoking Club, and when they were engaged in these sacred operations, it had to be worn in the buttonhole; otherwise there was a fine of a halfpenny, which helped to fill the coffers of the club, and was spent in cigarettes. But only last week Bags, who did not belong, happened to see his badge, and said casually, " Hullo, you belong to the Sick Club, do you ? " This was annoying, because it not only implied a knowledge of the club, but darkly alluded to its rules. David had been ready enough on this occasion, and had answered smartly, " If you belonged to an S.C., it would be the Sneak Club," and the shot had gone home, for Bags had sneaked once. Of course it was ever so long ago, the term before last, before Bags had become a decent chap, and the incident had been suitably buried. But the thought of its possible resuscitation made Bags extremely civil for several days.

Certain words, " the horror of sin, the infamy of evil," caught David's ears at this moment, and he attended for a little. It seemed to him rather poor stuff, and why the Head should sway about and shout like that was impossible to conjecture. But it gave him a hint, and David, closely listening, intended to reproduce some of it in dormitory that night. A night-shirt made an admirable surplice, and a pair of trousers hung over the shoulders would make a ripping stole. He himself would be the Head, as he had thought of it, and Stone and Ferrers should be stuffed with pillows to represent Goggles and Carrots, with his bed as the organ. David would march the whole way down the dormitory, after the matron had gone, with the Head's rocking walk and some cotton-wool for a beard, preceded by a small boy carrying a poker. . . .

Then suddenly the Head's voice changed ; it became extraordinarily solemn and beautiful, as it did some-times when he read to them. And the words were beautiful, and they affected David in that puzzling, incomprehensible manner in which words did. Words and the pictures, dim and only half-conscious, that they produced in his mind, often had that effect on him ; they gave him a sort of homesick yearning, and an ache, as if his mind were hungry. And it was clear that what he was saying moved the Head in the same sort of way ; his voice shook and grew lower yet, reminding David of something he had felt once when he woke early and heard the chirruping of birds before daybreak. . . .

"So prepare to be men," he said, "and when manhood dawns on you, let it dawn on you as on the clean dewy grass, with birds singing in your hearts and innocence still looking from your eyes. Never contemplate evil, and the desire of it will fade from you. Run away from it, if by staying near it you would yield, and 'Whatsoever things are lovely, whatsoever things are of good report, think on those things.'"

David gave a little gulp; not only were these beautiful words, but they meant something. . . .

But the sermon was over, and it was impossible not to remember that in a few minutes now he would be having tea in the housekeeper's room, while the wretched Dubs was doing the Head the honour to wait on him. It had been "jam" to see the Head stamp on that yellow-covered book! And, with any luck, the fragments of it would be in the grate of the museum to-morrow. David determined to get up early, and see what it was about. It was in French, which was a bore, but it was worth while, even at the trouble of looking out heaps of words, to see what it was that had made the Head in such a wax. . . . Or had it something to do with the things the Head told them they must run away from? . . .

Rum old bird, the Head. But he did say jolly things sometimes.

CHAPTER III

THE tea which (with the Head's compliments) Mrs. Lowe provided after chapel was an apotheosis of tea. The Head's dinner was going on simultaneously, and the most delicious remainders were brought in from it for the boys, ending with an ice pudding that at its entrance was practically untouched, though soon there was nothing left to touch. It had really been worth while to voyage at such peril over unknown seas and lands, if this was to be the eventual haven, and when, at the end, Ferrers proposed the health of Iconium, his toast was drunk with acclamation. Thereafter was a little quiet ragging, but David had not joined in this, for when he was seized by somebody he had said in plethoric tones, " For God's sake, don't bend me, or I shall be sick," and for fear of that untoward result he had been left alone. Bags also was not disposed to active exercise, and David had taken the opportunity to be agreeable, according to his resolution in chapel.

" I say, I hope I didn't hurt you, Bags," he said. " You see I had to kick you just once to make it all square. Is it *pax* ? "

Bags looked sideways at David, with his shallow, goat-like eyes, before he answered.

" Oh, rather," he said. " It wasn't anything. You hardly touched me."

This was surprising, for David had the distinct impression in his toe and instep that this particular kick had been a juicy one.

"Right oh, then," he said. "I say, there's one piece of cake left. Shall we halve it?"

"Couldn't," said Bags, getting up.

Though he could not be bent, David thought that a cautious attack might defeat the one piece of cake, and strategically accomplished this. But it was funny that Bags should not have tried, too, and for a moment he had suspicions.

"It is *pax*, then?" he asked.

"Oh, rather," said Bags. "And your lip's all right, isn't it, Blazes? Quite clean, I mean. I think the Head only gassed about that on the spur of the moment. Will you swear I washed it, if necessary?"

"Oh, yes," said David. "Gosh, I'm full. And I'm going to preach in dormitory, night-shirt and trousers for a stole. I can remember lots of the sermon."

"Oh, may I come?" asked Bags.

"Right, but don't be sarcastic and spoil the show. It'll be in my cubicle."

"Rather not," said Bags, moving away. "May I be Goggles or Carrots?"

"Sorry; Stone and Ferrers have bagged them. But you might blow the organ, and let it go out with a squeak, same as it did this evening."

"Oh, thanks; that'll be ripping," said Bags, beginning to practise squeaking in a realistic and organ-like manner.

Now Bags's mater was, as all the world knew, a Jewess. Bags had volunteered that information himself on his first day at school, adding loftily that she was of the tribe of Judah. This, if it was meant to be impressive, had singularly failed in its object, and the only consequence was that, for his first term or so, Bags had been the butt of various embarrassing questions as to whether he was allowed to eat sausages, or observed other Levitical injunctions. David, as a matter of fact, had not joined in these painful catechisms, holding that it wasn't fair to consider a fellow responsible for his mater, but he had always secretly felt that this might account for there being something rather odd about Bags. For Bags had a retentive and vindictive memory, and was ever on the look-out to repay antique scores, though other people would have forgotten all about them. It was therefore not likely that he would have overlooked a scene so recent as this kick, and after Bags had gone, David said to himself that he was being " too infernally genial "—a jolly sounding word, which he had just learned—to deceive the wary. In fact, though Bags had definitely agreed that it should be *pax*, David was subconsciously a little suspicious of him, and this attitude was confirmed by Bags having said that that one beautiful kick had hardly touched him. It absolutely must have : there was no mistaking the quality of the touch. But he did not dwell on it much ; should Bags prove to be bellicose still, in spite of the treaty, he felt the utmost confidence that he could deal with him.

David woke next morning very early, with a sense of immense interest in things in general. It was still only the hour of faint and early dawn, and he lay quiet a little while, drawing his knees up to his chin, and clasping his legs with his bare arms in order to multiply the consciousness of limbs and body and life generally. Just behind him was the open window, through which the fresh breeze of morning came, coolly ruffling his hair, and on each side the varnished pitch-pine of the walls of his cubicle, gay with wonderful decoration. His face was turned to the partition close to his bed, and thus, the earliest object that his eye fell on was the

school eleven cricket-cap which he had won last week,
hung on a nail. On another nail beside it was his
watch and chain, his father's birthday present to him
on attaining the immense age of thirteen, and on the
same nail, though not conjoined with this jewellery,
the mystic badge of the Smoking Club. A little farther
on was another gift of his father's, a small chromo-
lithographic reproduction of the Sistine Madonna, by
a " fellow " called Raphael, whose name somehow
appealed to David, though the picture itself was " rather
pi," and close beside that a photograph of Carrots,
exchanged for one of his in those happier days before
she sneaked. Now, Carrots's intelligent features were
turned face to the wall, and David wondered whether
she ought not to be deposed altogether. Anyhow, it
had been Carrots who had asked him for his photograph,
promising hers; the exchange had come from her side.
Then there was a photograph of Ferrers Major, un-
framed, but tacked to the wall, and one of Hughes,
David's great friend, who had left a year before, and
gone to Marchester, where David hoped to follow him
at the Michaelmas term. . . . Hughes was altogether
godlike, and David adored him. Then came a small
fretwork bracket, home-made in the holidays, with a
sort of petticoat of crimson silk hanging round the
edge of its shelf, on which was placed a small china lamb
lying down among amazing flowers, which David assured
his friends was " jolly valuable."

He cuddled his knees for a little while, contemplating these precious things, and forbearing to turn
round and look the other way, because even more
agreeable objects (with the exception perhaps of the
photograph of Hughes) would meet his eyes there, and
the zest for them was to be sharpened by abstention.
To begin with, there was the chair which last night

had made so perfect a pulpit, and even the sight of his trousers now lying on it, which last night had made so lovely a stole, would make him giggle again at the thought of his highly successful sermon. There also was the photograph of the two elevens in last week's match, and, more precious still, a snapshot of himself standing at the wicket, which Ferrers's sister had taken, had developed, and had sent to him the very next day. " Jolly cute of her," thought David.

He longed to turn round and assure himself by ocular evidence of the permanence of these things, but teasing himself, went on with his enumeration of them. There was his cricket-bat and one right-hand batting-glove which he had bought second-hand. Most people did not rise to gloves at all; indeed, Stone's glove was the only other one in the school, and for the moment the idea of staggering humanity by purchasing a left-hand glove also with Aunt Eleanor's five shillings flashed across him. Probably nobody at Helmsworth had ever had two batting-gloves before; fancy being snapshotted with two gloves! Then there was a pill-box filled with the yellow dust from the cedar-cones in the grounds, which he had collected and labelled " Cedar-sulphur"; and, lastly, there was his washing-basin in which, ever ineffectually trying to climb up its slippery steep sides, were the Monarch of the Glen and his spouse. David could resist that no longer, rolled round in bed, and got up.

" Good morning, Monarch," he said politely. " How——" And then he stopped. There were two or three elm-leaves in the basin and a half-eaten strawberry, but otherwise it was empty. There was no Monarch, there was no wife.

For the moment David could not believe it : he felt that they must be there, and that for some curious sleepy reason (although he was not sleepy) he could not see them. Again and again he turned over the leaves, and looked underneath the strawberry (as if the Monarch had been made little by his meal, like Alice in Wonderland), but there was no sign of them. Then he searched about his cubicle, scrutinizing the varnished walls, examining the floor, searching in his blankets in case they had strayed there. And all the time he felt the futility of this, for he was convinced in his own mind that neither the Monarch nor his lady could have climbed the glazed ascent of the sides of the washing basin. Often had he watched them attempting to do so ; even the gradual slope at the base was beyond the adhesive power of their feet, and as for the precipice of the sides themselves, they were hopelessly incapable of surmounting it. They *could* not get out themselves : some one must have——

Then a sudden suspicion struck him, and he went softly and barefooted to the far end of the dormitory where Bags slept, and shook him awake. This had to be accomplished with silent caution, since no boy was allowed to leave his cubicle till the dressing-bell sounded.

"I say, Bags, have you taken my stags ? " he whispered. "If you tell me you have, and give them up, I swear I won't do anything to you."

Bags sat up in bed and yawned heavily, to give himself time to think.

"Do you really think I would touch those filthy crawlers ? " he asked.

"Doesn't matter what I think," said David. "I want to know if you did."

Bags was considerably astounded by David's having so instantly suspected him, considering that he had agreed to *pax* yesterday evening.

"Well then, I didn't," he said. "So that's flat. Where did you put them last night ? "

" In my basin," said David.

Suddenly Bags saw the stout figure of the matron in the ante-room just outside the dormitory, while David, facing towards him, could not see her. If he could detain David in talk here for a minute, it was more than likely that she would hear voices, and find him out of his cubicle, in which case she would certainly report him to the Head. He had not forgotten about the incident as they went into chapel last night, and the temptation was too strong.

He laughed silently into his bed-clothes.

" What are you laughing at ? " said David, raising his voice. " What's the blooming joke ? "

Bags did not answer, and David repeated his question. At that Bags saw that the matron had heard the talking, and was advancing in her felt slippers up the dormitory. She was already past David's cubicle, and retreat was cut off. He sank back gently into bed. " Cave," he whispered, " there's Glanders coming ! and stag-beetles can fly. Fancy not knowing that ! "

And he closed his eyes and sank apparently into a refreshing sleep.

David turned round. Glanders was coming straight up the dormitory, and had already seen him. Since there was no hope of concealment, he went out to meet his fate.

" Out of your cubicle before dressing-bell," said Glanders bleakly. " I shall report you, Master Blaize. Not the first time, either."

David got back into bed again in a very different mood from that in which he had awoke half an hour ago. The week was beginning just about as badly as it could, and the sight of his cricket-cap and batting-glove failed to console him in the least, or bring back the sense of his happy awaking. He had two maps of

the second missionary journey to make, he had to
stop in between twelve and one, when he should have
been practising at the nets, to learn his Catechism, the
Monarch and his wife had vanished, and he was to
be reported for being out of his cubicle before the
dressing-bell sounded. That was a serious breach of
school-discipline, and Glanders might have gone further
when she so feelingly reminded him that this would
not be " the first time either," for it would not be
the second either. On the last occasion the Head had
told him precisely what would happen if it occurred
again. The colours of the new cricket-cap had faded,
the glove looked ridiculous, and the washing-basin was
like the house of some one lately dead. He felt furious
and exasperated against fate, and it was bitter to be
reminded by Bags that stag-beetles could fly. In a
general way he supposed he had known it too, but it
had not occurred to him that the Monarch and his
wife would dream of such a thing. Then there was a
good fine caning to look forward to : it hurt hideously
at the time, and you couldn't hold a bat all day afterwards, because your hands were so sore. There was
an awful legend, too, in the school that the Head had
once broken a fellow's finger, and who knew that he
would not repeat that savage feat to-day ? First one
hand, then the other, and the same bruised and smarting
hands again, just in the same place, and blood-blisters
rising there. . . .

The dressing-bell sounded, and it was necessary to
get up. It was just the sort of morning, too, that
made a fellow wild with mysterious delight, if things
were going well; but when things were black, it seemed
an added insult that the sunlight and the sky were
in such excellent spirits. There was the cricket-

professional in the field outside, whistling as he put up the nets for practice, but there would be no practice for David to-day. Instead, from twelve to one he would be making maps and staring at the Catechism, and his hands would be tender and bruised and lumpy, and there were no stags to cater for. . . .

He went down to his bath feeling utterly wretched and dispirited, with that completeness of emotion that only children know, who are unable to look beyond the present and immediate future, the happiness or misery of which possesses them entirely. Other boys were splashing about and throwing sponges at each other, and he was hailed with the derisive taunts indicating general good spirits and friendliness.

" Hullo, here's Blazes. 'What, reported again, Blaize ! Don't bully me, sir ! The other hand, sir.' Whack, whack ! "

" I say, Blazes, how's the Monarch ? Flown away, Bags says. Dirty vermin anyhow, so what's the odds ? Come and practise at No. 1 net at half-past twelve with me and Ferrers."

David chucked his sponge into his bath and kicked off his slippers.

" Can't. Catechism to learn, thanks to Stone."

" Oh, yes, so you have. I expect you wouldn't be able to hold a bat either. Never mind, buck up. All the same in a hundred years. Besides, Hughes was caned two mornings running last year, and he didn't blub even at the second helping."

The goat-like Bags entered at this moment.

" I say, rough luck," he said to David. " I warned you as soon as I saw Glanders. Found the Monarch yet ? "

This was rather too much. David felt suddenly sure that Bags was at the bottom of all his misfortunes, and, already goaded by high-spirited sympathy, turned on him.

"No, I haven't," he shouted; "and I'm jolly well going to search your cubicle. I believe you stole him. Look here, you chaps, I believe Bags took the Monarch, and I believe he saw Glanders coming when I was talking to him, and didn't warn me."

Stone took his brown head out of the towel in which he had been rubbing it.

"Why? What evidence?" he asked.

"Unless you're too blooming omniscient to want evidence," said Bags.

"Because you're a sneak. Because I jolly well hurt you last night, and you said I hadn't, to put me off the scent," said David with a sudden inspiration. "Why, you've got a bruise as big as a football," he cried, pointing to the injured part of Bags's anatomy, "and yet you said it didn't hurt. It must have hurt: it's all rot to say it didn't. And you said it was *pax* in order to put me off the look-out."

"Bosh: that's not evidence," said Ferrers, whose father was a K.C., and was much looked up to on points of school-law. "That's only your blooming guess."

"Well, it would be evidence if I found the Monarch in his beastly cubicle," said David. "Or perhaps you'd say that stags can fly, and that the Monarch had only flown there."

This was sarcasm of the deepest dye, and produced its due effect on all the boys who, in various stages of undress, surrounded the two, except Stone, who never could understand what sarcasm meant.

"Oh rot, Blazes," said he. "At that rate the Monarch may have flown to my cubicle, but I'm not going to have you search it and turn everything upside down for the sake of a sickly stag-beetle."

The man of law considered the points.

"I don't see why you shouldn't make a challenge out of it, Blazes," he said, disregarding the obtuse Stone. "If you're so certain of it, you can challenge Bags to allow you to search his cubicle, and if you don't find the Monarch there, he gives you three cuts of the hardest with a racquet-handle and *pax* immediately afterwards."

David was standing in his bath, and, slipping, plumped down into it heaving out solid water.

"Sorry, you fellows," he said to those who were wettest. "Right then—I challenge."

Bags had moved away, in the general stampede caused by David's plunge, and on the instant, with fresh suspicions teeming in his head, David jumped out, and got between him and the door of the big bath-room.

"I say, Bags, you haven't had your bath," he said; "and were you going back without it? Aren't you going to have a bath? Not feeling dirty? Anyhow, I challenge. Do you accept it?"

Bags took off his dressing-gown.

"Oh, you thought I was going back to dormitory to put them in your cubicle again, did you?" he said. "It just happens to be my bath there by the door."

"Well, but do you accept?" cried David, executing a sort of Indian war-dance round him.

"No," said Bags. "I don't want to give you three with a racquet-handle, as we made it up last night. And I don't want you turning everything upside down in my cubicle."

Ferrers put on his dressing-gown with the solemnity of a judge assuming the black cap.

"Then it simply proves the plaintiff's case, if you won't have your cubicle searched," he said. "It's all rot about your not wanting to whack Blazes because it was *pax* last night. He's challenged you: it isn't *pax* any longer. State of war!"

Ferrers was in his element, and it seemed to the court generally even as to him, that never at the Old Bailey had the net been woven in such impenetrable fashion round the most palpable criminal. Bags, too, felt that, but the net that really enmeshed him was of very different sort from what it appeared to be. Certainly he was in a hole, but not the hole that every one thought he was in.

The majesty of the law proceeded.

" If you don't accept the challenge," said Ferrers, " it proves you are guilty."

The plaintiff continued to dance.

" I'll let you give me six cuts if I don't find the Monarch in your cubicle," he shouted. " You must be guilty if you refuse six. Mustn't he, Ferrers ? "

Ferrers tore his sock in trying to put it on to a wet foot.

" Not for a cert," he said. " Bags is beastly cunning. He may be running you up to a higher figure."

"Then I'll let him have twelve cuts," said David, feeling absolutely sure about it, " if I may search his cubicle and not find the Monarch. Oh, and search his dressing-gown, too," he added quickly, conjecturing a perfectly demoniacal piece of cunning on the part of Bags.

Bags stepped out of his bath with dignity, feeling there was no escape.

" Then I accept Blazes' challenge of three cuts," he said, " just to show I didn't want to run him up. If I did, I should take twelve."

" Done," said David. " I'll go and search at once; there's another quarter of an hour before school. I may as well search his dressing-gown first. No, not there. Oh, blow! what shall I say if Glanders finds me in his cubicle again ? I know : Bags is in the bath-room, and wants his liniment. If Glanders doesn't think that likely, she can come and look at him."

Now Bags's dilemma, the net in which he was really involved, was this. He had lain awake for two hours last night in savage anger with David, whom, in secret boyish fashion, he adored, and who had been so beastly to him. Open vengeance was out of the question, because, if it came to a fight, David was more than his match, and thus his revenge for that infernal kick must be done stealthily. Plan after plan suggested itself to him, but none were suitable until he thought of the very simple one of taking the Monarch and his wife, which, as he knew quite well, lived in David's washing-basin at night. That was accomplished very easily, without disturbing their owner. But a few hours later he was awakened by David himself, who had conceived the revolting suspicion that Bags had done precisely what he had done. Then at the same moment almost, while he was hot with indignation at being justly accused, he had seen the matron at the far end of the dormitory, and could not resist the temptation to get David into further trouble. This, too, had been successfully accomplished, and David would certainly be caned after morning school. And then Bags began to regret his success : his affection for David, whom no one could help liking even when he was being beastly, and his sense of his own meanness pointed the finger of scorn at him, and, having ensured David a caning, he wished he had not, at any rate, taken his beloved stag-beetles as well. So, lingering behind till the rest of the dormitory had gone to the bath-room, he induced the Monarch and his wife, who were scratching about in his soap-tin, to crawl on to his sponge, and, as he passed David's cubicle, he had shaken them off on to his bed.

Then had come the bath-room complication. He had been forced eventually by Ferrers's resistless legal acumen to accept the challenge, and he would have to whack David, for any one might search his cubicle till Doomsday and never find a stag-beetle there. And each one of those cuts would be unjust : he had taken the stag-beetles, and David was perfectly right. The fact of having put them back did not ease a troubled conscience.

David rushed upstairs again to his dormitory, and with clatter and publicity went straight to Bags's cubicle, and began a violent and intimate search. He searched in his pockets, he examined the lower tray of his soap-dish, he peered behind pictures, and ransacked the receptacle, usually called the synagogue-box, where Bags kept family-letters and such-like, but nowhere was there the faintest trace of the Monarch to be seen. These operations Glanders observed—and David observed that she was observing them—with her bleak and stony eyes, and just as he was very busy she approached.

" Do you want to be reported twice, Master Blaize ? " she asked.

" Oh, certainly, if you like," said David. " But Crabtree asked me to get his liniment."

"And why can't Master Crabtree get it himself, then ? " asked Glanders. " And why does he want liniment ? "

" Oh, don't be tedious," said David. " He can't get it himself, because he hasn't got any clothes on, and is afraid of shocking you, and he wants it because he has got a bruise, which you can see if you aren't afraid of being shocked. Anything else I can tell you ? "

Muffled laughter sounded from various directions as Glanders sniffed, which was her congenital way of acknowledging the legality of doubtful proceedings, and David finished his search, turning over the pillows of Bags's bed without further hindrance. But there was

no Monarch to be found, and he had to go back to the
bath-room to report that he could find no liniment and
had lost his challenge. This was depressing, because
the beloved Monarch was still missing, also his wife,
the hope of the race, and because the loss of the challenge meant three nasty cuts from Bags and his racquet-
handle. And the Head was going to let fly at him
first, and there was the missionary-map to be made,
and the whole blackness of this dreadful Monday
morning, dissipated for the moment by his certainty
that he would find the Monarch, overcast the sky again.

On his way back he passed his cubicle, and, pausing
to throw his sponge and towel down, his eye fell on
his bed, and there on the blanket were two black blots
of familiar shape.

David gave a great sigh.

" Oh Monarch and missus," he said affectionately,
" you little devils."

The travelling-carriage of the royalties was to hand,
and in a moment the black pair were safe again. How
they had got on to his blanket he did not pause to
think, and the three cuts due to him were " jolly
cheap at the price." He made but a couple of leaps
down the stairs to the bath-room.

" I say, I've lost the challenge, Bags," he said ; " but
I've found the Monarch. He was on my blankets, and
so was she. And—I say, I'm sorry I suspected you.
When'll you take your cuts ? "

Bags's inconvenient conscience and affection gave him
a nasty prod at this. If David had only not said he
was sorry he suspected him, he would not have felt
so " beastly." On the other hand, it was dangerous to
try to stifle his internal beastliness by magnanimity, since
this might lead to fresh suspicions on David's part. But
magnanimity salted with sarcasm might serve his turn.

" Oh, I don't want to whack you," he said, " as you say you were sorry. As if I should have touched your filthy stags ! Clip their wings, and take them to Marchester next half, and see if Hughes is proud of his pal who keeps vermin."

David stared in blank surprise. To forgo the pleasure of chastisement was not in the spirit of Shylock.

" Oh, well, thanks awfully," he said. " If you don't want to take your cuts, I'm sure I don't mind not getting them. But why don't you ? "

Bags was struggling into his shirt, and speech was for the moment extinguished.

" Simply because the challenge was too silly for words," he said, as his head emerged.

The repetition of this silly reason did exactly that which Bags desired should not happen. Suspicion, vague and unformulated as yet, again sprang up in David's mind. Such magnanimity was simply childish.

" I think I'll take the cuts then, Crabtree," he said, to mark the complete severance of friendly relations.

That roused Bags : the rejection of his spurious, but highly superior, motives quite stifled the prods of his inconvenient conscience.

" All right, then, you shall," he said. " Gosh ! I'll let into you. I'll put beef into them, Blaize. I've got a racquet-handle that'll do nicely. I bet I break it. You'll want some liniment afterwards."

The ten-minutes bell sounded at this moment, and the boys ran upstairs again to finish dressing and say their prayers. For the last five minutes of these ten they were bound to be on their knees at their bedside, while Glanders patrolled the dormitory. But with care and discreet peeping through fingers it was possible to get through some neglected dressing during the

devotional five minutes, and David, who was a good
deal behindhand, buttoned his collar, put on his tie,
and laced one boot without being detected.

Mr. Dutton was in an unusually docile mood during
this hour from seven to eight, and it wanted little
penetration on the part of his pupils, when they remembered the visit he had done the Head the honour to
pay him last night, to guess the cause of that. David
felt chagrin at the fact that he had been detained in
the bath-room, and had not been able to take the dismembered yellow-back from the grate, to find out
what made the Head so waxy, but there was no doubt
that it was the Head who had made Mr. Dutton so mild.
Indeed, it had often been a debated question as to
which was really the worst, a caning or a proper " jaw "
from the Head, for the hardiest were reduced to unwill-
ing tears by the Head's tongue, when he really chose to
apply it, so convincing and dismal a picture could he paint
of a boy's satanic iniquity, and the inevitable ruin that
such courses fashioned for him in this world and the next.
But it was a point of honour not to cry at any application of the cane after you were twelve ; kids might cry,
but not elderly persons. The cane might break your
hands, and make you set your teeth, but it was not
allowable to let it break your spirit. But a " jaw " broke
your spirit into smithereens, and no doubt that disin-
tegrating process had happened to old Dubs. Anything
in the way of construing was sufficient this morning,
and the grammatical questions were mere child's-play.

It was already ten minutes to eight, and the school
sergeant, a whiskered veteran, who visited the different
class-rooms during early school, with orders from the
Head, and summonses for boys who had been reported,
had already passed the museum door without coming
in, and David's heart rose. If Glanders had reported

him, it was quite certain that the sergeant would have
conveyed the summons that he was to go to the Head
after chapel, to his class-room, and yet he had passed
without delivering it. From time to time these remis-
sions happened. Glanders occasionally forgot to report,
even when she had promised it; sometimes even in the
act of complaining, the stoniness of her bosom relented.
Then, with a sinking of the heart, proportionally greater
owing to its premature uplifting, there was a tap on
the door, and the sergeant entered, saluting.

" Beg your pardon, sir," he said to Mr. Dutton,
handing him a small slip of blue paper; " but I forgot
this as I went by."

Mr. Dutton glanced at it.

" Blaize to go to the Head after chapel," he announced, and David thought he detected a faint smile
showing the malicious glee of a fellow-sufferer.

Chapel, usually tedious, was not long enough that
morning, and the psalms, the lessons, the hymns, and
the prayers passed in a flash. Ferrers, as they went
out, administered spurious consolation.

" If you stick your hands in cold water," he said,
" it'll numb them a bit. I remember, last winter, I
held mine in the snow for five minutes, and it didn't
sting nearly so much."

" And there's such a sight of snow about in July,
isn't there ? " said David bitterly.

Ferrers shrugged his shoulders.

" All right, then," he said, feeling slightly hurt.
" And you've got your three cuts from Bags, too,
haven't you ? I bet Bags lays on."

A minute afterwards he was in the awful presence.
Even as he entered he heard the jingle of keys, and
when he advanced to the table, where its occupant was
looking vexed, he saw that the fatal middle drawer was

already open. That it could have been opened for any other reason did not strike him; he supposed that his case was already judged.

For the moment the Head seemed unaware of his presence, and continued to read the letter that apparently annoyed him.

" Pish ! " he said at length, in a dreadful voice, and, looking up, as he tore it in fragments, saw David.

" Ah, Blaize," he said, " I sent for you—yes, I want you to answer me a question or two."

This looked as unpromising as possible. The drawer was already open, but it seemed that a " jaw " was coming first. Why couldn't he cane him and have done with it ? thought the dejected David.

The Head rapped the table sharply.

" Question one," he said. " Is it the case that my daughters have incurred the wrath of the first form ? "

David's head reeled at the thickness of the troubles.

" Yes, sir," he said.

" Good. Question two, which you need not answer if any sense of honour forbid you to. Why have they deserved this—er disgrace ? And why do you join in inflicting it ? "

David drew a long breath ; there was no sense of honour that would be violated in telling the Head, but to do so was like taking a high header into unknown waters, when it required all the courage you were possessed of to go off a low board into four feet of familiar swimming-bath.

" Please, sir, it's quite obvious that Car——"

He had begun with a rush, and the rush had carried him too far.

" Carrots," said the Head suggestively.

(Lord ! how did he know ? thought David.)

" Please, sir, we felt sure that Miss Edith had got

Ferrers into a row, because she saw him in Richmond the week before last," said David.

" And—and sneaked to me ? " suggested the Head.

" Yes, sir, told you."

" I dare say Miss Edith saw him," said the Head, " but I haven't the slightest idea whether she actually did or not. I saw him myself. Miss Edith had nothing to do with it. Kindly tell your friends so."

" I'll tell them," said David. " They'll be awfully glad, sir."

" Why ? " asked the Head.

Again David dived off the high header-board into dark waters.

" Because nobody wanted to think she was a sneak, sir," he said. " We always thought she was a good chap—young lady, I mean, sir."

The Head nodded, and for the next half-minute busied himself with the reports that had come in that morning.

" I think there was something else I wanted to see you about," he said. " Yes : here it is. You are re-ported for being in Crabtree's cubicle before dressing-bell this morning. Any explanation ? "

" No, sir," said David.

" You knew it was against the rules ? "

" Yes, sir."

The Head drew a large and dreaded book towards him, which contained a list of all the boys' names, and against each the number of times they had been reported for any misconduct during the current term. Next the name of Blaize was that of Bellingham, and, glancing at it hastily, he credited David with Bellingham's stainless record.

" I see you have not been reported before this term," he said.

The moment he had spoken he saw his mistake ; on the line below was David's record, showing that he had

been reported twice.　But he waited for David's answer.
He had not considered what he should do if David accepted the statement, but he believed, and wanted to
prove to himself, that David would not.

A joyful possibility whirled through David's mind;
it was conceivable that previous reports against him
had not been entered.　And then, not really knowing
why, he spoke.

" No, sir, I have been reported before," he said.

" For the same offence ? "

" Yes, sir."

" Once before ? " asked the Head, feeling that his
test stood firm.

" No, sir, twice," said David, squeezing his hands
together.

The Head closed the book.　He put it in the middle
drawer and closed that also.

" Thank you for telling me the truth," he said.　" And
now I want you, as a personal favour, to make an effort
to keep school-rules.　They are made for that purpose.
Good-bye, my boy.　Ah, you are late for breakfast, so
come and have breakfast with me.　If you are late for
school afterwards, explain to Mr. Dutton."

David was joyfully late for school, and not only explained briefly then, but categorically afterwards to his
form in the interval at half-past ten.

" Sausages," he said, " and poached eggs and bacon,
and sloshy buttered toast and strawberries.　Gosh, the
Head does himself well.　He has breakfast like that
every day, I expect.　Didn't I tuck in ?　Oh, and another
thing : Carrots didn't sneak at all, it was the Head
himself who saw Ferrers in Richmond.　He told me so."

" Don't believe it," said Ferrers, who had misogy-
nistic tendencies.

" Well then, you've got to. The Head never fies, and so Carrots is all right. And the Head's my pal."

" Can't think why he didn't whack you, though,'? said Ferrers. " Perhaps he knew you were going to catch it from Bags. He's been binding his racquet-handle, too, to get a firm grip."

This was slightly malicious on Ferrers's part, but what with special tea last night, and special breakfast this morning, and the recovery of the Monarch, and the re-mission of a caning, he thought David a little above himself. But even this information about Bags did not appear to depress him, and he cocked his yellow head on one side, like a meditative canary, and half-shut his eyes, as if focussing something.

" Blow it, if I hadn't forgotten all about Bags," he said. " Ferrers, there's something rummy about Bags's show. Why did Bags not want to take up my chal-lenge, if he knew the Monarch wasn't in his cubicle ? And why didn't he take a dozen cuts at me ? It's all rot of him to say that he didn't care about whacking me. Any decent chap's mouth would water to lick a fellow who had accused him of stealing."

The two boys had wandered away in this half-hour's in-terval between schools to a distant corner of the field below the chestnut-tree. There David lay down flat, and Ferrers flicked the fallen flowers at his face. But he stopped at this.

" You see, I caught him a juicy hack, too, last night," continued David. " And he's a revengeful beast in a general way."

" Perhaps it's the Day of Atonement or something," suggested Ferrers.

David sat up.

" No, that can't be it," he said. " Else he'd want to make me atone. Hallo, here he comes across the field, racquet-handle and all."

He suddenly gave a shrill whistle through his broken front tooth.

" I say, will you back me up whatever I say ? " he asked. " I've thought of something ripping."

Ferrers peered short-sightedly across the field. He did not often wear his spectacles, since they were supposed to give him a resemblance to Goggles, which was the rise of intolerable comment. So they seldom graced his freckled nose.

" Yes, here he comes," he said. " I'll back you up. But, what is it ? "

" Oh, you'll see," said David.

Bags made a truculent approach, swinging his racquet-handle. He had done all that could humanly be done in the easing of his conscience, and since he had been literally unable to get out of the rôle of executioner with honour, he had wisely determined to dwell on the bright side of it, and hit as hard as he could in the same place.

" I'll lick you now if you like," he said brightly.

David turned a cold face on him.

" Thanks, awfully," he said, " but we settled it for twelve. You see, a good deal may happen before twelve. Ferrers and I were just talking it over. Wasn't it a pity that Ferrers Minor slept so badly last night ? "

This remark seemed slightly to disconcert Bags, but he carried it off with fair success.

" The point ? " asked Bags politely, slapping his leg gently with the racquet-handle.

" Oh, thought you might see it," said David. " The point is that he didn't go to sleep before—when was it, Ferrers ? "

" He heard the clock strike one," said Ferrers, at a venture.

A shade of relief crossed Bags's face, which the Machiavellian David noticed.

" I still don't see the point," said Bags.

David pursued his ripping plan.

" No, you've mixed it up, you goat," he said to Ferrers. " Your minor told me he awoke and heard the clock strike one, and lay awake till dressing-bell. Bang, wide awake, like—like toothache."

" Sorry; of course it was," said Ferrers, backing his fellow-conspirator up.

Bags shrugged his shoulders, and began to walk away.

" Afraid I can't see the point," he said. " So I'll whack you at twelve, Blazes."

David lay down again with complete unconcern.

" Right oh," he said. " But, of course, if you've got anything to say about it all, you might be wise to say it yourself, and not let—well, somebody else say it for you. Ferrers Minor hasn't told anybody yet, except his major and me. Not yet, you know," he added.

Bags appeared to take no notice of this, unless he strolled away rather more deliberately than before. Then David turned quickly to Ferrers and whispered in his ear.

" Go and find your minor," he said, " and don't let Bags talk to him. I'm going to stop here. I shouldn't wonder if Bags came back."

" But what on earth is it all about ? " asked Ferrers.

David's eyes sparkled with devilish intrigue.

" Can't explain now," he said. " Just go and stick on to your minor, and don't let Bags question him. There's something up."

Ferrers obeyed the bidding of the master-mind, and by a rapid flank march got in front of Bags, who called to him. But he took no notice, and presently David saw him lead off his minor like a policeman. At that his habitually seraphic face grew a shade more angelic, and any one who did not know him must have been surprised that wings did not sprout from his low slim shoulders.

The Machiavellian device which he had practised had come to him like an inspiration : if Bags's conscience was clear, he would not mind a scrap for the wakefulness of young Ferrers, and David was morally (or immorally) sure that Bags's conscience was not immaculate. He had had something to do with the disappearance of the stag-beetles, though exactly what David had no idea. Then he gave a little cackle of delight, for he saw that Bags had stopped in his indolent stroll with the racquet-handle; then that he turned and was coming back towards him. David lay down at full length and whistled in an absent manner. Without looking, he became aware that Bags was standing close to him.

"I say, Blazes, I want to tell you something," said that conscious-stricken one at length.

David sat up with an air of great surprise.

"Hallo: that you ?" he said. "Tell away then, if it won't take too long."

"Well, it's private. You must swear not to tell any one."

David shook his head.

"Oh, I couldn't do that," he said.

"Why not ?"

David turned on him an indulgent glance.

"Oh, I expect you know," he said. "It's partly because I know already what you're going to tell me, and partly because you're a swindling, stealing liar, and the sooner other chaps know that the better."

Bags made a swinging blow in the air with his racquet-handle.

"Well then, I don't care," he said. "I'll give you three of the jolliest cuts you ever had at twelve."

"Will you ? After Ferrers Minor has told his story ?" asked David.

"Well, I tried to get out of it," said the unhappy Bags

"There was an awful bright moon last night, Crabtree," said David thoughtfully. "But about what you want to tell me. It might make a difference if you told me voluntarily."

Bags capitulated.

"Well, then, I took your beastly stag-beetles, and put them back on your bed when you had gone to your bath."

"Oh, that was the way it was?" said David. "Pretty cute. But then, you see, I was cuter. Ferrers Minor didn't lie awake a minute, as far as I know. But I saw you had a bad conscience. Can't think why you didn't accept my challenge straight off. Why didn't you?"

He looked at the dejected Bags, and his funny boyish little soul suddenly grew perceptive.

"What's the row, Bags?" he asked.

Bags sat down on the grass by him.

"I feel perfectly beastly," he said. "You're always horrid to me, and—and I like you so awfully. You kicked me fit to kill last night, just because I threw an ink-dart at you. I only did it for a lark, just because I felt fit. And after I had taken your stags I was sorry, and I tried to get out of your challenge, though I knew you would lose it."

David ceased to sit in the seat of the scornful. Whatever Bags had done (and he really had done a good deal) he had blurted out that "he liked him so awfully." It was no time to inquire whether he had seen Glanders and not warned him, or to examine further into "the bally show." What Bags had said in all sincerity took rank over anything Bags might have done. And with that he wiped the whole affair clean off his mind, and held out a rather grubby hand.

"I bet we get on rippingly after this," he said hopefully.

CHAPTER IV

DAVID was swaggering about—neither more nor less—
in the new school blazer and eleven-cap on the morning
of the cricket-match against Eagles School, which was
the great event of the entire year. But, as a matter
of fact, this swagger was but a hollow show, and though
he was completely conscious of being an object of
envy and admiration in the eyes of the small boys, or,
indeed, of anybody who was not in the eleven, he did
not envy himself in the smallest degree. To begin
with, he had that which in later life is called an attack
of nerves (though at present it came under the general
comprehensive head of " feeling beastly "), which made
his mouth dry and his hands damp and his inside
empty but not hungry. And, to make this worse, his
father had announced his intention of coming down
to see the match. That might not sound tragical, but
to David it was the cause of awful apprehensions, which
require a true sympathy with the sensibilities attaching
to the age of thirteen fully to appreciate.

To begin with, his father was an Archdeacon, and
since he wore a shovel-hat and odd, black, wrinkled
gaiters even when, as during last summer holidays, he
climbed the hills in the Lake District with a small
edition of the poems of Wordsworth in his pocket,
from which he read aloud at frequent halting-places,
David had not allowed himself to hope that on the
present inauspicious occasion he would be dressed like

any other person, and so escape the biting criticisms that his curious garments would be sure to call forth. But there was much worse than this, for his father was going to stay with the Head over Sunday, and was to preach in school chapel in the evening. That had occurred once before, and the thought of the repetition of it made David feel cold all over, for his father, among many other infelicitous remarks in the course of an infliction which had lasted over half an hour, as timed by the indignant holders of surreptitious watches, had alluded to the chapel and the services there as the central happiness of school-life. David had barely yet lived down that fatal phrase; everything connected with chapel had been rechristened: the chapel bell had been called " the central happiness bell "; it was time for " central happiness "; one was late for " central happiness." The school had been addressed as " lads in the springtime of hope and promise "; it was the most deplorable affair. And he might easily, in this coming trial, give birth to more of these degrading expressions, which David felt to be a personal disgrace.

But it was not even his father's dress nor his possible behaviour in the pulpit that David dreaded most: it was the fear that he would again, as he had expressed it before, " take part in their school-life." On that lamentable occasion he had had dinner with the boys, not sitting at the masters' table, which would have been bad enough, but side by side with David at the table of the sixth form. As ill-luck had it, there was provided for dinner that day beefsteak pudding, otherwise known as " resurrection-bolly," since it was firmly (though mistakenly) believed that it was composed of all the scraps left on the plates during the last week. This tradition was beyond all question of argument and conjecture; it was founded on solid proof, since

Ferrers had distinctly recognised one day, in his portion of resurrection-bolly, a piece of meat which he himself had intentionally left on his plate four days previously. Consequently, however hungry you might be, it was a point of etiquette never to eat a mouthful of resurrection-bolly; and David's misguided parent had not only eaten all his, but, like Oliver Twist, had asked for more, and unlike him had obtained it, and eaten that as well with praise and unction. Of course he could not be expected to know that he had been eating scavenged remains (so much justice was done him), but he had remarked on the excellence of it, whereas it was popularly supposed to " stink." Clearly, then, that was the sort of food which Blaize was regaled on at home in the holidays, and witheringly sarcastic pictures were drawn of Blaize's pater in gaiters collecting scraps from the dustbin in his shovel-hat, and gleefully taking them to the kitchen.

These miserable forebodings, well founded on bitter experience, were interrupted by the arrival of the team from Eagles School, and the home team took the visitors off to the dormitories to put on their flannels. It fell to David's lot to be host to a boy called Ward, of trying deliberation in the matter of dress, who parted his hair four times before he arrived at the desired result, and looked, with a marked abstention from comment, at the decorations in David's cubicle. Consequently, when they got down to the field again, the rest of the two elevens were practising at the nets, the grass was dotted over with groups of boys whose parents had misguidedly determined to visit their sons, while the happier class, unhampered with the dangers and responsibilities attaching to relations, were comfortably dispersed on rugs in the shade of the elms. David cast an anxious glance round to see if his own responsibility had yet arrived, when his eye fell on the figures at the nets, and the appalling truth burst upon him.

There was no possibility of mistake. Mingled with the crowd at the nets on the other side of the field was a figure in gaiters and a shovel-hat just taking off his coat and betraying—an added horror—a brown flannel shirt. He held up a cricket-ball to his eye a moment, in the manner of fifty years ago, and, taking a short stodgy run, delivered it. His hat fell off and the ball was so wide that it went, not even into the net for which it was intended, but into the next adjoining.

David's companion saw (for that matter, David felt that all Europe saw), and laughed lightly.

" I say, look at that funny old buffer in a flannel shirt ! " he said. " He bowled into the wrong net. I wonder why he wears such rummy clothes."

David felt his heart sink into the toes of his cricket-boots, and leak out. But there was no help for it : his father was perfectly certain to kiss him when he joined the fellows at the nets, and the truth might as well come out now.

" Oh, that's my pater," he said.

" Oh, is it ? " said Ward politely, with a faint suppressed smile. " But I expect he's—he's awfully clever, isn't he ? My guv'nor played cricket for England one year, and made fifty."

Just then David was beyond the reach of human comfort. At any other time it would have been a glorious thing to be walking with the son of a man who had made fifty for England, but just now such glory was in total eclipse. There, fifty yards away, was his own father putting his shovel-hat on again : he wore gaiters and a flannel shirt, he bowled into the wrong net, he would preach to-morrow, and perhaps again

eat twice of resurrection-bolly. But a certain innate
loyalty made him stand up for this parody of a parent.

"Oh, my father doesn't know a thing about cricket,"
he said, "but he's frightfully clever. He writes books
about"—David could not remember what they were
about—"he writes books that are supposed to be jolly
good. He took a double-first at Oxford, too."

The Archdeacon had seen his son, and, to David's
great relief, did not bowl any more, but came towards
him. There were bad moments to follow, for he kissed
him in sight of the whole school, at which Ward looked
delicately away. Also he had turned up the sleeves
of his brown flannel shirt (as if brown flannel was not
bad enough) and revealed the fact that below it he
wore a long-sleeved Jaeger vest. How hopelessly impossible that was words fail to convey. Nobody ever
wore vests in the summer : you had your coat, waistcoat and shirt, and then it was you. It was "fuggy"
to wear a vest in the summer unless you had a cold,
and everybody would see that he had a fuggy father.
And, oh, the idiocy of his attempting to bowl! It was
pure "swank" to try it, for at home he never joined
in his children's games, but here the deplorable habit
of "joining in the life of the place" asserted itself.
The same habit made him, when at the seaside, talk
knowingly to bewildered fishermen, before whom he
soon exposed his ignorance by mistaking a mackerel
for a herring, or, when in Switzerland in summer holidays, walk about the milder slopes of the Alps with
a climber's rope about his shoulders and a piece of
edelweiss stuck into his shovel-hat. If he would only
stick to the things at which he was "frightfully clever,"
and not go careering about in these amateur excursions !

Presently the field was cleared for the match; the
home side won the toss, and poor David, who was going

in fifth wicket, endured the tortures of the lost. His father sat next him on a bench in front of the pavilion, still with his coat off, and continued to enter into the life of the place by pouring forth torrents of the most dreadful conversation. There were crowds of boys sitting and standing close round them, every one could hear exactly what was being said, and every one, David made no doubt, was saving it up for exact reproduction afterwards.

"And Virgil," he said, " you wrote to me that you were reading the story of Dido, *Infandum regina jubes*—but we must attend to the cricket, mustn't we ? Ha! There's a fine hit ! Well played, sir ; well played indeed."

The fine hit in question was accomplished by Stone. To any one who knew the rudiments it was perfectly plain that he intended to drive the ball, but, mishitting it, had snicked it off the edge of his bat through the slips, where it should have been caught. Instead of which it went to the boundary.

" Four, a fine four," said the Archdeacon enthusiastically. " Ah, butter-fingers ! The wicket-keeper should have fielded that."

"It was only being thrown in to the bowler," said David.

" Ah, but if the wicket-keeper had fielded it, he might have stumped the batsman," said his father knowingly, suddenly and pleasantly recalling fragments of cricket-lore long since forgotten. " The batsman was yards out of the—the popping crease."

Quite without warning a small boy standing close behind where they sat burst into a bubble of irrepressible giggling, and walked rapidly away, cramming his handkerchief into his mouth. Otherwise just close round them was dead silence and attention, and David looked in impotent exasperation at the rows of rapt faces and slightly quivering mouths, knowing that this priceless conversation was being carefully stored up. He was aware that his father was being gloriously funny, that if it had been anybody else's father who was enunciating those views, he would have listened with internal quiverings, or, like Stephens, would have found himself compelled to move away from politeness. But, agitated and nervous, waiting for his innings, he could see nothing funny about it. Wearily he explained that you could not be stumped off a hit to the boundary, that you were given four runs without running for them; but his father thought it an arguable point, and argued. . . .

Two wickets fell in rapid succession after this, and David began putting on his pads. Aunt Eleanor's five shillings had been spent in a left-hand glove, and even at this dark and anxious moment it afforded him a gleam of consolation. But the donning of these protective articles awoke further criticism.

" Why are you putting all those things on, my boy ? " asked the Archdeacon. " You shouldn't be afraid of a knock or two. Why, we never thought anything of a shooter on the shins when I was a lad. And gloves : surely you can't bat in gloves."

Firm, fixed smiles illuminated the faces of those round. David had rubbed the second glove in, so to speak, rather profusely during this last week; the school generally had heard a little too much about it. But David was hearing a little too much about it now . . . and a shooter on the shins ! how could a shooter hit your shins ? Blazes' pater was talking through his hat, that very odd hat.

" Oh, every one wears pads, and gloves, if they've got them," said David rather viciously.

" Well, well, I suppose we were rather too Spartan for these days," said his father. " Ah, well blocked ; well blocked, sir."

Things were going badly for the home side; four wickets had fallen for thirty, and David was feeling colder and clammier every moment. This was far the most important match of the year, and he knew quite well that it largely lay on him to stem the tide of disaster. He knew too, even more keenly, that he did not like the look of one of the bowlers in the very least. The wicket was fiery, and he was bumping in the most nerve-shattering manner. He himself was, primarily, a bowler; but, owing to the twenty-five runs he had made last week, was put in fifth wicket, instead of being reserved for the tail, when, the sting being taken out of the bowling, he would have been quite likely to make runs. But this morning the sting had not at all been taken out of the bowling; it was still detestably steady, and he saw, in the agonised period of waiting for the next wicket to fall, that he ought to play a careful game, and wait for opportunities of scoring instead of running any risks. On the other hand, with his nerves in this condition, he felt that nothing could give him confidence except one or two proper slogs. With them duly accomplished he thought he could wipe off the paralysing effect of his father's presence and conversation. Then came a shout of " How's that ? " from the field, and Stone was out, caught at the wicket.

There were three more balls in that over, to be delivered, not by the bumping terror, but by a slow bowler, and, as David walked out to the pitch, he abandoned prudence, and determined to hit out, if possible, at once, and so get the confidence he needed. He looked carefully round the field; and stood to receive his first ball.

If he had been able to choose, he would have selected no other ball than that. It was a half-volley, clear of his off-stump, the very ball to smite at. He did so, and in the very moment of hitting he heard that he had

mistimed it. Somehow or other he got right underneath it, and it soared and soared almost straight up
in the air. As he ran, he knew the feverish clapping
of one pair of hands, and his father's voice shouting,
" Well hit, well hit, David."

Then the ball was easily caught by cover-point, and
David was sure that never till the end of his life would
he be able to get over what had happened. He was
out, first ball, off a simple half-volley in the match of the
year. Everybody, from Jessop downwards, would know
and would despise him. And it was the boy whose
father had made fifty for England who had caught him.

It is falsely said that the serious troubles of life only
begin when manhood is reached. There was never
anything so grotesquely untrue. When manhood is
reached, on the contrary, the apparently irremediable
nature of most events almost ceases. The man, though
bitterly disappointed in one direction, has the power
of seeing that there are other directions ; he knows also
that, though he is acutely unhappy at the moment,
his misery will be alleviated not only by his own efforts
but by the mere passage of time. But to any boy whose
keenness and enthusiasm promises well for the future,
no such alleviation is possible. He has no knowledge
of the healing power of time in these crucial years, no
realization that other opportunities will come; his misery,
like his happiness, is exclusive of all other considera-
tions. The moment to David was completely horrible :
he was out on this monumental occasion without scoring, while his hopeless father, though with no sarcastic
intention, had shouted " Well hit, David." And there
was this added sting in that simple phrase, that now
every boy in the school would know what his Christian
name was. For Christian names at Helmsworth were
hidden secrets : if you liked a boy very much you

might tell him what your Christian name was, but to have it publicly shouted out, so that every one knew, was quite horrible. And as he walked back to the pavilion the world contained no more for him than that he was out first ball, and that his name was David. All sorts of stories from the book of Kings, which, most unfortunately, was being read just now at morning chapel, would be treasured up against him. They would ask after Jesse, and as likely as not his stag-beetles would be known as Bathsheba and Uriah.

The innings of the home side proceeded disastrously. The whole team was out before lunch for seventy-two, and Eagles made twenty before the interval without loss of a wicket. David, at present, had not been put on to bowl, and was fielding deep, near where the Archdeacon was sitting talking to Goggles and Carrots, who were apparently instructing him about the disposition of the field, while the Archdeacon, in his manly way, deplored the fact that the wicket-keeper wore gloves and pads. Also he thought that boundaries were an effeminate institution; in his day everything had to be run out (" and a jolly lot of running you had to do," thought David). But with optimistic hospitality, Helmsworth hoped that lunch would worry the batsmen, though Helmsworth's bowling apparently did not, and were as-siduous in filling their visitors' plates and glasses. David's acquaintance of the morning, who had made fifteen out of the twenty runs already scored, proved himself as distinguished at table as he was at the wickets, and ate lobster-salad in perfectly incredible quantities.

During the last fortnight friendship had prospered, as David had thought probable, between Bags and himself, and Bags, who did not, so to speak, know a bat from a ball, and so was not called upon to defend the honour of Helmsworth, had a wise thought that

day. He had been of the group that had listened re-
tentively to the Archdeacon's preposterous conversation, and had seen David's inglorious and fruitless
innings. Then came the wise thought: " it must be
jolly difficult to play cricket if your pater is making an
ass of himself," and directly after lunch Bags proceeded
to tempt the pater away from the field. He got hold of
the key of chapel, listened with sycophantic interest to
legends about the saints in the windows, and managed
to inveigle him into a long stroll round the grounds.
There was something heroic about this, for, though
Bags could not play cricket, he wanted to watch it,
and in especial to watch David. For when he was nice,
he was, in Bags's unspoken phrase, " such an awfully
fetching chap." He had all that one boy admires in
another : he was quick and ready of laughter, he was
in the eleven, which was an attraction, he was very
good-looking, which was another, and in point of fact,
at that portentous moment when it was made matter
of common knowledge that Blaize's Christian name
was David, Bags would have rather liked it if some one
had proclaimed that his own name was Jonathan. But,
as it was only George, it might as well remain a secret.

Now David was a bowler of the type known as
" wily." In other words, he bowled balls apparently
so slow and stupid and devoid of all merit that a batsman who did not know quite all about them felt insulted and tried to do impossible things with them.
So, the score having risen to thirty without the loss of
a wicket, Stone said, " Try an over this end, Blazes."

David had seen the departure of his father with Bags
from the field, and felt enormously better. Another
opportunity in a new direction had come, and as he
took up the ball his fingers tingled with possibilities.
He had a few practice-balls, sauntering up to the

crease, and pitching them slow and high without any spin. Then epical matters began.

He took an enormous prancing run at top speed, and delivered a ball of surpassing slowness. Ward, who received it, suspected there was something funny about it (which there wasn't), and, as it was clearly off the wicket, he left it alone. The next one was a slow, straight half-volley, which he very properly hit for four; so also was the next, with which he did likewise. Then came the wile: David's fourth ball, for which he did not take nearly so long a run, was considerably faster than the other two. Ward completely mistimed it, and was bowled. Off the last ball of his over, a really fast one, he caught and bowled the incomer.

This was better, though still bad. Two wickets were down for thirty-eight, whereas none had been down for thirty. Then ensued an hour of tip-top excitement, at the end of which nine wickets were down for seventy, of which David had taken seven. As it was a one-day's match, it was to be decided on the first innings, if there was not time for two, and at that rose-coloured moment David was probably the most popular person in Surrey.

It was his over again. His first two balls each narrowly missed the wicket, the third was gently spooned into his hands, and he promptly dropped it. The fourth was hit for four, and Eagles had won by one wicket. With his next ball David captured the remaining wicket; but he had already lost the match for them by dropping the easiest catch ever seen.

Two exultant batsmen and eleven miserable fielders went towards the pavilion. Stone, with spurious consolation, slipped his arm into David's, as they walked.

"By Jove, well bowled, Blazes," he said. "You took eight wickets for about thirty. Jolly good for your average."

"Oh, blast my average," said David. "As if I didn't know I lost the match."

David's comment was more in tune with the popular verdict than Stone's. It was quite certain that Helmsworth would have won had not that ass Blazes (David Blazes) dropped the "pottiest" catch ever seen. Exactly as in the world afterwards, his achievement in having so nearly won the match for them by his bowling was entirely wiped out by his subsequent mistake. Criticism, in fact, had nothing to argue about; it was all so clear. And, as tea was in progress in the tent, Bags and the Archdeacon, in a state of high animation, appeared on the lurid scene. They were instructed as to the result.

"Somebody caught you, you couldn't catch him?" said David's father playfully.

"Yes, just that," said David, wanting the earth to open . . . he could have caught that ball with his eyes shut. . . .

The Archdeacon found himself next Goggles, who had told him that morning the difference between point and short-leg.

"I have been seeing the chapel-organ," he said; "my young friend Crabtree tells me you will play to-morrow. A noble instrument. And now we have returned to see some more cricket. I am afraid the Blaize family have not helped you much to-day, but to-morrow we will try again. David is in the choir, is he not? One of us in the choir, the other in the pulpit. Tea? Thank you, a cup of tea after the excitement of the match would not be amiss."

David felt as if he was being publicly insulted, though all that was really at fault was his father's friendly adaptability. He had been markedly interested in cricket, when cricket was predominant, but, the excitement of that being over, he transferred his mind to the

next engrossing topic, which was Sunday, when the
Blaize family would make another effort. But he
erred in not adapting himself to the age and outlook
of those with whom he strove to identify himself, and
in thinking that it was possible for a boy in the school
eleven who had nearly won and then quite lost the
match for his side to treat a tragedy like that lightly,
or feel the smallest interest in pulpits or choirs.

An hour of cricket succeeded tea, but, since it was
impossible to arrive at a finished second innings, this
was but a tepid performance, and, after the Eagles
eleven had been speeded with cheers, in which David's
father joined with wavings of his curious hat, he turned
to more serious concerns again, and took David off
for a stroll in the grounds to have a paternal talk to
him. There was comedy in some of these proceedings,
for when they had put a hundred yards or so between
them and the cricket-field, the Archdeacon took out a
cigarette-case.

"I should not like to be seen smoking," he said,
"by any of your companions, but I think we are unobserved now."

David nearly laughed, but managed not to. As luck
would have it, his father had stopped on the very spot
which was sacred to the meetings of the Smoking Club.

"The Head smokes," he said encouragingly. He
saw, too, that his father's brand of cigarettes was that
preferred by the Smoking Club.

Then ensued the serious talk. Cricket was com-
mended in moderation, but as an amusement only, not
as an end in itself. David's school-work was gone into,
and he gave again the information he had put into his
Sunday letter a few weeks ago. Then, it appeared, his
father had heard a boy swear as he watched the cricket-
match, and hoped that such a thing was a rare if not

a unique occurrence, and David, with the barrier of
age rising swiftly and impregnably between them,
hoped so too. Transitionally, noticing the blue of the
July sky, the true meaning of the Latin word *caeru-
leus* was debated, and David cordially agreed that it
probably meant grey and not blue. Then his prayers
were touched on, which, as a rule, were not very fer-
vent performances. This morning, however, he had
said one prayer with extreme earnestness to the effect
that Helmsworth should win the cricket-match which
they had just lost, and David, after the views that had
been expressed on the subject of cricket, felt it better
not to give details on this subject. Take it all together,
the talk was hardly a success, David's father feeling
that the boy was not " being open with him," which
was perfectly true, and David feeling that his father
didn't understand anything at all about him. This
happened to be true also ; at any rate, his father had
no conception of what it felt like to be thirteen, any
more than David had any conception of what it felt
like to be forty-five. Then came the one bright spot.

" The Head is very well satisfied with you," said his
father as they turned.

Instantly David's eye brightened.

" Oh, is he really ? " he asked. " How awfully
ripping ! Even after——"

He stopped, knowing that his father would not
understand.

" Even after what ? " said he.

David blushed.

" Oh, it was nothing," he said. " I only was going to
say after missing that catch. But—but I suppose he
would think that didn't matter. Though, of course, he's
awfully keen for the school to win the Eagles match."

He left his father at the Head's house, and walked

back across the field to the museum class-room, where he was already late for preparation, as the lock-up bell had sounded ten minutes before. He knew quite well that his father was fond of him, and was anxious about his well-being, but somehow the serious talks froze him up, and he could not feel all the things he knew he was expected to feel. It was so odd not knowing that fellows swore when they jammed their fingers in doors, or were suddenly annoyed at anything. Probably grown-up people did not, but that was because they were grown up. He was afraid it was a distinct relief that the " jaw " was over, and on the top of that, in a way that he did not understand, he was sorry he was glad. And then suddenly he swept all those puzzling regrets off his mind, and he became alertly and absolutely thirteen again.

Walking across the field towards him came Mr. Dutton, who, on his approach, as David's extremely observant eye noted, put something in his coat-pocket in an interesting and furtive manner. Without doubt he had been smoking his pipe, as he came from common-room, a thing which all the school knew was forbidden to masters in the school precincts, for fear of the bad example to the boys. This was interesting; it might lead to something ; and David, knowing that the fact that he had been walking with his father neutralized all possible penalties for being late for lock-up, advanced timidly, as if he thought he was detected in some breach of rules.

Mr. Dutton had just come out of meat-tea with the other masters, and was feeling autocratic. He called David in a peremptory and abrupt manner.

" Come here, Blaize," he said.

Now Mr. Dutton was not at all a nice young man, and his unpopularity in the school was perfectly justified. He had favourites, usually pink, pretty little boys, whose

misdoings he treated with leniency, while those who
were not distinguished with his regard he visited with
the hundred petty tyrannies which his mastership gave
him the opportunity of exercising. He also had an
effective trick of sarcastic speech, which is an unfair
weapon to employ to those who are not in a position to
answer back. And of all those under his charge there
was none whom he so cordially disliked as David, who
returned the aversion with uncommon heartiness. Mr.
Dutton was often not quite sure whether David, under
a polite demeanour, was not "cheeking" him (though he
need not have had any doubt whatever on the matter),
and he was also aware that all the impositions which he
set the boy did not make him in the least an object of
reverence. However, in a small way, he could make
himself burdensome.

"It's after lock-up, Blaize," he said. "What are you
doing out ?"

"Only walking about, sir," said David.

"Did you know it was after lock-up ?"

David looked guilty and shifted from one foot to another.

"Ye-es, sir," he said.

"Then you will write out two hundred lines of the
fourth "Æneid" and bring them to me on Monday evening. I suppose you thought that your heroic performance
to-day, that splendid innings of yours which came to
an end a little prematurely, perhaps, and the wonderful
catch you so nearly held, entitled you to place yourself
above school-rules."

This was excellent Duttonese, cutting and insulting,
and impossible to answer without risk of further penalties
for insolence. For the moment David's face went
crimson with anger, and Mr. Dutton rejoiced in his
mean heart, and proceeded to pile up irony. He had
forgotten the pipe in his pocket, the smoke of which

curled thinly up. But David had not forgotten it, nor did he fail to see that the Head was coming up across the field towards them with his swift, rocking motion, and a vengeance of a singularly pleasant kind suggested itself to him. Had not Dubs made himself so gratuitously offensive, he would not have dreamed of taking it; if he had even only stopped there, he might not have done so. But the disgusting Dubs, intoxicated with his own eloquence, and rejoicing to see David writhing under it, did not stop.

" It was a grand day for you, was it not ? " proceeded this odious man, " with your father to look on, and call out ' Well played, Blaize '—I beg your pardon, ' Well played, David.' And to finish with being late for lock-up is a fine achievement."

The Head was close to them now, coming up silently, on the grass behind Mr. Dutton. At a few yards distance he joined in the colloquy.

" What is all this ? What is all this ? " he inquired. Mr. Dutton turned.

" Blaize is late for lock-up," he said. " I have just set him two hundred lines."

" Well, Blaize ? " said the Head.

David shook off the guilty slouch, and stood erect and confident.

" Please, sir, I was walking with my father," he said. " Mr. Dutton didn't ask me to explain, as he went on about my being out first ball and missing that catch."

" You have only just left your father ? " asked the Head.

" Yes, sir, two minutes ago."

The Head nodded.

" We will remit that imposition," he observed.

Then David suddenly stared at that which he had been secretly glancing at, namely, the whorl of smoke from Mr. Dutton's pocket.

" Please, sir, you're burning," he said, anxiously pointing at it. " Something is burning in your pocket."

The Head transferred his awful eye to Mr. Dutton, and sniffed with his omniscient nose.

" You may go, Blaize," he said. "Well, Mr. Dutton?" David scuttled off.

" Scored off, you cad," he said to himself, still hot with indignation at these insults.

But, as David had expected, there were far worse things to be faced than the sarcasms of Mr. Dutton. Since the conclusion of the match, David's performances, heavily handicapped by those of his father, had been subjected to serious debate, and had been found to be wholly unsatisfactory. It was true that he had captured a quantity of Eagles' wickets at small cost, but with the match in his hands, literally in his hands, he had let it go. Taking his record as a whole, therefore, his futile innings being also brought under scrutiny, it was fair to make unkind allusions to his father. There were dissentients from the general view, the chief of whom was Bags, who said hotly that it was a " chouse " to rag Blazes, considering that if it hadn't been for him Eagles would probably have won by eight wickets instead of one, for who stood the slightest chance of getting out the fellow whose father had made fifty for England, even weighted as he was with salad of many lobsters ? But this view was that of a small minority, and an untrustworthy sort of hush settled down on the first-form class-room as David entered with simulated composure. No master was in charge during this hour of preparation on Saturday evening, and though every boy had to sit at his desk, talking was allowed. Sometimes a sort of patrol-master visited them, and occasionally, for a pleasant surprise, the Head came round, the knowledge of which possibility checked any exuberance; but, provided that no row was made, there was nothing to be feared.

So there was an uncomfortable silence when David entered, the sarcastic intention of which was not lost on him, for there was no mistaking the chilliness of his reception. Bags, it is true, greeted him with a " Hullo, Blazes," but otherwise nothing was said. Then trouble gently began to accumulate, like the quiet piling up of thunder-clouds, with Old Testament allusions.

" I say, Jesse must have been a fine old chap," said somebody. " He had such lots of sons."

" Oh, did he ? " asked somebody else politely. " How many ? "

" 'Bout ten. But the elder ones didn't seem to matter much."

There was a dead silence, and David gathered himself up within himself. Then conversation began again, with rustling of the leaves of Bibles, to refresh memories.

" I suppose Jesse was a Jew."

" Oh, rather. That's why Bags is so keen about his kids. I say, it's sausages to-morrow, isn't it ? "

" Yes, Bags and Jesse and the kids won't have any breakfast. Bad luck."

David looked up, and caught Bags's mild eye, which was gleaming with sympathetic martyrdom. Then the attack became more direct.

" I say, Da—I mean, Blazes—I hope you had a good blow-out to-night."

David had got a certain fighting-light in his eye, which Bags altogether lacked. He replied briskly :

" Yes, thanks," he said. " But why ? "

" Oh, I didn't know. As there are sausages for breakfast——" and a subdued giggle went round.

David opened the lid of his desk.

"I say, Mullins," he remarked to the last speaker, "if you don't know, you'd better find out. I'll ask you about it when we go up to dormitory."

"Right oh," said Mullins, strong in the consciousness of numbers to back him; "but lots of chaps will tell you."

"Then I'll ask them all," said David. "Two at a time, if they funk."

His heart quaked, but the essence of courage is not that your heart should not quake, but that nobody else should know that it does.

"Jesse had younger sons as well," said somebody else, while Mullins was thinking about this. "There was one who was ruddy. I should think it was beastly to be ruddy."

"Oh, yes. He was an awful corker, and kept sheep. Don't suppose he could keep wickets or anything like that. Probably he couldn't hold the simplest catch, either. But I expect he could spoon them up himself, all right. Old Jesse would like that. He would probably say ' Well played.' "

"I say, *what* was the name of the kid ? " asked a voice in tones of the intensest interest.

David had been rummaging in his desk in a meaningless manner, not in order to find anything, but to have something to do to cover his self-consciousness. But when this direct question was asked his hand closed firmly on a tight, solid classical dictionary, and he waited for the answer.

"I think he was called David," said Mullins, who had plucked up again after David's threat, which had silenced him for the time. "Yes, David, I think," he repeated.

"Oh, do you ? " said David, and before Mullins had time to guard, the classical dictionary, discharged with low trajectory, hit him violently on the nose, which proceeded to bleed.

"And if anybody else wants to talk about David, that's what he'll get. Chuck it up here, Bags."

Bags gave a shriek of exultation, as he returned the dictionary.

"Jolly good shot," he said. "Bang on the proboscis."

Though David had followed that excellent maxim of war, "If in an inferior position, attack," he probably would have thought twice, had he not completely lost his temper before attacking, for almost everybody but Bags seemed to have coalesced against him, and he was taking on rather a large order. But the very suddenness and savageness of the attack certainly surprised the hosts of the enemy for a moment, and the gore-streaked Mullins retired to comfort his nose amid dead silence. But David's cause was an unpopular one, and he knew it. The Eagles match was won, except for him, and no one was level-headed enough to reflect that it would have been much more decisively lost without him. Under the circumstances, though he had silenced Mullins altogether (for Mullins certainly would not want to be hurt again, and David in his present mood did not care two straws whether he himself was hurt or not), he knew that he must expect a disagreeable evening.

David would have supplied that night an excellent concrete example to any philosopher who wished to study the unstable nature of popularity. During that exquisite hour when he was tying up and confusing the Eagles side with his "wily" bowling there was no bounds to his popularity, and in one moment, by the insufficient closing of his hand, he had forfeited it all. Bags alone was faithful, and though that shot with the classical dictionary had silenced one of his tormentors, it had been a great mistake. For any one who had lost the match so palpably as he had done must expect to have sarcastic remarks made, and if David had only taken them with the meekness that their justice demanded there would probably soon have been a truce to his punishment. But meekness, unfortunately, was one of those Christian qualities which he was totally devoid of, and, though his summary hard-cornered answer to Mullins had been successful enough, he found that, even if it had been possible to continue making violent assaults on everybody, he had not the heart to do so, so chilly and dispiriting was the general attitude towards him. Stone, for instance, though he had congratulated David on his bowling directly after the match, was swayed by popular feeling, and when, on going up to dormitory, David offered him one of his supper biscuits, which was highly sought after, Stone said " No, thanks," in a tone that would have chilled a salamander. No one definitely cut him, and there were no more direct allusions to the son of Jesse, for the portent of Mullins's nose was a danger-signal which it would have been folly to disregard ; but if he spoke, he was answered in polite monosyllables, and if he joined a chattering group, the chatter ceased until he went away again. No one but Bags came to sit on his bed, and though he made pretence of being particularly communicative and cheerful, he jested with a hollow heart.

Next morning was Sunday, and, in lieu of early school, the boys were allowed to spend the hour before breakfast at the bathing-place. But when David asked Stone to come and bathe with him Stone replied that he was engaged to Mullins, and it was bitter to see Ferrers lend Mullins his towel (though after he had finished with it himself) and find that Mullins, fat, stupid Mullins, was regarded not only as an injured person, which anybody could see who looked at his face, but an unjustly injured person And in the middle of David's bathe, who should appear but the Archdeacon

himself! It is true that he went to the far end of
the bathing-place, which was known as the masters'
bathing-place, where the Head himself sometimes
swam fiercely about; but the stout apparition of his
father, clad in a striped jersey cut off at the knees and
shoulders, standing on the header-board was a distracting affair. Even the loyal Bags, who had followed
David down to keep him company (for Bags was not
allowed to bathe, having a weak heart), even Bags gazed
in dismay at that squat, square form, and said " Lor'."
Simultaneously somebody behind David remarked:

" Anyhow, he takes his gaiters off."

David felt too desolate to resent this; also he was
watching his father, almost praying that he should
take a neat header. But a loud, flat smack was heard
as he fell into the water.

And Ferrers said to Mullins:

" I say, can your pater take belly-floppers ? "

Then Mullins (with a watchful eye on David), as he
dried himself with Ferrers's towel, began to whistle
" Once in royal David's city." Other boys began to
whistle it too. It was all deplorable.

The day had begun badly and continued badly.
David offered to share his hymn-book with the boy
who sat next him in chapel, who appeared not to see
what he did. He asked Stone to come for a walk
with him after chapel, and again Stone was engaged
to Mullins. But all the time Bags was waiting like a
dog to divert and console his master if only his master
would allow him, eagerly braving the unpleasantness
of alliance with the unpopular side; and though, twenty-
four hours ago, David would have scouted the idea of
Bags consoling him, he turned to him eagerly now,
and even allowed him to have the Monarch's travelling-
carriage in his pocket at dinner. And though all the

slights and sneers which surrounded them were of the
general nature of chaff, they were of the species of chaff
which is meant to hurt. As Bags had once acutely
remarked, you can hit a fellow over the head just to
show you like him, but you can do the very same thing
in an opposite spirit, and it was this spirit just now
that animated these small boys. It was " a rag," no
doubt, but a rag with a sting in it, for David was
paying the penalty of having been popular, as well as
of having disappointed his admirers.

But an eye, wholly unsuspected, was watching the
situation. The Head was perfectly aware that David
had lost the match against Eagles (though he had so
nearly won it); he was aware also what manner of impression David's father would make on his irreverent
school, and when all day he saw David no longer the
centre of groups that were making rather more noise
than was necessary, but either alone, or with Bags, he
took counsel with himself and stroked his grey beard for
several minutes. Then he went across to the museum,
where the first form were sitting under Mr. Dutton, about
the time that the Catechism would be finished and the
third missionary journey embarked on. There, having
excused Mr. Dutton, he suddenly addressed David.

" Blaize," he said, " though it is Sunday, and we are
in school, I must just congratulate you on your bowling performance yesterday. I have watched a good
deal of cricket at Helmsworth for the last twenty years,
and it was by far the finest piece of bowling I can remember. The school ought to be proud of you. Now,
for our work. Antioch! Stone, where is Antioch?"

There was no getting round this. Stone, Ferrers,
David, and Bags walked arm-in-arm to chapel together.
And Mullins's nose suddenly became the subject of un-
kind and universal comment.

CHAPTER V

DAVID returned from the station on Monday morning,
where he had been permitted to go, in order to see his
father off, in extremely good spirits, with his straw hat,
trimmed with the school eleven colours, well back on
his head, his hands in his pockets, where one caressed
five distinct shillings, the other the travelling-carriage
of the Monarch, while fragments of cheerful tunes
came piercingly forth from the aperture caused by
his broken tooth. The shape of this orifice no doubt
had something to do with the deafening quality of his
whistle, which went through the head of the hearer
like the chirping of a canary in a circumscribed room;
and when deeds of infamy, such as illicit feasts, were
going on in the bushes at the far end of the second-
club field, he was often suitably bribed to keep watch
at the railings nearest the school buildings, for his
whistle carried that distance quite easily. There was
therefore, when his melodies were heard, time to remove
all traces of debauch before Dubs or any other incarna-
tion of danger could arrive. So desirable, indeed, was
the gift of a really resonant whistle that Ferrers had at
one time begun operations on one of his own front teeth
with the file on his nail-scissors in order to get a similar
configuration, but increasing tenderness had made him
desist before he had got far.

David was conscious of a great many things that
made for cheerfulness. His father, to begin with, had

put himself gloriously right with the school, and had, very wisely, left in the hour of supreme popularity, so that there was no fear of his forfeiting, by gaiters or Christian names or flat headers at the bathing-place, or any such tragic follies, the esteem he had won. For, greatly daring, as it seemed to the boys, he had asked the Head to grant an extra half-holiday, and the announcement that it would be given this afternoon, " in honour of his visit," had duly appeared on the school notice-board. It was supposed by some one who had seen his flat header that the phrase " in honour of his visit " must mark a sarcastic intention on the part of the Head, but whether that was so or not there was no doubt about the half-holiday, which was all that mattered. Even David, when quite respectfully appealed to, had no clear idea as to why his father's visit was an honour, but supposed it must have something to do with the books he wrote, which were printed by the Clarendon Press at Oxford. In any case, he felt quite certain now that all the errors of which his father had been guilty would be pardoned and forgotten, and that he would never hear any more of his hat or his gaiters, of his excruciating performance at the cricket-nets, of his belly-floppers into the bathing-place, of his betrayal of his own son's Christian name, or finally of the disastrous discourse he had unfortunately delivered at school-chapel on Sunday evening. For the moment, as he remembered that, David's whistle ceased, and he clutched at the five shillings and the Monarch's travelling-carriage for comfort. It had been too awful : not only had he talked the most dreadful rot about the joy and peace of the chapel services (same as last year, only worse) under the influence of which all troubles and anxiety melted away, but he had gone on and on and on in a manner quite

unparalleled. For forty stricken minutes he had detained them, (Stone said forty-two) which beat all
known records by at least nine minutes, and it was no
wonder that the boy next David had written "AND
NOW" in capital letters on the fly-leaf of his hymn-
book and passed it to him. . . . But that was all
over; he had made the most honourable amends, and
David knew that his father would be considered a
credit to him. Indeed, that "he was a first-rate old
buffer" was quite a moderate estimate of him, and
one given by the most critical.

There were other satisfactory points about him also.
He had asked that David should be allowed to see him
off at the station, so that he could have a further talk
with him. This meant missing half an hour (or more,
if he lingered on his way back, as he was doing) of
repetition of Latin prose. David had not been certain,
at starting, that he would not sooner do prose repetition than have more "jaw"; but the "jaw," when it
came, was of the most delightful kind. Not only was
he certainly to go to Marchester in September, but,
after consultation with the Head, it had been settled
that he was to go there next week to try for one of the
scholarships, a wholly lovely adventure. Apparently
—this was news to David—his work had shown great
improvement during this last term; it showed signs
of perception and taste, and, though greatly wanting
in accuracy, which, the Archdeacon reminded him,
could always be attained by the industrious and pains-
taking, it might prove up to scholarship-level. David
did not attend much to these generalities: the point
was that he would go to Marchester for a three-days'
examination next week.

Finally, as a cause of happiness, his father had on
the platform presented him with the five shillings that

now he clutched in his pocket, to commemorate his
having got into the school eleven. That presentation
had been so sheer a surprise that David could have
fallen flat on his face with astonishment. He would
have expected, if the fatal topic of cricket was to
occur again, to be reminded that it was only a game,
and to be bidden to take thought of it just as such and
no more; but to be tipped on such a scale had not
entered into his most sanguine calculations. Then the
train had come in, and David submitted to be kissed
publicly without shying, even though a small vendor
of papers, with whom he had slight differences before
this, ceased shouting " Dily Mile," and squeaked " Kiss
me, ducky," in perfectly audible tones. He could be
dealt with after the train had gone. . . .

So his father waved his shovel hat from the window
and David his straw hat from the platform, after
which he twitched off the paper vendor's cap and rubbed
his face upwards with it, and hit him on the hands so
that he dropped all his papers, and strolled back to
school again in the highest spirits. And not only were
his spirits high, but, for the first time in his life, he was
conscious of how happy he was, instead of just being
happy. This morning he seemed to stand away from
himself and envy the boy (only it was himself) who was
going to try for a Marchester scholarship next week,
and was certainly going there in September, and had
five shillings and two stag-beetles in his pocket, and
was in the school eleven. Child though he was, consciousness of self had come to him : he knew that his
head was full of delightful plans, that his limbs were
taut and strong, that he was set in the enchanted
garden of the world. He said, " By Gosh ! " and
saluted the discovery by kicking an empty tobacco-tin
that lay in the road with such firm accuracy that it

flew with a whirring, gong-like sound over the fence of
the house where the assistant masters of the school
lodged, and David thought it wise to go swiftly away,
and not look behind.

He dropped to a sober pace again after putting a
corner between himself and the masters' house into the
garden of which the empty tin had so pleasantly flown,
and from mere happiness made a quantity of good
resolutions, one of which he immediately put into effect
by not going into the tobacco-shop where he had
originally intended to buy a packet of cigarettes as a
present for the Smoking Club. Just now the solid
satisfaction of life rendered unnecessary such minor
adjuncts, and, since he did not like smoking, it was
convenient that it happened to be contrary to school
rules. There were such hosts of things pleasant and
not against school rules, that he wished, by way of a
thank-offering for them, to resolve on a virtuous life.
He really would get up at the sound of the first bell
in the morning for the future, he would not smoke any
more, he would not look up the answers to sums before
he wrestled with them, nor copy out on his shirt-cuff
the principal rivers of Russia. They were there now
in fact, and in this sudden access of being good because
he was happy, he stopped then and there, and, with a
piece of india-rubber, expunged the Volga and the
Vistula and the Don and the Dnieper. And, as if to
reward him, just as he got to the school-gate eleven
o'clock sounded, which meant that Latin prose repetition was over, and since to-day was a half-holiday,
there was only one more hour of school, and that was
English literature, the one lesson of the week which he
actively enjoyed, and, though the Head usually took it,
was not in the least terrifying. He asked but few
questions, or sometimes there were no questions at all,

but he would read to them a poem, with explanations
of difficult words or sentences, so that any one could
understand it, and then perhaps shut the book and
repeat it very slowly in his deep, smooth voice, so that
the magic of beautiful words wove its spell round
David's wondering mind.

To-day, on his way to the museum, just as David
passed the long French windows of the Head's study,
he stepped out and called him.

"So you've seen your father off, Blaize?" he
asked.

"Yes sir; thank you, sir," said David, beaming.

"Ah! Well, we'll take a little stroll across the field,
you and I, before we begin our English literature."

It was one of those days when Rhadamanthus un-
bent, when the man who could be so terrible became
wholly enchanting, a man not to fear but to love.
These days were not common, but when they came they
were golden.   And now that tremendous person, who
had been a rowing-blue at Oxford, who was the in-
carnation of fate and retribution, laid his arm over
David's shoulder and put aside his terrors.

"I had a long talk to your father, David," he said.
"No, no one can hear me call you David—don't be
alarmed; and no doubt he has told you part of what
we said, that you are to go up for a scholarship at Marchester next week.   Do your best, won't you, and be
a credit, not to me, which doesn't matter so much, but
to yourself.   And I told your father I was proud of you,
and I meant it.   You and I have had what they call
words before now, haven't we?   In fact, I'm afraid
that sometimes it has come to blows.   You have often
been most unsatisfactory, idle and careless and dis-
obedient; I dare say there's not a single school rule
that you haven't broken.   But I told your father that

I had never found you mean nor bestial. I look upon
you as a boy I can trust."

David's young skin flushed with pleasure, and then went
white again with a resolution that frightened himself.

" I—I've done lots of things you don't know about,
sir," he said. " I don't think it's right you should
think me good; I've——"

The Head stopped, and David's heart sank into his
boots. What an ass he had been to say that! Why
not have received this handsome tribute, however un-
deserved, without disturbing the misplaced faith that
prompted it? And yet he knew that he had done
it deliberately and because he had to.

" Do you wish to tell me about them ? " asked the
Head. But his voice was still quiet and kind. David
seemed to himself to be going mad. He just heard his
voice in a quaking whisper say :

" Yes, sir."

" Well, then, David, I don't want to hear about
them," said this astounding man, " though I thank you
for wishing to tell me. I feel sure you have broken
rules of school often enough, but I don't think you
have broken rules of character. They are much more
important, though school rules have got to be kept as
well."

Suddenly his grip on David's shoulder tightened,
and his eye fixed itself on the back of a small boy who
was sitting on the wire railing at the edge of the field,
unconscious of their approach.

" Ferrers Minor, I think," he called out in an awful
voice.

The Head thought right, and Ferrers Minor presented his startled and dejected countenance.

" Did you, or did you not, know the rule about sitting
on the railings ? " demanded the Head.

" Yes, sir," said Ferrers Minor.

" Then this is wilful disobedience," thundered the Head. " I will not be bullied by you, Ferrers Minor, nor have you disregard the rules with which you are perfectly well acquainted. I suppose you wish to make a fool of me, to hold me up to ridicule for having the impertinence to frame rules which Mr. Ferrers Minor keeps or not, as he finds convenient. Was that your plan ? "

" N-no, sir," said Ferrers Minor.

" Then I will make a plan for you instead, and it is that you write out in your best copy-hand ' I will not sit on the railings like an ass ' a hundred times. You may go, Ferrers Minor."

But Rhadamanthus, the inexorable terror, had only mounted his judgment throne for a moment, and came down off it again. His grip relaxed, and he patted David's shoulder.

" And now for our literature lesson," he said. " It's too hot to hold it in the museum, isn't it, Blaize, when we can sit under the trees instead. Let's have it out here : go in, will you, and tell the class to come out. And, personally, I shall take my coat off, and anybody else who likes to do the same of course may."

The boys trooped out at David's summons, peeling off their coats, and grouped themselves in the shade of the four big elms that stood in a quadrilateral clump at the edge of the field. The Head had taken off his coat, and, leaning on his elbows, lay on that part of his person which in ordinary mortals is called the stomach, with a book or two in front of him.

" All comfortably settled ? " he said. " That's all right. Now to-day I'm going to talk to you about a man whom very likely you have never heard of, and read you something he wrote. His name was Keats, John Keats. Has anybody heard of him ? "

Nobody had.

" He was a chemist's assistant," said the Head, " and if some ninety or a hundred years ago, you, Stone, or you, Blaize, had gone into a doctor's little dispensary near Hampstead to get a dose because you had a pain in your inside, from eating too many strawberries, or from having shirked into Richmond and devoured more than a sufficiency of Maids of Honour, you might have had your medicine given you by one of the greatest lyrical poets who ever lived. The doctor's assistant, a pale young man with a bad cough, might perhaps have mixed it for you, and if you were wide awake you might have seen that when he got up to give you your pill or your powder, he laid down a pencil and a piece of paper on which he was scribbling. Stone, if you leave that wasp alone he will not get angry and sting you, or lose his head and think it was me who was annoying him. Yes, and then when you had paid your twopence and gone away with your pill, you may be sure he would have taken up his pencil and paper again. No doubt, if you had asked him, he would have copied out for you what he was writing on another piece of paper, in which he was accustomed to wrap up parcels, and wondered that you cared to pay another twopence for it. But if you sold that piece of paper to-day you would get, not twopence, but hundreds of pounds for it. For on it would be written lines by John Keats, in his own hand. And what you might have found on that piece of paper is this :

> " My heart aches, and a drowsy numbness pains
> My sense, as though of hemlock I had drunk,
> Or emptied some dull opiate to the drains
> A minute since, and Lethe-wards have sunk.

"Lethe we had in our Homer not long ago. Lethe, the water of forgetfulness. Sometimes I think Blaize and others of you have drunk it.

> " 'Tis not through envy of thy happy lot,
>   But being too happy in thy happiness
>   That thou, light-wingèd dryad of the trees
>   In some melodious plot
>   Of beechen green, and shadows numberless,
>   Dreamest of summer in full-throated ease."

He read on, occasionally stopping to explain a word; once and again his voice trembled, as it did sometimes when he preached; once it nearly stopped altogether as he came to the lines:

> " Perhaps the self-same song that found a path
>   Through the sad heart of Ruth, when, sick for home,
>   She stood in tears amid the alien corn.

" In tears amid the alien corn," he repeated.

The entire informality of these proceedings, the absence of the sense that they were being taught and had got to learn, disarmed the boys, and before this stanza was reached the fact that it was the portentous Head who was reading to them had quite vanished. They were all sitting or lying about at ease on the grass, one or two of them listening intently, the others, for the most part, feeling just lazy and soothed and comfortable. But among the intent listeners was David, and as the Head paused and repeated " alien corn," he rolled over on to his back, absorbed and lost.

" Golly," he said quietly to himself. " Oh Golly ! " Then he became aware that he had spoken aloud, but scarcely wondered whether the Head had heard or not, so completely did the magic of the words possess him. And in some mysterious way they added to his store of happiness : they became part of him, and thus part of the fact that he was going to Marchester

next week, and would see Hughes, that there was a
half-holiday this afternoon, that he was in the eleven.
Keats's poem was part of the whole joy of life, it, and
its music, and the sense of longing for something he
did not know about, which it produced in him. Then
his attention was completely diverted by the feeling
of a slight vibration in his trouser-pocket, caused by
the movements of the Monarch and his wife who were
there in their travelling-carriage, and, now that he
recollected them, became part of the beneficent joy of
things in general. So for fear of their not getting their
proper share of the oxygen of the world, he withdrew
the box from his pocket, laid it on the grass, and forgot
about them again, in hearing of the " foam of perilous
seas."

The Head finished the Ode, and invited questions.
Stone wanted to know what Hippocrene was, thinking
this an intelligent question, but Ferrers's inquiry as to
what the " magic casements " were earned stronger
approbation from the Head, who mysteriously told him
that no one could tell till they looked out on to the
" perilous seas." It was not like the "Commentaries "
of Julius Cæsar, this which he had read them, because
it could mean different things to different people.
Each sentence of the " Commentaries " meant one thing
and it was the business of boys to find out, with the aid
of a dictionary, what it was. But music and poetry
were altogether different : they meant to you what
you were capable of finding in them. Then he turned
to David, who alone of the class had not asked any
questions, intelligent or otherwise.

" Nothing you want to know, Blaize ? " he asked.

" No, thank you, sir," said David. " But would
you read it us again, sir, as you do sometimes ? "

The Head sat up, clasping his knees with his arms,

and without answering David began the Ode again in
that extraordinary voice of his, this time not looking
at his book.   He began in tones so low that it needed
an effort to hear him ; it boomed out over " charioted
by Bacchus and his pards " ; it sounded like a breeze
at night in the stanza " I cannot see what flowers are at
my feet "; again it shook with emotion over the " sad
heart of Ruth," and David felt a lump rise in his throat,
a mysteriously blissful misery took possession of him.
And when the Head finished he found himself smiling
at him with mouth that trembled a little.

There was silence a moment.

" That will do for to-day," said the Head.   " You
can go."

The group rose from the grass with alacrity, for
though Keats was all very well, an extra half-hour at
the bathing-place, for the lesson had been very short,
was even better.   But in spite of the permission David
lingered.

" Did he write much else, sir ? " he said.

The Head handed him the volume.

" You may see for yourself," he said.   " Give it me
back when you've finished with it."

David deposited this in his desk in the museum,
and then ran after the others to the bathing-place, with
lines still ringing in his head, but untying and un-
buttoning as he went so as to lose as few seconds as
possible before the first heavenly plunge out of the heat
and baking sunlight into the cool arms of the water.
That, too, on this morning of vivid life was more consciously delicious than ever before, when with a long
run he sprang, an arrow of gleaming limbs, off the
header-board which he left vibrating with his leap,
and burrowed into the cool embrace of the water.
Some flower must have opened in his brain to-day,

quickening his sense of living, and though no whit less boyish than before, he was far more conscious of the water and the sun, and above all of himself.

He swam and floated and dived, came swiftly up behind Stone, who swam in rather a water-logged manner, and with a firm hand placed suddenly on the top of his head sent him down to the bottom of the bath, and before he came up again, spluttering and more water-logged than ever, was floating with arms and legs spread star-fish fashion, gazing serenely and unconsciously into the sky. Stone concluded mistakenly that it was Ferrers who had done this thing, and raised a storm of splashing in his indignant face, and got ducked again for that, and so precisely flicked with a wet towel when he came out that he cried on the name of his Maker and danced with the shrewdness of the touch. Upon which David, forgetting that his mouth was submerged, laughed, and thereon swallowed so much water that he had to come out and lie face downwards on the grass in order to disgorge it. That was pleasant also, and he lay there on the grass with his forehead on his arms till his back was dry and baked. Then, making a compact parcel of himself with his hands clasped round his ankles, two friends lifted him and swung him into the water again.

Bags the unbathed had brought down some strawberries and newly baked buns, and David, having filled himself up with those things, took to the water again in spite of Ferrers's warning that if you bathed directly after a heavy meal you got cramp in your stomach and sank like a stone to rise no more. It was necessary to test the truth of this remarkable legend, and it was found to be wholly untrustworthy. . . . And all the time the magic casements and the alien corn wandered fragmentarily in his head.

The first eleven played the next sixteen that afternoon, and still that happy tide of the consciousness of
life and the beautiful jolly things of life bore David
along. He made a catch of an unparalleled order off
his own bowling from a hit so smart that he had only
meant to put up his hands to protect his face, and the
ball stuck in them to his great surprise and hurt more
than anything had ever hurt. Subsequently he made
thirty runs after being missed three times, which added
zest to the performance, and took the Head's volume
of Keats up to bed with him. But, Glanders being
ill, and the dormitory unpatrolled, he had a wonderful
pillow-fight with Bags instead of reading, and did not,
as his custom was, go instantly to sleep when at length
he got into bed. Instead he lay in a lump with his
hands round his knees saying " Jolly happy, jolly, jolly
happy ! By Gad, ' fairy lands forlorn ! Fairy lands
forlorn.' Gosh, how that catch hurt ! but what frightful
sport ! Marchester next week too . . . five bob. . . ."
    And these images lost their outline, and became
blurred with the approach of sleep.

    One of the house-masters at Marchester was an old
friend of the Archdeacon, and it had been arranged
that David should stay with Mr. Adams when he went
up for his scholarship examination. Hughes, David's
great chum of a year ago, was in Adams's house, and
by permission met him at the station, and, after the
first greetings, looked David over with an eye made
critical by the adamantine traditions that bind junior
boys at public schools. Hughes was extremely glad
to see him, but he had certainly been very anxious to
get an early and private view of him to see if he came
up to the standards and ordinances then prevailing,
and make such corrections in his bearing and attire as

were necessary. It would be an awful thing, for instance, if David turned up in a straw hat with his school eleven colours, as those were identical with the Rugby fifteen colours at Marchester, and to be seen walking about with a small alien boy in fifteen colours was a nightmare possibility. But there was a lot, as he saw at once, to be said in David's favour : his clothes were neat, he looked exceedingly clean (not grubby, a thing which Hughes, from his faded reminiscences of Helmsworth, was dismally afraid of), his hair was short behind and well inside his collar, and he stood straight. On the other hand, there were certain details that must be altered.

" I say, have you been travelling in a smoker ? " he asked. " Second, too."

David wished he had spent his last shilling in going first.

" Yes, first was so frightfully expensive," said David.

" Oh, I didn't mean that : all the fellows go third. Yes, the bus will take your luggage up, and we'll walk, shall we ? It'll take the fug of the smoking-carriage out of your clothes."

David marvelled at this : he had thought a smoking-carriage must be the manly thing. He had a packet of cigarettes also in his coat-pocket.

" Don't fellows smoke here ? " he asked, looking up in timid admiration at Hughes, who had grown enormously.

" Oh yes, in some scuggy houses," he said, " but not in Adams's. It's thought frightfully bad form in Adams's ! "

David fingered his packet of cigarettes nervously, conscious suddenly of the enormous gulf that yawned between a private and a public school, and yearning to bridge it over by every means in his power.

" I've got some cigarettes in my pocket," he said.

" Oh, chuck them away," said his friend, " or give them to a porter. It would be a rotten affair if any of the fellows in the house knew. You'd come here with a bad name."

David's face fell for a moment, for those were gold-tipped cigarettes, which he had thought would probably be so exceedingly the right thing. Hughes noticed this, and gave consolation, for really Blaize was extremely presentable.

" I say, Blazes," he said, " I'm awfully glad to see you, and we'll have a ripping time. But it's best to tell you what's the right thing and what isn't, don't you think ? "

David responded cordially to this.

" Rather," he said, " and it's jolly good of you. Thanks, awfully. Do tell me if there's anything else."

Hughes gave him another critical glance, as solemn as a tailor's when looking at the fit of a coat that he wants to be a credit to him.

" Oh well, that buttonhole," he said. " I think I should take that out. Only tremendous swells wear them, and even then it's rather ' side.' "

David instantly plucked out the offending vegetable. He probably would have torn out a handful of his hair, if crisp yellow locks showed " side." Hughes nodded at him approvingly.

" Now you're first-rate," he said. " Oh, just send your stick up with your luggage. Now come on. You look just as if you were at Marchester already. You see I got leave for you to come and brew—have tea, you know—in my study this afternoon, and it would have been beastly for both of us, if you weren't up to Adams's form, and it turned out that you smoked, or kept white mice, or something hopeless."

The two handsome boys went on their way up to

the Mecca of David's aspirations, and he thought with
the deepest relief of his decision not to bring the
Monarch and his wife with him.   It had been a wrench
to part with them even for a few days, and an anxiety
to leave them even in the care of the assiduous Bags,
to whom he had given a paper of directions about
diet and fresh air.   But if it was hopeless to keep
white mice, how much more dire would have been his
position if he had been found possessed of stag-beetles,
or if, as might easily have happened without this
oblique warning, he had incidentally mentioned to
some of Hughes's friends that his tastes lay in those
verminous directions! And Hughes proceeded, inspired by that authoritative conventionality which
public schools so teach, that every well-bred junior
boy of fifteen or sixteen in any house is in character-
istics of behaviour exactly like every other.   At one
time buttonholes and smoking are *de rigueur*, at another
they are quite impossible ; at one time it is the fashion
to be industrious, and every one works, at another to
be as idle as is possible.   Morals are subject to the
same strict but changeable etiquette ; for years perhaps the most admirable tone characterises a house,
then another code obtains, and Satan himself might be
staggered at the result.

" Jove, it was a good thing I came to the station,"
he said, " and I wanted to, too.   Else you might have
appeared with a stick and a buttonhole and a cigarette,
and a slow-worm for all I knew.   Do you remember
we had a slow-worm, you and I, at Helmsworth ?   Of
course some fellows go in for natural history, and
Maddox, who's the head of our house, collects butterflies.   But then, he's such a swell, he can do just
what he likes.   I'm his fag, you know, and he's awfully
jolly to me.   Damned hot it is ; let's walk slower."

David was extremely quick at picking up an atmosphere, and he made the perfectly correct conclusion that, though smoking was bad form, swearing was not. But the mention of Maddox roused the thrill and glamour of hero-worship—a hero-worship more complete and entire than is ever accorded by the world of grown-up men and women to their most august idols.

"Oh, go on, tell me about Maddox," he said.

"I dare say you'll see him. Sure to, in fact. He's not very tall, but he's damned good-looking. He's far the finest bat in the eleven, and the funny thing is he says cricket's rather a waste of time, and hardly ever goes up to a net. He's editor of the school-paper, and played racquets for us at Queen's last year. But what he likes best of all is reading."

"That's queer," said David.

"'Tis rather. He makes all our juniors work too, I can tell you. But he'll help anybody, and he'll always give you a construe of a bit you don't understand, if you've looked out all the words first. And he's only just seventeen—think of that—so that he'll have two more years here. He never plays footer, though he can run like hell, and says Rugby is a barbarous sport; and in the winter, when he's not playing racquets, he just reads and reads. His mother was French, too; rum thing that, and the point is that H.T. (that's Hairy Toe, an awful ass) who teaches French, is English, and Maddox knows about twice as much as he. He makes awful howlers, Maddox says, and pronounces just as if he was a cad. But that's all right, because he is."

David skipped with uncontrollable emotion.

"Oh, I say, how ripping!" he said. "But I wish Maddox liked cricket and footer."

"Well, footer he detests; but he only means that

thinking of nothing but cricket is a waste of time. By the way, you're in luck : there's a two-days' match begins to-morrow against Barnard's team. Friday's a whole holiday ; some frowsy saint. They say Jessop's coming. Wouldn't it be sport to see him hit a dozen sixes, and then be clean-bowled by Cruikshank ? "

" Oh, and who's Cruikshank ? " asked David.

" Well, that's damned funny not to have heard of Cruikshank. Fastest bowler we've ever had, and he's in Adams's too. He and Maddox don't get on a bit, though of course they're awfully polite to each other. Cruikshank's awfully pi : fit to burst. Here we are."

Hughes again cast an anxious eye over David, for the moment was momentous, as the whole school would be about. But he really felt that David would do him credit. They paused a moment in the gateway.

" If you like we'll stroll round the court," he said, " before we go down to house. There's chapel, you see, and hall next beyond it ; foul place, stinks of mutton. Then two more college boarding-houses—what ? "

" But which is Adams's ? " asked David.

" Oh, that's not here. These are all college houses, in-boarders, and rather scuggy compared to out-boarders. Then there's fifth-form class-room, and sixth-form class-room, and school library up on top. I dare say Maddox is there now. Big school behind, more class-rooms and then the fives-court. Like to walk through ? "

No devout Catholic ever went to Rome in more heart-felt pilgrimage than was this to David. It was the temple of his religion that he saw, the public school which was to be his home. His horizon and aspirations stretched no farther than this red-brick arena, for, to the eyes of the thirteen-year-old, those who have finished with their public school and have gone out from it to the middle-aged Universities, are already

past their prime. They are old; they are done with,
unless the fact that they play cricket for Oxford or
Cambridge gives them a little longer lease of immor-
tality. But to be a great man, a Maddox or a Cruikshank in this theatre of life which already his feet trod,
was the utmost dream of David's ambitions, and if at
the hoary age of eighteen he could only have played a
real part in the life of the scenes that were now un-
rolling to him he felt that an honoured grave would
be the natural conclusion. Everything that might
happen after public school was over seemed a post-
humous sort of affair. You were old after that, and at
this moment even the Head, for all his terror and
glamour, appeared a tomb-like creature.

Hughes exchanged "Hullo" with a friend or two,
and said "Right: half-past four" to one of them,
which made David long to know what heroic thing was
to happen then, and took him past the east end of
chapel without further comment. David, quickly and
quite mistakenly, drew a conclusion based on his
private-school experience.

"I suppose chapel's pretty good rot," he said.

This was worse than buttonholes.

"Chapel rot?" said Hughes. "Why, it's perfectly
ripping. Maddox's uncle was the architect. It's the
finest school-chapel in England, bar Eton perhaps.
You'll see it to-night. You never saw anything so
ripping."

"Oh, sorry," said David, flushing; "but I didn't
know."

Hughes paused a moment and looked at him again.

"I say, Blazes, it's awful sport your coming down
like this," he said. "Do sweat your eyes out over
this exam. It would be ripping if you got a scholarship. We're all working like beans in the house:

that's Maddox's doing. Work's quite different, if you take an interest in it, you know. Yes, that path goes down to the bathing-place, and there are nightingales in the trees. Then hall : fuggy spot—we all have dinner there, both out-boarders and in-boarders. See that don there in cap and gown? He takes the fifth form. He's frightfully polite, and is learning to ride a bicycle. Consequently you always touch your cap to him as he goes wobbling along, and he takes a hand off to return your chaste salute, and falls off. Good rag. There's his class-room, with the library up above. We'll just go down there, and I'll answer to name-calling on my way."

They turned out of the big court into an asphalted square full of boys. A master was standing on a raised dais at one end, calling out names with extreme deliberation.

" Oh, damn, he's only just begun," said Hughes, after listening a moment. " We won't wait."

He touched another boy on the shoulder.

" I say, answer for me, Plugs," he said. " You owe me one."

" Right oh ! What's your voice now, Topknot ? Treble or bass ? "

" 'Bout midway. Something with a crack in it. Thanks, awfully."

Plugs, whoever Plugs was, saw Hughes's companion.

" Who's your friend ? " he asked.

" Scholarship-chap from my t'other school. Decent ! "

That was an aside, but clearly audible, and David swelled with pride, and tried to look abnormally decent. . . .

They made their way through the crowd that was collecting and dispersing as the roll-call proceeded,

and went back down the long, empty passage past the
steps leading up to the school library. Even as they
approached them there was a clatter of feet on the
concrete floor above, and a boy came flying down them
four steps to his stride. Beneath one arm he carried
a sheaf of books, and his straw hat was in the other
hand. "Maddox," said Hughes quietly, and on the
moment Maddox took his last six steps in one leap,
and nearly fell over them both.

All the hero-worship of which David was capable
flared up : never did hero make a more impressive entrance than in that long, lithe jump that landed him
in the passage. He nearly knocked Hughes down, and
dropped all his books, but caught him round the shoulders and steadied him again. There was a splendid
crisp vigour about every line of his body, his black,
short hair, his dark, full-blooded face.

"Topknot, you silly owl ! " he said. " Don't get in
a man's light when he's in a hurry. Haven't hurt
you, have I ? I'd die sooner than hurt you."

David picked up the scattered books, and Maddox
turned to him.

" Oh, thanks awfully ! " he said. " You're Topknot's pal, I suppose, come up for the scholarship-
racket. Good luck ! "

He nodded to David, flicked the end of Hughes's
nose, and went off down the passage to the sixth-form
room, whistling louder than even David thought possible.

" Gosh ! " said David. There was really nothing
more to be said.

" Oh, he's always like that," remarked Hughes, feeling that the meeting could not have been more impressive.

" And he wished me good luck," said David, still

feeling dazzled. "Wasn't that awfully jolly of him? And he flicked your nose, same as you might flick mine."

"Oh, Lord, yes," said Hughes.

After this all that immediately followed seemed but the setting and stage from which the chief actor had departed, for that glimpse of Maddox had been to David like some appearance of the spirit itself of public school. Soon they left the college buildings and walked down some quarter of a mile to where the red roofs of Adams's rose between full-foliaged elms. They had to cross a broad, swift-flowing chalk-stream where rushes twitched in the current, and cushions of star-flowered water-weed waved, and Hughes pointed out the wagging tail of a great fat trout who was supposed to have baffled the wiles of all fishermen from time immemorial. Arrived at the house, they had to part, for David, as a guest, must present himself formally at the front door while Hughes went round through the yard, where stump-cricket was going on, to the boys' quarters. There were cheerful cries of "Hullo, Topknot!" and David, waiting for the bell to be answered, thrilled again at the thought of being part of all this. The idea of Mr. Adams was no longer formidable, though he had pictured him as being rather taller than the Head.

He was shown through a big oak-panelled hall, into Mr. Adams's study, and even if he had entered in trepidation, his fears would have been at once set at rest. In a long chair by the open window, with a pipe in his mouth, while two boys were leaning over the back of his chair, sat his master, clerical as to collar, but with a blazer on instead of a black coat. Just as David entered, one of the two boys, scarcely older than himself to all appearance, and with a shrill voice yet unbroken, was expostulating with him.

" Oh, I say, do go back and construe that again, sir," he said. " I wasn't attending. Sorry."

Adams held out a hand to David.

" That's right," he said. " Delighted to see you. Just wait half a moment. Now, Ted, if you don't attend this time, I will not go over it again."

Ted took an injured tone.

" Well, there was a wasp," he said. " It wasn't my fault. Please get on quick, sir."

David thought he had never seen so pleasant a room, nor one which less suggested " school " as he had known it. The windows looked out on to a big lawn, in the centre of which two boys and a tall, black-haired girl, whom he conjectured to be Adams's daughter, were playing croquet. Round the edge were cut five or six golf-holes where other boys were putting, slightly to the derangement of geranium beds, and half a dozen more were sitting in the shade of lime-trees reading and talking. Here inside, two occupied the sofa, and, as David waited for Ted to be construed to, another tall fellow strolled in and lay down on the hearthrug with an illustrated paper. The walls were lined with low bookshelves, on the top of which were strewn cricket-balls, books, and straw hats, while on the table in the centre was a litter of papers, and in the middle a great bowl of roses. Honeysuckle trailed trumpeted sprays over the spaces of open window, and the dark-stained floor was bright with Persian rugs.

The construing was soon over, and Adams gave the book back to one of the boys. Then he who had lain down on the hearthrug looked up from the paper.

" Sir, Jessop's coming down," he said.

Adams got up from his chair.

" Then get him out at once with the very fastest ball ever bowled, Crookles," he said.

Some one from the sofa joined in.

" Oh, don't be too hard on him, Crookles," he said. " Let him hit you over the pavilion a bit first."

David's eyes took on their most reverential round-ness. Without doubt this must be Cruikshank, the fastest bowler the school had ever had. And yet he had a casual private life of his own, and was called Crookles.

" And here's Blaize come down on purpose to see it all," said Adams, " and incidentally to get a scholar-ship—eh, David ? "

Horrors ! The Christian name again ! But nobody appeared to think it the least ridiculous, any more than that Ted, who was climbing out of the window, should be known as Ted.

Adams looked rather unfavourably at one of the two boys on the sofa.

" Ozzy, go and wash your hands at once," he said. " I won't have fellows in here with dirty paws."

" Sir, mayn't I just finish——" began Ozzy.

" No : finish when you're clean. Come out into the garden, David. How's your father ? Topknot met you at the station, didn't he, and you're going to have tea with him. We might find some strawberries."

David was packed off early to bed that night in order that his brain might be in its most efficient mood for his examination next day, in a whirl of happy excitement. Never in all his day-dreams had he con-ceived that Adams's could be like this. It was not like a school, it was like some new and entrancing kind of home, with the jolliest man he had ever seen as a master and father, and for family these friendly boys, and the black-haired girl, Adams's daughter, whom everybody called by her Christian name. And yet the

glamour of public school lay over it, and among this
happy family there moved, like ordinary mortals, the
great ones of the earth, Maddox and Cruikshank, and
Westcott, captain of the school fifteen, behaving like
everybody else and seemingly unconscious of their
divinity. And these heroes had been seen with his
mortal eyes, and he had been taken by Hughes into
Maddox's study after tea, where he had been permitted
to help in washing up his tea-things. That to him was
the Vatican, a room some twelve feet by ten in material
dimensions, but a shrine, a centre. There were books
everywhere—not school-books merely, but novels, books
of poetry, books in French which Maddox read for his
own amusement. Cricket-bats and a press of rackets
were piled in the corner, and such space on the walls
as was not filled with books was a mosaic of school
photographs. And, perhaps most astounding of all,
though Maddox had his school cricket colours, his
racket and fives colours, there was no trace of those
glories anywhere ; instead, on a nail behind the door,
was hung a straw hat with just the house-colours on
it, which David himself would be allowed to wear next
September. Somehow that was tremendously grand :
it was like a king who had the right to cover himself
with stars and garters, preferring to go out to dinner
in ordinary evening dress. . . .

David's bedroom was in the private part of the
house, but next door was one of the boys' dormitories.
Merry, muffled noises leaked through the walls, and
from the open window of the dormitory there came
into his room whistlings and cheerful riot, and from
time to time the clump of boots kicked off on to the
floor. By degrees these sounds grew quiet, but he
still lay in wide-eyed contemplation and expectancy.
The most trifling preoccupation was always sufficient

to make him forget to say his prayers, and to-night he had got into bed without their ever occurring to him. But, as he lay awake, among the million surmises that came to him about life in this enchanted place, he wondered whether fellows in the house said their prayers, since chapel apparently was a thing to be proud of, and on the moment he tumbled out of bed and knelt down. But only one petition seemed possible, and he made it.

" O Lord, let me get a scholarship and come to Adams's," he said very fervently.

He thought for a moment, but really there seemed to be nothing else that his heart desired.

" Amen," he said, and, jumping into bed again, fell asleep.

CHAPTER VI

IT was the morning of the day before Helmsworth broke up; examinations were over, lists had been read out, and places and removes assigned to those who would reassemble in September, and just now the whole school was employed in the joyful task of packing play-boxes. This was not an affair that usually demanded anxious consideration : it consisted in shying your books into your box and shaking it until the lid consented to close or burst in the attempt. But David on this particular occasion was not sure that it was very joyful, and, as an outward and visible sign of his doubts, he was actually packing his books, fitting them in one with another, that is to say, instead of making salad. Glorious things had happened, and a dazzling future was no doubt to follow, but he was dimly aware that a chapter in life was closing, which in spite of its drawbacks and terrors and annoyances had been jolly. He had been happy, he was aware, without knowing it, and whatever the future held it would not hold this again. No such scruples afflicted Ferrers, who was emptying his locker into his play-box in the manner of a cheerful cataract, holding up for competition anything he did not want.

"Old Testament Maclear," he said. "*Quis* for an Old Testament Maclear ? List of kings of Israel and Judah in it, with lots of noughts and crosses over it.

Lord, I'd like to make a parcel of it and send it to Dubs without any stamps on."

David was considering the question of a catapult. In the famous visit to Marchester he had discovered that catapults were scuggy inventions, but he had at present been unable to bring himself to part with this one, so great was its calibre. The stag-beetles he had given to Ferrers Minor the day after his return, and their new owner had sat down on them with total loss of life, a few hours subsequently. And now he hardened himself again.

"*Quis* for a catapult?" he said heroically, and a chorus of "Ego" answered him. He threw it to Stone, who had clearly been first with his "Ego."

"Rotten things, catapults," he said, to strengthen himself; "only scugs use them at Marchester."

Then he came upon the Smoking Club badge. Since his return from Marchester he had broken with the S.C., but since, as a leaving gift, he had made the club a magnificent present of twenty-five cigarettes and a cherry-wood holder, his defection had not roused unpleasant comment. But the badge had still something of the preciousness of the past about it; he remembered the pride with which, by the assistance of a pair of tweezers, he had shaped the copper wire into the mystic letters. He slipped it into his play-box.

There was a loose cricket scoring-sheet, which he had craftily torn out of the book, because it showed his own analysis on the day of the Eagles match, and did not record the fact that he had missed the catch which lost them the game. Well, there was no use for that now, any more than for catapults or stag-beetles, since the fellows at Marchester would care precious little what his bowling-analysis had been against a private school of which nobody had ever heard. They had not

heard of him either, and at that thought David saw
just where his vague regrets and melancholy came from.
He had to start all over again on a new page, to part
with everything that for its own sake or from familiarity
had become dear, to be a nobody again instead of being
a big boy in his circle. He had been used to consider
himself rather a swell, with an assured position; now
he was nobody again, with no position at all. . . .
The school sergeant, the minister of fate who brought
round the slips of blue paper on which the Head had
written the name of culprits whose attendance was required, looked in at this moment.

"Master Blaize to go to the Head at once," he said.

David's heart stood still, not with fear but with
suspense. For the last three days he had hourly
expected that news would come of the result of the
Marchester scholarship examination, and perhaps this
meant its arrival. But his friends thought otherwise,
and Ferrers Major rattled his keys and slapped a book
with suggestive resonance.

"Don't bully me, sir," he said. "The other hand,
sir. Whack, whack, whack, all in the same place!
The fellow who was going to take all the wickets in the
old boys' match won't be able to bowl a ball. Whack,
whack. Sobs and cries!"

"Oh, piffle," said David getting up.

That was a word he had brought back from Marchester and was new to the Helmsworth vocabulary.
He had distinctly overworked it, with the result that
two days ago there had been a " piffle conspiracy "
against him. Whatever question, that is to say,
David asked anybody was answered by " Piffle," which
became rather wearing to the nerves. But the conspiracy was short-lived; it had lasted, indeed, only a
few hours, since David distinctly announced that he

would firmly hit in the face the next fellow who said
" Piffle " to him. That checked off the juniors at once;
but unfortunately there were others, and when David
the moment after said to Stone, " Will you come and
bathe ? " Stone said " Piffle." Immediately afterwards Stone had a black eye, and David a bleeding nose. But he went for the next piffler with un-
diminished zeal, and the thing had dropped, for it was
not worth while fighting David over a little thing like
that. He also had dropped the use of the word, and
this time it slipped out by accident.

" And if anybody says ' Piffle,' " he remarked cheerfully, " there's heaps of time to smash him silly before
I go to the Head."

This was too high-handed.

" One, two, three," said Stone, and the whole class-
room simultaneously shouted " Piffle ! " at the tops of
their voices. That was a manœuvre previously agreed
on, in case David used the word again, and he was
scored off.

" Oh, funny asses," he said witheringly, which was
about the best thing that could be done under the
circumstances.

David walked down the path that led to the Head's
study with a suspended heart, feeling certain that this
was scholarship news, and not one of his private misdeeds that was to be set before him, but yet hurriedly
attempting to recollect the omissions and trespasses
of which he had lately been guilty. But he credited
himself with so stainless a record that he was really
open to the damning imputation of having become a
saint. For the effect of that glimpse of public-
school life had been magical on his conduct : he had
literally not cared to do the sort of things any more
that spelt trouble at Helmsworth. At Marchester, for

example, only scugs smoked, and therefore the temptation of so doing (especially since he did not like it, had ceased to beckon him. The only reason for indulging in it had really been the notion that it was grand, and if by a higher standard it was not grand at all, the point of it was gone. Again, the fact that at Adams's house it was the thing to work, had made industry a perfectly palatable mode of passing the time. Or where, when he had once seen a master like Adams, was the use of cheeking that dreary ass Dubs ? You couldn't cheek Dubs any more : it was beneath you to do any such thing. Dubs was pure piffle.

There had been a paralysing row in the school a few days before, at which the Head had appeared in his most terrific light; but David had had nothing to do with that. A series of small thefts had been going on, and the culprit had eventually been caught red-handed in a dormitory deserted for cricket, had been held up to public execration, and expelled. That scene had made David feel sick with terror : personally he did not in the least desire to steal other fellows' things, but he quaked at the thought of being made the scorn of the assembled school, as had happened to Anstruther. He supposed that his whole subsequent life would be cursed and blasted, as indeed the Head had assured Anstruther that his was.

David tapped at the door, and entered in obedience to a stern, gruff permission. The Head looked up, frowning.

" Blaize ; yes, wait a moment."

He finished a letter, re-read it and directed it, and threw it on the floor. That was one of his great ways : he just threw letters on the floor, if he wanted them to be posted, and they were picked up and stamped.

" I have just heard from Marchester," he said.

" You have done well, but you have not got a scholarship. There were six given, and you were eighth on the list. Don't be discouraged; you have done well. But I am recommending your father to send you to Mr. Adams's house, anyhow. It is more expensive than an in-boarder's, and I wish you had got a scholarship, so as to begin helping in your own education. But I think you may consider that you will go to Mr. Adams's next September."

The Head suddenly took his keys from his pocket, and rattled them in the lock of the drawer that held the canes. But he was doing it, so it seemed to David, in a sort of absence of mind and not to be thinking of what lay within. Then, leaving them there, he got up and rocked across to the fireplace, where he stood on the hearthrug, looking gigantic. He began a portentous, terror-breathing discourse.

" David," he said, " a few days ago you saw a schoolfellow publicly expelled. I saw you turn white; I saw your horror at the task that was forced on me. Now you are on the point of going out into the bigger life of a public school, and when you have been a week at Marchester you will look back on the time you have passed here as a sort of babyhood, and wonder whether it was you who smoked half a cigarette now and then, and cheeked Mr. Dutton, and put—er—put resurrection-pie into envelopes and burned it."

(" Good Lord," thought David. " Is it going to be a caning for sundries ? ")

Apparently it wasn't.

" But you will find," continued the Head, " that there are worse things than smoking, and all the misdeeds you may or may not have been punished for, and you will find out that there are even worse things than stealing, and that many quite good chaps, as you

would say, don't think there is any harm in them.
Do you know what I mean ? "

David looked up in quite genuine bewilderment.

" No, sir," he said.

" Thank God for it, then," said the Head. Then he
moved across the room to his cabinet of cigars, and
broke his own rule, for he took one out and lit it and
smoked it in silence for a moment in the sacred presence of one of the boys. Then he turned to David
again.

" You don't understand me now," he said, " but you
will. And when you do understand, try to remember
for my sake, if that is anything to you, or for your
own sake, which certainly is, or for God's sake, which
is best of all, that there are worse things than stealing.
Things that damn the soul, David. And now, forget
all I have said till the time comes for you to remember
it. You will know when it comes. And don't listen to
any arguments about it. There is no argument possible."

" Yes, sir," said David blankly.

He could not understand why it was the Head had
thanked God; but there was no time for wonder, for
instantly the Head's whole gravity and seriousness
vanished.

" That is all I wanted to say to you," he said, " and
I feel sure you won't forget it. Now when does the old
boys' match begin ? Twelve, isn't it ? I hope you'll
be in form to-day with your bowling. We haven't
beaten the old boys for six years, but I don't think
we've ever had such a good chance as we have to-day.
The wicket ought to suit you, if the sun comes out."

Gradually the sense of this dawned on David, its
tremendous import. He flushed with incredulous pride.

" Oh, but fellows like Hughes will hit me all round
the clock, sir," he said.

" They will if you think they are going to," remarked the Head. " That's all then, David. Hughes
is staying with me over the night. You'll sup with
us."

" Yes, sir; thank you, sir," said David.

In spite of his failure to win a scholarship David
walked on air as he went back to the packing of his
play-box, for far more important, from his own point
of view, than the getting of a scholarship was the fact
that he was going to Adams's. For a minute he wondered about what the Head had said concerning things
that were worse than stealing; but, having been told
to forget all about it, instantly proceeded to put the
question out of his mind in favour of more agreeable
topics. And there was no doubt that the Head implied
that it was he who might win the old boys' match for the
school. Jolly decent of him, considering that it was
he who had certainly lost the Eagles match for them.

Soon after the great men from Eton and Harrow and
Marchester began to arrive, and each appeared more
enormous than the last. To-day, however, there was
no baleful father to trouble David's peace, and in the
half-hour before the match began he went and bowled
to Hughes at the nets, who incontinently hit him three
times running out of the field. But David had the
true temper of the slow bowler who expects to be
hit, while he studies the hitter, and observed that
Hughes was not nearly so comfortable with a slightly
faster ball pitched a little outside the leg stump, and
(if luck accompanied the intention) breaking in. He
quite mistimed two that David sent down, upon which,
having got this valuable hint, David bowled no more
of that variety, lest Hughes should get used to them.
Then, as there were plenty of bowlers at Hughes's net,

he went on to the next, where Cookson, who had left two years before, was batting. There, again, the wily David tried the ball which Hughes did not care about, but found that Cookson had a special affection for it, and hit it juicily to square leg. But he was less confident with a very slow ball, such as Hughes had hit so contemptuously; so here was a second bit of information. David committed that to memory, and tried a third net, where he had no success of any sort or kind.

There had been six school matches before this; Stone had lost the toss on five occasions, and on the sixth, when he had won, had put the other side in with disastrous results. To-day, however, having, contrary to all expectation, won the toss, he took the innings, and by lunch-time six wickets were down for a hundred and three, while Cookson, the only bowler of any real merit, was losing his sting, and David, in the last over before lunch, had hit him impertinently for twelve, thus bringing his own contribution up to twenty. During lunch he made a beautiful plan that he would really go in for hitting hard afterwards; but this miscarried, and he lost his wicket off the first ball he received, owing to his hitting hard at it at the moment when his bails were already whizzing like driven partridges through the air. Three-quarters of an hour later the innings closed for a hundred and thirty-five, a total which might have easily been worse, but undeniably should have been better.

David's heart sank when he saw two immense figures coming out of the pavilion to open the innings of the old boys, and found that he had to begin bowling to one with a moustache and a forearm that seemed about as big as his own leg. But, as the Head had augured might happen, the sun had come out during lunch-time, and this, after the rain of the night before, which had rendered the wicket easy this morning, might render it very difficult (and also very suitable for his mode of attack) during the afternoon. Without doubt the turf would cake, and a ball, if judiciously handled, might do very odd things indeed. He felt as if the Head had ordered the sun on purpose for him, which was a kind thought, and, suddenly glowing with optimism again, pranced up to the crease with his usual extravagant action, and was immediately hit clean out of the ground. The Head had appeared in front of the pavilion just in time to see this done, and David candidly reflected that it was worth seeing. It didn't often happen that the first ball of an innings was slogged for six. Juicy hit, too !

David approached the crease again in a much more staid manner, and delivered a second ball exactly like the first. There was really no reason why it should not have been treated in exactly the same way, but the giant carefully blocked it instead, for it looked different. That thoroughly pleased David : he was creating an atmosphere. He did not use that phrase to himself, he merely thought that the batsman suspected something.

Again he altered his action, and took hardly any run at all. But this time he delivered the slightly faster ball which had puzzled Hughes during the practice at the nets. And it was feebly returned straight into his hands, where it remained till he buzzed it vertically into the air.

" Gosh, I'm devilish deep," said David to himself in a spasm of odious pride.

By six it was all over. Helmsworth had won by twenty runs, and David had taken eight wickets. And though, since his return from Marchester, he had often told himself that this was only a scuggy little private

school, this was a moment worth living for, for not
only did the scuggy little private school roar at him as he
came to the pavilion with the rest of the team, but the
disgraced and vanquished giants of public schools, people
of sixteen and seventeen, came out shouting " Well
bowled, Blaize," with the most generous appreciation.
The Head was there, too, clapping his hands, and
Goggles was there, beaming through her large round
spectacles, and Carrots, with her hair shining in the
sun . . . they were all there.

David came up the steps to the pavilion all alone,
for the rest of the eleven suddenly stood away from
him and shoved him forward, crimson in the face with
exertion and joy.

" Oh, 'twasn't me, sir," he said to the Head, who
patted his shoulder. " It was just the ground : it
played awfully queer."

And he buried his delightful confusion in a quart
of lemonade.

So in delicious triumph the last hours of David's
school-life passed, and from the train next morning he
saw between the trees the fleeting glances of the roofs
which for three years had been his home.

CHAPTER VII

DAVID's father lived in a grey, rambling house in the
close at Baxminster, a plan of his that, as far as David
went, had something to be said both for and against it.
In its favour was the fact that the house contained
a whole top-story of dusky and mysterious attics,
roofed in the dimness by cobwebby beams, and used
only for lumber-places and cisterns. Here it had been
delightful in years gone by to find pleasing terrors
in these dark and doubtful corners, amid the gurgles
of water-pipes. Here he and his sister (in those years
gone by, or in other words until a few months ago)
had often passed entrancing wet afternoons, daring
each other, particularly at the closing in of dusk, to
explore the farthest recesses even to that last attic of
all, which contained a large coffin-like box and a cistern
that unexpectedly gave sudden and mirthless goblin-
chuckles to itself, most harrowing to nerves already
keenly on edge. The rules generally in force were that
one of them had to go and sit alone in that very spooky
chamber, with face turned honestly away from the
door, while the other dressed up in any horrific garb
that might suggest itself to a fevered imagination, and,
having stealthily entered, frightened the watcher with
this hideous apparition, accompanying it by any such
noise of screaming or groaning that might appear
suitable. With the victim looking steadily away from
the door, these noises might go on, like an artillery

121

attack, until his nerves were thoroughly shaken, though he had not yet seen what the apparition was to be. David had once frightened Margery into hysterics here, having entered the room in silence, swathed in a sheet, and wriggling snake-wise along the floor. He had coloured his face purple from Margery's paint-box, and, having serpentined along till he was in front of her, suddenly yelled and disclosed the horrors of that apoplectic countenance. On that occasion the gurgling cistern had been useful, for he swiftly washed his own face to reassure her. But, by a varia-tion of the rules, it having been ordained that the frightener should enter the room first and get himself up to receive the frightened on entry, Margery had got back her own again, for she had chalked her face and put her tongue out, and lain down in the coffin-shaped box, closing the lid as usual. David had looked for her with quaking tremors behind the cistern, and found her not; he had peered into the darkest of all corners, where an empty bookcase concealed a dan-gerous recess, when suddenly the lid of the coffin-box, which he had not suspected, flew open, disclosing Margery lying quite still, with white face and protrud-ing tongue. . . . David had run as far as the nursery-landing before he could master the panic of his legs.

Clearly, then, there was, or rather had been, advan-tages in this house, but to-day as Margery and David sat idly beneath the mulberry-tree in the garden, from which every now and then a fat sun-ripened fruit plopped on to the grass, David announced that there was no more savour in these childish things. Margery was a year older than he, but, being a girl, and already turned fifteen, and he a boy who had but last week celebrated his fourteenth birthday (his father had given him a copy of the " Christian Year," for which he had very little use), she was essentially some five years his senior, and knew how David felt.

" Yes, it used to be ripping," he said discontentedly, in allusion to those years, " and I used to be awfully excited, but I don't care now. You see the point was that we *were* frightened : that was the ripping part of it. Besides, you know, if any of the fellows at Adams's asked me what sort of games we played at home, it would be sickening to have to say that we just hid behind boxes in a frowsty attic. 'Tain't no use any more ! So what are we to do all this afternoon and to-morrow and the next day ? It's funny that you can't suggest something else."

Margery gave a long sigh and ate one of the fallen mulberries. She would have given anything to be able to suggest something else. In appearance she was so like David that if brother and sister had dressed in the other's clothes, and corrected the discrepancy of hair and broken front tooth, either might have passed a frontier with the passport of the other.

" Well, I've suggested heaps of things, and you say they are all rot," she said. " I'll play anything you like. We used to have rather fun playing cricket. Wouldn't you like to play cricket ? "

" Oh, what's the use ? " said David. " I should hit you into the Deanery garden all afternoon, and always bowl you first ball. I took eight wickets against——"

Margery had a good deal of David's spirit, as well as his bodily aspect.

" I know—you told me that," she said. " Twice."

David had a certain sense of being ill-used, common to his sex at his age.

" Oh, all right," he said with dignity. " But you *used* to be interested in my things."

Margery had probably never heard of women's rights; she only knew that her beloved David was rather unfair sometimes. On these occasions she never by any chance took refuge in pathos.

"Silly gubbins," she said. "You told me twice, and I was interested even the second time. David, do buck up! Go and smoke a cigarette, won't you? It's quite disgusting of you to smoke, and some day father will smell it and there'll be trouble. But it used to make you feel—feel starched."

"Given up smoking," said David morosely. "Ages ago."

"Hurrah! Did it make you feel extra-special unwell?"

"No, you ass. But it's scuggish to smoke. Only scugs smoke at Marchester."

Margery nodded at him approvingly.

"I always told you you would cease to think it grand when you got with nice boys," she said.

"Oh, shut up," said David.

Margery melted completely under this. She felt that he was only a little boy, in spite of all the wickets he had taken, and that she was a woman. Instinctively she took up the glory and burden of her sex.

"Oh David, what's the matter?" she said. "I am sorry you feel beastly. What is it?"

David slid off his chair, and lay down flat on the grass, staring up into the thick green leaves, chinked with blue sky. Almost immediately a ripe mulberry dropped on his nose and burst, and though it was immensely funny, Margery continued quite grave. David said "Damn," and solemnly wiped it off. Then she sat down on the grass by him.

"What is the matter, David?" she repeated.

David blew away a fly that wished to settle on his face.

"Oh, it's so dull," he said. "I am so bored! And fancy being stuck here all August, as father's in residence. You're a ripper, all right, but then you're a girl. I expect you can't help. I'll come and play cricket if you like."

"I don't," said Margery. "Go on."

"I don't suppose you would understand," said the superior sex, "but you see I've got to start again. It's scuggish to smoke or to keep stag-beetles, and I shan't see any of the chaps I was friends with again (and some of them were jolly decent, in spite of what you say about smoking) except Bags. It's . . . it's like emigrating. Of course, it's perfectly ripping going to Marchester, but . . . oh, well, I feel rotten this afternoon."

"Oh, is Bags going to Marchester?" asked Margery.

"Yes. I heard from him this morning. He's going to Adams's too."

David's tone was not that of one who finds a consoling circumstance, and Margery felt her way.

"But you're tremendous friends with him, aren't you?" she asked.

"Oh yes, I suppose so. He was jolly decent to me last half when a lot of the fellows were against me. But he doesn't play games, you know, and has got a weak heart, and he's rather an ass in some ways . . . and he says he has persuaded his governor to let him go to Marchester, just because of me."

"Well then, he's very fond of you," said Margery.

"I know he is. That makes me feel rather a cad. Of course it'll be awfully nice to have Bags there and all that, but . . . oh, I can't explain, and you can't understand."

But Margery, being a child herself, could completely understand the unfathomable mind of childhood.

"I shouldn't worry about that, David," she said.
"Even if Bags can't play cricket, perhaps you'll find
he can do something else that'll make him all right."

David regarded the roof of mulberry-leaves severely.

"Well, I suppose I've just got the hump," he said.
"I don't care for the old things, and I haven't got any
new ones yet. Look at these holidays! I hate cathedrals, and we're going to stop here all August. I don't
want to grub in the attics any more, or to play pirates,
and there's no cricket except one match against those
rotten little choir-boys. And father talks the most
awful tosh about cricket. Says he never wore pads
when he was a boy—I dare say they weren't invented—
and, anyhow, he could never have played for nuts.
I can't argue with him; it isn't any use, because he
doesn't know!"

David sat up in a despair of indignation.

"Only the other day," he said, "at the county
match, he asked me where Jessop was fielding. So of
course I said, 'At cover-point,' which he was. And
father said, 'Perhaps.' It wasn't 'perhaps'; it *was*
cover-point. There wasn't a 'perhaps' in the whole
blooming show. Why, even you know that! That
makes it so unfair. If father tells me that dog-tooth
ornament comes in Norman architecture I don't say
'Perhaps.'"

The wise Margery continued her course of consolation.

"Oh, but David," she said. "There are a lot of things
you like besides cricket. There's that ripping poem
you read me the other day, Keats's 'Ode to the Nightingale.' I loved it. Was he head master of Eton?"

David wiped the final remains of the burst mulberry
from his face in a magisterial manner.

"Head master of Eton!" he said. "Why, he was
in a sort of doctor's shop, where you might have got

something for stomach-ache, the Head said. And all the time he was writing that ode. Isn't it rummy?"

The boy is father to the man, so also is the girl to the woman. Margery, with secret glee, saw that David was feeling better, and inclined to be interested.

" Yes, you did tell me," she said penitently; " but I forgot. Sorry, David."

" Oh, that's all right. I forget lots of things. I say, it's an awful pity you're a girl, Margery. You would have been such a ripping boy."

" I dare say I should have got on all right," said she. " Or perhaps you might have been a girl."

" Me a girl?" said David. " But I couldn't. Think of the things girls have to do. It's ridiculous."

Margery felt she must stand up for her sex.

" I don't see that the things we have to do are more ridiculous than your smoking, or keeping those beastly stag-beetles," said she, for she shared Bags's horror of that which crawled.

David got up with extraordinary dignity.

" Those are the things I told you in confidence," he said.

" Well, and whom have I told?" demanded Margery.

" Besides, they're all finished," said David. " You shouldn't bring them up against me."

" I didn't; I was only arguing."

" Then let's stop arguing," said David. " Lord, it's only just three. There's that beastly cathedral clock striking. I suppose that's Norman, too, isn't it? What are we to do?"

Margery made a little sympathetic grimace at David.

" Oh David, I do understand," she said, " and I'm so sorry you're bored. I know exactly what's the matter with you."

" Wish you'd tell me," said David.

" You know too, really.   You've dropped one lot
of things and haven't got the next lot yet.   Then
there's this.   Do you remember that green snake you
used to keep, and how, when it was changing its skin,
it used to lie quite still, not eating or drinking, and
seeming awfully depressed ?   I expect that sort of
thing is happening to you.   I shouldn't a bit wonder
if our minds changed their skins now and then, just like
snakes."

David was interested in this, but it was necessary, in
his present humour, to be rather depreciatory.

" Girls do have such rum notions," he said.   " I can't
think where you get them from.   But what then ? "

" Just that.   You have been a little boy up till now,
although you were no end of a swell at Helmsworth,
and you're just beginning to see it.   You know you
would have been furious with me if I had told you, even
only last holidays, that you were only a little boy.
But you don't mind now because you know it yourself.
You're changing your skin.   What—oh, I forget that
word of yours, the Marchester one."

" Piffle ? " suggested David.

" Yes.   What piffle you would have thought the
Keats Ode only a few months ago, and at that time
you thought it grand and grown-up to smoke."

David sat down again, thoroughly interested in his
own metamorphosis.

" Yes, that's rum," he said.

" No, not really.   It's just growing up."

" It sounds sort of philosophical," said he.

Margery picked up two or three fallen mulberries, and
put them into her mouth absently, one after the other.

" I dare say," she said.   " Oh, David, do be quick
about changing your skin, and let me see the new one.
And now let's go and do something.   I vote we go and

look at that old bookstall by the Priory Gate. We
might find a Keats among the cheap lots in the tray.
You asked me to come and look for one this morning."

She held out her hands to her brother, and he pulled
her up.

"Right oh!" he said. "I say, Margery, you're
not a bad sort."

And Margery was extremely content.

The garden where they had been sitting was one of
peculiar charm, though to David it ranked rather high
among the disadvantages of the place, for the lawn was
not big enough to play any game into which hitting
hard or kicking hard entered, and, as that was the para-
mount requirement demanded of pieces of grass, there
was really very little to be said in favour of this garden.
Balls always went into bushes or flower-beds ; it was a
very second-rate arena. The house itself, rambling
and grey-stoned, lay between it and the road that
circled round the close, and to north and south the
garden on its longer sides was bounded by brick walls
which centuries of sun and wintry weather had mellowed
to an inimitable softness of hue. Below the southern-
facing wall a deep flower-bed, the grave of many balls,
ran the whole length of the grass, which on the other
side came up to the wall, flush as a carpet to a wains-
cotting. A few rose-beds sunned themselves below
the low stone terrace that bordered the house ; but the
most distressing thing, from David's standpoint, was
that this kindly thick-leaved mulberry-tree, propped and
strutted like a very old man taking the air, stood bang
in the centre of the lawn, so that lawn-tennis was out
of the question. Along the far end of the garden was
a collection of sculptured stones (" Roman or something
beastly," was his verdict there) probably unearthed
when the garden was first made. Here a gate in the

middle of the third brick wall led into the kitchen-
garden, which, of course, from the orthodox athletic
view of gardens, was also quite futile.

But to the unorthodox nothing could have been more
charming. The brick walls were starred with stone-
crop and self-sown wallflower, and over the grey-tiled
roof of the house rose the Norman tower of the cathedral,
grave and gracious against the sky. The care of the
flower-beds had lately been given into Margery's hands,
who had adopted radical measures against the dreadful
rows of geraniums, calceolarias, and lobelias with which
the gardener had been accustomed to make gay the
long border, and she had gone back to happier jungle-
methods. Sweet-peas stood in clumps like stooks of
flowering corn, pansies and heliotrope and love-in-mist
were lowlier citizens, and behind hollyhocks and sun-
flowers kept sentinel. And over all, pervasive and
mellow as the August sunshine, brooded that atmosphere
of studious serenity which belongs to such ancient homes
of peace as cathedrals and monastic places. But,
æsthetic as such an atmosphere is, it is not greatly
appreciated by the young, nor indeed is there the
smallest reason why it should be. Everybody and
everything (such was David's view) was old here, and
for some inscrutable reason age was considered an ad-
vantage. An old Bishop lived in an old palace, and
the venerableness of both appeared to the inhabitants
of the close to be equally admirable. Elderly rooks
(at least they talked in an elderly and boring way)
cawed in immemorial elms. Roman remains were
constantly being dug up, and put in the museum, or,
if not worthy of that fate, carefully grouped, as here,
into the form of an outrageous rockery. And now for
seven weeks, since this year the Archdeacon was in
residence in August and September, the monotony of

six deadly week-days was only to be broken by the even deadlier monotony of Sunday.

Such was the pessimistic outlook over life that David took to-day, and, since pessimism was of uncommonly infrequent occurrence with him, it was more than possible that Margery's reference of it to skin-changing was a correct one. This "sort of philosophical" explanation on her part had already done something towards restoring him to more normal levels, and the inspection of the boxes of books outside the window of the second-hand shop, with the events that followed, completed the process. For there, by the most apt dispensation of Providence, they found (Margery actually found it, and instantly passed it on to David) a rather battered and dog-eared copy of Keats. This was a triumphant affair, showing that good could come even out of Baxminster, and they hurried inside to complete the sixpenny purchase. Coming out again into the street, they saw outside a straw-hatted figure turning over the boxes they had just left, and suddenly David's heart leaped, for he saw that the colours on it were those of Adams's house. The moment after—wonder upon wonder!—he saw who it was.

Maddox turned round as they came out, and frowned for a second, wondering where he had seen David before. Then he remembered.

"Why—why, you're Topknot's pal, aren't you?" he said.

Then he saw that David was with a girl.

"I beg your pardon," he added quickly, raising the enviable hat.

David took his courage in his hands: probably it was awful cheek, but after all it was in the holidays, and they were not at school.

"Oh, this is my sister," he said. "Margery, this is Mr. Maddox."

Maddox shook hands, and turned to David again.

" Do tell me your name," he said, " for the only piece
of it I can remember is ' David.'　You came down to
try for a scholarship and stayed at Adams's."

It seemed wonderful to David that anybody so great
should remember anything.

" Blaize," he said.

" Of course.　And so you and David live here, Miss
Blaize, in this ripping town.　I never saw such a jolly
place.　I could prowl about the close and the cathedral
for weeks."

" Yes, my pater's Archdeacon," said David.

" I wish mine was," said Maddox.　" But I've got
some right here.　I came down two days ago to stay
with my uncle, who's Bishop.　I expect you know him,
don't you ?　He's got one of those gorgeous houses in
the close."

David again made a stupendous call on his courage.

" I say, won't you come to tea ? " he blurted out,
" if you like these houses in the close.　We live in one,
you know.　Margy, do ask him."

" David and I would like it awfully if you would
come," she said.

Maddox laughed, and he tilted his head back a little
as he laughed, and on the moment that appeared to
David the only possible way to laugh.

" Thank you very much," he said.　" We should all
three like it awfully, then, so why shouldn't we do it ?
But may I just look through this box ?　I love looking
through old book-trays.　You never know what you
mayn't find, though personally I never find anything
but volumes of antique sermons printed by request
of a few friends.　Have you been buying something ? "

" Yes, but only an old Keats," said David, holding it
out to him.

Maddox looked at the title-page, which was intact, and his eyes grew round.

"My goodness, you lucky beggar!" he said. "And you bought it just this minute?"

"Yes; why?"

"Only because it's a book that a book-lover would give a lot for. Second edition of Keats, that's all. O Lord, if I hadn't sat down doing nothing after lunch, instead of coming here!"

"Oh, I say, please take it then," said David. "I didn't know anything about it. I just thought I would like a Keats. Any other one would be all the same to me."

Maddox looked at him gravely a moment, and then began to smile.

"Thanks very much," he said, "and I will then sell it you, if you like, for ten pounds."

Then he laughed again.

"I'm a greedy brute," he said, "but there are limits. Take it back quick, or it will grow on to my fingers. You are a lucky chap."

"Ten pounds?" said David incredulously.

"I should think about that, but I don't really know. I'm not in the habit of buying second editions of Keats. Let's look again a minute; I'll try to give it you back. Yes, it's quite complete."

Suddenly David remembered that the find was not his, but Margery's.

"I bang forgot," he said. "Margery, you found it Congrats."

For a moment his face grew troubled.

"And I offered it you, not remembering," he said to Maddox. "I really did mean it. Do take it. Margery, you understand, don't you?"

Maddox laid his hand on David's shoulder and looked at him.

"It's quite ripping of you, David," he said (and at that moment David loved his Christian name), "but whether it's your sister's or yours, I couldn't possibly. But thanks, most awfully."

"But are you sure?" asked David.

He laughed.

"Why, of course I am. What do you take me for? Oh, I can't bother about these beastly books, now I know what's come out of that tray. Shall we go, then?"

But on the way the question of the rightful possessor of this treasure had to be laid before him. Margery's contention was that David had suggested going to see if they could find a Keats, and that she had merely accompanied him, and therefore the book was his. David, on the other hand, contended that she had found it, and you couldn't get over that. They both referred the decision to Maddox with his seventeen years' experience of the world.

"Depends what you are going to do with it," he said. "If you mean to sell it, I really think I should divide the proceeds. If not—well, I should have a box made for it, with two keys, one for each of you. Anyhow, I shouldn't suggest the Solomon-trick, and cut it in half!"

The immenseness of all this momentarily obscured the honour and glory of taking Maddox home to tea, and the fate of the Keats was warmly debated. David was rather inclined to sell it, and revel in gold, but Margery hinted that if they were each possessed of five pounds, it certainly would not be they who revelled in gold, but the savings bank. Before the question was settled they had got back to the close, and David pointed out his father's house, a little way ahead of them.

Maddox clicked his teeth with his tongue, in a show of impatience.

" This is rather too much," he said. . " You find a second edition of Keats, and bring it home to the most beautiful house in Baxminster. I call it rotten. May I see all over it before tea, and the garden ? "

David felt he must apologize for the garden. " Oh, the garden's an awful hole," he said, " though Margery doesn't think so. There's no room for anything, as you'll see."

So the Fairy Prince was led in and taken all over the house, and as they went merits and glories undreamed of dawned on David. What had been dark, ugly wood turned out to be A1 Jacobean panelling, and a frowsy old picture of David's great-grandmother in a mob-cap was pronounced the most ripping Romney, who in his line appeared to be up to the high standard already set by Keats. And most astounding of all was Maddox's verdict on the attics, which David had abandoned as a proper playground for anybody who was going to Marchester in September. But the Fairy Prince thought otherwise.

" What awful fun you could have playing horrible games like hide-and-seek up here," he said. " I hope you do. Lord, what's that groan ? Oh, a cistern, is it ? I thought it must be a ghost. How ripping ! "

David instantly dismissed his resolution of not playing games here any more.

" Oh, there's a worse room yet," he said. " Do come and look at it. There's a box like a coffin in it. Margery and I used to play gorgeous games up here, dressing up and frightening each other, you know. Wasn't it fun, Margery ? "

Margery was the soul of loyalty. She would no more have reminded David that only to-day he had

come to the conclusion that these games were silly
than she would have had him led out to instant execution.

" Yes, when it begins to get dark it's awful up here,"
she said. " You can't see anything distinctly, and the
cistern suddenly groans, and you can't tell what's
coming next ! "

Maddox, in spite of his seventeen years and Olympian
elevation, did not seem to be unbending. David, in
fact, if his utterances this afternoon were to be taken
literally, had to unbend to him.

" I love being frightened," said Maddox. " You
ought to read ghost stories to each other here, and the
one who reads may make any sort of noise he chooses
at any moment. Just when the ghost is going to
appear, you know. Lord, I hope I shall never get
beyond that sort of thing ! "

He, Margery, and David were standing in a row
opposite the coffin-shaped box. Just then the cistern
in the room behind gave one of its best goblin-groans,
and Maddox looked awfully round.

" Oh, what's that ? " he said. " That's not the
cistern. That's a man bleeding to death in there, that
is. His throat's cut from ear to ear."

" No," said David. " I'm sure it was the cistern."

" Are you ? It may have been the cistern before,
but I don't believe it was that time. Pity it's not a
little darker. There's too much light really just now."

Already to David the attic bristled again with entrancing possibilities, under this stimulus. It was queer
that any one of Maddox's age and attainments should
see sport in what a few hours ago had seemed childish
and savourless to himself, but since this was so, it was
clear there must be something in it. But schoolboy
hero-worship made him see through his hero's eyes,

and all that Maddox did or said was invested with
authority. True, he had seen him perhaps half a
dozen times altogether, but that was quite sufficient to
make this matchless glamour. In all the world there
was no one so instinct with romance and glory as this
boy three years his senior who realized for him all he
wanted to be.

Of course they went downstairs again on the pro-
nouncement that it was not dark enough.

"I'm afraid you'll think the garden is rot," said
David. "There's a beastly mulberry-tree bang in the
middle of the lawn. But it's not so bad to have tea
in: Margery, can't we have tea out there?"

So the Fairy Prince was escorted downstairs and out
into the garden, to give his verdict on that despised
spot, and looked round with those quick movements
of his eye from side to side without turning his head,
which again seemed now the only possible way of
looking at things.

"But what on earth *is* good enough for you,
David?" he said. "You can't read Keats except out
of a second edition, and you told me the attics were rather
fun once, and you say the garden is rotten! Look at
those brick walls, look at the house, look at the mulberry-tree! Oh, I say, what are those stones in the
corner? Isn't that a Roman altar?"

"Yes, I believe so," said David. "Do you care
about those things?"

Maddox and he walked down to the collection of
old stones which had appeared to David the dullest of
the antique things of Baxminster. Some of the letter-
ing on one of these was still distinguishable.

"Yes, 'Optimo Maximo,'" said Maddox. "I expect
that gap is 'Jovi.' Then, lower down, do you see,
'P. Aelius': that must be the chap who dedicated it.

Funny that it should stand here now for you and me to read, while the cathedral tower squints at us over the attics where the ghosts live."

Maddox had seated himself cross-legged on the grass to examine the altar, and David leaned over him following the letters as he traced them with his smooth brown finger. And at once the subject even of Roman altars leaped into interest. Maddox shaded the lowest line of the inscription with his hand to catch the shape in the weather-worn letters.

" Can't read any more," he said. " But anyhow one day, long before the cathedral was built, Publius Aelius set that up, because the gods had been good to him. What a lot of jolly things there are! And some fellows go mooning along never looking at anything."

" I'm afraid you mean me," suggested David modestly.

Maddox looked up at him over his shoulder.

" Well, I don't," he said. " And there's a bit of an arch. Perhaps that came from the temple where P. Aelius put his altar."

Maddox asked for (and was given) another look at the Keats before he left, and proposed to David that he should walk with him as far as the old palace.

" Best afternoon I've spent for ages," said the Idol, as they parted. " I wish I wasn't going away to-morrow, or I should ask to be allowed to come again. Anyhow, we meet at Adams's in September."

A haunting doubt had been present in David's mind at intervals all that heavenly afternoon. Now it had to find expression.

" I say, I hope it hasn't been awful cheek of me to have asked you to have tea, and all that ? " he said.

" I can stand lots of that sort of cheek," said the other.

CHAPTER VIII

It was the afternoon of such a November day as the pessimistic call typical : a cold, south-westerly gale drove streaming flocks of huddled cloud across the sky, like some fierce and boisterous shepherd, and the whole of the great court at Marchester stood ankle-deep in gravelly pools of wind-flecked, rain-beaten water. The gale had stripped bare of their few remaining leaves the avenue of lime-trees which ran between the gate and the in-boarders' house at the far end of the court, and to-day they stood, stark pyramids of dripping branches and twigs, that whistled as the wind hissed through them. Though the day was Saturday, and in consequence a half-holiday, there were but few signs of outdoor animation, for the conditions of the weather were sufficiently diabolical to tinge with some touch of respect the contempt in which healthy boys hold the vagaries of climate. One occasionally, with collar turned up, fled splashing across the court from one house to another, or now and then a small company of drenched enthusiasts would trot in, in dripping shorts and sweaters, from their training run along the London Road, or a couple of figures, with racquets protected under their coats, would dash across from the racquet-court. But football had been officially announced to be " off," since the field was neither more nor less than a morass, and without doubt the most comfortable conditions of

life were to-day to be obtained in front of a fire with
a novel to read, or, under stress of necessity, arrears of
work to be overhauled and demolished.

There was, however, in one of the open fives-courts
near the porter's lodge a notable exception to this
indoor tendency.   There two boys, capless and streaming with water, were absorbingly engaged in playing
squash, a most apt occupation, since they and the earth
and the sky generally seemed to be in a condition of
squash.   Even in the drier parts of the court the
ball, as it bounced, sent up a squirt of water; at other
times it pitched in more definite puddles, and so did
not bounce at all.   But the two, David and Bags, were
quite undeterred by such small drawbacks, and David
talked without the least intermission.

" Six all," he said; " and, as I gave you six, I've
caught you up before you've scored.   Have some more
points, won't you ?   Very well, if you're proud, you
needn't, but if I played squash at all like you, I should
be damned humble.   O Bags, you ass, I don't believe
you'll ever be the slightest good.   Why can't you hit
the ball with the middle of your racquet for a change ?
There, look at that : exactly one-eighth of an inch
above the line.   I like them like that.   Seven, six.
Oh, good shot, jolly well got up, but observe !   You
can't get that, so what's the use of throwing yourself
against the wall ?   Eight, six . . . oh, damn !   Puts
you in : six, eight. . . . I'll give you two hands if you
like.   Oh, you'll take that, will you ? . . . one hand
out then. . . . Oh, do get on : run, can't you ? it's
raining.   There ; suck it !   You expected it the other
side of the court, and that's exactly why I didn't send
it there.   Puts me in. . . . I'll play you for sixpence
if you like, next game, and give you eight and two
hands . . . No ?   Prudent fellow.   I wish the rain

wouldn't get into my eyes, though it's sweat as well, I expect. Lord, I am hot! Isn't it ripping?"

David paused a moment both from talk and athletics, a truce gladly accepted by the panting Bags, and pushed his dripping hair out of his eyes. He was a completely dishevelled and yet a very jolly object, and was quite altogether wet, his knickerbockers clinging like tights to his thighs, the skin of which showed pink through them, while the water trickled steadily down his bare calves into the dejected socks that lay limply round the tops of his shoes. They and his legs were stained with splashes of watery gravel, his shirt, open at the neck and slightly torn across the shoulder, lay like a wet bag glued to his back, and his hair was a mere yellow plaster from which the water could have been wrung in pints. Bags was in similar plight, except that he wore a thick woollen jersey over his shirt, which gave him a slightly less drowned aspect.

The game, and with it David's running comments, were resumed after a minute or two, and neither of the two saw a figure with trousers much turned up and a large golfing umbrella who had paused on his way to the gate, just behind them.

"Yes, I'm going to play racquets for the school some time next century," David was saying, "and squash is jolly good practice. Nine, six: that's rather a sell, Bags! Oh, I say, look at that for a half-volley. Just a shade Maddoxy, I don't think."

The half-volley in question, that clung close to the left wall of the court, finished the rally, and David turned to run to pick it up, and found that Maddox was the spectator.

"David, you juggins, why haven't you got a sweater on?" asked he.

"Hullo!" said David. "Oh, because I couldn't find mine. Some brute's collared it, I suppose."

" Well, by rights you ought to get pneumonia, and be prayed for in chapel, and die in spite of it."

David pushed back his hair again and laughed.

" Thanks awfully, but otherwise engaged," he said.

" Are you going up to house after you've finished being drowned ? " asked Maddox.

" No, I was going to have tea with a fellow in college," said David. " But I'm rather wet, I'm afraid."

" You'll go up to house and change first, do you see ? " said Maddox. " And you might bring up a parcel there will be for me at the lodge. Hasn't come yet, but it'll come any minute."

" Right," said David.

The game was resumed, but Maddox still lingered. Both boys played with redoubled keenness before so honourable a spectator, but David's artless and incessant conversation was felt by him to be unsuitable. Maddox watched in silence for a minute.

" No, let the ball drop more," he said, Bags having made an egregiously futile return. " Don't take an easy ball like that till it's quite low. David, you play with your whole arm like a windmill, whereas you only want your wrist. Just keep flicking it : look here."

Maddox gave David the large umbrella to hold and, taking his racquet, knocked up down the left-hand wall of the court, sending each ball parallel and close to it, with easy accuracy. " Like that more or less," he said. " Now I'm wet, blast you both."

He took his umbrella again, reminded David of the parcel, and splashed off across the quadrangle.

Familiarity and closer acquaintance had not in the least made David get over the glory and wonder of Maddox.

" By gad," he said, " fancy his taking the trouble to coach two scugs like you and me. Isn't he a ripper ? Come on, let's have one more game."

" Oh, I vote we stop," said Bags. " It's too wet for anything."

" Rot ! We can't possibly get wetter than we are."

David, of course, had his way, and it was not till twenty minutes later that they trotted off down the Bath Road, on their way to Adams's, David going by preference through the larger puddles. Bags's mind, and no doubt David's also, still ran upon Maddox.

" Does he always call you David ? " he asked at length.

" Lord, yes, when we're alone," said David, " and I suppose he thought you didn't count. I remember how sick I was when my father called me ' David ' at Helmsworth. Sort of disgrace to have your Christian name known. What beastly little scugs we were, with smoking and keeping stag-beetles ! "

" I never did either," said Bags, in a rather superior manner.

David jumped with both feet in a particularly large puddle, and covered Bags with splashed water.

" I know you didn't," he said. " You were such a scug, you see, that you didn't do those things when it was scuggish not to. But now, when it's scuggish to do them, I believe you do. I bet you smoke. You and Plugs went out smoking yesterday after hall."

" Well, what if I did ? " said Bags. " And how did you know ? "

" Because I stunk you when you came back, Simple. What a funny chap you are ! You never smoked at Helmsworth where it was the right thing, and yet you do here where it's the wrong thing."

Bags plodded on for a little while in silence.

" Adams doesn't really mind our smoking," he said. " He chiefly wants not to have it brought to his notice."

" Yes, but Maddox does," said David. " I wish he'd

catch you at it. You wouldn't sit comfortable for a
week or two."

David pranced into the footpath ; there was a limit
to the amount of mud that it was convenient to carry
on your shoes.

" Let's walk a bit," he said ; " I'm blown."

They moderated their pace to a walk, and David
squeezed his hands into his pockets—a difficult operation
as they were glued together with wet.

" Several fellows have asked me about Maddox," he
said, " and I don't know what the deuce they're after.
Hughes has, for instance. Hughes used to be a ripper,
but he's different somehow now. He asked me the
other day if Maddox had become a saint, and if I'd
converted him. What the devil was he talking about ?
I don't like Hughes as much as I used. He told some
filthy tale in dormitory the other night, and some of the
fellows laughed. I laughed too : I supposed it was
polite, but I didn't see a hang what it all meant."

" What was it ? " asked Bags.

" God knows ; some awful piffle. Sounded filthy, too.
He wanted to explain it to me ; came and sat on my bed
and wanted to explain. But just then Maddox came
to bed : he'd been sitting up late working, and he
hoofed Hughes out again in less than no time. It was
the day after that that Hughes asked me if Maddox
had become a saint. Lord, wait a minute."

For some inconjecturable reason known only to the
feline mind, Mrs. Adams's cat had thought good to
sit out in the rain this afternoon, on the top of one of
the brick pilasters which stood at the entrance of the
passage up to the house. There she sat unconscious of
David and Bags, contemplating the scenery. With
infinite craft David, having picked up a small pebble,
threw it with such accuracy of aim that it passed through

the fur at the top of her head between her ears. She threw up her paws and looked wildly round in startled dismay, and was there no more.

"Slap between her ears!" shrieked David. "Lord, didn't she look funny when she threw her hands up! Blow, I've forgotten Maddox's parcel. What an ass you are not to have reminded me! Hot bath, anyhow Then I'll go back to college and fetch it."

This cloud-laden gale had caused the dusk of evening to close in very early, and the passage leading from the dormitories to the big room with its rows of baths was already nearly dark. On either side of the passage were the studies of the prefects, and David had to tiptoe delicately through the danger-zone, since he owed fifty lines to Cruikshank, and had not yet written them though they were overdue. But he reached the bathroom without encountering the enemy, and wallowed in a heaven of water so hot that if he moved he must almost scream. Bags was in a neighbouring bath, but finished his washing first, and left David intent, as the water cooled a little, on matters of soap and mud between his toes. Then his rain-soaked head did not seem satisfactory, and he washed the showers out, emerging eventually, towel-girt, to rub his head into a semblance of dryness. This was a tingling, exhilarating affair, and he accompanied it by bouts of piercing whistlings.

Next door to the bathroom was Maddox's study, and about this time he perceived that David had not filled his kettle for tea. Since David—for his whistle betrayed him—was next door, it was simpler to go and fill his kettle himself, than to go in and fetch David to do it. There, on the end of the bench below the steam-clouded windows, was David sitting, his head enveloped in a towel, violently scrubbing, and whistling whenever the towel was not in actual contact with his

mouth. He had not noticed his entry, and **Maddox**
thought it would be rather amusing to sit down without speech close beside him, holding out, in mute re-
proach, the empty kettle that David should have filled.
This he did.

In a minute David's head was sufficiently dry to
satisfy him, and it emerged from its towel. He looked
round astonished to find any one there, for Bags had
gone.

" Hullo, Maddox ! " he said.

" Yes : got to fill my kettle myself," he said.

David jumped up.

" I say, I'm awfully sorry," he said. " I bang forgot. Give it me ! "

But Maddox still held it, looking at him.

" Oh, it doesn't matter," he said. " Just having a
bath, were you ? "

David paused. There was Maddox only looking at
him, only smiling. But instantly he had some sense
of choking discomfort. He looked back at him, frowning and puzzled, and his sense of discomfort hugely
increased. He merely wanted to get away.

" Oh then, I think I'll go and dress," he said hurriedly,
and, picking up his sponge, left the room and ran away
down the dark passage to his dormitory.

David sat down on his bed for a minute, feeling as if
he had escaped from some distant nightmare that had
vaguely threatened to come near him. Then, very
sensibly, running away from it instead of thinking
about it, he began to dress in a great hurry. He
washed his hands over again, went on rubbing his hair,
did anything to occupy himself. In a few minutes
Bags came in dressed from his dormitory next door,
but David had no voluble conversation on hand, as

he had half an hour ago in the fives-court, and continued dressing in silence. Bags tried a few amiable topics, but got no more response than grunts and monosyllables, which were quite unlike David's usually rampageous loquacity. After three or four thwarted attempts it was borne in upon his lucid mind that there was something the matter.

" What's up, Blazes ? " he inquired.

" Nothing. Why ? " said David savagely.

" Oh, I don't know. You haven't got as much to say as usual."

" Well, who wants to talk to a chap like you ? " asked David, getting his tie in a knot, and venting himself in irritation.

Bags felt slightly hurt, for he was unaware how he could have caused this, but since David did not want to talk to " a chap like him," the most rudimentary sense of self-respect forbade the " chap like him " to make any further overtures.

David cracked his nail over his collar-stud, failed to get any sort of parting in his hair, and broke a bootlace. These material adversities somehow sobered him, and he began faintly to see that really Bags had nothing to do with his own mood.

" Sorry, Bags," he said at length, having tied the ends of the broken bootlace together.

Bags was the most amiable of mankind, and besides, this was David.

" Right oh," he said at once. " But do tell me what's up, if I can be of any use."

" Good old Bags, but you can't; thanks awfully. Don't ask me anything about it, if you don't mind."

Suddenly the fact of the parcel at the lodge which he had forgotten to bring down for Maddox presented itself. He felt that he couldn't see Maddox again just at once.

"I say, there is one thing you might do," he said. "I wish you'd come up to college with me, and get that parcel of Maddox's. I should be frightfully obliged if you would. I'm going to tea with a fellow there, and I should have to go up and down twice."

Bags felt that, if David offered this as an explanation of his ill-humour, it was a pretty thin one.

"Oh, is that all you're so sick about?" he asked.

David's irritability returned.

"All right, don't come then," he said.

David was ready by now, and without another word he marched to the door. He would have to bring the parcel up himself, but he was determined to get some-body else to take it to Maddox's study.

"Wait a second," said Bags in a slightly injured tone. "Of course I'll come up with you."

David took his arm.

"You are a brick," he said. "But don't ask me anything more. It isn't anything. I expect I've made a fool of myself."

"Shouldn't wonder a bit," said Bags pacifically.

"Funny fellow! Don't strain yourself."

Maddox had gone straight back from the bathroom to his study, without filling his kettle. He sat for ten momentous minutes in front of his fire without doing anything, without thinking even, but looking with open eyes, so to speak, on himself. All these weeks that intense friendship which was springing up between himself and David had been splendidly growing, and till now his influence over him had been exerted entirely for David's good. He had constantly shielded him, as on the night when he had found Hughes sitting on his bed, from all that could sully him, he had checked any hint of foul talk in David's presence, for, of all his lovable

qualities, there was none so nobly potent to the elder boy
than David's white innocence, his utter want of curiosity about all that was filthy. It didn't exist for him,
but the danger of it (though, thank God, it had passed)
he knew that he himself had brought near to him. . . .
Then he got up and looked at himself in the mirror
above his mantelpiece, hating himself.

"You damned beast," he said. "You deserve to
be shot."

Presently there came a tap at his door, and he remembered that he had told David to bring up a parcel
for him. Probably this was not David, for he usually
whistled and hardly ever tapped. On his answer Bags
entered.

"Oh, it's your parcel, Maddox," he said. "Blaize
forgot to bring it down after we finished playing squash,
and so I went back with him and brought it."

Maddox held out his hand for it.

"Thanks," he said. "Did—did Blazes ask you to
bring it me ? "

"Yes, he was having tea in college."

"Has he gone there ? "

"Yes, we went up together."

Maddox got up.

"Right," he said. "But he's forgotten to fill my
kettle. Would you mind, please ? "

That was exactly like Maddox. He always thanked
fags who did things for him, and treated them politely.
Bags, in consequence, retired with pleased alacrity, and
returned.

"Getting on all right, Crabtree ? " asked Maddox.
"No troubles ? "

"Oh no, thanks. I like it all awfully."

"That's right. I forget who your fag-master is."

"Cruikshank."

"Oh, yes. He'll look after you. Thanks for filling my kettle."

Bags went delicately and rather proudly away. Cruikshank never thanked him.

Maddox put his heel into the fire to make a level place for his kettle, and sat down again to work. But other thoughts kept interposing themselves between him and his books, claiming precedence. He knew from David's abrupt exit just now that he scented danger, or, if that was too strong an image, just turned his back on the miry road that had been in Maddox's mind, and his getting Bags to do the forgotten errand confirmed that. Vaguely, perhaps, David had guessed something of the nature of that muddy place, and had gone clean-footed from it. With much greater sureness Maddox saw that, if their friendship was to continue, he must turn his back on it too, and convince David that he had done so. He was ashamed: he hated himself.

The kettle boiled over, sending a puff of steam and light ash into the grate, and he took it off and put it in the fender. And still he sat there, looking backwards into his life and finding no comfort there; and then looking forwards, seeing a gleam of saving hope. At last outside his study there came a familiar step, but there was no whistling, and after the step paused there came a tap at his door. David entered, looking shy and frightened.

"Oh, I came to clear your things away and wash up," he said hurriedly.

Maddox did not want to shirk what lay before him. The friendship that had become so intimately dear to him was at stake.

"Will you shut the door a minute, David?" he said, rising and standing by the mantelpiece, with his face turned away.

David did so, and remained by the door.

" I want to say just one thing," said Maddox. " I'm damned sorry, and I apologize. You needn't be frightened of me. It shan't happen again. That's all. There's nothing to wash up : I haven't had tea."

Some subconscious horror still lingered in David's mind. He had been obliged to come back here, to see to Maddox's washing-up, else perhaps Maddox would have sent for him, and that would have been worse. At the moment he had no other desire, in spite of what Maddox had said, but to get away.

" I'll go then," he said quickly.

" All right."

David left the room, but he had gone only a little way down the passage outside, when his feet simply refused to carry him any farther, or to allow him to leave Maddox like this. All his love and his loyalty insisted that he was wrong not to trust the regret and the assurance that had been given him, that he was doing a mean and a cowardly thing to retreat like that. But the talk that he had had with the Head on his last day at Helmsworth was very vivid in his mind ; the Head had told him there was no use in arguing about certain things, and his instinct, in spite of his innocence, told him that such, vaguely and distantly, were the things about which the Head had spoken. But the Head had never told him to turn his back on a friend, or to refuse to trust that which his heart knew was sincere. And so once more from inside Maddox heard a familiar step return and once more David tapped and entered.

" I don't know why I went away," he said, " or why I was frightened when you said I needn't be. So—so I came back. Sorry."

Then he had the instant reward of his confidence.

He saw Maddox look up at him with unshadowed eyes of affection. He came and stood close to him.

"It's bang all right," he said. "I'm—I'm awfully glad it's all right."

Then a positive inspiration seized him. There was nothing more to be said on this subject, and the sooner it was dismissed the better. He instantly became Maddox's fag again.

"I say, you're awfully late having tea," he said. "Why, your kettle's not boiling any longer."

Maddox followed his lead.

"No, I took it off and forgot," he said. "Put it on again. And there's a cake in the parcel Bags brought. Take it out, will you ?"

David tore open the bag.

"Two cakes," he said. "Which do you want now ?"

"Either. You can stop and have tea with me if you like."

"Thanks awfully, but I had tea with a chap in college."

"Well, have another."

David considered this proposition simply on its own merits.

"Well, I think I will," he said. "But you've got a rotten fire. Shan't I take your kettle to the gas-stove ?"

"Yes ; good egg. Pour a little into the teapot first, though. Hi ! Not over my fingers.

"Sorry. It didn't really touch you, did it ?"

Maddox laughed.

"No, of course not. I should have smacked your head if it had. Thought it was going to."

"Just for safety," said David. "I always swear before I'm hurt. Then they take more care."

"Yes ; stick my kettle bang in the middle of the gas-stove. Say it's mine if any one objects."

"Right," said David. "It'll be boiled in two shakes."

CHAPTER IX

DAVID had been placed in one of the two parallel forms just below the lowest division of the fifth form when he entered Marchester at Michaelmas, but failed to get his promotion at Christmas, and now in the middle of the Lent term he was face to face with the fact that nothing in the world was more unlikely than that he should get out of it at Easter. There would be not more than half a dozen boys out of each remove promoted then, and, as his place was seventeenth in the list of the half-term results lately published, only a first-class miracle, the sort that does not occur, would do it for him.

He had just received a letter on the subject from his father, who, as usual, David thought, failed to grasp the situation altogether. But as David had not dreamed of telling his father what the situation really was, it was not much to be wondered at that the Archdeacon failed to grasp it. But there were things you couldn't tell your people, and this was one.

At the moment David was reading extracts to Bags from this letter with comments interspersed.

" He must have been an absolute infant phenomenon," he said, " if he really got his promotion every term, as he says. Nobody does now : it simply isn't done. And he's written to Adams about my work, blow him."

" Bad luck," said Bags.

" And has asked whether I hadn't better have a private tutor in Latin in the holidays," continued the

outraged David. " It's really too sickening, just as if
one didn't have enough of the dreary fellows in the
term. And of course I had to lie about what goes on
in the form. He asked me at Christmas whether there
was any cribbing, and I looked as if I simply didn't
know what cribbing meant."

" Perhaps nobody cribbed when he was an infant
phenomenon," said Bags.

David scratched his head.

" It's all rather rotten if you come to think of it,"
he said. " I only crib sufficiently myself to get off
impots, and very often I run it too fine and don't crib
enough. But I do think it's rot to crib your way to
the top of the form. Cribbing wasn't meant for that.
Plugs got full marks last Euclid lesson, just by copying
the propositions slap out of the book. He didn't have
the decency to make a howler or two ! "

Bags inserted a lump of sugar in a small hole which
he had bitten in the rind of an orange, and began to
suck the sweetened juice. He had come on amazingly
during this last half-year, and David was no longer in
the least ashamed of him as a pal. He wasn't any
good at games, and consequently would have been an
entire nonentity in any house except Adams's. But
in Adams's, so the rest of the school thought, even the
juniors took an interest in all sorts of queer things like
reading books which had got nothing to do with school
work, and knowing the difference between Liberals and
Conservatives. Such topics and pursuits were held to
be laudable affairs for the occupation of the mind in
Adams's, and the daily paper was not merely the source
from which it was discovered who had made a century
in a county match. Adams had half the house in and
out of his study all day, and the conversation was
generally supposed to be of the most abstruse type.

An odd thing was, too, that the house was just as keen on games as any other, and was possessed of most of the competitive cups. But, having trained and practised and won their cup, the house did not make this the sole topic of interest and congratulation. This was not the usual plan, and the consideration that Bags had won at Adams's would certainly not have been his elsewhere.

Bags considered this short disquisition on the proper sphere of cribbing for a little. He himself was in the parallel remove to David's, where it so happened that no cribbing went on. This was merely a question of fashion, and was as arbitrary and inexplicable as all other fashions, but as binding. Some forms cribbed, some didn't. Local fashions, not any sense of honesty, directed it.

"'Tisn't a satisfactory state of things, though," he said. "If everybody cribbed everything, it would be all right, because then everybody would get full marks."

David laughed.

"But old Tovey is a suspicious dog," he said, "and in that case he might suspect something. He's as blind as a bat, and you can have your crib spread out on the desk bang in front of his nose, and he won't see it. He didn't ought to be a beak at all. I put out my tongue at him the other day, right out like that, and held it there, and he never saw. I think beaks ought to have their eyesight tested every year or two, like they do for the army to see if they're competent. He makes up for his eyes by his ears, though. If you try to prompt a fellow right at back of the room, he hears like—like a megaphone."

Bags continued to suck his orange till David had finished and then went on.

"I repeat, if everybody cribbed everything it would

be all right," he said. "And the only proper alternative is that nobody should crib nothing."

"Oh, ah," said David. "Case of 'Jerusalem the Golden,' as applied to Tovey's. When we're all saints we'll wear nightshirts, 'stead of pyjamas, and golden crowns and bare hoofs——"

"Don't be profane," said Bags. "You're going to be confirmed."

David wrinkled up his nose.

"Right oh," said David. "Lord, do you remember the catechism classes at Helmsworth?"

David finished his father's letter and tore it up.

"Grown-up people seem to think that we think the same way as they do," he said. "That's such rot. We might just as well expect them to think the same way as us. They've forgotten about being fourteen, and we never knew about being forty or fifty. Do you remember my pater's sermon, too, about the chapel being the centre of school life, just because the cathedral is the centre of his? I think he's forgotten a lot about being a boy."

Bags had a certain persistency about him.

"Cribbing," he remarked—"I don't see why it's any worse to get full marks for a thing by cribbing than to avoid an impot by cribbing. Either you crib or you don't. If you crib, why not crib it all? I don't see that Plugs is a bit worse than you. Blazes, why don't you tell Maddox all about it? You're such pals with him, though you are his fag."

"My word, you do have rum notions," he said. "It would be sneaking; Maddox always whacks fellows if he finds they crib!"

"But just confidentially," said Bags.

"Simply imposh!" said David briefly.

The door of their study was open, and at the moment

Plugs, the wholesale cribber, came whistling by. His real name was Gregson, and he was freckled. He put his head in and said " Frowsy beasts," for no particular reason except that he felt cheerful.

" I say, Plugs, come in a minute," said David. " Have—have one of Bags's oranges ? "

" Don't mind if I do," said Plugs politely, " that is, if Bags doesn't mind. What's the row ? "

" Oh nothing, but we're just jawing about cribbing. Thought you might help."

" Not much to jaw about," remarked Plugs. " It's a dead cert that nobody ever got out of Tovey's without, if you mean that. Why ? "

" That's your mistake," said Bags. " If nobody cribbed, fellows would get out of Tovey's just the same."

" Didn't say that," said Plugs, " and the mistake's yours. I said nobody ever had got out of Tovey's without cribbing. No more they have. What would happen if nobody cribbed, ain't the question. Every one always has cribbed in Tovey's since the year one. You can't help it with an owl like Tovey. Blazes cribs, and he's three-quarters way down. Where'd you be without it, Blazes ? "

" Bim," said David promptly.

" There you are, then ! Can't think why you don't crib more, and get higher."

" But it's such silly rot," said Bags. " You'll crib yourself into the lower fifth some time. Nobody cribs in lower fifth. Where'll you be then ? "

" I shall be in the lower fifth," remarked the astute Plugs. " That's what I crib for. Then I shall stop cribbing, and we all start again fair. Besides, there's a sort of sport in cribbing. You may always be nabbed. It—it sharpens the faculties. Oh, there's a lot to be said for it ! "

" It would sharpen them just the same to learn your work," said Bags.

" It might, but it would take longer. I can learn a thing in half the time if I use a crib. I say, Blazes, there's extra confirmation class this evening. Whole of the second part of the catechi."

" Oh, blast ! " said David.

Plugs got up and left an arid orange-skin on the table.

" Jolly good orange," he said. " And now I've got a squash court. Want to play ? "

" Can't, with this extra confirmation-racket," said David. " Don't know a word of it."

" Crib it," said Plugs. " It's quite short, though tricky. Just like the third hole on the links. Lots of little bunkers."

David jumped up.

" Yes, I think I will," he said. " I'll do catechi after dinner. I'll be changed in two shakes."

Bags's ideas in this discussion about cribbing were limited to the possibility of its being made systematic. It must be at once premised that no sense of the dishonourableness of the practice so much as entered his head, but it was absurd that there should be no standard about it. At present everybody in Tovey's cribbed according to his lights, some to get full marks, others, more half-heartedly, like David, to avoid impositions. And that owl Tovey, in his view, was responsible for it. It was not a fellow detected in cribbing who ought to get into a row, but Tovey who made such a state of affairs possible. As stated before, in the parallel form which Bags graced by his presence, cribbing was unknown ; this was probably owing to fashion, but no doubt the extraordinary quickness of eye possessed by Bills (Williams, the form-master) had something to do with it. There it was, anyhow : nobody cribbed in Bills's; everybody cribbed in Tovey's, and the same number of boys were terminally promoted from each division into the lower fifth. Bags himself ran a decent chance of promotion this half, whereas David had none, but he knew that he had not David's brains, nor yet the half of them. David, for instance, had been *proxime accessit* in the scholarship examination last summer, whereas there had been no question of Bags going up for it. It was a rum world.

Bags and David shared their study together, presumably in equal quantities, but it was easy to see which was the master-mind, or, from certain aspects of it, the master-body. The room measured some ten feet by twelve, and appeared to be chiefly given up to David's possessions and implements. There were a couple of racquets in a press, and a bag of racquet-balls, a squash racquet (for which he presently rushed in, buttoning his shirt), a cricket-bat, an old deflated football, and a bag of golf-clubs. There were school-books about equally divided, a few cribs belonging to David, and on the walls some half-dozen rather thin watercolours of the Archdeaconry and Cathedral at Baxminster, executed post-haste by Margery after the famous day when Maddox had declared that it was the rippingest cathedral in England, and David's house the rippingest house in the close. There was also a pen-and-ink drawing made by David himself of the tower of the cathedral, which leaned in an unsatisfactory manner till he had framed it slightly crooked in a cardboard mount, which restored its dangerous want of equilibrium. The two tables, supposed to belong severally to them, had been chiefly annexed by David, since golf-balls, fives-gloves, and such paraphernalia usurped the one, while the other was littered with his books, Bags excavating a corner for himself when occasion abso-

lutely demanded. But this predominance of David's
belongings was not accomplished so much by greed on
the part of David as by Bags's consistent self-effacement
when David's interests clashed with his own. Indeed,
it indicated one of the most popular points in Bags's
character, namely that, as everybody said, he was so
deucedly easy to get on with. David was easy to get
on with too, owing to his intense appreciation of the
humour of life in general. And even when it was not
humorous he thought it was, which was a cheering
way of looking at things. But of the two, David, both
publicly and privately, was the substance, and Bags
the shadow : the shadow danced in obedience to that
which threw it.

But this morning Bags—the nickname had stuck to
him in the new school, for it was simpler than " Crabtree " and there was not anything else in particular to
say about him—Bags was meditating a dance of his
own, independently of David. He felt certain that if
David had been in his division, parallel to the one that
he mildly cribbed in, where cribbing happened not to
be the vogue, he would probably be somewhere near
the top of the form, though, as it was, he was three-
quarters of the way down. David himself bore the
weight of " things as they were " with complete equani-
mity (for there they were) and he cribbed sufficiently
to avoid the tedium of impositions, but not sufficiently
to secure himself a decent place. He appeared to be
quite content with this state of affairs, except in so far
that it might lead to having a private tutor in the
holidays, whereas to Bags it all seemed a gross miscar-
riage of justice. No doubt if David turned to and
worked with industry and zeal he might make his
difficult way upwards, but it was a tremendous handicap to be obliged to sweat your eyes out in order to get

on level terms with people who slowly and correctly construed out of an English translation of the lesson. and David would have been the first to turn up his nose at such a proposal. It was less trouble to sit seventeenth in the form, and avoid impositions.

Bags was not very good at independent action : his line was action that fell in with other people's wishes, and he meditated over any possible idea that might suggest itself to him in his new rôle. He would have liked to tell Adams (confidentially, of course) that Remove A relied so largely on Tovey's well-known shortsightedness, but, apart from the general feeling that this would be sneaking, there was a considerable doubt in his mind as to how Adams would take it. Adams was a splendid chap, of course—that was the only possible view to hold of him ; but it was undeniable that he didn't want to be bothered. He liked things to be pleasant ; he liked fellows to come and sit about in his study with clean hands and a parting in their hair, and to be happy and contented. He liked them also to be interested in general topics, and to bring their work to him for help ; but he did not like to know that school-rules were being broken, or that the house was not getting on in a saintly and successful manner. He wanted it to manage its own affairs, while he, like a genial father coming home in the evening to his family, saw only bright and cheerful faces round him. Once, Bags remembered, Cruikshank had consulted him on a case where bullying was suspected, and Bags, at Cruikshank's invitation, had been present as a witness. But Cruikshank's reception, though perfectly cordial, had not been of a sort to encourage confidence. Adams had thanked him, had appreciated his good intentions, but had told him that he was sure the feeling of the house would prevent any such occur-

rence in the future. The feeling of the house was the
best jury, and he wished to leave the matter in the
hands of the prefects. Bags conjectured quite easily
from his recollection of this what was likely to be his
own reception if he informed Adams confidentially
that Remove A consistently cribbed. No; that
would not do, and David had been horrified at the idea
of Maddox being told. . . .

Then quite suddenly all scheme of independent action
was taken from Bags. Somewhere down the passage
a door was opened, and David's name was shouted.
David, in any case, was not here, having gone to play
squash, and, though the voice was Maddox's, Bags
saw no reason for going to tell him. If David did not
answer, he would conclude that David did not hear.
Probably Maddox only wanted him in a general sort of
way. Then came a step along the passage from the
bathroom, where the prefects' studies were, and along
the corridor and round the corner, and Maddox entered,
genial and cordial as usual.

" David out ? " he asked. " Why didn't you
shout ' Not at home ' ? But when he comes in you
might tell him——"

Maddox's eye wandered round the study.

" I say, what a God-forsaken mess you and David
keep your room in," he said. " Piles of books and golf-
balls in between. What's this ? "

Maddox suddenly took up from the table a book in
a dark blue cover. It was an English translation of
Thucydides, edited by the obliging Mr. Bohn.

" Is this yours ? " he asked.

" Yes," said Bags instantly.

" Well, I shall confiscate it, and I shall whack you.
Better come and be whacked now, and get it over.
But it's a damned bad plan to use cribs, Bags. When

you get into the fifth form, you'll find you're no end of a way behind fellows who've worked their way up, instead of cribbing their way up. Got any more of these silly things ? Let's have them all. I don't want to search your study, you know. I would much sooner you gave me them, all of them, and told me there aren't any more. Word of honour, you know."

Bags thought feverishly a moment.

" There are several more," he said.

" Right ; let's have them."

Bags got down from the table where he was sitting, feeling rather limp physically, but quite resolved to see this through. Meantime, unfortunately, Maddox had opened the volume of Bohn's Thucydides, with the idle habit of the book-lover, and turned to the title-page.

" And you wrote David's name in it, though it was yours ? " he asked.

Here was an awful complication. And what an unspeakable ass was David, so thought Bags, to write his name in a crib. He remembered his doing it now, in Greek characters. He quite intensely wished he had not said it was his own. But that he proposed to stick to, and if Maddox chose he might think him guilty of the unutterable meanness of owning a crib and writing a pal's name in it.

" Yes, I wrote Blaize's name in it," he said, " in Greek."

But he did not say it particularly well. Or Maddox was confoundedly sharp. Probably both.

" Oh, that's a lie, isn't it ? " he said.

Bags was between the devil and the deep sea, and any other uncomfortable neighbours that are possible to a boy. He had been quite prepared to take a whacking on David's behalf, and, though the flesh was weak, his spirit really embraced the opportunity. But now just as likely as not, he was going to take a whacking on his own behalf, without getting David off. It was all pretty bad, but how could he have foreseen that Maddox would look at the title-page, or have forgotten that David had been such a juggins as to write his name there ? So, being landed in this awkward place, he made up his mind to stop there.

" No, that's all right," he said. " I wrote Blaize's name there."

Maddox looked at him, so it seemed to Bags, with a certain respectful sympathy.

" And in David's handwriting ? " he asked. " Makings of a forger. And are you doing Thucydides this half ? David is, I know, because I've often given him construes. But you're in the other remove, aren't you ? "

It was no use lying about this. Bags surrendered and told the truth.

" Yes, in Remove B," he said.

" Then you can't be doing Thucydides, because they always do different books. Oh, cave in ! Out with it ! "

" Well, then, it's Blaize's crib," said the unsuccessful Bags.

" So I knew. Why did you say it was yours ? "

" I don't know," said Bags.

" Think, then."

Bags threw his sucked orange, the third of them, into the waste-paper basket.

" Because I thought you'd just whack me, and there wouldn't be any more bother ! " he said.

Maddox again looked sympathetic.

" Just to save Blaize a whacking ? " he asked.

Bags suddenly took courage. Maddox was such a ripper, he would understand.

" No, not altogether," he said. " But I felt I'd sooner let you think it was mine than his. He's so awfully proud of you. I didn't want you to know that . . . oh, blast it all," he added desperately.

Maddox kicked the door shut.

" You didn't want me to know he cribbed," he said, " because then I shouldn't think him such an awfully decent chap ? "

" About that," said Bags.

Maddox nodded.

" You're a good chap, Bags," he said; " but I've found out that David cribs in spite of you, and I shall whack him for it. 'Tisn't your fault. You did your very best, and a rather good one too, to prevent it. But cribbing is all rot. I hadn't an idea David cribbed. Do other fellows in Remove A crib much ? "

Then Bags saw his opportunity made for him from beginning to end. Here was Maddox, who mattered so much more than Adams, or any one else, asking for information, instead of being reluctantly saddled with it. For a moment he hesitated, since David had been so horrified at the thought of Maddox being told; but then Maddox said:

" 'Tain't sneaking, Bags. I'm not going to make visitations 'cept on David. In fact, I want to clear things up."

Bags's hesitation vanished.

" Yes, they all crib in Remove A," he said. " It's —it's just the fashion. Blazes doesn't crib much, only enough to avoid impots. Other fellows crib to get marks; that's why he's so low."

" Never thought of that," said Maddox.

" No, why should you ? But there it is."

" And do the fellows at the top of the form crib ? "

asked Maddox. "Remember you're not giving any-body away in the sneaking sense."

"Rather; that's why they're there."

Maddox had sat down on a pile of books and golf-balls, and there was a rolling-about and spilling as he got up.

"Thanks," he said. "I'll think what can be done, and remember you know nothing about it all. But the fact that I've found a crib of David's is another matter. Send him to me when he comes in."

There was a piercing and cheerful whistle outside at this moment, quite unmistakable, and David burst gaily in.

"Hullo, Maddox!" he said.

"Hullo! I say, I've got a Thucydides crib of yours here, with your name written in it, you silly ass. Collect all the cribs you've got, and bring them to my study. I'm going to whack you!"

He waited a moment, just to make sure that David was not going to say that everybody cribbed in Remove A. Of course David said nothing of the kind, and he went back to his study.

"Bags, you ass!" said David, innocent of all that Bags had attempted to do. "Why didn't you sit on it or something, when he came in?"

"Couldn't. There simply wasn't time."

David searched his shelves, swearing softly to himself, and the result was a rather voluminous load.

"I shall simply descend to the bottom of the form," he said. "Private tutor too, in the Easter holidays. Oh, damn, I think you might have managed something. Maddox lays on, too. It's a blasted affair."

David had grown in breadth no less than in height during this last half-year, but it was an extremely limp figure that appeared in Maddox's study a few minutes afterwards, with eight volumes of Mr. Bohn's classical series. He had felt rather queer all morning, and the sight of a racquet-handle on the table gave him an unpleasant qualm.

Maddox took the books from him.

" These are all, David ? " he asked.

" Yes. That's the lot."

" Anything to say ? " asked Maddox.

David might have had something to say, namely, that everybody cribbed in Tovey's. But it never occurred to him, however remotely, to say it.

" No," he said, " 'cept that I've got beastly thin flannels on."

" So I see. I'm not going to jaw you as well as lick you, but cribbing's an utterly rotten game, and I always whack anybody whom I find doing it. So get over that chair. I shall give you six."

" Gosh," said David quietly, presenting himself.

Maddox gave him four, and not in fun ; it was not meant to be fun, and David felt the cold sweat stand on his forehead He could just prevent himself from crying out, but there was not much to spare, and he felt doubtful if he could stand two more. But Maddox, at the same moment, felt that he certainly couldn't, and he threw the racquet-handle into the corner.

" That's enough," he said.

David straightened himself up and turned round, wiping the sweat from a very white face.

" You—you can whack," he said. " I say, I feel rather bad. May I——"

There was a sudden singing in his ears, and Maddox caught him as he reeled, and put him gently down into a chair, as he leaned on him. But David's faintness was only momentary, and, recovering almost instantly, he saw that Maddox was looking almost as queer as he himself felt.

"I'm all right again," he said. "I say, thanks awfully for not giving me six. Rotten of me to feel squeamish, but I couldn't help it."

"I say, for God's sake don't crib again, David," he said, "or anyhow, don't let me catch you."

David smiled and got up rather gingerly. He understood nothing of what was in his friend's mind, knowing only that he had been caught with a crib, and that summary retribution had been most effectively carried out.

"I'll jolly well try not to," he said.

"Right. Shake a paw, then," said Maddox. "By the way, Bags tried to make me think the crib was his— told me so in fact—but then I found your name."

David stared.

"Jolly decent of Bags," he said. "But whatever did he do that for?"

"I expect he's rather fond of you," remarked Maddox.

Maddox gave two days' consideration as to the question of the next step to be taken, and found the rival claims of honour and justice rather hard to reconcile. As far as he himself was concerned, he cared not one farthing what the Remove A would think of him if, as he thought he might have to do, he went to Adams or the Head Master with the information that cribbing was the fashion in that form; but he realized that it would never do if it came out somehow that Bags was the source from whom his information had been derived. Remove A would argue, with irrefutable logic, that somebody must have sneaked, and would take all steps with all the ingenuity that was theirs to find out who had done so. Again, there was David, on whom suspicion might fall. It would be certainly known that Maddox had licked him for cribbing; it would very likely be inferred that he in self-defence (though the self-defence had proved singularly ineffective) had tried to justify himself by saying that the practice was a universal one. And that was precisely what David had refrained from saying ; it would be the rankest injustice that he should be executed for cribbing and disgraced by the supposition that he had attempted to justify himself. On the other hand, cribbing was a rotten system, and Maddox intended to do his best to stop it.

It was not easy to decide what to do, and he turned all his acute boyish brain to the solving of the problem, which to him seemed one of the utmost delicacy and importance. It made all the difference to the well-being of the house, which, quite rightly, was to him the world, that Remove A should cease to crib, and that they should be unaware how the news of their habits had come to the authorities. He wanted to take the wisest course, and, had he considered the matter a trivial one, he would have been in his sphere, and for his age, every whit as culpable as the Prime Minister of a State who shrugs his shoulders at some astounding national abuse. It mattered immensely, and, indeed, more than he knew, for the right management of the affairs of such small kingdoms as a house or a form in a public school goes to build up the foundations of the right management of the affairs of big kingdoms. Character and judgment are formed there ; a responsible boy takes into the big world exactly that which he has learned in smaller spheres. Maddox, it may be remarked, not being a prig, did not indulge in those edifying reflections, but only said to himself, as he scratched his curly head, " I'm damned if I know what to do ! " But his wise boy's brain worked and explored and burrowed, and two days after he went to his house-master.

"I hate bothering you, sir," he said, "but I'm in a fix."

"Cruikshank?" asked Adams who knew there was not much cordiality lost between the two. For himself, he respected Cruikshank, but loved Maddox.

"Oh no, Crookles and I are getting on all right, thanks. It's another thing."

Adams, as has been stated, disliked exercising his authority. He held the slightly dangerous creed that a house managed itself best when left alone, and that public opinion was the most effective check on irregular practices.

"You always manage house affairs much better than I could, Frank," he said.

"Don't know about that, sir. But this affects more than the house."

Mr. Adams lit his pipe. He rather wanted to play golf, but Maddox seldom bothered him with problems, and it might be well to listen.

"Fire ahead, then," he said.

"Well, sir, I had to lick David a couple of days ago for having cribs," began Maddox.

"Why isn't the little beast higher in his form then?" remarked Adams.

"I was coming to that. I learned from—well, from another fellow—that everybody cribs in Remove A, that it's absolutely the regular thing, which is rotten. Also I learned that David cribs only about enough to avoid impots, whereas other fellows crib their way to the top of the class. It isn't fair, sir."

Adams decided to go into this.

"Shut the door, Frank," he said. "Of course, all you say is confidential, unless you give me leave to mention it. Go on!"

"Well, sir, it's really all old—it's Mr. Tovey's fault,"

said Maddox. " You see, he's so jolly blind, that fellows practically must crib."

" Then David has been suffering vicariously for Mr. Tovey," remarked Adams.

Maddox laughed.

" Yes, sir, about that," he said.

Adams relit his pipe.

" Funny thing this should have happened just now," he said, " for Mr. Tovey has been sent to bed with flue."

Maddox gave a cackle of delight.

" Gosh, what luck ! " he said.

" Why ? "

Instantly a scheme lit itself up in Maddox's head.

" Why, sir, you might suggest to the Head that some of the prefects—particularly me, I mean—should take some of Mr. Tovey's work. He's rather keen on that sort of thing ; don't you remember he told me to take your form for a couple of days when you were laid up last half ? Well, sir, if you could manage that I descended on them out of the blue, say, to-morrow morning, before they know that Mr. Tovey's gone sick, I bet I can reap a lot of them in. They're sure to have learned their work with cribs ; and then, you see, I've got David's cribs, and I can tell if their construing comes out of cribs. O Lord, I see it all ! "

Adams considered this.

" And how about telling the Head that the form cribs ? " he asked. " Perhaps he'd join in and take some of the work himself ! "

Maddox laughed again.

" Gosh, what a time Remove A's going to have," he said. " But the Head mustn't make it retrospective. It must all be found out afresh, sir, if you see what I mean."

Adams nodded.

" Yes," he said. " The Head will understand that."

Later in the day a conference between the powers hostile to Remove A was held (the powers in question being the Head, Adams, and Maddox) and a diabolical plan of campaign was hatched. The classical work of the form, hitherto presided over, blindfold, so to speak, by Mr. Tovey, was to be taken with the suddenness of a thunderstorm by Maddox. Not a word was to be said; he was simply to march in at early school next day, and open fire on his own system. The lesson was Virgil, and that evening he closely studied the excellent translation as given by Mr. Bohn in the volume he had confiscated from David.

Construing began from the top of the form, and boy after boy translated with extreme elegance and fluency, and Maddox was beaming and complimentary. Among his other weird accomplishments he knew shorthand, and, screened by the sloping cover of his desk, he made an accurate transcript of what the translation of each boy had been.

" Yes, very good, very good indeed," he said when this was finished. "Quite a lot of you have got full marks."

He opened the lid of his desk, and took out of it the Virgil crib which he had confiscated from David three days before.

" I hadn't time to mug it all up," he remarked, " and so I shall just read you through a translation out of a crib which—which came into my possession a few days ago."

He began; read a line or two, then stopped and consulted his shorthand notes. Then he nodded to the top of the form.

" Just the expression you used," he said genially.

He went on a little farther.

" I think that is how you translated it, Plugs—I mean, Gregson," he observed to the second boy.

This was not quite comfortable, and uneasy glances passed about. Who could possibly have expected that Maddox would bring a crib into form? There was a really distressing parallelism between it and the renderings given by most of the boys, and in consequence there were pensive faces. But Maddox made no further comment, and proceeded to ask a few questions about grammar.

" And now," he said, " you will turn on a hundred lines farther and translate on paper the twelve lines beginning at line 236. You will use no books at all for this, neither dictionaries nor—nor any other."

There was a quarter of an hour's silence, broken only by the scratchings of labouring pens. The unlucky Gregson, who had been positively brilliant over the prepared lines, could make neither head nor tail of the fairly elementary passage that Maddox had set, and ventured on a protest.

" I say, Mr. Tovey never gives us unseens," he said.

" I dare say; but I do," remarked Maddox.

Suppressed giggles: this was rather a score.

" Nor do I allow laughing," he added.

Decidedly this hour was not going very comfortably, and no alleviation was possible, for it was somehow quite hopeless to think of ragging Maddox; it was also very nearly hopeless to translate this unknown passage. And then a thing far more dreadful happened than any that had gone before.

The door of the class-room opened, and the Head entered in rustling silk gown. He nodded to Maddox, who got up.

" All going well," he said, " in Mr. Tovey's absence?"

The form did not think so: but, unfortunately, the Head had not asked them.

" What are you doing with them, Maddox ? " he said.

" Virgil lesson, sir," he said. " We've had the prepared lesson, and I've set them a short unseen."

" Very good practice," said the Head. " And the marks for the seen translation were satisfactory ? "

" Yes, sir, very," said Maddox.

" Excellent. Please take the unseen translations over to my house after school, and I will look them over myself. It isn't fair to give you all the work."

" Yes, sir," said Maddox.

The Head still lingered by Maddox's desk, in a rather beastly fashion, and peered (he was a little short-sighted) at Maddox's shorthand notes.

" And what are those cabalistic symbols ? " he asked.

" Just notes I took in shorthand of the fellows' translations, sir," he answered.

" Ha ! I shall like to compare these with the unseen. Write them out for me, Maddox, will you, and bring them over to me. And this ? "

He took up the volume of Bohn's translation which Maddox had been reading out of.

" It's a Bohn, sir," said Maddox. " I brought it in myself. I hadn't time to learn up the lesson, and I thought I'd better have a crib by me."

The Head, so thought the eager audience, looked rather stern for a moment. Then, quite naturally, he laughed.

" I shall confiscate that," he said, looking pleasantly round. " Better practice for you, Maddox, to get up your lesson without one."

He rustled out again, leaving uneasiness behind him. It had been rather sport to see Maddox's crib taken from him, but behind that somewhat superficial pleasure there was a vague idea that dangerous things were getting into dangerous hands. Maddox had been bidden to supply the shorthand notes of the prepared translation, which would reveal the parallelisms between Mr. Bohn's renderings and that of the Remove A. It would be a dreadful thing if the Head, in an abstracted moment, consulted Mr. Bohn also. Added to that there was the fact that the Head was going to look over the unseen work, and would no doubt be struck by the amazing contrast between that and the prepared lesson. It was almost too much to expect that he would credit the form with such extraordinary industry and taste as to have prepared their set piece so perfectly, and yet to be so lamentably wanting over an unseen. Such, at least, was the private meditation of most of Remove A, who wished severally and collectively that they had not been so brilliant over the first part of the lesson.

Breakfast and desultory confabulation when the form assembled again for the next lesson had not tended to make things more comfortable. But there was nothing whatever to be suspicious about as to the manner in which those ill-omened decrees of fate had unfolded themselves. Mr. Tovey had happened to have influenza, the Head had happened to tell Maddox to take his place, and Maddox had happened to set them an unseen and to take shorthand notes of their previous translation, and the Head had happened to come in to see how Maddox was getting on, and had taken for his own delectation a crib, shorthand notes made manifest, and those dreadful attempts at an unseen. All this was hurriedly debated after Remove A assembled for second school, awaiting the arrival of Maddox, who was a little late, and, so it was sarcastically said, was probably mugging up the Thucydides lesson in another crib. Then the uneasiness increased into

dismay, for the door opened, and there appeared, not
Maddox at all, but the Head himself. He had a packet
of papers in his hand, which were rightly and instantly conjectured to be the Virgil unseen of the hour
before.

Dr. Hamilton did everything rather quietly and
slowly, and was distinguished for a politeness of manner
that on occasion became terrible. He had never been,
as far as the school was aware, notable for athletic
prowess; but, in spite of this defect, he was always a
keen observer of cricket and football matches, and was
certainly intelligent about these matters, so that his
heart was felt to be in the right place. It was quite
certain also that his head was in the right place, for he
had been the senior classic and Chancellor's medallist
at Cambridge, a fact which was viewed in the light of
a strong testimonial in favour of the dead languages.
But, quite apart from any of his accomplishments was
the cause of the awed respect in which he was held,
and, though the Sixth themselves could not have told
you why he was so impressive a person, the reason, except to boys, was not far to seek. It was the justness
and the bigness of him, his character—a thing not
definable by those whose characters are not yet formed,
but quite clearly appreciable by them. To please the
Head was worth effort; his praise was of the nature
of a decoration. It may be added that it was quite
as well worth an effort to avoid displeasing him.

He went, with his rustling gown gathered up in his
arm, straight to the desk that Mr. Tovey was wont to
occupy, and for five awful minutes, without the slightest
allusion to Thucydides, continued reading from the
sheaf of papers he carried with him. He did not look
at all pleasant, as occasionally he made a note, or
occasionally drew his thick blue pencil across a page.

And all the time the hapless Remove A sat in a state of confirmed pessimism.

It was noticed that he had divided his sheaf into two packets. He came to the end of it, and tore up, across and across, the larger packet of the two. The rest numbered perhaps half a dozen sheets. Then he spoke.

" I have never seen a worse set of unseen translations than those which the form showed up to Maddox this morning," he said. " Some half-dozen are passable, and one, that of Blaize, is good, or nearly so. Blaize ! "

" Yes, sir," said Blaize.

" What is your place in the form by the half-term marks ? "

" Seventeenth, sir," said David, from his lowly abode.

The Head glared at him and spoke very advisedly.

" That is a disgraceful place for a boy who can make such a decent unseen translation," he observed.

This had precisely the effect that that diabolical Head had intended. Rather bad luck on Blaize, reflected the form generally, to be whacked for cribbing, and then to be slated by the Head for being so low.

The Head paused a moment.

" You may close your books for the present," he said, " and listen to what I have to say to you. It is an extremely serious matter. Before doing your unseen you construed a piece of prepared work, and out of the twenty-four boys in the form, sixteen got practically full marks for it. You may remember that at last lesson I took away from Maddox the crib he had brought in with him, and I also took the transcription of the shorthand notes he had made. I see, by referring to the crib, that all, or, I think, nearly all of the boys who got full marks, had used that crib. They had not even the sense to alter their translations so

that their indebtedness to it should not have been so
glaringly obvious.   They are fools, in fact, as well as
knaves, and I have no use in Remove A or in any
other part of the school for either.   Now I have not
the slightest intention of asking any of you if you
used a crib or not, because, without your telling me, I
know that you did.   I will just take one instance, the
first that comes to hand.   Gregson translated his
prepared lesson perfectly, and in it used three expressions which were identical with expressions in Bohn's
translation.   His unseen, on the other hand, was
simply beneath contempt.   I use his name only as
the first that occurs to me, and I do not single him out
as being a worse offender than many others.   Nor do
I wish him or any of you to confess, still less to deny
that he used a crib.   He and you alike are a very
rotten set of fellows."

The form generally, during this quiet and biting
address, was growing stiff with horror, and Gregson,
who, as Plugs, had conversed so lightly in Bags's study
about the advantages of cribbing, was feeling singularly
empty.   It was one thing to talk airily about the
merits of the system; but they were not so apparent
when the Head spoke like this about its demerits.

He let this sink in for a bit, without looking at poor
Plugs any more than at anybody else.   Then he continued:

"I have looked through the marks of the half-term,"
he said, "and it is quite inconceivable to me that such
high marks as those earned by the boys who are at the
top of the form could have been come by honestly.   I
am therefore going to cancel the whole of the marks
which to-day determine your places, and begin a fresh
with the marks for the unseen which I have just looked
over.   You will therefore now take your places in the

new order which I shall read out, and the whole of the marks of the term hitherto are cancelled. If any boy, high or low, in the newly constituted form has the slightest protest to make, he will please state it fully, and I will listen to it with respect. I am not talking sarcastically, and I only want to do justice—roughly, no doubt, but to the best of my power. I dare say you have all used cribs to a certain extent, but I do not want to go into that unless any one wishes me to. It is dishonest to use cribs at all, and there is the end of the matter. I will, however, go into any individual case, for the purpose of doing justice. You may talk it over among yourselves if you wish, and, while you do so, I will leave your class-room and come back when you have made up your minds. If any boy wishes me to go, he will please hold up his hand, and go I will. No notice will be taken by me of the owner of any hand that is held up."

They could appreciate that; there was a justice about it that commanded respect. But though the Head's promise was implicitly trusted by all present, not a hand was held up. The Head gave ample time for this.

" I take it, then, you are satisfied," he said at length. " You will therefore take your places in the new order. And do not take any books out of your desks before you take your new places. I will read the list, and each boy will take his place according to these marks as his name is read."

There was the scraping of boots, the stir of changed places, and in a couple of minutes the new order was established.

" And now," said the Head, " every boy will look in his new desk, and give to its previous occupant all its contents with the exception of any cribs that there may be there. Now make the exchanges, and place all cribs you find in front of my desk."

There was an impression at this point that the Head was showing ignorance. He should have known that most cribs were not brought into school at all, and that the large majority of them were securely reposing in their owners' studies. But here they reckoned without their host.

Some dozen books were given up, a very meagre total, and the form generally (wrong once more) expected that the Head would make a desk-to-desk visitation himself. He did nothing of the kind.

"You will now," he said, "each of you, go to the house and the study of the boy whose place you now occupy, and bring me all the cribs you find there. I have told Maddox to go round after you. I sincerely hope—sincerely—that he will find nothing to do. If he does the consequences will be quite serious. I shall come back here in exactly twenty minutes, and shall expect to find the books ready, piled here. Maddox will go his rounds after you have finished and report to me. You all of you share studies with other boys, and you will understand that all cribs found therein will be brought here, whether belonging to members of this form or not. Now you had the opportunity of consulting each other before, and you must not consult now. If any of you don't know the house to which the owner of your present desk belongs, ask."

The Head got up, rustled down the room, and went out looking neither to right nor left. A perfectly silent form dispersed.

They were back again in their places before he reappeared. In front of his desk was a solid pile of books. He did not even glance at them.

"We will now do our Thucydides," he said. "Who

is the top boy of the form? You, Blaize. What chapter of what book are you at?"

"Book three, sir," said David. "Chapter fourteen."

"Read the Greek then, aloud, till I stop you, and then construe."

A rather trying half-hour followed. The form generally was addled with emotion, and it was almost a relief when Maddox appeared from his search. He had no fresh and incriminating volumes with him, but he might have left them outside.

"Well?" said the Head.

"No, sir," said he, "I couldn't find any more."

And his eye fell almost respectfully on the appalling pile already found.

"Thanks," said the Head. "I am glad. Please take the lesson to-morrow morning."

He instantly resumed Thucydides.

"Gregson, read and translate," he said.

Poor Plugs! . . .

At the end the Head got up.

"There is no need to speak to you further," he said, "because I think you all understand. I may say, however, that any boy found using a crib in the future will be flogged and degraded into the fourth form. You will find it unwise to try. At least I think so."

He gathered up his gown, and for the first time, apparently, saw the heap of books piled in front of his desk.

"The lowest six boys of the form will bring those silly volumes across to my house," he said. "The head boy will count them here, and then come across when they are all removed and count them again to see that the numbers tally. You understand, Blaize?"

"Yes, sir," said David.

"And I am ashamed of you all," said the Head.

CHAPTER X

DAVID'S soft grey hat with house-colours on it was tilted over his eyes to screen them from the sun, and he lay full length on the hot dry sand above high-water mark on the beach at Naseby, stupefied and simmering with content. His arms, bare to the elbow in rolled-up shirt sleeves, were extended, and he kept filling his hands with sand and letting it ooze out again through the interstices of his fingers in a pleasant, tickling manner, hour-glass fashion, though the action evoked in him neither edifying nor melancholy reflection on the subject of the passing of time. Beside him lay two coats and two bags of golf-clubs, for he and Maddox, with whom he was staying, had just come back from a morning round of golf, and had gone down to the shore to bathe before lunch. They had tossed up as to which of them should go to fetch towels, and, Maddox having lost, had just disappeared up the steep, crumbling path that led to the top of the sand-cliffs, where was perched the house his mother usually took for the summer holidays. A few hundred yards farther north these cliffs broke into tumbled sand-dunes and stretches of short, velvety turf, where greens nestled in Elysian valleys surrounded by saharas.

Maddox would be absent some ten minutes, and David let his lazy thoughts float down the stream of the very pleasant thinkings which made up his extreme contentment. He did not direct them, but let them drift, going swiftly here, eddying round there, while the memory-shores of the last few months glided by. In the first place, and perhaps most important of all, he was staying here with his friend—this was an eddy; he went round and round in it. Though he had been here three days already, passing them entirely with Maddox, playing golf with him, playing tennis with him, bathing with him, and quite continuously talking to him, David could not get used to this amazing situation. He called him " Frank " too, just as if he was nobody in particular, and at the thought of it David rolled over on to his side, wriggling, and said " Lord ! "

It was but a little more than a year ago that he had been, in his own phrase, " a scuggy little devil with stag-beetles," capable, it is true, of hero-worship, and able to recognize a hero when he saw him, for had not his heart burned within him when, going up for his scholarship examination, the demigod had thrown a careless word to him ? It was quite sufficient then that Maddox, the handsomest fellow in the world, the best bat probably that Marchester had ever produced, and altogether the most glorious of created beings, should have noticed him at all : indeed, that was more than sufficient ; it was sufficient that Maddox should exist. And since then only a year had passed, and here he was calling him Frank, and leaning on his arm when so disposed, and tossing him who should get towels, and staying with his mother. Often she would say something to him in French, unconscious which language she talked, and Frank would answer in French, which seemed wonderfully romantic. Though their ages were so diverse (for Frank was eighteen and David fifteen, and three years, when the combined total is so small, make a vast difference) here, staying with him, David hardly felt the gap. At school it was otherwise, a hundred seasons sundered them, but here they were equal. All difference was swallowed up in friendship, friendship even swallowed up hero-worship sometimes.

David dwelled gluttonously on the steps that had led up to this. There was that meeting at Baxminster, with the splendid adventure of the second edition of Keats, and here he made an agitated excursion into the fate of that. He and Margery had decided to sell it, and had got the enormous sum of twelve (not ten) pounds for it. But the glory of that had been abruptly extinguished, for their father had insisted that their equal shares should be invested in the savings bank, to roll up at some beggarly rate of interest, and do no good to anybody. Really, grown-up people were beyond words. . . .

He dismissed this distressing topic and hitched on to Maddox again. Public-school life began with his installation as fag, and there hero-worship had soared like a flame day by day, until that afternoon when, after playing squash with Bags in the rain, he had gone back to the house for a bath. David had always avoided the thought of that; it remained a moment quite sundered from the rest of his intercourse with Frank, embarrassing, and to be forgotten, like the momentary opening of a cupboard where nightmare dwelt. Anyhow, it had been locked again instantly, and the key thrown away. Never a sound had again issued therefrom.

Thereafter came a flood of jolly things to swim in. After the new arrangement in Remove A, consequent on that monumental cribbing-row, he had got into the lower fifth at Easter, and would, when he went back at Michaelmas, find himself in the middle fifth. Frank had made him work with intelligence and industry as well, though the distractions of the summer half had been frightfully alluring. For David was really coming on as a wily left-hand bowler, and it had been extremely difficult to give more than casual attention to the "Commentaries" of Julius Cæsar, when his inmost mind was wrapped up in cricket. It was not hundreds of overs, but thousands of them that David delivered in imagination when he ought to have been crossing the Alps with Hannibal, or challenging Medea's strange use of the pluperfect when that infuriated lady was in the act of stabbing her children. But he had got his remove, and a satisfactory report of his work, so that there was peace and joy at Baxminster, and his father sanguinely prophesied that he would go up into a fresh form every term, as he himself had done.

Half-way through the summer half had come the most intoxicating possibility, namely, that he had a chance of getting his house-colours for cricket, his very first year at school. This was a thing nearly unheard of (though, of course, Maddox had done it), but he had been tried in house-matches, and had done rather well. Then that hope had gone to the grave, for when Maddox put up the list of the completed house-eleven his name did not appear. But he had known that it was not going to do so already, and the manner of its exclusion was, secretly to him, almost a greater gratification than its appearance would have been. That, too, lying on the hot sand, he turned greedily over in his mind, licking the chops of memory.

It had happened thus. He had come one afternoon into Maddox's study, just before the final promotions were made, and Maddox opened the subject.

" David, would you be fearfully sick if I didn't give you your house-colours ? " he asked abruptly.

David had already allowed himself to hope for, even to expect them, and the sunshine went out of life.

" I think I should," he said. " Not that it matters

a hang. . . . I say, I'm going up town.   Do you want
anything ? "

"No, thanks.   But just wait a minute.   Oh, don't
look like that ! "

David's face had taken an expression of the most
Stygian gloom.

"Sorry," he said.   "Of course I was an ass to hope
it."

"No, you weren't," said Maddox.   "But I've been
bothering about it, and I thought I'd talk to you.   It's
like this : you and Ozzy have about equal claim, and,
if we weren't such pals, I think I should toss up which
of you I gave colours to.   But the house would think I
was favouring you if I put you in.   There's another
thing, too : it's Ozzy's last year, and your first.   I don't
know that that matters so much; so, if you find yourself left out, it'll be because we're pals.   See ? "

David moved a step nearer ; the woe had gone from
his face.

"Gosh, then, leave me out," he said.   "I—I prefer
being left out, if that's it."

"Really ? " asked Maddox.

"Yes, rather, and—and thanks ever so much."

There had been no need for more than these jerked
telegraphic sentences, but David went up town, tread-
ing on air, with a secret heavenly pride that was certainly among the "rippingest feelings" he had ever
had.   He congratulated Ozzy with complete sincerity.
. . . And here was Frank himself sliding down the crumbling sand-path with towels.

Frank threw a towel at him and knocked off his hat.

"Mother's lunching out," he said, "so we can bathe
just as long as we please without being late.   Oh,
and she said to me, ' need you '—that's you—' go away
on Saturday ? '   I said I'd ask you."

David had no hesitation over this.

" No, of course I needn't," he said. " At least——"

" At least ? " said Frank, emptying the sand out of his shoes.

" I mean, are you sure I'm not being a bore? I should love to stop, of course. But won't you and your mother get blasted sick of me ? "

" Don't think she will," said Maddox gravely. " I shall rather, but it doesn't matter. In fact, I was wondering whether perhaps you'd mind going on Friday instead of Saturday."

David laughed.

" That's a poor shot at getting a rise out of me," he said. " Absolute failure. I shan't go away on Friday or Saturday."

Frank just shrugged his shoulders, and stifled a yawn with dreadful verisimilitude. David gave him one short, anxious glance.

" And that wasn't such a poor shot after all," said Frank. " Just for a second you wondered if I was in earnest."

" No, I didn't," said David promptly.

" And that's a lie," said Frank.

David gave it up, and lay back on the sand again, beginning to unbutton.

" I know it is," he said. " You yawned jolly well."

Frank picked up a handful of the dry powdery sand and let it trickle gently into the gap of shin that showed between the end of David's trousers and the beginning of his sock. This caused him to spring up.

" Lord, what's that ? " he said. " Oh, I see. Funny ; I thought it was a bug of sorts."

" Well, if you will grow so that your trousers only reach half-way down your legs, what else is to be done with the intervals ? " asked Frank.

" I grew two inches last half," said David. " I shall be taller than you before I've done."

" Very likely. You will be the image of a piece of asparagus, if you like that. And certainly, if you grow up to the size of your feet, you'll be big enough. I shall call you Spondee."

David's shirt was half over his head, but he paused and spoke muffled.

" Because why ? " he asked.

" Because a spondee is two long feet."

David gave a great splutter of laughter, as his shirt came off.

" Oh, quite funny," he said. " Wish I had guessed. Jove, doesn't the sea look good ? I'm glad it was made, and—and that I didn't die in the night. You didn't bring down anything to eat, did you ? Isn't it bad to bathe on an empty tummy ? Or is it a full one ? "

" Don't know. I'm going to bathe on my own, any-how. David, there's a sharp line round your neck, where your clothes begin, when you've got any, as if you'd painted your neck with the sprain-stuff, Iodine."

" I did," said David fatuously, standing nude. " Come on ; the ripping old sea's waiting for us."

The tide was high and the beach steep, so that a few steps across the belt of sand all a-tremble in the heat, and a few strokes into the cool, tingling water, were sufficient to snatch them away from all solid things, and give them the buoyancy of liquid existences. The sea slept in the windlessness of this August weather, and, as if with long-taken breaths, a silence and alternate whisper of ripple broke along its rims. Far out a fleet of herring-boats with drooping sails hovered like grey-winged gulls ; above, an unclouded sun shone on the shining watery plains, and on the two wet heads, one

black, one yellow, that moved out seawards with side-
stroke flashings of white arms clawing the sea, amid
a smother of foam. Farther and farther they moved
out, till at last David rolled over in the water, and
floated on his back.

" Oh, ripping," he said. " Good old mother sea ! "

Frank turned over also and lay alongside.

" It's like something I read yesterday," he said.
" ' As the heart of us—oh, something and something—
—athirst for the foam.' I seem to remember it well,
don't I ? "

" Yes. What is it, anyhow ? Who did it ? "

" Fellow called Swinburne. Good man is Swinburne,
at times. Lord, you can lie down on the sea like a sofa,
if you get your balance right. Oh, dear me, yes ; Swinburne knows a trick or two. For instance, ' when the
hounds of spring are on winter's traces, the mother of
months in meadow and plain fills the shadows and
windy places with lisp of leaves and ripple of rain. And
the bright brown nightingale'—oh, how does it go ? "

He lay with head awash and eyes half closed against
the glare, and the spell of the magical words framed
itself more distinctly in his mind.

" O listen, David," he said. " Drink it in ! "

> " ' For winter's rains and ruins are over,
>   And all the season of snows and sins,
>   The day dividing lover and lover,
>   The light that loses, the night that wins :
>   And time remembered is grief forgotten,
>   And frosts are slain and flowers begotten,
>   And in green underwood and cover
>   Blossom by blossom the spring begins.' "

David would have appreciated this in any case, but
never had any poem so romantic a setting as when
Frank repeated it to him here, as they lay side by

side right out away from land, away from anything but
each other and this liquid Paradise of living water.

"Oh-oh," he said rapturously. "And what's the
name of it ? Go on, though."

Frank thought a moment.

"Can't remember the next verse," he said. "But
it's 'Atalanta in Calydon.'"

"Oh, she's the chap that went out hunting with her
maidens," said David confidently.

"She is. Look out, there's a jelly-fish. All right,
it's floating by. I say, the water's as warm as—as—I
don't know."

"I think you're babbling," said David. "Go on
about Atalanta. Did she have good sport ?"

Maddox laughed, forgetting that he was balanced in
a briny sea, and swallowed a large quantity of it.

"What's the row ?" asked David. "What did I
say ?"

Maddox ejected as much of the water as was acces-
sible.

"Oh, you are such a kid," he said, "and I keep forgetting it."

David kicked himself into a perpendicular position
and trod water.

"Well, I'm getting older as quick as I can," he said in
self-defence. "Blast ! I wish it could go on for ever."

"What ?"

"As if you didn't know ! Being in the sea, and
being with you, and being alive, and so on."

"Same here," said Frank. "Lord, but I wish I
could *be* the sea as well."

"Rather jam. But I don't think I'd allow everybody to bathe in me," said David. "Dogs, yes, and
some people, not all. Or should we charge a shilling,
and let anybody ?"

Maddox pushed himself upright in the water.

" 'Fraid we ought to come out," he said. "It must be latish. I'll race you to shore."

" Right oh. Give me twenty yards start."

" Measure them very carefully," said Frank.

" Well, twenty strokes then," said the wily David, shoving from Frank's shoulder to get a movement on, and then, taking very long, slow strokes, letting his impetus exhaust itself.

" Now," he said.

Both boys swam with the overhand side-stroke, breathing whenever their heads happened to be above water, and ploughed landwards with waves of bubble and broken water behind them. Frank overtook the other in the last thrilling ten yards, won by the length of an arm and a head, and panting, but still cool, they lay for a little in the shallow water, and then reluctantly went up over the beach to where their clothes lay. There the hot sun soon rendered superfluous the towels Frank had been at pains to fetch, and presently after they laboured up the sandy path to the house, slack and hungry and content, with the half of the wonderful day still in front of them. Once on the upward ascent David paused, his mind going back to the magic of words.

" O-o-oh," he said again rapturously. " 'Blossom by blossom the spring begins.' I shall read some more of that after lunch."

Lunch took a considerable time, for David's appetite, like his bones and muscles, seemed but to grow larger with the food he ate, and it was not till he had taken Frank's evil advice and drunk a second bottle of ginger-beer that he declared himself able to turn his attention to literature again. They were going to play golf once more in half an hour, and David staggered out on to

the lawn to lie on the shady terrace-bank for a short
spell of Swinburne, which Frank went to fetch from
his bedroom.   Letters had arrived during lunch, and
he found one for himself and one for David, which
with Swinburne and the daily paper that would contain one important matter, namely, the result of the
county match between Sussex and Surrey, he took
out with him.

"There's a letter for you," he said, "and there's
Swinburne and the *Daily Telegraph*.   What order of
merit ? "

"Oh, *Telegraph* first," said David.   "I bet you that
Surrey—oh, this letter's from Margery.   Might just
see what's going on.   I say, I know exactly how a bal-
loon feels.   But it was jolly good ginger-beer."

Frank flopped down on the bank by him, and began
opening his letter.

"What else do you expect," he said, "if you inflate
yourself with gas, as you did at lunch ? "

"Don't expect anything else," said David thickly.
"And it was you who suggested it.   I think I must see
what happened in the match first."

"Well, let's have a look too, you selfish devil," said
Maddox, putting down his half-opened letter.   "Can't
you turn over, and put the paper on the grass here, so
that we can read it together ? "

"Lord, no," said David.   "At least it'd be a risk.
But I can sit up if I do it slowly."

Sussex, which had the good fortune to be David's
county, and for which he felt rather responsible, had
done him credit on this occasion, and had won by half
a dozen wickets.   The rest of the paper did not seem
to contain anything that mattered, and, throwing it
aside, he and Frank began on their letters   Margery's
was quite short, though good of its kind, and, having

finished it, David looked up, and saw that Frank was reading his, and that there was trouble in his face.

" Oh, I say, is anything wrong ? " he asked.

Frank did not reply at once.

" I've heard from Adams," he said at length. " There's been a row. Some letter has been found, and Hughes isn't to be allowed to come back in September."

" Why ? What sort of letter ? " asked David.

Then, as Frank was still silent :

" Oh, something beastly, is it ? " he asked. " What an ass Hughes is ! He was such a nice chap, too, at my other school."

Frank had finished reading, and was looking out over the Surrey garden, biting his lip.

" I say, Frank, what's wrong with you ? " said David.

Frank gave Adams's letter to him.

" Read it," he said.

David took it. It spoke of the letter written by Hughes to a boy in the house, a letter disgusting and conclusive. . . . Then it spoke of the disgrace Hughes had brought on himself, and the misery he had brought on his father and mother. He read it and gave it back to Frank.

" Well, I'm awfully sorry, just as you are," he said : " but if fellows will be brutes—— Old Adams seems no end cut up about it. But somehow, I'd ceased to be pals with Hughes. Where's the Swinburne ? "

But still Frank did not answer, and David knitted puzzled brows.

" What's up ? " he said.

Maddox turned over on to his back, and tilted his hat over his eyes till his face was invisible.

" I might have been Hughes," he said.

Again the memory of what David always turned his face from came into his mind.

" Oh, rot," he said lamely, hating the subject.

Maddox was silent a moment.

" 'Tisn't quite rot," he said. " But then there came a thing, which I dare say you've forgotten, only I haven't. You came in from playing squash one wet afternoon, and you and your innocence made me suddenly see what a beast I was."

David could not help giving a little shudder, but the moment after he was ashamed of it.

" I don't care what you were like before," he said. " But what I'm perfectly sure of is that since then—I remember it very well—you ve been all right."

" Yes."

" There you are, then ! " said David.

Frank was still lying with his hat over his face, but now he pushed it back and looked at David.

" It's all serene for you," he said, " because you've always been a straight chap.   But it's different for me. I feel just rotten."

David scratched his head in some perplexity. The whole matter was vague and repugnant to him, and he did not want to hear more or know more. There were such heaps of jolly proper things in the world to be interested in and curious about. But he understood without any vagueness at all and with the very opposite of repulsion, that his friend was in trouble, and that he wanted sympathy with that. So the whole of his devoted little heart went out there.   It was bad trouble, too, the worst trouble a fellow could have.

" It must be perfectly beastly for you," he said, " and I'm as sorry as I can be.   But you're sorry yourself, and what more can a chap do ? If you weren't sorry it would be different.   There's another thing too,

to set against what you've done, and that's how you've
behaved to me.   You've been an absolute brick to me.
You've kept that sort of filth away from me : I know
you have."

David paused for a moment.   This morning alone on
the hot beach his mind had dwelt long and eagerly
on this wonderful friendship, and now, just when it was
the very thing that was wanted to comfort Frank, this
aspect of it struck him.   He remembered how often
Frank had, by a seemingly chance word, discouraged
him from seeing much of certain fellows in the house ;
he remembered the night when Hughes came and sat
on his bed, and with what extraordinary promptitude
Frank had ejected him ;   he remembered how his
dormitory had been changed, and he had been put in
Frank's, and had since then slept in the bed next him.
All this with swift certainty started into his mind, and
with it the policy that lay behind it.   Frank had consistently kept nasty things away from him ; here was
his atonement.

So he went on eagerly.

" I know what you've done for me," he said.   " You've
always—since then—had an eye on me, and kept filth
away.   I'm no end grateful.   And since you've done
that, chalk it up on the other side.   You've made it
easier for me to be decent.   Oh, damn, I'm jawing."

David suddenly became aware of this, and stopped
abruptly, rolling over on to his side, with his face to his
friend.

" Haven't you been doing that on purpose ? "   he
demanded.   " I could give you heaps of instances."

" Well, yes."

" Then let's chuck the whole subject," said David.

" In a moment.   I just want to tell you : I tried,
instead of corrupting you, to uncorrupt myself.   But

you did it; it was all your doing. You made me ashamed."

David gave a shy little wriggle towards him.

" I never heard of anything so ripping," he said. " Though it sounds rather cheek."

Maddox sat up.

" That's what you've done," he said. " And if it was cheeky, the other name of that is salvation."

There was silence a moment, and probably David had never known such intense happiness as he tasted then. And, just because he was feeling so deeply, the idea of anything approaching sentiment was impossible. It had been said, and the harvest was garnered.

Frank felt that, too; they could not feel differently from each other just then, and away went the whole subject, a mountain a few minutes ago, and now light as thistledown on a summer wind.

" It's done," he said. " Oh, what was the other thing we brought out ? ' Atalanta in Calydon,' wasn't it ? First chorus."

" Yes, that would be ripping," said David. " At the same time it's just struck three, and we were to play golf at three."

" Jove, so we were ! How you must have jawed ! "

For one second David was not quite certain whether Frank was trying to get a rise out of him or not, with such naturalness did he speak.

" Sorry," he said quickly. " I'm afraid I did."

Frank laughed.

" David, it's no sport trying to get a rise out of you," he said. " You simply rise at anything. I really didn't think you'd rise at that."

" Oh, all right," said David; " then it was a nice surprise for you. Come on. If you'll give me a stroke hole. I'll—I'll probably get beaten," he added, in a

sudden accession of modesty most unusual. " I say,
what a ripping day it's being."

" 'Tain't bad. And you're not such a bad little devil."

This bordered on past conversation again, and he
hastened away from it.

" Go and get our clubs, David," he said. " I lost
the toss about the towels this morning."

"That's not fair," said David. " We tossed this morning, and that's finished. We'll toss again. Heads ! "

" Well, then, it isn't. It's tails. But I'll go if you
like ! "

It was still very hot, and the links, although the
usual August crowd was at Naseby, were nearly deserted,
since it seemed to most of the world to be the better
part of wisdom to sit quiet till the heat had a little
abated, and resume activities again after tea. The two
boys, therefore, had an empty green before them, and
since finance in both their cases happened to be pre-
carious, and there was no need to keep their places on
the green, they took no caddies. On the right along the
first hole lay the sea, shimmering and still, so near
that it was easily possible (to say the least of it) to slice
a ball on to the beach, and in front lay the fairway of
the course, stretches of velvet grass, interrupted by
tossing seas of sand-dunes, fringed and bearded with
coarse bents, while a flag planted thereon showed
where lay the direction of the desired haven. Then
came trudges through sandy places, with breathless
suspense to see whether the balls had carried the last
of the bunkers and in other cases the equally vivid
conviction that they had done nothing of the sort,
and would be found nestling in little, steep, bare hollows
and bedevilled hiding-places. David, in especial, found
himself frequently in amazing and awful places, of
which Satan had certainly been the architect.

But, in spite of the intimate nature of all that had passed between the two so few minutes before, their unbroken solitude together did not produce in either of them the least wish to reopen the subject. It had been closed; a door had been triumphantly slammed on it, so that even if golf had not been so absorbing, they would neither of them have mentioned it again. And yet, deep down in each, and unknown to them, all that had passed had taken root, and was silently germinating, making fibre in their unconscious minds, building up the stem on which character bursts into blossom. Many words were consciously spoken, and many thoughts thought, and all the words and all the thoughts did not stray beyond the fortunes of the little white india-rubber balls.

At Marchester golf was a recognised school game, played on their own links, for the two winter halves, when it did not interfere with cricket, and Frank—it was just like him, so thought David—had become a fine player with really no trouble at all. He had only played for two years, but at school he was a scratch player, and here at Naseby had just won a medal prize, starting from four. He confessed that it had come easy to him (everything seemed to), and to David's observant eye he did not seem to do anything particular that caused him not to top one drive, and send the next spouting in the air like a geyser. When it came to approaching, it was with the same supple ease that he flicked the ball high with a little fid of turf flying after it. It all appeared so perfectly simple: you merely hit the ball with the middle of the club. At times, if you were playing against him, the thing became almost monotonous.

Whatever could be said about David's play, it could not be called monotonous. He gave an excellent ex-

ample of his methods this afternoon at the third hole,
slicing far and gorgeously from the tee out on to the
sand.   There had been no interest in Frank's drive;
it had merely gone straight, and a very long way, and
so he came with David to walk up his ball, which was
found to be lying fairly well.

" Silly ass," he said to him as David took out an iron
and prepared to play with it.   " Take your niblick and
make certain of getting back on to grass."

" But I could get on to the green with an iron, if I hit
it," said David excitedly, " and then I should be there
in two, and you can't get them in less than two, and I've
got a stroke and should win the hole off you, if I putted
my first near it."

" Right oh," said Frank.   " Never mind the ' ifs '."
" Not an atom ! " said David.

The ball was not lying so very badly, and there was
really a certain excuse for David.   So he took his iron
and hit the ball rather firmly on the head.   It went
about fifteen yards in an injured manner, and settled
itself in the moat of what had been a child's sand-castle.

" And it'll take the deuce of a putt to get near the
hole from there," remarked Frank.

David, as always, took his game very seriously, and
for a moment felt merely wild with rage, impotent,
ineffective rage.   Nobody cared.

" Hell——" he began.

Then his admirable temper asserted itself before he
settled what hell was going to do.

" Oh dear, you're always right, Frank," he said.
" Niblick it is, and I wish it had been before.   Now I'm
going to take trouble."

He shifted with his feet in the loose sand, as Frank
had told him to do, till he got a firm stance.   Then
(which Frank had never told him to do) he took the

most prodigious wipe at his ball and shut his eyes as
the sand fell in showers round him.

" Didn't see it ! " he said.　" What happened ? "

Somehow or other he had hit the ball clean and hard
and perfectly straight for the green.　It wasn't a niblick shot at all ; nobody, David least of all, knew how
it had happened.

" Well, of all the almighty flukes," said Frank.
" Probably on the green."

David bubbled with laughter.

" Oh, I say, what sport ! " he said.　" Now I know
how to play golf.　If you lie rather badly, take an
iron and make it worse.　Then take a niblick and hit
it home."

They went back to the course to walk up Frank's
ball.　It was lying impeccably twenty yards short
of the shored-up bunker that guarded the green.　And
for once he was not monotonous ; he chipped at it
with a lot of back-spin, and it bounced against the
boards of the bunker and fell at their feet.　Thereafter
he played racquets against the boards.　Then he gave
it up, and David, the reckless and unreasonable, was
lying just a foot beyond the bunkers.

In such wise the hot, heavenly afternoon went by.
Dreadful and delightful things happened.　Frank, after
long consideration as to whether he could get over the
brook with a drive at the tenth hole, decided to play
short with a cleek, and pitched full into it.　David, with
two strokes in hand, putted four times at the eleventh
before he got down, and, both of them trying to carry
the far bunker at the thirteenth, topped into the near
one instead.　But there were delightful incidents to
balance these distressing ones : Frank holed a mashie
shot at the sixteenth, and at the next David ran through
two (not one) bunkers off a topped drive, and a third

with his second shot. But, deep down below, the basis
of their enjoyment was their friendship, and neither
thought how easily that priceless possession might have
foundered and been lost in quagmires. . . .

Frank won : a wholly loathsome putt on the last green,
which went into the hole not by the honest front door,
nor even with a kick at the honest back door, but with
a stealthy, sideway entrance, after circling round the
hole, decided the match.

" Oh, good putt," said David politely, and instantly
the politeness broke down. " Gosh, what a fluke ! "
he added.

" Rot ! I tried to hole it, and did," said Frank.

" Well, I said ' good putt ' once," said David. " And
I can't say it again. Simply can't."

After tea at the club-house, it seemed a necessity to
play again, and this time, regardless of financial strin-
gency, Frank treated David to a caddy, and they went
forth with pomp, now playing seawards into the
hazy east, now westwards into the blaze of the de-
clining sun, absorbed in their game and yet absorbed
in their friendship of boy-love, hot as fire and clean as
the trickle of ice-water on a glacier. The knowledge of
their talk had made Frank able to turn himself away
from all the bad business of Adams's letter, and instead
of brooding on the irremediable worst of himself, he
took hold of all that was best. And by his side was
David, the friend of friends, now with his arm linked
in his, now excitedly addressing a cupped ball with his
largest driver, now brilliantly slicing among untrodden
sand-hills, now dancing with exultation at the success
of a shot that was wholly beyond expectation, now half
whispering to him, " Oh, it's the rippingest day."

Then followed lawn-tennis, till it was so dark that the
ball could hardly be seen at all, and in consequence

David, standing at the net, got hit full on the end of his nose, which bled with extraordinary profusion. Indeed, had murder been committed that night at Naseby, as Frank said, when they went down for a hurried dip before dressing for dinner, it would have required no Sherlock Holmes to draw the certain but quite erroneous conclusion that the deed had been done in David's bedroom, and the body carried down to the beach afterwards with the idea of its being taken away and out by the ebbing tide and the seaward current. A slop-pail with blood-stained water (analysed by Professor Pepper and found to be Mammalian) would be discovered in his bedroom, and at intervals down the path to the beach, further traces of the same incriminating gore.

The cool sea-water put an end to David's bleeding, and as he dressed he began to feel delightfully uncomfortable (as in the attics of Baxminster), so grimly and gravely did Frank reconstruct the history of the crime with fearful imaginative details thrown in. A little way from them on the beach was something vague and black and humped up, and Frank suddenly pointed at it.

" Do you know what that is ? " he asked David in a whisper.

" That black thing ?   No.   What ? "

" It's the body," said Frank.

Of course this was all nonsense, but David peered at it through the gloom, and Frank suddenly gave a deep and hollow groan, which startled him quite awfully.

" It wasn't utterly dead," he explained. " It tried to call for help, but it couldn't call loud, as its throat was cut from ear to ear. But it just groaned. The body was that of a boy of fifteen, tall for his age, David, and well nourished."

David could not help it ; he had to run in his bare

feet to where the supposed corpse lay, kicked it, and came back.

" Only seaweed," he said. " Now the murderer did it in my room, you say—I mean he cut the well-nourished boy's throat there, and then carried it down to the beach. That won't do. There are only quite a few drops of blood on the way down, If its throat had been cut from ear to ear, there'd be more blood."

" Not at all," said Frank. " The murderer held the two edges of the wound together—no, he'd want both hands to carry the body—he pinned the edges of the wound together with—with safety-pins, so that it only just leaked. He carried it down to the beach like that, and then took out the pins, because he had a saving disposition, and this let the boy bleed to death. As I said, he thought the tide would carry it away, but it didn't, and it was found there next morning. Lobsters had got at it though, and howked pieces out of it. There's lobster for dinner to-night. Then the police traced the bloodstains to your bedroom, and found the slop-pail, and you were kept in prison till you were sixteen, and then hung at Norwich."

" And what did he—I—I don't know which I am, the corpse or the murderer——"

" You're both," said Frank. " The pins ? They were put back in the pin-cushion on your dressing-table, where I saw them just now. There were stains on them that looked like rust. But they weren't rust, they were——"

" They were blood," said David. " Mammalian."

Frank looked hastily round for more material for horror, and saw a fisherman coming down the steep path just behind them carrying two lobster-pots. This was luck, for David had not seen him, being employed in putting his shoes on. Frank went on without pause.

" After that the beach at Naseby," he said, " was not a place where prudent people cared to be after sunset, especially during the month of August, and particularly on—on August the tenth, which was the exact day when the murder was committed. Prudent people avoided it, for there was no doubt it was haunted. A figure was often seen coming down that steep path just behind us, carrying a ghastly burden."

David looked quickly round with the intention of reassuring himself that there was no one there. That was a dreadful mistake. There was. Frank, after his one glance at the figure, had not looked at the path again.

" Good Lord," said David in a whisper. " There's something coming down it now. It's coming straight towards us ! "

Then he saw more distinctly, and gave a great cackle of laughter.

" Oh-oh-oh, it's only a fisherman with lobster-pots," he said. " But you did give me such a turn. You said that awfully well. When I looked round and saw that old buffer coming down I could have screamed. I say, do lobsters really eat deaders ? "

" Whenever they can get them. There are a good many about now, too. The cook told me that the one we're going to have for dinner to-night had a man's finger in its claws when they brought it up to the house. The best ones——"

" Oh, dry up," shouted David. " You've a foul mind."

Frank laughed.

" Oh, you kid ! "

Nor was the immortal day over yet. The man-eating lobster was in turn eaten by man, and after dinner Frank read to his mother and David the neglected

"Atalanta," after which they played ridiculous games till bedtime. Frank's room and David's communicated with each other, and, as they undressed, further details and embellishments of horror were added to the murder story, through the open door. But to one of Frank's most gruesome inventions there had been no response, and, looking in, he saw that David was kneeling by his bed. And at that he went back to his room again.

The silence was not of long duration, and in a moment David called to him.

" What was that last, Frank ? " he said. " It sounded jolly beastly, but I wasn't attending."

Frank repeated it, and David squealed as he drew his bedclothes up to his chin.

" I think that's enough," he said. " I shall have gory nightmares. Oh, hasn't it been a jolly day ? "

" Ripping. Good night, David."

" Good night. What a pity it can't be this morning again."

Frank lay long awake that night. Before he slept he slid out of bed and followed David's example.

CHAPTER XI

DAVID, with the tip of his tongue stuck out at the corner of his mouth, was engaged in the delicate, and apparently (until you know the reason) meaningless task of lashing two pens together with a piece of cotton, so that their respective nibs should be fixed at a particular distance apart from each other. The distance, as he took pains to measure accurately, was exactly that between the first and fourth line on a piece of scribbling paper. If this is neatly done—and David with his deft fingers was doing it very neatly indeed—it will be clear that, if both pens are dipped in ink, and one writes certain words along the first line of the paper, the second pen, duly adjusted, will simultaneously be writing the same words along the fourth line. Similarly, when the first pen is engaged in the second line, the other will be engaged on the fifth. Thus, provided the pens are securely lashed and behave reasonably, a sheet of scribbling-paper of the sort that holds twenty lines can be filled with hexameters from any given part of the highly overrated adventures of the pious Æneas in the time that, without this contrivance, it would take to transcribe ten of those lines. Any boy, moreover, and such adults as still preserve a brain of moderate ingenuity, will easily guess why those pens, in David's very superior contraption, were lashed together at a distance of three lines, for were they lashed together at the distance of one or even two lines apart, this engaging scheme by which two lines were written simultaneously would be much more easily detected. As David had to write out no fewer than five hundred lines of this piffling "Æneid," he thus hoped to be quit of his task in the time that it would take a less ingenious devil to write two hundred and fifty.

It was already getting dark at the close of a half-holiday afternoon towards the end of February, and Bags, while David was engaged in these preparatory processes, was making tea for them both in the study they shared together. It was a considerably larger one than that which they had inhabited during their first year, but David's belongings seemed to have grown proportionately to his own limbs, and they still usurped by far the greater portion of the available room. His task, though tiresome, was not one that required much concentration of attention ; it was mere dull transcribing work, and he could quite well converse as it was going on. Besides, it was a very short time since he had copied out these same pages before ; he had a certain familiarity with them.

He finished adjusting the pens, found that he had got their distance to a nicety, and, gripping them on the place where their handles crossed, he dipped them in the ink. . . . Then, as a refinement of ingenious engineering, he took Bags's inkpot and put it in such a place that the two pens were dipped simultaneously.

" ' Infandum regina jubes,' " he said. " What an awful gasser Æneas was ! He talked straight off for two books, and I suppose Dido didn't go to sleep, 'cause she was so mad keen on him. Why can't I copy out something decent, like Keats or Swinburne, instead of this mouldy old Johnny ? I should really rather like that."

" Perhaps that's why they don't let you," said Bags, giving him a cup of tea.

" Shouldn't wonder if it was.   Thanks awfully, Bags :
did you put four lumps of sugar in ?   Oh then, two
more, please.   But, as regards the patent pen, of course
there is a certain risk that Owlers (this, of course, was
Mr. Howliss) will spot it and I shall have to do it again.
But it ain't likely three lines apart.   Great security in
three lines apart."

" You've spent most of your time this half writing
lines," said Bags.

" I know.   I don't seem to be able to keep out of
rows.   I don't want to be late, or cut chapel, or go out
of bounds, but I don't seem to be able to help it.
Adams jawed me this morning ; said he didn't know
what to do with me, and I'm sure I couldn't tell him.
Maddox is rather sick with me too, which matters
more ; says I play the goat too much.   And he doesn't
know about the seal and this last impot yet.   I shall
have to tell him, though ; it's the best rag I've had yet.
Yes, more tea, please."

" I think you're rather an ass, unless you prefer
writing out the ' Æneid ' to any other ploy," said Bags.

" I dare say.   But I can't help it.   I simply can't.
I should never have gone to that silly old fair up town
last week if they hadn't put it out of bounds ; but
when they put it out of bounds I had to go.   It wasn't
because I wanted to see the fat woman and the skeleton
dude.   If I take to smoking, which I haven't done yet, it
won't be because I like it, which I don't, but just because
it's against the rules.   That's good enough for me."

Bags took up the first page which David had
written, and which resembled some loose sort of
triolet with its repetition of lines.   In spite of the difficulty of managing two pens with success, it was wonderfully uniform, and written in David's neat and
vigorous hand,

" I'll get on with another page of them, if you like,"
suggested Bags; " all the fellows say I write exactly
like you."

" Thanks ; that's jolly good of you," said David.
" And you do write awfully like me. I wonder why.
You used not to, as when Maddox spotted my hand-
writing in that crib."

" Oh, I suppose it's being with you and all that,"
said Bags vaguely, knowing quite well that he had
long tried to write like David, out of affection and
admiration for all that pertained to his pal. " I'll
begin at line one hundred, shall I, so that when you get
there you can skip the next hundred and go on at line
two hundred ? "

" Yes, that's the trick," said David. " Thanks
awfully. Sure it doesn't bore you ? I say, shall I
lash a couple more pens for you ? "

" Don't think I should get on well with them," said
Bags.

The Lent term, about half of which was now over,
seemed to David a very poor affair in comparison with
other terms. Rugby football was finished with ; cricket,
of course, did not exist ; the weather had been consistently diluvian, so that the golf-links where he had
intended to pass most of his leisure, were generally
half flooded. Other fellows, it is true, were busy on
athletics, but David, seeing through Frank's eyes, had
no sympathy with just running when there was no
ulterior object except to run quicker than anybody
else. In fact, there were no games except fives and
racquets, and, the demand for courts being largely in
excess of the supply, he could not get one as often as
his energy needed. Thus, since there was so little that
might legitimately be done, he had chiefly occupied
himself in breaking school-rules, and, as Bags had said,

he had really passed most of the half in writing lines, which, though it took time, merely bottled up instead of relieving him of his exuberant vitality. Furthermore, since there was not the slightest chance of his getting out of the middle fifth at Easter (only geniuses, of whom he was certainly not one, did that) David had argued that the less time he spent over work the better.

The worst of it was there was so very little to do, and Maddox had jawed David on this subject of "playing the goat" before, suggesting that the devil had entered into him. It was not quite that really : it was only the rampageous energy of David's youth seeking an outlet. He was growing enormously, and, as sometimes happened, this process did not make him languid and slack, but seemed only to increase the vitality that stirred and bubbled in him as in some long-legged colt, making him throw up his limbs and scamper simply because he was vigorous and growing. But his escapades and general obstreperousness somewhat exercised his friend as well as his house-master, who at the present moment, while David and Bags were writing lines together, was talking to the prefect about the house in general, and the affairs of David in particular. His general line, as has been said, was to let the senior boys run the house, while he enjoyed the tranquillity that their management brought him. But David's persistent adventures had protruded themselves into his notice, and a consultation with Maddox seemed to him desirable.

"About David," he said. "It's only energy, Frank, and not viciousness. You gave just the same sort of trouble yourself, when you were his age."

"Sorry, sir," said Maddox. "But I don't believe I was ever quite such a nuisance as David is. If ever there's a crash in the house, it's always David breaking a window or throwing his boots at somebody."

" Can't you do anything with him ? " asked Adams. " He'll listen to you when he won't attend to a word I say."

" Oh, he listens to me all right," said Maddox; " but then, he forgets. Besides, he's so awfully funny: he makes me laugh."

Adams lit his pipe and sat down on the floor in front of the fire, for Maddox happened to be occupying his particular arm-chair. At the moment all the electric lights went out.

" I'd bet a shilling," said Maddox, " that David's at the bottom of that. Shall I go and see, sir ? "

" Yes, do, and then come back."

Maddox felt his way along the passage to David's study, and knocked. He always knocked before he went into other people's rooms.

" Come in," shouted David. " But take care of yourself, whoever you are. There are inkpots about, and it's as dark as hell and smells of cheese. Good old Bags; fancy finding a candle in this den. Hullo, Frank ! "

" Have you been fooling with the electric light ? " asked Maddox.

" Yes, of course. This beastly plug didn't work and so I dug a knife into its bowels, and something went off, and gave me an awful start."

" Ass ! " said Maddox. " You've put out the lights all over this passage and Adams's study."

" Oh, what larks ! " said David. " Let's have a procession of the unemployed, who want to work like good little saps, and can't work in the dark. Let's——"

" Let me just get at you," said Maddox, as David dodged round the table. " I'll teach you——"

David squealed with hideous resonance.

"Well, it wasn't my fault," he said. "I only jabbed it with a knife. Wow! Spare me! Have mercy upon me! Wow!"

Frank drove David to a corner and punched him heavily in the ribs, and boxed his ears, and smacked his head. Summary and effectual justice being then done, he observed David's patent lashed pens.

"I know that trick," he said. "What! is the virtuous Bags doing lines too?"

"Oh yes," said Bags airily. "Some of the fourth 'Æneid'."

"For David, I suppose, eh?"

"Well, yes," said Bags.

"How many lines is it this time?" asked Maddox. "And what for?"

"Five hundred," said David. "A present for a good little Owlers. Gosh, I wish you wouldn't hit so hard."

"Do you? And what has good little Owlers done?"

David began to laugh.

"Oh, Lord, it was funny," he said. "It was worth five hundred lines. He's just as blind as possible, blinder than Tovey, you know; and I thought it was very likely I shouldn't be put on construing——"

"Why?" asked Maddox.

"Oh, I don't know; it seemed likely. Well, he was taking us in the museum, so I fetched down a stuffed seal, and stuck it up in my place, so that if he counted heads I should be there, and then I went to play squash. Bags, you go on. I didn't see."

Bags took up the wondrous tale.

"There we all were," said Bags, "with the seal sitting up in David's place, I saw Owlers count heads, and then we began construing. Then it didn't quite

pan out as David expected, for after a bit Owlers said
' Go on, Blaize,' and of course the seal didn't say anything whatever."

" Poor thing, how could it ? " said David.

"And then Owlers said, looking very kind, ' Perhaps you haven't prepared quite as far, Blaize.' But
the seal had nothing to say to that, and Owlers asked
him why he didn't answer. And then Owlers gave
him a long jaw, and told him he was sulky, and there
the seal sat with his glass eyes fixed on the ceiling.
Finally Owlers got awful sick with him, and set him
five hundred lines."

It was no use trying not to laugh : the idea of Owlers
jawing the seal was too much for Maddox, and the
three went off into peals of laughter.

"And didn't he spot the seal at all ? " asked Maddox
at length.

" Rather not. He went tottering out at the end of
the hour, just reminding the seal to show them up
to-morrow."

David took up his double pen again.

" Oh I wish somebody else had done it," he said,
" for I missed Owlers jawing the seal. But it was my
idea."

Maddox got up.

" Well, you'll get into worse trouble if you don't look
out," he said. " I'm talking you over with Adams."

" Oh, may I come and listen outside the door ? "

" You may not."

" Well, stick up for me," said David encouragingly.

Maddox went back to his house-master, still giggling.

" Well, did David make the darkness ? " he asked.

" Yes, sir, rather. He investigated the electric plug
with a knife, and something went off, he said. So I
hit him about. They're putting another fuse in."

He laughed again.

" David was writing five hundred lines as usual," he
said, " with Bags helping. I think I must tell you
why."

Adams made no attempt at gravity and shook with
laughter.

" But it can't go on," he said. " David's becoming
a nuisance, and gating him and giving him lines to write
is no earthly good. What he wants is a good licking
and plenty of exercise. There's not an ounce of harm
in him."

" Oh, he's the straightest chap in the world," said
Maddox.

" Well, you might warn him. Tell him next time
he's reported to me, I shall send him to the Head with
a request that he shall be swished. And how's the
rest of the house ? "

" Oh, pretty slack, sir. It's rotten weather, you see.
Weather makes a lot of difference to us."

" I know. There's always more trouble this half
than any. Try to keep them up to the mark, Frank."

" I'll do my best, sir. But I've got an awful lot of
work with this Trinity scholarship exam. coming on
in a fortnight. I'm as rusty as nails over my history."

Adams smoked his pipe for a little in silence.

" By the way, you pull all right with Cruikshank
now, don't you ? " he asked.

" Rather. I used to bar him awfully, but we—well,
we had a talk after Hughes was sent away, and decided
to get on better together. Crookles is a good chap."

" Glad you've found that out," said Adams. " You
never would believe me when I told you so. Well, tell
David that the wooden eye of Nemesis is on him, and
see if you can't make him less obstreperous. He
thinks more of what you say than of what any one else

says. He simply jumped down my throat the other day in your defence."

" What about, sir ? "

" Because I ventured to criticise your play in that house-racquet tie, when we were nearly beaten by Thomas's. I said I thought we should have won more easily if you had served with more care and less force. David turned quite purple, and said, ' I shouldn't wonder if he knew what he was about.' "

" Frightful cheek," said Maddox.

" Well, I don't know. He only reminded me that you know more about racquets than I do, which is perfectly true. Well, are you off ? Tell David not to make himself so conspicuous."

Maddox went upstairs again after this to his study, where his fag was putting out his tea-things. David, of course, after his promotion into the fifth form, had ceased to be in a state of servitude, and his successor was a small bony youth called Jevons, who usually had a cold in the head, and an inky handkerchief with which to minister to it. There was no kind of brisk-ness about him ; he was timid and slovenly and melan-choly, and went about his duties as if laying out the bake-meats for the funeral of a dear departed friend. Maddox did his best with him, tried to encourage him to look the world in the face a little more, and wash a little more, and not drag his feet as he walked ; but it was a dismal change from being attended to by the adroit and willing David. David, it is true, sometimes smashed things by running with them, or from excess of zeal in cleaning the inside of a teacup, but that was better than finding forgotten tea-leaves in the pot one day, or crumbs and other foreign substances in the sugar, and little bits of butter sticking to the bottom of the plates. But though Maddox was kind to this

spiritless youth, David, on the occasions when he came
across him, was severely critical. It seemed to him a
dreadful affair that his place should be filled by so
abject a specimen, and, mixed with his contempt for
Jevons, there was a certain jealousy that he should
go in and out of Maddox's study as he chose, and joy-
lessly perform all the offices in which David had delighted. Fifth-form boy as he was, he would have
loved to continue fagging for Maddox, for the sake of
seeing that he was properly looked after, and for the
intimacy which that would give him. Now, since their
ages and places sundered them so widely in ordinary
school-life, David necessarily saw much less of him
than before. He knew that this must be so, but it did
not make him like Jevons the more.

There was the sound of cheerful whistling going on
from the bathroom where David was washing up on
his own account, when Maddox came up to his study,
but it ceased as Jevons went in to fill his kettle, and a
half-cracked admonitory voice took its place.

" Well, have you put a nice bit of butter in the milk-
jug to-day," it asked—the voice was as unmistakably
David's as the whistle—" or have you rubbed it round the
edge of the teacup ? Lord, rinse out the kettle before you
fill it, can't you ? Here, give it me. I say, you really
should smarten yourself up a bit, Jevons. Wash your
hands while I get the kettle ready. I wonder Maddox
can eat a thing when you've touched his crockery."

" David ! " shouted Maddox.

" Want me ? " asked David.

" Yes, come here a minute. I've got something to
say to you."

David went to his study followed by the depressed
Jevons, who shuffled about the room for a bit, dropped
a knife, and then left them.

" Jove, it's jolly in here," said David appreciatively, " though how you can stand that scug mucking about, I can't think. I used to run you much better than this, Frank. What do you want me about ? "

" I've been talking to Adams about you," said Frank. " and I should advise you to try to go steadier. Adams told me to tell you that the wooden eye of Nemesis is on you, and next time you're reported he's going to send you to the Head to be swished."

David shrugged his shoulders.

" Wooden eye is good," he said. " But I don't much care. I'm not sure I wouldn't sooner he swished than be writing lines to all eternity. I never get them done ; there are always some more."

" Finished that five hundred ? " said Maddox parenthetically.

" Lord no, but I was just washing up and taking an easy. Bags is going on."

" Well, I said I would pass on Adams's message. Of course you can be swished if you like : nothing easier. But the Head makes you feel a bit cheap first, and afterwards lays on."

David sighed heavily.

" I suppose I ought to promise you to be an absolute record for saintliness," he said, " but it's no use. Something goes ' fizz ' inside me, and I can't help playing the fool. I wish I was older or younger. If I was older I suppose I should see what a rotter I am, and if I was younger I should simply do what you told me. I know you're right, but then comes a minute and I can't help doing something foolish on any account, if you know what I mean."

David looked round the study again, and it made him feel rather melancholy. He hadn't seen much of Frank this term, for Frank had been working hard, and

again the sense of the distance they were apart in the
world of school severed them. It was greater now
that he was an independent person in the fifth than
it had been when he was Frank's fag, and in Remove A.
And the intimacy which had been theirs at Naseby
was no longer possible at school. At that moment,
also, a tooth began suddenly to ache and gave him a
series of staccato stabs with a really brilliant touch.

" Gosh, and I've got the toothache," he said. " It's
suddenly begun hurting like hell."

" Sorry," said Frank.

David leaned back in his chair, with his long arms
and legs sprawling.

" It ached yesterday," he said, " but then I didn't
mind, as I was having a good time over the seal. But
it's rot having toothache when other things are beastly.
Why should this blighter decay ? My other teeth don't.
What a rotten show it all is ! "

" What's up, David ? " asked Frank.

" Oh, I don't know. There's a sort of conspiracy
against me. Whatever I do gets found out, and I'm
writing lines and being gated the whole blooming time.
And the sight of your study gives me the hump. I
haven't been here for a week I should think, and now
you're sick with me, and so's Adams."

" Well, don't play the goat," said Frank.

" Yes, it's easy to say that," observed David, " but
it isn't as if I set out to play the goat. It just comes :
it just happens. Oh, Lord, the seal was so funny,
sitting there on its sloping bim, and staring with its
glass eyes at the ceiling, and all my books spread out
in front of it. Soon as I'd got it fixed, I hopped out of
the window, you know. There it was looking at the
ceiling all moth-eaten, and the Owlers never guessed
it wasn't a boy."

David gave a shrill laugh that began in a high treble and ended baritone, for his voice was cracking. Then he became quite grave again.

"Things are rotten," he said. "I get amused like a kid, and suddenly in the middle of it, I remember I'm not quite such a kid. I know it really, but I can't help skipping about and butting round. Why can't I be your fag instead of that mucky Jevons, and, if not, why can't I be a sensible person? I made Jevons wash while I made your kettle decent again; you should have seen his fingers. And then he sniffs and blows his beastly nose with a sort of tight sound. And I'm no better; I've got the toothache and I'm gated at five, and I've the best part of five hundred lines to write still, and you're sick with me, and I shall get swished if I don't take care."

Frank had been through this: he knew the transitional disquiet of being fifteen, which has just got to be lived through. He poured out a cup of tea and handed it to David.

"I think I won't," he said. "I've just had tea. Isn't it rum how you can be no end cheerful, as I was when I jabbed the electric light, and then suddenly go rotten? I dare say it's only toothache."

Frank got up.

"There's some chloroform somewhere," he said, "which I used for killing butterflies. If you stick some on cotton wool, and jam it in your tooth, it'll be all right."

He rummaged in his cupboard, and with the aid of a pin put the soaked wool into David's tooth.

"Gosh, that's better already," said David after a minute. "Thanks, awfully. Perhaps if I drank some tea the other side, it wouldn't hurt it."

There was a cake also, and David was induced to try this as well.

"Better," he said at last.

"That's good. More?"

"Well, just a little. Then I'll wash up for you properly, just for once."

"That'll be ripping of you. And, as we're pretending you're my fag again, I shall just jaw you. You see, I know quite well what it feels like to do something goatish, just because it's against the rules, but that wears off, David. You'll get to know that most rules are pretty sensible. You see you couldn't have a whole division of stuffed seals. Therefore you mustn't have any."

David laughed in a full-mouthed manner.

"Oh, but wouldn't they look ripping?" he said.

"Yes, but things couldn't go on if every one behaved like you. Therefore you mustn't. See? By the way, I told Adams you were the straightest chap in the world."

David flushed with pleasure.

"Oh, did you really?" he said.

"Yes, why not? But he'll send you to be swished just the same if you bore him."

David got out of his chair.

"Well, I'll try not to," he said; "so I'd better get on with those lines."

"Perhaps you had. I must work, too. And don't get any more. You've only got to stump along, and be ordinary. By the by, I've got a racquet court to-morrow at twelve, and I can't use it. You may have it if you like."

"Oh, ripping," said David. "Tooth out first, then racquets. Thanks awfully."

He lingered a moment.

"What jolly good days those were at Naseby," he said.

"I know that. They're all alive too. There'll be lots more of it."

David put his hands on Frank's shoulders, as they stood together for a moment by the fireplace.

"I believe they are," he said. "And I believe I'm as tall as you."

"Oh, you're getting a big lout," said Maddox.

But the evil star continued to shine balefully on David next day. The device of the double pen was promptly detected by Mr. Howliss, his lines were torn over, all to be done again, and Bags's friendly help was vain labour also. Bags had been opposed to the patent-pen system, on the ground that it was liable to detection, and though theoretically it saved time, it didn't save so much, as nobody could wield the double pen with the same swiftness as the single one. Consequently he made no renewed offer of help with regard to the re-imposed imposition, and David had to stop in at twelve next day after an excruciating interview with the dentist instead of playing racquets. And this parsimonious dentist quite refused to whip out the aching tooth, and have done with it (a pang to which David had strung himself up); he said it could be saved, and the salvation thereof included a whizzing drill, and the stuffing of it with something painful to the feelings and obnoxious to the taste, and implied a further visit the day after to-morrow.

Then followed a brief interval of delightful happenings, while the baleful star hid itself. The tooth was comforted and reinforced, so that it could be bitten on again even with nuts, an unexpected mid-term largesse of ten shillings from his father, and half a crown from Margery, which was almost insanely noble of her, turned up, and with Bags for a partner David won the

school junior-fives competition. This was a triumph
of the juiciest kind, for all Europe must have known
that Bags was a fives-player of no class at all, and that
portion of civilised Europe which saw the final were
aware that David practically played it single, butting
about from side to side of the court, while Bags effaced
himself in the manner of a shadow against the wall,
so as not to be in the way. That meant another sover-
eign, which had to be expended in the purchase of a
small silver commemorative cup, and to that sum he
added five shillings out of the tips from home, and
bought for it a black polished stand of pear-wood with
a plated shield on which was engraved his name and
that of his innocuous partner.

" First of my cups," he announced when it came
home, " and it jolly well will not be the last. Won't it
be ripping when I have a whole shelf-full of them?
No, I'm blowed if I have my tea in an ordinary cup.
Pour it in here, Bags, and I'll drink your good health for
getting out of the way so well! Lord, how hot it gets!"

Simultaneously with these propitious events, came
the early rounds of the house handicap golf competition.
David had adopted a wise policy over this. For ten
days before the links had been practically unplayable
owing to floods, but he had remembered a word of
Frank's. " If you want to improve, go out with half a
dozen balls and practise mashie shots on to a green.
When you've got them all there, putt them all out."

So for the last week David had " slacked out " with
a mashie and a putter, found a green that was not
under water, and had put this hint into practice. It
was dull, but then there was nothing else to do, and
the reward looked within reach. He had been entered
with a handicap of fifteen, but, thanks to his practice,
he was already a stroke or two better than that. He

had met Maddox in the second round, and receiving eleven strokes had beaten him. Then he encountered Gregson, whom he played on level terms, and, emerging by the skin of his teeth from that, had wiped up the floor with Cruikshank, who gave him six. This brought him to the semi-final.

Then from behind the clouds out popped the baleful star again, and shed its dreadful beams on him with peculiar effulgence. First of all Maddox went up to Cambridge for his scholarship examination, and David, who had never known what school was like without the sense of his being there, who was the first person he saw when he woke in the morning, and the last before he went to sleep at night, felt lost and rudderless. Next him in dormitory was the empty bed, and all day long he knew there was no chance of Frank's dropping in, or calling him to his study. Then Bags got influenza and disappeared also, leaving David bereft of his two great friends, to find out for the first time how solid and comfortable a pal Bags was. Then came the semi-final of the golf-handicap, in which he was completely off his game, and got beaten on level terms by the mild and spotty Joynes, to whom David felt competent to give four strokes in the round. But such proved, on this fatal afternoon, not to be the case.

It was a gusty, boisterous day, and David, liable at all times to be rather wild and given to exuberant slicing, sliced in a manner probably without parallel. With his loose arms he could drive a very long ball, but to-day that was a disadvantage rather than otherwise, since he sent it to remote cover-point. This was exasperating, and Joynes, who usually had the honour, exasperated him further, for, having himself gone not far, but straight up the middle of the course, he overwhelmed David with a sort of envious condolence.

"By Jove, what a long ball!" he would say, as David's drive started on its insane career. "I wish I could drive like that. Oh, the wind's catching it; bad luck. Look where it's going, miles away! It'll be rotten bad luck if it's on the road."

Or, again, David would make an astonishingly feeble putt, and Joynes again showed sympathy.

"Pity it wasn't a little harder; it was dead on the line. I wish I could putt as straight as that. Hullo, you've missed the second one, too. That leaves me three for it. You'd much better make me putt them out. I can miss anything. Hullo, it's gone in. Sorry."

This sort of thing goaded David to madness, and presently he could bear it no longer.

"I say, would you mind not talking quite so much," he said politely. "It's awfully rotten of me, but I think it puts me off."

Upon which Joynes hermetically sealed his lips, till they came to the fourteenth hole, where the match came to an abject end. . . .

All this was sufficiently depressing, and there was no quietly sympathetic Bags to be a comfort. Nor was there Bags to get tea ready, and it struck David really for the first time to-day how invariably Bags did that. And he could not find his milk-jug, and when he did it smelled sour, for it had not been washed up . . . and there was nothing to eat, and he would have to go up to school-shop to get a cake. It was all deplorable, and on the way he met Gregson, his victim in the third round.

"Suppose you disposed of Joynes all right, Blazes?" he asked.

"No, he disposed of me. Easily as anything," said David.

"Hurrah!—I mean sorry. But you see I bet a shilling he would."

" Congratters," said David insincerely.

The wind had turned bitterly cold, and spikes of sleet half frozen had begun to fall as he came back from the shop. That, again, seemed to David part of the conspiracy to make his life as disagreeable and uncomfortable as possible : Nature herself had joined in. He did not want to be unreasonable, but if, on the top of all these things, it was going to snow, he felt that even Job's patience would break down. Snow ruined everything ; it was incompatible with any form of exercise, and mournfully he went back to his solitary study.

But when he had drawn the curtains, and pulled his chair up to the hot-water pipes, so that he could rest his feet on them, and divided his attention between " Ravenshoe " held in one hand (he had got to where Gus and Flora were naughty in church), and tea in the other, things seemed to cheer up a little. Outside evidently the weather had got worse, for the wind squealed round the corner of the house, and on his panes, behind the thick red curtains he could hear the muffled patter of the driven snow. And, after all, there was a bright side to snow, for it would mean that there would be prayers in the house to-night, and he would not have to turn out to go to chapel. And Maddox would be back on Saturday, and it was Thursday evening already. Also Bags had written to him from the sick-room, saying that he was better, and expected to be out again by Sunday. David's spirits began to improve, and he kicked off his shoes, in order to enjoy a greater intimacy with the hot-water pipes, and burst into a shout of laughter as Flora announced that she had left her purse on the piano. . . .

It would have been a poor heart that did not rejoice next morning, for during the night the wind dropped and so smart a frost had set in that the snow lay hard and crusted on the ground, and it would be clearly possible to go tobogganing on the slopes of the down at twelve. At breakfast, moreover, there was a post-card for him from Frank, with a highly coloured photo-graph of the great quadrangle at Trinity on the back, and a couple of lines to say he would be back by mid-day on Saturday, and that Cambridge was a topping place. It warmed David's heart to think that Frank should have remembered him, and, with the prospect of tobogganing at twelve, and the cheer of the frosty-shining sun, his spirits went up to a pitch of inexpres-sible buoyancy as he slid along the trodden path to go to ten-o'clock school.

Paths had been swept in schoolyard between the various class-rooms, but the rest of the broad space lay white and untrodden. David got there while it still wanted five minutes to ten, and hung about with a few friends outside the class-room door till the hour should strike. There was a quiet exchange of small snowballing, furtively delivered, for it was very strictly forbidden in the quadrangle, and David had just lobbed one not bigger than a racquet-ball with extraordinary success, just between the collar and neck of Joynes, who had not the vaguest idea who had done this. Now he was moulding another larger one in his hand, with an absent eye in Joynes's direction, and his shoulders trembling with suppressed laughter, for Joynes's at-tempts to scoop the snow out were really very funny, when Gregson came up to him.

" Jolly good shot," he said. " I saw. But I bet you can't chuck a snowball right across the quad."

" Bet-you-I-can," said David all in one word.

He put down his books, took a couple of quick steps, and discharged the snowball he had prepared. He had aimed it, a high howitzer sort of shot, at the blank wall opposite. But it went rather to the left, and at the exact second of his throwing it, the door of the masters' common-room opened, and out came Owlers.

"Lord, I've got him," squealed David, though he had not intended to " get " anybody. And immediately behind Owlers came the Head.

David was quite right : the snowball " got " Owlers just in the middle of the waistcoat, and the Head saw. Very quickly and delicately the group of boys among whom David was standing dispersed into the two class-rooms that stood side by side, David with them, and amid stifled sniggers took their places. Immediately afterwards the Head entered, stiffly rustling.

"Did any boy here throw a snowball across the court just now ? " he asked.

David stood up at once. It was no good not doing that, for, unless he gave himself up, it was quite certain that there would be punishment for the whole of the two forms in their corner of the court, and that was not to be thought of.

"You, Blaize ? " said the Head.

"Yes, sir."

"Very well. You knew that snowballing in court was forbidden ? "

"Yes, sir," said David.

"Who is your house-master ? "

"Mr. Adams, sir."

That was all for the present, but after school David saw the Head talking to Adams, and, remembering Adams's warning, felt prepared for the worst, and tobogganed without any particular zest. Subsequently that day Adams remarked laconically, " So you're determined to have your way, David," and next morning the school porter entered his class-room with a

small blue paper, which he presented to Owlers. He
peered at it in his short-sighted manner.

" Blaize to go to the Head at twelve," he said.

Going to the Head at twelve implied knocking at the
door of a small empty class-room, barely furnished,
next the sixth-form room. The Head was there waiting, standing in front of the fire, and looking vexed.

" Blaize, I have been talking to your house-master
about you," he said, " and he tells me that you have
given a great deal of trouble this term. He tells me
also that he had warned you that the next time you
made a nuisance of yourself he would send you to me.
Did you get that warning ? "

" Yes, sir," said David.

" Very well, then, I shall give you a good whipping,"
he said. " It isn't for just throwing a snowball, you
understand, but for all the accumulation of silly, dis-
obedient things you have done. You have been gated
several times this term, and you have had frequent
impositions. Your form-master gives me exactly a
similar report of you. These punishments don't seem
to have made any impression on you, so I shall try
another plan. It's no use your going on like this, and
I'm not going to have it. Rules are made for you to
obey, whereas you seem to think you may break them
or not exactly as you please. They were not made
without a purpose, and I am going to show you that
they cannot be broken indefinitely without great in-
convenience."

David had not quite allowed for the horrid effect of
the Head's tongue. He had faced the fact that he was
going to be swished, but he had not faced the fact that
the Head would take all the stuffing out of him first,
so to speak, just when he wanted the stuffing.

" I am not going to whip you for my amusement,"

he continued, walking towards a cupboard, "far less
for yours. I am whipping you because I wish to give
you something by which to remember that you must
keep rules instead of breaking them. Reasonable
methods have been tried with you, and they don't
succeed, and I am going to treat you as if you weren't
reasonable, and hurt you. I don't like doing it, you
will like it much less, and I want you to understand
that it's a lower method of treating a boy like you,
who is quite big enough and clever enough to know
better. You have been behaving like an unreasonable
animal instead of a sensible boy. You are going to be
sharply reminded to have more sense in the future.
Now get ready."

David had not imagined it would be pleasant, but it
was a great deal more unpleasant than he had antici-
pated. The Head never swished unless he meant it;
there was no such thing as a light swishing, and that
fact was most clearly comprehended by David during
the next minute. Nor was there any consolation from
his executioner when it was over.

"That will do," he said. "You richly deserve what
I have given you. Don't let me have to send for you
again."

David went out, biting his lip. It had really been
very hard not to cry out under those stinging blows,
considering how very abject he felt before they had
begun, and almost the worst part of all was the waiting
between the strokes, which were delivered with pauses
for thought. But he got through without giving himself away, and went down to his house, feeling rather
glad that Bags was in the sick-room, since an interval to
pull himself together again in solitude was certainly
desirable. But hardly had he got into his study when
there came a tap at the door, and Maddox entered.

" Hullo, David," he said; " I've just got back. Did
you get my postcard ? I half wondered whether you
would come up to the station. I say, what's up ? "

" Just been swished," said David.

" What for ? "

" Accumulations, so that blasted Head told me.
Throwing a snowball finished it."

" Oh, you infernal ass," said Maddox. " You jolly
well deserved it."

At that the devil, no less, entered into David.

" Anyhow, I never deserved being expelled," he said
very evilly.

Frank looked at him a moment ; then, without a
word, he left the room.

For a few seconds David was not in the least sorry
for that speech. He was smarting himself, and if all
Frank had to say was that he deserved it, he was glad
to have made Frank smart too. . . . And then with a
sudden sense of sick regret, he remembered who Frank
was, and all that Frank had been to him. And on
the moment he was out of his study, and off down the
passage to Frank's. He went in without knocking.

" I say, I'm a damnable chap," he said. " I'm
frightfully sorry. I don't know if you can forgive me."

He put out a rather timid hand. Instantly it was
clasped and held.

" I didn't mean it," he said. " I felt mad."

" David, old chap," said Frank.

They stood there for a minute in silence, for really
there was nothing more to be said. Then David smiled.

" I think I'd better not make an ass of myself any
more," he said.

" Beastly good idea," said Frank.

CHAPTER XII

DAVID was sitting on the steps in front of the cricket-pavilion in school-field, with a pad on each leg and a glove on each hand, and an icy lump of nervous fear inside his canvas shirt to take the place of a heart. But nobody paid the least attention to him, or gave him a single word of encouragement, or cared at all for his panic-stricken condition, because everybody was utterly absorbed in what was going on at the wickets. The whole school and the whole staff were there watching the end of the final tie in house-matches in absolute tense silence, except when a run was scored, or a smart piece of fielding prevented one being scored. Then a roar went up from all round the ground, cut off again suddenly, as if a hand had been placed over all the mouths of some many-throated beast, as the bowler received the ball again. During the pause between overs a buzz of talk rose as if the cork had been taken out of a bottle where sonorous bees were confined ; this talk was silenced as the next over began.

Probably such a final as this had been seen before, but that did not detract from the tenseness of the excitement. The present position, arrived at through many delightful adventures, was that Adams's wanted twenty more runs to win, with two wickets to fall. Maddox, luckily, was in still, and Cruikshank (a miserable performer with the bat) was in with him. If either of them got out, the forlorn and trembling David had to take his place, last wicket, to totter down the steps

231

and walk apparently about twenty miles to the wicket, in the full light of day, with the eyes of the world on him. Maddox, of course, was the only hope of salvation; neither David nor Cruikshank could, even by their most optimistic friends, be considered as capable of doing anything but getting out against such strength of bowling as they had against them. And, in order to make David quite happy and comfortable about it all, there was indelibly written on the tablets of his memory the fact that he had got out second ball in the first innings "without," as the school paper would record on Saturday, "having troubled the scorer. . . ." What if the paper added that in the second innings he proved himself as independent of the scorer again? So, while the groups of boys round him, regaling themselves the while on bags of cherries and baskets of strawberries, seethed with pleasant, irresponsible excitement, David was merely perfectly miserable, as he waited for the roar that would go up round the field, to show another wicket had fallen. That would not be abruptly cut off like the tumult that succeeded a run or a piece of fielding: the Toveyites would go on screaming "Well bowled" or "Well caught" until he marched out across the field. All that he could think of in this hour of waiting was the fact that he had been completely bowled by the second ball he received in the first innings after having been completely beaten by the first. Tomlin, who had kindly sent down that fatal delivery, was bowling now, and no doubt he would be bowling still when he went in.

The match had been full of entrancing and agonizing vicissitudes. Adams's had batted first, piling up a respectable total of a hundred and eighty-two, which gave no cause for complaint. Then Tovey's had gone in and had been ignominiously dismissed by Cruikshank and Mellor for eighty-one, and the sages were inclined to think that the match was as good as over. They had followed on, but, instead of being dismissed for eighty-one again, they had amassed the huge total of three hundred and twenty-nine. Cruikshank, the demon of the first innings, had been hit completely off his length, and David had been put on as first change, not having bowled at all in the first innings. But the glorious personal result of that afternoon's work gave him no encouragement now, for his mind was filled to the exclusion of all else with the fact that in his previous appearance with the bat, and not the ball, Tomlin had beaten him twice and bowled him once. But yesterday, when he was bowling, Tovey's could do nothing with him; he bowled their captain, Anstruther, in his first over (after being hit twice to the boundary by him) and had proved himself altogether too much for the rest of the side. The wicket was fast and true, and there was no reason for their not being able to play him, except the excellent one that he bowled extremely well. He was left-handed, with very high action, and had (as an accessory) cultivated a terrifying prance up to the wickets, with a crooked run and a change of feet in the middle of it, like a stumbling horse. After this he delivered a slow high ball, while every now and then (but not too often) he laced one in as hard as ever he could with precisely the same delivery. In the end he had taken seven wickets for ninety runs, while the rest of the three hundred and twenty-nine had been scored off the other bowlers of the side, who had captured two wickets (one being run out) between them.

There came a roar from the ring of spectators round the field, and shouts of derisive laughter from a group of Adams's boys standing near, and David, forgetting everything else for the moment, added a piercing cat-

call whistle to the general hubbub. Tomlin had changed
his field with the obvious intention of getting Maddox
caught in the slips, sending mid-on there, making the
fourth of them. Then he proceeded to bowl a little
wide of the off-stump. Maddox had let three balls go
by, but the fourth he pulled round to exactly where
mid-on had been, and scored four for it. Oh, a great
stroke, and no one could tell, perhaps not even Maddox,
how it was done.

There was one more ball of this over, and it was
wonderfully important that Maddox should score one
or three or five off it, so as to get the bowling again.
But it was no use attempting to do anything with such
a ball, it was all he could do to play it. So Cruikshank
got the bowling. Well, it was better that Cruikshank
should face Crawley than Tomlin. If only Tomlin
could receive a telegram saying that his father and
mother and his three brothers and his four sisters (if
he had any) were all seriously ill, and that he had to
go home absolutely this minute. . . .

It was clear that Cruikshank was nervous—David
knew of somebody else who was nervous, too—but he
presented a dull solid wall to two straight balls. Then,
with extreme caution, he lobbed one up in the direction of
long-off, and ran like the devil. "Come on," he shouted
to Maddox, for he was just as anxious that Maddox
should get the bowling as were the rest of Adams's.

Maddox wanted a run as much as anybody, but he
was completely taken by surprise at the impudence of
this. But there was Cruikshank half way up the pitch,
and it meant a wicket lost, if he told him to go back.
So he, too, ran like the devil.

The situation only lasted a couple of seconds, but it
made up in quality what it lacked in quantity. If
long-off, who already had the ball in his hands, had

thrown it in to the end from which Cruikshank had started, he had a good chance of getting Maddox run out, while if he threw it in to the bowler, close to him, he had the practical certainty of running Cruikshank out, which was not nearly so important. Simultaneously both wicket-keeper and bowler shouted "This end!" and he threw it wildly to about the middle of the pitch. And there were fifteen more runs to get to win.

It seemed to David, as he watched, forgetting himself for a moment or two, that Maddox himself was feeling the strain, especially after this last and unmerited escape. He spooned a ball feebly in the air short, but only just short of point; and the next, though he scored two off it, was the most dangerous stroke, and as unlike as possible to his usual crisp cutting. Still, it might be only that there was something dreadfully unexpected about that ball, which caused him to mistime it. But if only he would kindly *not* mistime balls for a little while longer. Then came the last ball of the over, which he hit out at, completely missed it, and was nearly bowled. So Cruikshank had to face the fatal Tomlin.

There ensued some piercing moments. There was an appeal for a catch at the wickets, confidently made, which was not upheld, and Cruikshank proceeded to play like a clockwork doll, imperfectly wound up. After failing to play two balls altogether, he hit out as hard as he could at the third, intending to drive it, and snicked it between his legs for one. But that gave Maddox the bowling again, and off the last ball he scored one, and thus secured the bowling again.

A little faint glimmer of hope came into David's heart. There was a bye for two, which left eleven runs only to get, and perhaps, perhaps he would not have to bat at all. If only Maddox would hit three fours in succession, a feat of which he was perfectly capable, the match would be over, and David thought it would be quite impossible ever to stop shouting again. For nothing in the whole world mattered to him now, except that they should win, and nobody mattered except those two white figures at the wicket. Yet one was Frank, and David so far mastered his trembling knees as to go to the scoring-box to see how many he had made. His score was just eighty, so that he could not get his century, even if he scored the rest himself. Rather a pity, but certainly nobody would care less than Frank.

At the third ball he opened his shoulders, and gave a little skip out to drive, and a celestial stroke it was. The ball flew along the ground, rather to the right of long-off, and it seemed as if it must go for four; but that odious fellow just reached it, stopping it with his foot, made a beautiful return, and instead of four it was a single only. And Cruikshank had the bowling.

A roar had gone up on account of the smart fielding of the last ball, and was instantly silent again. Now there went up another, not so soon coming to an end, for Cruikshank's leg-stump had been sent flying. And there were ten more runs to get.

David got up, put on his cap and then with great deliberation took it off again. He didn't know if he wanted a cap or not, and it was immensely important to settle that. It was sunny, but the sun was still high, and would not really come in his eyes. But he certainly wanted something to drink, for his throat had suddenly become gritty and dry like the side of a match-box, and he wanted to run away and hide, or to do anything in the world rather than cross that interminable stretch of grass, across which Cruikshank was now walking. But as soon as Cruikshank reached the pavilion he would have to go. That impossible feat had to be accomplished

Bags had been sitting by him, thoughtfully eating cherries, after David had refused them, but it was long since he had had any clear consciousness of Bags or of any one else except those white figures in the field. But at this awful moment Bags proved himself a friend in need.

" Oh, David, how ripping it will be," he said, in a voice of complete conviction, " that you and Maddox win cock-house match for us."

Up till that moment the possibility had literally not entered David's head : he had been entirely absorbed in the prospect of losing it for them. But this suggestion put a little bit of heart into him, instead of the cold fear.

" By Gad," he said, and, drawing a long breath, went down the steps on to the level field.

The moment he got moving, even though he was only moving to the place of execution, he found that it was not so impossible as it had appeared in anticipation. It had seemed out of the question at this crucially critical period in the history of cricket, which was more important than the history of the world, to face this. But now there he was, going out all alone, bat in hand, and he did not sink into the earth or fall down with a few hollow groans. And then two other things encouraged him further, neither of which he had contemplated. As his tall, slight figure detached itself from the crowd in front of the pavilion a real cheer went up, not from the boys of his house only, but from the school in general. He told himself that they were not cheering him, David Blaize, but only the last actor in this enthralling piece of drama, in spite of which he felt much the healthier for it. And the second thing that encouraged him was far better, for Maddox, leaving the wicket, had come half-way across the ground to meet him and walk back with him.

" David, old chap, isn't it ripping," he said (even

as Bags had said), " that it's you and me ? Just the
jolliest thing that could happen. Don't bother about
runs; they'll come all right. Just keep your end up,
and don't take any risks. The bowling's absolute
piffle, so long as you don't try to hit it."

Then they had to part company, each going to his
wicket.

There were, so David remembered with hideous dis-
tinctness, two more balls of the over, and after taking
middle and leg he had a look round. The two points
that struck him most were that the other wicket seemed
nightmarishly close to be bowled at from, and that
there were apparently about thirty fielders. But then,
as Crawley walked away to get his run, the rest of
David's nerve, now that the time for action had come,
was completely restored to him. He had never felt
cooler nor clearer of eye in his life.

He received his first ball. At first he thought it was
going to be a full-pitch, but then he saw it was a yorker.
He saw it in time and he heard, sweet as honey to the
mouth, the chunk with which it hit the centre of his
bat close to the end.

There was no doubt whatever about the second ball :
it was a half-volley well outside his leg-stump. David
made one futile attempt to be prudent and resist the
temptation, but he was quite incapable of it, danced
out a yard, and smote for all he was worth. He heard
the solid impact of the bat, telling him he had hit it
correctly, and—there was the ball, already beyond and
high above mid-on. It was not worth while starting
to run, since this was a boundary-hit, if ever there was
one. And—almost more important—this was the end
of the over. Opposite he saw Maddox shaking his fist
at him, as the roar of applause went up, mingled with
shouts from his particular friends of " Well hit, Blazes !

Smack 'em about, David," and he swaggered out of his ground, to slap a perfectly true place on the wicket with his bat.   He looked up with a deprecatory smile at Frank.

" Sorry, I had to," he said.

" You little devil ! " said the other.

A silence more intense than ever settled down over the ground, as the last shouts consequent on David's immortal feat died away, for Tomlin proceeded to send down perhaps the best over he had ever bowled in his life.   Once he completely beat Maddox, and must have shaved the varnish off his bails, and from the rest the batsman made no attempt to score, being quite satisfied with stopping them.   At the end Anstruther looked round the field.

" Wace, take an over at Crawley's end, will you ? " he said.

Then that period, deadly for a newly arrived bats-man, had to be gone through, when the fresh bowler has a few practice-balls, and rearranges the field, and it made David fret.   Long-on had to be moved two yards nearer, and one yard to the right : cover-point had to go much deeper, point had to come in a little, and the slips went through a mystic dance.   This being concluded, Wace proceeded.

David opened with an appalling stroke, that would have been easily caught by cover, if only Wace had not moved him, and thereupon Wace brought him in again. So David, with an even worse stroke, spooned the ball over his head, so that if he had not been moved the second time, he must have caught it.   For this he scored one amid derisive and exultant yells, and Maddox hit at him with his bat as they crossed each other. And there were four more runs to get.

Then the end came.   Maddox played two balls with great care, and the unfortunate Wace then sent him a full pitch to leg. There came the sound of the striking bat ; next moment the ball bounded against the palings by the pavilion. And Maddox had played his last house-match.

Frank waited to see the ball hit the palings, and then ran across the pitch to David.

" Didn't I tell you so ? " he said. " And wasn't it ripping that you and I should do that ? Hullo, they're coming for us. Let's run."

All round the ground the crowd had broken up wildly shouting, some going towards the pavilion, but others, headed by a detachment from Adams's, streaming out on to the pitch. The two boys ran towards the pavilion, dodging the first few of these, but both were caught and carried in starfish-wise. Then again and again, first Maddox alone, then both together, they had to come out on to the balcony, while the house and school generally shouted itself hoarse for this entrancing finish. Indeed, the honours were fairly divided, for if Maddox's batting had saved the situation to-day, the situation would have been impossible to save if it had not been for David's bowling yesterday. Then by degrees the crowd dispersed, and the shouting died, and the two sat for a while there, the happiest pair perhaps in all England, blunt and telegraphic with each other.

" David, you little devil ! " said Frank. " Frightful cheek, your hitting that four. Second ball you received, too."

David gave a cackle of laughter.

"Don't rub it in," he said. "I apologized. Juicy shot, too. I say, Tomlin sent you down an over of corkers after that."

" Nearly spewed with anxiety," said Frank. " Absolute limit of an over."

" Wicked fellow, Tomlin," quoth David. " Glad I
didn't get any of them."

" So'm I, damn glad. Else——"

" Of course nobody can bat except yourself," said
David.

" You can't, anyhow."

" But we've won."

" Have we really ? Don't interrupt. I should have
added that you can bowl."

" You can't," said David, getting level.

" No, filthy exercise. I'll take you down to bathe, if
you don't bar washing, and then I'll take you to school
shop, and you may eat all there is. Lucky I'm flush."

" Right oh, thanks awfully," said David. " But you
won't be flush long."

They got up to go, but at the door Maddox paused.

" Best of all the days I've had at school, David," he
said.

" Same here," said David.

School bathing did not begin for another hour, but
Maddox had the sixth-form privilege of bathing whenever
he chose, and Adams, whom they ran to catch up on their
way down, gave David leave to go with him. He had
dutifully and delightedly watched every ball of the
match, and had helped to carry David into the pavilion as there was no chance of assisting at the entry of
Maddox.

" Yes, by all means, yes, you—you blest pair of
sirens," he said, quoting from the Milton Ode which was
to be sung at concert at the end of the term. " And
take care of David, Jonathan, and don't let him sink
from being top-heavy with pride. We shall want him
to bowl next year."

They trotted on for a little, in order to arrive at the
bathing-place in the greatest possible heat.

" I say, wasn't that ripping of him ? " said David.
" Didn't know he knew we were pals."

" Jolly cute," observed Maddox.

" But how did he know ? We don't go about together
in public. Lord, here's the Head coming. Lucky I've
got leave."

They had gone through the gate into the master's
garden, beyond which lay the bathing-place. This
was penetrable only by masters and by the sixth-form,
and there was no turning back, or avoiding what was to
David a rather formidable meeting. It was quite illo-
gical that he should find it so, since he had leave, but
he had not met the Head since the interview in the
disused class-room, and the halo of terror still shone
about his head.

He nodded kindly to the boys as they dropped into
walking pace and took their caps off, and then stopped.

" Fine innings of yours, Maddox," he said. " I congratulate you. You too, Blaize. A lot to expect,
wasn't it, that you should bowl Mr. Tovey's eleven
out one day, and keep up your wicket to win the match
the next ? Very glad you did it successfully."

David, still rather awed, shifted from one foot to the
other.

" Thanks awfully, sir," he said. " I—I've got leave
to bathe from Mr. Adams."

The Head looked at him a moment, with a certain
merriment lurking below his gravity.

" Quite sure ? " he asked.

David saw this was a joke, and laughed.

" I want just a word with you, Maddox," said the
Head. " Will you go on, Blaize ? "

The Head waited a moment.

" It's about Blaize I wanted to speak to you, Maddox," he said. " How is he getting on ? I had to

give him a good whipping last term. Is he more—more rational?"

"He's come on tremendously, sir," said Maddox. "He's getting on excellently."

"I'm glad you think that, because I believe he's one of the most promising boys we've got, and you know him, I should think, better than any of us."

Maddox wondered how on earth the Head knew that. Adams might know; but how did the Head?

"I don't want his cricket to interfere with his work," he said. "The middle fifth had to write an essay last week, and I told Mr. Howliss to send them in to me to look over. All but two or three were dreadful rubbish, but Blaize's was excellent. And, as you're a Trinity scholar as well as being captain of the eleven, you can see my point of view. Do you think he's getting cricket out of focus? He ought to be higher in his form, you know."

Maddox shook his head.

"Oh, I don't think Blaize is a bit unbalanced about his cricket, sir," he said. "I always rub it in that cricket doesn't matter. At least I usually do, though I didn't to-day, because I couldn't after he'd bowled like that. But I'll rub it in again after to-morrow."

"Why after to-morrow?" asked the Head.

"Because I was going to put him into the twenty-two to-night sir, though he doesn't know yet, and I must let him enjoy it a bit. And then there's the eleven against the sixteen on Saturday next, and after his whole record in house-matches, it's just a question whether he oughtn't to play for the eleven. There are four places left."

The Trinity scholar had certainly got absorbed in the captain of the eleven.

"You mean he has a chance of his school-colours?" asked the Head.

" Yes, sir, if he goes on developing like this," said Maddox. " It's five weeks yet to the Lords match, and it's easily possible he may be the best slow bowler in the school."

Maddox paused a moment.

" He'll have to practise a lot," he said, " and he'll have to think about it a lot. Three-quarters of a slow bowler is brains, you know, sir. Or would you rather I didn't try to bring him on at cricket ? He wouldn't notice ; he hasn't the slightest idea how good he is. And even if he had——"

" Well ? " said the Head.

Maddox dropped the surname altogether.

" You see, David's the best chap who ever lived," he said, " and we're tremendous friends. If I didn't put him in the twenty-two even he'd think it was perfectly all right. As you've talked to me about him, sir, I want to tell you that I'll do what you think best for him. I should naturally put him into the twenty-two this evening, because he deserves it, and, as I said, I was thinking of his playing for the eleven next week. But if you think not, if you think it would do him more good all round to be kept back, well, I will. But there's no fellow in the school less uppish, if you mean that."

That was all the Head wanted ; he had got at David's character, as seen by Maddox, with far more completeness than Maddox knew.

" Do just what seems best to you as captain of the eleven," he said. " But there are lots of you fellows who want watching, and it takes work off my shoulders if I know that you elder and steady men are doing some watching for me. Good luck to both of you. If you live till ninety, you'll never find a better thing than a friend. At least I haven't."

Maddox found David wallowing in the tepid water,

and at intervals making hazardous experiments from the high header-board. This was instructive as showing the flight of heavy bodies through space, and was occasionally followed by further interesting results as showing what happened when these heavy bodies flatly met a flat and incompressible material. Thereafter they went to school shop, and David ate his way, so to speak, from in at one door to out at the other. This was a long and sumptuous process, for the place was full, and congratulations were hurled at them. Tomlin, the diabolical, was there among the crowd, taking his defeat in a wide-minded manner.

"Thought you had me once or twice during your last over," said Maddox to him. "Fiendish over, Tommy."

Tommy considered this.

" 'Twasn't a very bad one," he said. "I think I should have liked to have sent it down to Blaize instead of you. Jolly good match, though. Hullo, Blaize! You're a rotten bad bat, you know. I'll stand you both strawberry-mess."

It was perfectly impossible for David not to feel elated at sitting down to strawberry-mess with two members of the eleven, in the full light of day, and in sight of the school generally, or, having dreamed night and day of being "some good" in house-matches, not to feel exalted when those dreams had merged into realities that so far exceeded all his imaginings. But in a little while Maddox and Tomlin began to speak in undertones, and David rose, with the sense that private conversation was going forward.

"I think I'll be getting back to house," he said. "Thanks awfully for the strawberry-mess, Tomlin."

"Wait a minute," said Maddox. "I'm coming down in a second. Go and blow yourself out a little more."

David thought it the part of wisdom not to do that,

and strolled outside to wait for his friend. Glorious as all those things had been there was nothing so glorious as that Frank and he had been associated in them. That friendship meant more to him than cricket, or this sort of open recognition of itself. Till now their ages and places in the school had necessarily divided them in public; and so to-day it was best of all the delicious happenings when Frank joined him, and they went off together.

" The Head asked after you this afternoon, David," said Frank. " Made inquiries. I told him you were fairly rotten."

David did not rise at this.

" You always stick up for a chap," he observed. " Anything else ? "

" Yes. I may as well tell you, as everybody else will know by chapel-time. Fact is, I'm putting you into the twenty-two to-night. And on Saturday, next week, you're playing in the eleven and sixteen match for the eleven."

David stopped quite dead. And then he thought he saw. Frank had tried to get a rise out of him just now and failed, and of course was trying again. It wasn't really quite nice of him to try to get a rise out of him over such matters, but then he didn't know how dreadfully David cared.

" Oh ! Jolly funny ! " he said, and walked on again.

" David, do you think I'm such a brute as to try to get a rise out of you with that sort of thing ? " asked Frank.

" B-b-but do you mean it's true ? " asked David, suddenly stammering.

" Yes, you ass. That's what I wanted to consult Tommy about, and he agrees. We can't have a kid like you bowling the eleven out, so you've jolly well got to bowl the sixteen out instead. And I'll take away your twenty-two cap, if you don't."

" Oh, Frank, I can't quite believe it," said David.
" What's it all for ? What have I done ? "

" That's one of your bad points, as I told the Head,"
said Frank. " I said you were filthily conceited."

" Lord ! " said David.

" Well, congratters on your twenty-two. And you can
bring your preparation to my study if you like, and I'll
give you a construe. I haven't got any work to do myself."

" Comes of being a scholar of Trinity," remarked
David, and fled.

Frank had written out the list of promotions into the
twenty-two when David came to his study with a copy
of " Œdipus Coloneus," which was his lesson for next
day, and he pushed it over to hm.

" I've stuck you in first," he said, " to prepare for
your appearance next Saturday. Now we'll leave the
silly business alone. What's your work ? ' Œdipus
Coloneus ' ? "

" Yes ; twenty-five lines of a chorus that's simply
beastly," said David, finding his place. "There: line 668."

Frank looked over his shoulder.

" Oh, it's not without merit," he said. " Now look
out every word you don't know, and then try to make
something of it for half an hour. After that, I'll give
you a construe. No talking."

" Oh, won't you construe it first ? " asked David.
" It'll save me a lot of trouble."

" And did you suppose I wanted to save you trouble ? "
asked Frank.

David sighed.

" Thought you might," he said. " It's rather flat
working after this afternoon."

" No, it isn't. You've got to learn that people like
Sophocles matter more than any silly house-match."

" 'Twasn't a silly house-match," said David.

" Don't talk ! "

David looked round.

" Lend me your dictionary, then," he said. " I've left mine in my study."

David had a very vivid sense of the beauty of words, and though it took him some time to whistle his mind away from the splendours of the afternoon and from the glories of that list that lay on the table, which would soon be displayed before the eyes of the entire school, he became conscious before long that the words of the "beastly chorus" which was open before him were beautiful things, and that their meanings, so his dictionary told him, were beautiful also, for it was all about horses, and nightingales, and thickets, and ivy the colour of wine— this was rather puzzling unless perhaps it meant *crème de menthe*—and clustering narcissus. Then by degrees he became absorbed in it, and all the time was slightly ashamed at being able to be interested in a mere Greek chorus, when his name lay on the table as heading the list of promotions into the twenty-two. But his absorption gained on him.

" Why, it's ripping ! " he said to himself under his breath, and, whistling softly, hunted up another jewel of a word. Then he lost himself again, diving into wonderful translucent depths.

" Gosh ! I've done more than twenty-five lines," he said at length, " and I never noticed. I say, give me a construe, Frank; I've been more than half an hour. I want to hear how it sounds in English."

Frank drew his chair up to David's, so that they could both share the same book.

"Right oh," he said, " but let me read it through first."

This was the education of David, and Frank was tremendously anxious to construe the beautiful passage well, and he took some five minutes more going over it, while David's glance fed on the list of the twenty-two promotions. Then he began.

"Stranger," he said. "Blast it; that won't do: it sounds American."

"Guest?" suggested David.

"Yes; that's better. 'O guest in this land of horsemen, thou hast come to the most fair of earth's homes, to gleaming Kolonos, frequented by the nightingale that bubbles liquidly in the shelter of green glades, making his habitation amid the wine-dark ivy, and the untrodden bowers of the god, myriad-berried, unseen of the sun, where Dionysus, master of revels, ever treads, companied by the nymphs that nursed him.'"

"O-o-oh!" said David, pushing back his yellow hair, and still rather shy of liking this.

"'And, fed with heavenly dew, the sweet clusters of the narcissus are flowering morn by morn, the immemorial crown of the great goddesses, and the golden-beamed crocus is a-blossom. Nor dwindle ever the sleepless springs whence come the wandering waters of the Kephissus, but every day he flows in stainless tides over the plains of earth's ripening bosom, giving speedy increase, nor have the choirs of Muses abhorred the spot, nor golden-reined Aphrodite.'"

Maddox paused.

"That's your twenty-five lines," he said.

"Oh, ripping," said David. "It really is. Absolute A1. Do go on."

"I told you it had merit," said Frank, and proceeded to the end of the chorus.

"Why, it's better than 'Atalanta,'" said David at the conclusion, despite his barbarian instinct that things like the beauties of Greek literature might perhaps be thought about, but hardly talked of. Maddox, however, had no such notions.

"Of course it is," he said.   "And some time, if you
work frightfully hard, and love it all, you'll find, as the
Head told us the other day, that you simply laugh at
the thought of translating it at all.   You'll know it
can't be translated, and that will be the reward of your
work, for it will mean that Greek has got into your
blood, that it's part of you."

"Do you mean the Head's like that?" asked David.
"All the same, I think I would sooner translate it like
you."

"You don't understand, but you would if you had
heard him the other day.   We had a Plato lesson with
him, but instead of going through a single line of it,
something set him off, and he talked to us for the whole
hour about Athens and the life they led there.   You
never heard anything so splendid.   You could go up to
the Acropolis in the morning, and look at the frieze
Pheidias had put up in the Parthenon, a procession of
horses and boys riding to the temple on Athene's birthday.   He showed us pictures of it; some were mounted,
—oh Lord, they had good seats—and others were still
putting their horses' bridles on, and one horse was
rubbing its foreleg with its nose, or t'other way round."

"Pheidias?" asked David.

"Yes; biggest sculptor there's ever been, far ahead
of Michelangelo or Rodin or any one.   And when you
had seen that, you and your friend—you and me, that
is—would sit on the wall of the Acropolis looking over
the town out to the mountains, the purple crown of mountains, as they called them, Hymettus where the honey
came from, and Pentelicus where they got the marble
for the Parthenon, and another one—what's its name?
oh, Parnes.   Then to the south you would look over the
sea, all blue and dim, out towards Salamis which, as the
Head said, was the Trafalgar of Athens, where they beat

those stinking Persians; and then we should lunch off grapes and figs, and cheese wrapped up in vine-leaves, and yellow wine, and go down to the theatre just below to hear perhaps this very play by Sophocles, first performance, and no end of an excitement. Then perhaps we should see Pericles, awfully handsome chap, and the biggest Prime Minister there ever was, and a queer, ugly fellow would go by, who would be Socrates. And all the boys and young men were fearfully keen about games, quite as keen as we are, because they used to date the year by the Olympic games, same as we use A.D. or B.C. . . . Lord, I'm jawing; I wish I could tell it you as the Head did."

" Oh, go on," said David.

" Well, it wasn't only games that they were so keen about. They loved sculpture and painting and writing so much, that no one ever touched them at it, before or since. It was the consummate age, so the Head said. And then, when it came to fighting, a little potty place like Attica, no bigger than a small English county, just wiped the Persians up. In everything, so the Head told us, the Athenians of the great age were the type of the perfect physical and intellectual life. Oh, David, let's save up and go to Athens."

"Rather! But why did the Romans walk over them ? "

Frank got up; the bell for chapel had begun.

" Because they became corrupt and beastly."

" What an awful pity ! I say, you made me feel awfully keen with that construe, and telling me what the Head said. I haven't thought about the twenty-two for—for ten minutes. And one's got to try to get at it all by sapping ? "

" Yes ; that's how you'll get to love it."

" Sounds almost worth while," said David. " But they liked games as well. That's a comfort."

Frank took up his straw hat ; he took up also the list
that lay on the table.

" Come on," he said.   " I want to put this up on the
notice-board before chapel."

" Oh, don't," said David.   " All the fellows will see
it, and I shall turn crimson when we stand up for the
psalms."

" Bosh ; every one expects it."

David's volatile mind went back to the Greek talk.

" Pheidias, was it ? " he said.

" Yes : sculptor-man," said Frank.

David, usually a solid sleeper, could not take his
usual plunge into the dim depths that night on getting
into bed, but he did not make any particular effort to do
so, for it was really waste of time not to lie awake when
there were so many delightful things to think about.
Round and round in his head they turned, like some
bright wheel, and now it was the events of the last three
days (house-match, in other words), now the more immediate happenings of the evening, his promotion into
the twenty-two, and the much huger honour of playing
for the eleven next week that sparkled on the wheel,
or again this sudden illumination with regard to the
Greeks fed his contemplation.   Up till now it had not
been real to him that the people who wrote these tedious
or difficult things which he had to learn were once as
alive as himself, or that beauty had inspired them to
make plays and statues, even as beauty had inspired
Keats and Swinburne.   Until Frank had given him the
gist of the Head's discourse, he never thought of those
plays as being performed in a theatre, before an audience,
who had not to look up words and learn the grammar,
and consider what governed an apparently isolated
genitive, or account for an irregular aorist.   They were
not bookworms and scholars, but men and boys who

ran races and crowned the victor, and had their Trafalgar just as if they were English. . . . It was all vague,
but decidedly there was a new light on matters concerning Sophocles.

But, permeating all these things, was their inspiring
spirit, Frank, who lay in the bed next him, whose face
he could dimly see in the light from the unblinded open
window just opposite. And then for the first time it
was borne in upon David with a sense of reality that in
a few weeks more, five and a piece, to be accurate,
Frank would have left. At that thought all the pleasant
and interesting things which had so delightfully enter-
tained this waking hour were struck from his mind, and
he sat up in bed giving a little despairing groan.

" Hullo ! " said Frank softly. " You awake too ?
What's the groaning about ? "

" Oh, nothing," said David, lying down again.

" Well, then, what isn't it about ? "

David slewed round in bed facing him, as he leaned
on his elbow.

" It's only five weeks to the end of the half," he
whispered, " and—and you don't come back."

" I know ; it's foul. I was thinking of it myself.
It's been keeping me awake."

David was silent a minute ; then Frank spoke again.

" I'm sorry to leave for a whole heap of reasons," he
said. " One more than any."

" What's that ? " said David.

" Fellow called Blaize. Thought I should just like
to tell you. Now don't groan any more. Go to sleep,
you swell in the twenty-two."

" Right oh, fellow called Maddox," said David.

CHAPTER XIII

DAVID was sitting on the bank below the pavilion on the last afternoon of the term, waiting for Frank, who was paying certain bills in the town, to join him, and take his cricket things away. To save time, David had packed them for him, emptying his locker into his cricket-bag, and now it and his own, ready packed, lay beside him on the grass. The plan was to sit here and talk till chapel-bell began, when they would take their belongings down and leave them at the lodge in readiness for the 'bus to the station next morning. It was their last opportunity of being alone together, for after chapel they would have to go down to their house to dress for concert, and after concert was the house-supper in honour of their having won the cricket-cup. It would all be exceedingly public and rejoiceful, and Frank would have to make a speech, and David was afraid he would want to groan again instead of applauding, which was quite out of the question, as the occasion was one of uproarious mirth.

The last five weeks had passed with awful speed; he had worked a good deal, he had played cricket a good deal, and, though he had not got into the eleven, everything had been tremendously prosperous. He had been tried twice for the eleven, once against the next sixteen, once against a team of old boys from Cambridge, and in both matches he had bowled with considerable success. But then the weather had changed, and instead of the

dry, crumbling wickets which suited him, there had been
ten days' rain ; wickets were soft and slow, and certainly would be for the match at Lord's the day after
to-morrow, and David had become about as much use
as a practical bowler as a baby-in-arms would have
been. So Crawley, only this morning, had been given
the last place in the eleven, which was absolutely all
right, for Crawley could bat as well, and in the last
school match had both taken wickets and made runs,
the slow ground suiting his style in both respects. In
the same match Maddox had scored a hundred in his
inimitable style, and David had shouted himself hoarse,
and . . . and all these things were dead and done with.

Apart from cricket work had taken up a good deal of
his time, and work, mere silly work in a class-room taken
by Mr. Howliss, had assumed a different aspect. This
had all come out of that talk with Frank when he translated the chorus from " Œdipus Coloneus," on which
occasion David had realized that Pheidias was a real
person, and Pericles a real Prime Minister, and that
Socrates was jolly to young fellows, and told them
heavenly stories about the gods. They had all become
people who went to the theatre like anybody else, and
went to Olympia, just as anybody now might go to the
Oval, and had play-writers like Aristophanes who made
just the same sort of jokes as people make nowadays.
Out of that evening, too, had resulted the fact that
David, instead of occupying a modest and unassuming
place some half-way down the middle fifth, had heard,
to his great astonishment, his name read out at the top of
that distinguished form. A prize was the consequence
of that, presented him that morning at prize-giving by
a Royal Duchess, who said she was very much pleased,
which was distinctly civil of her. But all those things
were dead also ; they had happened.

There was but little more to happen, little that mattered. There was the concert, in which David was one of a group of tenors who would take part in the Milton Ode. That would be rather jolly; there was a delightful passage at the end about ' O may we soon renew that song.' And the name, ' Blest pair of sirens,' had an aroma about it. Adams had quoted it to him and Maddox just after cock-house match, when he had asked for leave to go down to bathe. What a good day that had been ! perhaps the best day of all these dead days.

Then, after the concert, would be the uproarious house-supper with a farewell speech from Frank. David felt empty inside at the thought.

The field was speckled with groups of boys straying about in the idleness of the last day. Some sat on the grass, some were playing stump-cricket, and all seemed unreasonably cheerful. Now and then two or three passed near him, and he exchanged friendly " Hullos " with them; sometimes they would ask him to join them in a stroll. But David's reply was always the same : " Sorry, but I promised to wait here for a chap." Then Bags detached himself from a passing group, and sat down by him. David could talk to him with freedom.

" Oh Bags, I feel beastly," he said. " What rot the end of term is ! "

" But you're going to have rather a decent time, aren't you ? " asked Bags.

" Oh, yes. There's a cricket week at Baxminster, and they've asked me to play in two matches. And it's awfully good of you to want me to come and stay with you. I'll let you know as soon as ever I can. Depends on my pater. Perhaps we're all going to Switzerland."

" Come whenever you like," said the faithful Bags.

"I shall be at home all the holidays. I think you might enjoy it. There's a lot of rabbit-potting in August, you know, and some partridges in September."

" Is it easy to shoot ? " asked David.

"Lord, yes. I get on all right, and I haven't got your eye ! "

" Well, it's awfully good of you. I should like to come if I may. But I don't care about anything to-day. Hump, I suppose."

Bags looked out over the yellow-green of the mid-summer field.

" Here's Maddox," he said, " almost running. Won-der what he's in such a hurry for."

David sat up.

"So he is," he said. " I say, let's sit next each other at house-supper. Take a place for me if you get in first. I'm a singer at concert, and singers always get out last."

" Right oh," said Bags.

He got up quite slowly, and it seemed ridiculous to David that he should not skip away at once. But he still lingered.

" I dare say Maddox is coming up to take his cricket things away," he remarked.

" I dare say that's it," said David.

By a stroke of Providence, Gregson and a friend came by at this moment.

" Ripping sport," said Gregson. " Come on, Bags. There's a terrier at school-shop, and they're going to put a ferret into the rat-holes. Place'll be alive with rats. Coming too, Blazes ? "

" No ; hate rats," said David.

Bags departed ; a moment after Frank joined David, just nodded to him, and sat down by him.

" Been waiting ? " he asked. " Sorry. I couldn't

get through with my jobs before. Have you stuck my
things into my bag ? Good work. We can just sit
here till chapel-bell."

" Yes ; I emptied your locker," said David. " I
stuck everything into your bag—old shoes, old twenty-
two cap, all there was. Afraid I didn't pack it very
neatly."

" Doesn't matter," said Frank. " Funny that there
should be an old twenty-two cap still there."

" Very curious," said David precisely.

Frank gave a short little laugh.

" It's all pretty beastly, isn't it ? " he said. " You
look rather depressed too. But there's the house-
supper to cheer you up."

" Oh, damn the house-supper," said David.

Frank's pretence at light conversation broke down.

" 'Tisn't as if we were going to lose each other," said
he. " And we're not dead, either of us, David. Do
buck up."

" Can't," said David.

" Then it's rotten of you. It isn't a bit worse for
you than me. You've lots of things in front of you :
you'll get into the eleven next year, you'll get into the
sixth at Christmas if you try. You'll swagger horribly,
you'll——"

Frank could not manage to pump up any more consoling reflections : they were all beside the point. So,
like a sensible boy, he left them alone, and went to the
point instead.

" David, old chap," he said, " I don't believe two
fellows ever had such a good time as we've had, and
it would be rot to pretend not to be sorry that this bit
of it has come to an end. I dare say we shall have
splendid times together again, but there's no doubt
that this is over. On the other hand, it would be equal

rot not to feel jolly thankful for it. The chances were millions to one against our ever coming across each other at all. So buck up, as I said."

David had rolled over on to his face, but at this he sat up, picking bits of dry grass out of his hair.

"Yes, that's so," he said. "But it will be pretty beastly without you. I shan't find another friend like you——"

"You'd jolly well better not," interrupted Frank.

David could not help laughing.

"I suppose we're rather idiots about each other," he said.

"I dare say. But it's too late to remedy that now. Oh, David, it's a good old place this. Look at the pitch there! What a lot of ripping hours it's given to generations of fellows, me among them. There's the roof of house through the trees, do you see? You can just see the end window of our dormitory. I wonder if happiness soaks into a place, so that if the famous Professor Pepper——"

"Oh, mammalian blood?" said David.

"What's that? Oh yes, the crime at Naseby. Same one. I wonder if he would find a lot of happiness-germs all over the shop."

"I could do with a few," said David, with a sudden return to melancholy.

"No, you couldn't. You've got plenty of them, as it is. . . . Lord, there's that rotten speech I have to make at house-supper. What am I to say?"

"Oh, usual thing. Say Adams is a good fellow, and we're all good fellows, and it's a good house, and a good school, and a good everything—hurrah."

"That's about it," said Frank. "Oh, there's one other thing, David. Look after Jevons a bit, will you? He's turning into rather a jolly little kid."

"Inky little beast!" said David. "All right."

Again they were silent for a while.

"Rather a ripping verse in the psalms this morning," said Frank at length.

"Was there? I wasn't attending."

"Well, it seemed rather applicable, I thought. 'For my brethren and companions' sake I will wish thee prosperity.' Just as if the other David, not you, was talking to *his* school. And there's chapel-bell beginning."

They sat still a moment longer; then Frank rose.

"We must go, David," he said. "Wouldn't do to be late, as it's the last time. Give me your hands; I'll pull you up."

David stretched out his great brown paws, and Frank hauled him to his feet. David stood there a second still holding.

"Good old psalm," he said.

CHAPTER XIV

DAVID was sitting in front of the fire in his house-master's study one afternoon late in November, occasionally reading the *Sporting and Dramatic* and otherwise listening with a strong inward satisfaction to the slinging of the sleet on to the window panes, which, as pointed out by Lucretius, emphasizes the warm comfort of present surroundings. He had a large foot on each side of the fire just below the chimney-piece, and a large cushion at the back of his head, and no intention at all of going into the foul, cold shower-bath called " out of-doors." What made his satisfaction the more complete was that a notice had been passed round at hall from Gregson, the captain of the house at football, that every one had to go out for a three-mile run with a view to keeping in training for house-matches, and it added to David's pleasure to think of all those poor wretches plodding through the rainy sleet and the mud and the puddles, while he, like the king's daughter in the psalms, was " all glorious within." Gregson—*alias* Plugs—who was a pal of David's, had called him by all the insulting names he could think of, when David had absolutely refused to obey orders, and the end of it had been that David had picked Gregson up (he was a little fellow, though an admirable half-back at Rugby football) and carried him all the way upstairs in his arms and round each dormitory in turn to show him that he was in perfectly good training already. Thereafter he had taken the *Sporting and Dramatic*

from the reading-room, against all rules, and retired to
Adams's study to spend a cosy time before the fire.

Adams himself came in before long, and David pushed
his chair back, and took down his large feet, so that
he did not usurp the whole of the hearthrug and the
entire warmth of the fire. He had, like half the house,
the habit of sitting in Adams's study, who wanted
nothing better than to have his boys about.

" Not gone for a training-run, David ? " asked he.

" No, sir. Plugs—er, gave me leave-off."

Adams lit his pipe, and sat down on the hearthrug,
which was his usual place.

" On what grounds ? " he asked.

David laughed.

" I carried him round the house, sir, to show him I
was in good training," he said. " He didn't mind
a bit."

" That'll do for my text," said Adams. " I wanted
to sermonize you. That's the sort of thing, David,
that I wish you wouldn't do. You are rather given
to undermining authority. It doesn't set a very good
example, and though you probably don't know it, the
house takes its tune from you and one or two others.
You are pals with Gregson, I know. And that's all the
more reason why you should support him. And, while
I'm on the subject, I want to ask you not to swear so
much."

David sat up in astonishment.

" Sir, I bet you've never heard me swear," he said.

" I know I haven't, but I've heard young Jevons,
and I draw the perfectly correct conclusion that you
do. I'm awfully grateful, by the way, for your taking
him up as you've done, and teaching him to wash his
hands, and not look as if everybody wanted to thrash
him. Did anybody suggest it to you ? "

"Oh, yes, Frank," said David.

"Well, you've done good work, though I didn't mean to praise you. But Jevons copies you: he brushes his hair like you, and whistles between his teeth, or tries to, and runs instead of walking, and, as I say, swears. Do stop it, will you? He was leaning out of his study window yesterday, exchanging compliments with somebody, and I never heard such an assortment of Billingsgate. It's such awfully bad form, you know. Also the sentiments expressed by bad language are not edifying."

"I'll try, sir," said David. "I—I never thought of swearing as meaning anything."

"I know you didn't; I never said it was the expression of a foul mind. But the house is becoming a perfect company of bargees. Try not to swear yourself, and kick anybody who does when it's convenient. That's all about that."

"Right, sir," said David.

"Then there's another thing," said Adams. "I want you to tell me about the Court of Appeal. I've only just heard about it, and I don't think I like it."

David frowned. This wasn't his idea of a comfortable afternoon indoors at all, and he wished he had gone out for a run instead of carrying Plugs round the house.

"I don't think I can, sir," he said. "There are other fellows concerned in it."

"Oh, I know that. The Court is you and Gregson and Bags; chiefly you. That's why I asked you. I heard about it from the Head. He doesn't like it, either. I said I would go into the matter. I don't promise that he won't as well."

"I suppose that little beast Manton told him," remarked David.

"I don't agree with 'little beast,'" said Adams,

" but I agree that probably Manton told him. I really don't see what else the head of the house could do. Now I want to hear what the Court of Appeal have to say about themselves, just as I shall want to know what the prefects say about them. Gregson and Bags are quite safe in your hands as *advocatus*—well, perhaps, not quite *diaboli*. You can trust me for that."

David raised himself and sat Turk-fashion with crossed legs in the big basket-chair.

" It's rather a long story, sir, if I'm to tell it from the beginning," he said.

" Never mind."

" Well, you see, sir, there was such an awful change in the house when Frank and Cruikshank left at the end of last half. You see, they were proper prefects; they used their authority properly, and it was jolly well necessary to respect it. You couldn't cheek fellows like them, when they gave orders; it simply couldn't happen. And it was so frantically different to get little clever squirts like Manton and Crossley in authority instead. They couldn't keep order a hang; the whole house would have been out of hand in no time. You'll see that the Court of Appeal was really meant to preserve order. Why, the very fags used to laugh at them. One of them put soap in Manton's kettle one day, and when it boiled it came bubbling out of the spout like blowing soap-bubbles. You never saw anything so funny. But the Court of Appeal stopped that."

Adams preserved his gravity.

" That's rather a new light," he said. " Go on, David. You needn't bring in names if you think you'd better not. But it's only fair that the Head should know your side of the question, as he has heard Manton's."

David got red in the face.

" Manton's a bl—— filthy little sneak," he observed. " Also, I bet he hasn't told the Head the truth."

" He probably told him the truth, as it struck him," said Adams. " It strikes you differently. But he didn't sneak as you think. The Head got his first news about the Court of Appeal from quite another source."

" May I know what source ? " asked David.

" Yes, I don't mind telling you, but you must be officially ignorant. Jevons went to breakfast with the Head the other day, and remarked, in an outburst of confidence, that you were far the biggest swell in the house, because you were the President of the Court of Appeal. He said it in all innocence, but the Head was naturally interested to hear more, and applied to—well, to the proper quarter, which was Manton."

David recovered from his spurt of temper.

" That funny little Jev probably thought it all quite regular," he said.

" Of course he did ; he wouldn't have given you away on purpose. Go on ; we've got to the soap in the kettle."

David laughed.

" Yes, sir, you should have seen it coming all rain-bowy out of the spout. So of course Manton sent for the—the fellow who did it, and he couldn't even cane him alone, but had to have Crossley in to help. It's perfectly degrading, sir, to have prefects like that. So Crossley held the fellow down, and, just as Manton began to lay on, the fellow kicked out, and Crossley slipped across to get out of the way, and Manton landed him an awful wipe over the shin. And so Crossley let go, and stamped about, and they made such a row between them that I had to look in. I'd gone on tiptoe to the door, sir, in case anything funny occurred, and so, as I say, I looked in, and there was Babbington—oh, name slipped out by accident—fit to burst himself with laughing, and the kettle boiling over again with soap-bubbles, and Crossley hopping about on one leg, and Manton apologizing to him. And then Manton turned on me, and told me I was undermining discipline; so I had to say there seemed a precious lot of discipline to undermine. And then Manton lost his presence of mind and whacked out again at Babbington, and missed him and smashed his electric light. O Lor'! I never saw anything so funny!"

David shrieked with laughter again at the remembrance, and Adams could not resist joining him as he turned to beat out his pipe against the bars of the fire.

"Well?" he said at length.

"I could tell you heaps of stories like that," said David, wiping his eyes. "Another time it was Crossley who told a fellow to write out fifty lines. So he wrote out 'Fifty lines,' just like that, on a sheet of paper, and showed it up. Fancy doing that to Frank, or Crookles! Why, you couldn't! And then Crossley told him to write them out twice. So he took another bit of paper and wrote 'Them out twice' on it. And then Crossley said he would cane him, so Jevons—Lord, there's another name; please forget it, sir—Jevons came and appealed. Precious lot of good that did him, for the Court were satisfied that he'd deserved his fifty lines, and so I gave him six frightful stingers myself, as I knew Crossley wasn't fit to, for cheek to a prefect. And yet you and Manton say I'm undermining discipline, sir," added David in a voice of outraged virtue. "Why, we're enforcing it. Jev had to write out his hundred lines, and got a whacking too. Though the Court of Appeal can reverse a prefect's decision, it also may enforce it, and then the—the appellant gets it twice as hot for having appealed. Same as in English law, sir."

"This is all rather news to me," remarked Adams.

"Well, sir, something had to be done," said David,

" or the whole house would have gone to pot. Why, the fags might have taken it into their heads to cheek fifth form next when they'd finished with the sixth, and there would have been trouble. You see, most of the big fellows in the house are in the fifth. That's the way the Court of Appeal started."

" Go on," said Adams.

" Well, the next thing was—oh, I must tell you this— one night a couple of juniors made an apple-pie bed for Gregson. Awful cheek ! So naturally he whacked them soundly and formally, and they went to Manton, and told him that Gregson had been whacking them. So round comes Manton and tells Gregson, before the whole dormitory, and him captain of football, that he'd no right to, as he wasn't a prefect. And of course Gregson said he'd heard that a little before Manton had caned Crossley (that was the Babbington affair) and that he hadn't any right to cane a prefect. That's the sort of thing that went on all the first weeks of this half, sir ; there'd have been a regular revolution unless we'd done something. And so I say that the Court of Appeal is more to support authority than the other way about."

" Well, now, we'll take the other way about," said Adams. " I mean I want to know about the cases in which you upset the prefect's authority."

David thought for a moment.

" Well, sir, those two, Manton and Crossley, did all sorts of things we're not accustomed to have prefects doing," he said. " When they went the round of the studies during preparation to see that we were working, they used to put on slippers and open the door quick to try and catch you doing nothing ; and of course they often did. Well, that's not playing the game, sir. Frank always came clumping along, and he always tapped at your door. It was just the same when they

went the rounds of dormitories after lights were out.
Slippers! You don't do any good by spying, you know;
you won't stop fellows ragging or—or anything else,
that sort of way. It only means that two can play at
that game, and if you want to do anything of the kind
that you shouldn't, you just put a sentinel at the door.
Spying just encourages fellows to break rules. Smoking,
too."

"Well, smoking?" said Adams.

"Crossley suspected a certain fellow of smoking, and
one day, when he was out, he went and looked in his
table drawer and found a pipe there. Now, sir, that sort
of thing's all rot. He wanted to whack him for it, and
the fellow appealed. So naturally we gave it in his
favour when it came out that Crossley had looked in his
private drawer. You wouldn't dream of doing it yourself, sir. Naturally not. So of course we reversed
Crossley's sentence, and wouldn't let him be whacked."

"Did you three appoint yourself the Court?" asked
Adams.

"Yes. I suppose it was about that. We were all
pals, you see, sir, and the rest of the house seemed satisfied that we'd take a fairish view of things, and so about
a month ago, after we'd settled that something must be
done, we just let every one know that they could appeal
against any impot or caning that those two, Manton and
Crossley, proposed to give, and we would decide. But
then, you see, sir, if any one appeals, as I said, and the
Court upholds the prefect, he gets it twice as hot.
Hundred lines instead of fifty, etcetera. We've written
it all out in a book. 'Constitution of the Court of
Appeal,' so as to have it regular, and in case we forgot."

"Good gracious, it's a constitution, is it?" asked
Adams.

David became slightly dignified.

" Yes, we thought it better to put it on an orderly footing, sir," he said, " and have everything regular, so that we shouldn't contradict ourselves, and do one thing one time and another another. Also the fellows know what to expect. And, what's more, we see that the impots are properly done if we confirm them. Canings, too. Why, one day Crossley caned a 'fellow "—David began to bubble with laughter again—" and he pretended to go to sleep and snore, and when Crossley told him it was all over, he pretended to awake, and said, ' Hullo, morning already ? ' Why, it's a farce, sir ; it's sheer childish ! What's the use of caning a fellow if you don't jolly well hurt him ? So we took that out of the prefects' hands and the impots get properly written, and fellows get properly whacked, if it's a whacking. I don't say it increases the respect in which the house holds those two little fellows at the top, but surely it's better to have some authority than none ! "

Adams thought over this for a while. The Head had apparently been given to understand by Manton that the authority of the two prefects had been wrenched out of their hands by these large, athletic upstarts of the fifth form, and that in consequence anarchy prevailed, and the house had become a sort of Medmenham Abbey. But David's account had put a perfectly different aspect on the affair, and one that was eminently reasonable. Adams was a fair-minded man, and, putting aside altogether the fact that he delighted in David and disliked Manton, he believed that David's version was the true one. It had always been his plan to let the house look after its own affairs as far as possible ; he gave it home rule, in fact, and certainly the transfer of government to the fifth form (though highly irregular and in defiance of school-rules) he believed to have been distinctly for the good of the nation. Again (a thing which bore out this

view), the first weeks of the half had been full of trouble
and worry; small boys were for ever appealing to him
against the prefects, and prefects were as constantly
invoking his authority to endorse their own lack of
it. Then, about a month ago, all these disturbances had
ceased, and Adams, with his habitual optimism, had
supposed that the house had shaken down together now.
But in the light of all this, it seemed far more reasonable
to suppose that the remedy had been brought about by
this brigandage of authority. Certainly the restoration
of peace and quiet was coincident with the establishment of this impertinent Court of Appeal, which would
have to come to an end as a recognized institution. But
during its existence it seemed to have been effective.

" Do you reverse many of the prefects' rulings ? "
asked Adams.

" Oh no, sir, not now," said David, anxious to do such
justice as could be done to those two impotent figure-
heads. " You see, neither of them liked their silly
rulings reversed, and they've become much more sensible. But you simply can't have a prefect looking in
your study when you're out, and wanting to cane you
because he finds a pipe there. Fancy Frank or Cruikshank doing a scuggish, low-down trick like that ! "

" You seem rather fond of that instance," said Adams.

" Yes sir, because it's so jolly typical," said David.

Adams got up.

" I'm considering what to say to the Head," he remarked. " I shall certainly tell him there's another
side to the question, besides Manton's."

" Oh, ripping ! " said David cordially. " I felt sure
you'd see it."

" I suppose you enjoyed the Court of Appeal a good
deal ? " he asked.

" Rather, sir," said David. " I should think we did.

Wish you could have heard one of the trials, with us
three on the bench, and Manton as defendant, and some
junior as plaintiff. You see, sir, Manton and Crossley
consented to it all; that's another point in our favour,
isn't it? Gregson planned all the ritual, because his
pater's a real judge in Appeal Courts, and we call each
other ' My learned brother Crabtree ' or ' Blaize,' for of
course there are no nicknames or Christian names in
Court. It's all quite serious; there's no rag about it.
We were thinking of appointing a permanent counsel to
plead for plaintiffs——"

Adams laughed.

"David, you don't suppose that the Court of Appeal is
going to be allowed to remain in existence?" he asked.

"That's as you wish, sir," he said. "But——"

"Well?" asked Adams.

"Nothing, sir. I was only thinking that there'll be
rather rows again."

"I hope not," said Adams. "That's exactly what
you and fellows like you have got to prevent."

"But how can we if you're going to stop it?" asked
David.

"In hundreds of ways: by backing the prefects up
without overriding them. You're sensible enough to
know that."

David considered this.

"Is the Head sick about it, sir?" he asked.

"He's never sick about anything till he's in full possession of the facts. He was prepared to be uncommonly
sick, when he had only heard the other side. In fact,
he said something about giving you another lesson
with regard to obeying authorities. But after what
you've told me I don't think you need be alarmed."

"Oh, I'm not," said David. "Of course he'll see
there's another side to it, same as you've done. Some-

thing had to happen when we got Manton and Crossley instead of Frank and Cruikshank."

At this moment a small and completely soaked boy burst into the room, not seeing Adams, who was sitting behind the door, but only David.

"Letter for you, Blaize," he said. "Oh, and I want to appeal. Sorry, sir, I didn't see you."

"You do now, Jevons," said Adams. "So go on, tell Blaize what the appeal's about."

"Well, sir, somebody put my sponge on the top of Manton's door, made a booby-trap, and because it's my sponge he says I'm responsible unless I find out who put it there."

Adams nodded to David.

"Go on, learned brother Blaize," he said.

"Notice in writing, Jev," he said.

He had seen the handwriting of his letter, and tore it open.

"Oh, I say, how ripping!" he said. "Frank's mother's ill, and is ordered out of England for Christmas—at least, it's beastly that she's ill—but Frank wants to know if he can stay with us for a week. I say, Jev, you're awfully wet, aren't you? I mean, you couldn't get much wetter, so I wonder if you'd take a tellywag just down to the office."

"Rather. And I'll put my appeal in your study, shall I?"

"Yes."

"Right. I'll be back in a second if you'll have your tellywag ready."

"Is the telegram to Frank saying he can come?" asked Adams.

"Yes, sir."

"Then hadn't you better write to your father first? It might not be convenient."

The impulsive David had already written " Ripping :
stay as long as you can," but he paused.

" Oh well, I suppose it would be best, sir," he said;
" I wish you hadn't thought of it."

David got up to go to his study, and write the note
which was so far outstripped by his desire.

" And may I talk to Bags and Plugs about the Court
of Appeal, sir ? " he said.

" Certainly. You can talk it over with Manton too,
if you like. In fact, I rather recommend it."

Adams's recommendation seemed to be rather sensible
when David thought over it, though not perhaps strictly
in accordance with Adams's idea in suggesting it. It
would give the Court an opportunity perhaps of finding
out what Manton had said to the Head, and, should
Manton not choose to tell them, it was easy to threaten,
as a counter-move, that the Court, when called upon,
as it undoubtedly would be, to appear before the Head,
would give a highly coloured account, strictly based
upon facts, of what had led to its formation. Also they
could put before Manton and Crossley a very depressing picture of what their position would be if the
Court was dissolved, and, privately, chose not to back
up their restored authority. It required but small
imagination to picture the status of those two unfortunate prefects if they had to enforce discipline in the
house without the support of what had been the Court.

Bags and Gregson had just come in from their run,
and Gregson, being in his bath and in the superior position of having no clothes on, could take reprisals by
water on David's having refused to go out. David, in
fact, had to dodge a soaking sponge thrown at him,
before he had time to begin to explain.

" Oh, *paw* a minute," he said. " There's a damned
—an awful serious thing happened, Plugs. The Head

knows all about the Court of Appeal, and it's goin' to
be gone into."

" Rot," said Gregson, filling his sponge again. " Now
who wouldn't go out for a sweat, David ? "

" 'Tisn't rot," shrieked David, snatching up a towel
to shield himself. " I swear it isn't. While you brutes
have been having an innocent happy sweat along the
road this nice weather, I've been jawed by Adams.
It's a solid fact. We're all going to be hauled up before
the Head, and he was disposed to be uncommonly sick
about it, so Adams said. Do shut up being funny with
sponges."

" Right oh," said Plugs, " if you swear you're not
lying."

" Swear ! " said David. " Hurry up and dress, and
come to my study, because you and I and Bags have
to talk. It's—it's a welter of politics."

The Court accordingly met in about ten minutes'
time in David's study, where he had made tea for them,
and where, on the table, lay Jevons's appeal. He laid
before the other two all his talk with Adams, repro-
ducing it with laudable accuracy.

" And as it's a dead cert that we shall appear before
the Head," he finished up, " we've got to agree exactly
what we say. We mustn't give different accounts
of it."

Bags caressed what he hoped was going to be a
moustache.

" Of course not," he said. " We've just got to say
what's happened. Truth, whole truth, and nothing but."

" Oh, I didn't mean we were to make things up,"
said David, " but the only question is, how much we tell
the Head. I vote for a conference—Adams suggested
it—with Manton and Crossley, and see if we can't let
each other down easily."

" Compromise out of Court ? " suggested Plugs.

" Yes : something of the kind. We can give them away hopelessly by saying how inefficient they were, and they can give us away by saying that we have undermined the prefects' authority. Don't you see ? It might all be toned down a bit."

" That's no use," said Bags, " if Manton's given us away already."

" But that's just what we don't know," said David. " I vote we try to get Manton to tell us what he told the Head. He may not have told him much ; he may have said it was an amicable sort of arrangement. On the other hand, he may have told him that our object was to undermine prefects' authority. Well, as I told Adams, there's another side to that ; we generally supported it, except when it was manifestly unfair. I want to know what Manton told him. That we have put ourselves above the prefects is true, but we did it in the cause of order, though of course we all enjoyed it frightfully."

" And the house accepted us," said Bags.

" Lot the Head will care for that ! I want to get Manton and Crossley to come and talk. Crossley doesn't matter, but Manton anyhow, as he's already seen the Head. You see, when the Head has us up, we can tell him a lot if we choose. He'll ask us for our account of it. Manton'll see that. He isn't a fool, though he is such a squirt."

With Plugs as well as Bags, David was the master-mind, and after a few minutes Bags went to Manton's study, and quite politely asked him to come round and confer with the Court.

Manton rather liked this : he promised himself a pleasant time in telling the Court that the Head was going into the whole matter himself, and that he had nothing more to do with it. He was prepared to be maliciously civil and courteous, and to express his regret the Court had made such an ass of itself as its spontaneous generation implied. He thought it would be rather fun, and came very blandly, with his spectacles on, and a book that he was reading. His finger kept his place in a cursory manner.

" Here I am," he said. " Hullo Blaize ! Hullo Gregson ! Yes ; the Court of Appeal. It wasn't I who went to the Head about it, you know ; it was that little fellow, Blaize's friend, who let it out. What's his name ? I forget."

" Oh, Jevons," said David.

" Yes, Jevons told the Head about it, and so of course the Head asked me more. He put it rather nicely : he said it was my business to tell him about it, as head of the house."

David was seated between his two learned brothers, just as if a regular Court was going on.

" Oh, we know about Jevons," he said. " We can leave Jevons out."

" Waive ! " said Plugs formally.

" Yes, we can waive Jevons," said David, " as my learned brother suggests."

Manton gave a little cackle of laughter.

" I shouldn't wonder if you had to waive everything," he observed pleasantly.

" Oh, we're not going to waive you just yet, if you count for anything," retorted David. " But perhaps you don't count for much."

Bags suddenly laughed in a hoarse manner.

" I beg pardon, brother Blaize," he said.

" Right oh, brother Crabtree, but just contain yourself. Well, Manton, you've been to the Head with your version, and next we go to the Head with ours.

We can make it pretty sultry for you if we choose, and
we shouldn't mind doing it a bit.   But it all depends on
what you have told the Head.   That's what we should
like to know."

Manton still felt in a very superior position.   All he
had told the Head was quite true—namely, that these
three fifth-form boys put themselves in a position above
the prefects, so that any order or punishment by the
two sixth-form boys in the house could be appealed
against, and if they thought proper could be reversed.
The Head had been extremely grave about it, and at
present there was no doubt in Manton's mind that he
was going to uphold the authority of the prefects in a
summary manner, and probably make it very hot for
those who had set themselves above it.   He felt quite
secure and comfortable, and smiled in rather a lofty
manner.

" I dare say the Head will tell you as much of what
I said as he thinks good for you," he observed.   " But
I really don't see why I should.   You see he takes the
view that prefects are not to be dictated to by two or
three members of the fifth form.   Bad precedent, you
know; it might lead to a couple of fellows out of the
fourth form dictating to you.   Jevons and a friend
might make a super-Court of Appeal.   Rather funny
that would be."

David passed the ghost of a wink to Gregson.   He
wanted to draw Manton on a little further, before he
unmasked his batteries.   It required some control to
assume an attitude of humility, when delicious sentences were beginning to seethe in his brain.   But it
was heavenly to see Manton's malicious little eyes
beaming at him through his spectacles, and notice
what an awful scug he looked with his hair, rather long
behind, lying outside his collar.   He gave a sigh.

" I say, I'm afraid we're in for it," he said disconsolately.

Manton let his mouth expand into an odious smile.

" Yes, I should say you were," he observed. " You see the Head's view is that the authority of prefects is an institution which has his support, and he doesn't quite see why it should be taken away by three fellows in the fifth. He asked me all sorts of questions, and so I had to give him a pretty full account. I should make a clean breast of it, I think, if I were you."

David could stand this no longer. He felt that he must burst if he had to listen to any more of Manton's advice.

" You say you gave him a pretty full account," he said, " though you have not chosen to tell us what it was. Well, I shouldn't wonder if we made it a bit fuller for you. I beg your pardon, brother Crabtree——"

Bags was leaning back, looking dreamily at Manton.

" Learned brother Gregson," he observed, " do you remember one day how Mr. Manton wanted to whack a little boy called Babbington, and how he had to call in Mr. Crossley to help ? "

Plugs assumed a portentous air.

" Yes, brother Crabtree," he said, " and how soap-bubbles came out of Mr. Manton's kettle, though he had not meant to wash."

David chimed in.

" And we all remember, my learned brother," he said, " how the house was a perfect bear-garden for the first month of this term before we started our worshipful Court, and how——"

David turned to Manton.

" Perhaps you didn't tell the Head that," he said. " We shall. We shall tell him how you couldn't get lines done for you, till we enforced the authority you hadn't got. We shall say how you walk round the house in slippers, and when you get back to your own fuggy studies you daren't walk straight in for fear of finding a booby-trap come down on your mangy heads. Jolly wise precaution, too, on your part. We shall tell the Head all that."

David licked his lips, as he warmed to his work. He took Jevons's appeal off the table in front of him.

" I shall take this to the Head, and read it him," he said. " Just listen : pretty dignified position for you, isn't it ? 'To the Court of Appeal. Please, Blaize, Manton got an awful soaker because somebody else put my sponge on the top of his door, which soused him; and because it was my sponge he says he'll whack me unless I find out who did it and tell him, which isn't fair, because it's not my business. So I appeal. M. C. Jevons.' "

Manton was getting a little rattled. Otherwise he would not have done anything so foolish as try to grab this paper. David whisked it away.

" I shall say, too, that you tried to get hold of this," he said. " Better sit down, Manton. That's right. And I shall tell him that your notion of authority is to look in a fellow's private drawer when he's out, to see if you can nail a pipe."

" I never did," said Manton wildly. " That was Crossley."

" Oh then, I suppose Crossley will explain that," said David. " Of course it may all be stale news to the Head, since you gave him a pretty full account, but I'll just see if the Head happened to listen to that part. You see, we don't in the least mind telling you what we're going to say to the Head, though you're too superior to tell us what you said. I've told Adams

about it already, and he thinks you're an awfully good
prefect, of course. And then, you see," concluded
David cheerfully, " when we've told him all that really
happened, why shouldn't we make up a lot that didn't ?
Probably you did the same. Gosh, the Head will have
a wonderful high opinion of you before I've done. I
shouldn't wonder if it isn't more than he can bear, and
he jolly well breaks down and sobs and kneels and gives
thanks that he has such a ripping couple of prefects in
this house, to keep us all in order."

" Well, you needn't be sarcastic about it," said
Manton.

" Yes, I need, because you began about having a
fourth-form Court of Appeal to override us. You think
that it's only you who can be so damned sarcastic and
superior, and give any garbled account you like to the
Head——"

" It wasn't garbled."

" It must have been, or do you suppose that a sensible
chap like the Head could have taken your side ? Perhaps you didn't invent things, but I swear you left out
some jolly important ones, like your not being able to
cane a cheeky junior without getting Crossley to help
you, and then whacking him on the shin instead. You
should have seen Adams shaking when I told him about
it. And I bet you said we set ourselves in opposition
to you. That's a lie. We backed your authority up
except when you made such utter squirts of yourselves that we couldn't. We helped you, you goat !
We did for you what you couldn't do for yourselves !
Lord, it makes me hot to talk to a chap like you. Go
on, Bags—I mean, Brother Crabtree."

Manton was beginning to present so ludicrous an
appearance that learned brother Blaize could hardly
prevent bubbling with laughter, which would have

spoiled the forcibleness of the situation. His finger no longer kept his place in his book; his tight little mouth no longer complacently smiled, but had fallen open in dismay at David's surprising remarks. And learned Brother Crabtree, with his suave style and slow sentences, did not reassure him.

"You see, there's nothing like fair play, Manton," said Bags. "I take it that you agree. And, as you've had an uninterrupted innings with the Head, and have run up a good score against us, I'm sure it is only proper that we should have our turn. Now, you were not wise in refusing to tell us what you had said to the Head; but the time for that is past now, and even if you wanted to, I don't suppose we should listen to you. It was foolish of you, because you make us guess what it was, and naturally we guess that you made up a lot of lies, since we think that is the sort of thing you would do. So when you leave us now, which will be very soon, we shall make up some rippers about you and Crossley—really awful things, you know. I began making some up when Brother Blaize was addressing you. They are beauties."

Gregson took up the tale with a wink at David in the eye away from Manton.

"And yet I don't know that we need bother to make things up, Brother Crabtree," he said. "It's easier to say just a few of the things that really happened. We will tell the Head the sort of thing that goes on in Manton's study when he thinks all the house are at preparation."

Now Manton, for all his feebleness and ineffectiveness as a prefect, was as blameless as the Ethiopian.

"But I don't know what you mean," he said.

Gregson gave a little laugh which he transformed into a cough.

"Oh really?" he said. "But the Head will soon know what we mean. David—I mean Brother Blaize knows."

David had caught the wink correctly. He put on a scornful face.

"Oh, *that!*" he said. "Yes, disgusting. You should be more careful about shutting your door, Manton. I and Gregson were walking about the house in slippers, following the example of the sixth form."

"But I don't know what you're talking about," said Manton.

"Right oh. We won't talk about it any more—to you."

It was in vain that Manton assured himself that, as was perfectly true, his conscience was as clear as noonday, for this wicked and subtly-acted fraud on the part of those fifth-form devils made him uncomfortable in spite of himself. And though he had not told the Head anything false about this beastly Court of Appeal, he certainly had not put their side of the case before him with the directness that it now appeared they were going to do on their own behalf. He had not, for instance, said that the Court of Appeal propped up, endorsed, supported the authority of himself and Crossley far more than they overrode it, though it was perfectly true (as he had told the Head) that they arrogated the supreme authority to themselves. Nor had it occurred to him to tell the Head that he and Crossley were quite incompetent to maintain discipline, that they got ragged to the point of having soap put in their kettles, that they toured the house in slippers. Truly the supplement to his tale was likely to be as voluminous as the tale itself.

Then David rose.

"Well, I don't think we need detain you," he said

politely, " in fact, we've got a good deal to talk over among ourselves. Thanks awfully for coming. I expect we shall all meet again at the Head's. That's all, then."

But Manton was not quite sure that this was all. Various remarks by one or other of the members of the Court were beginning to cause him somewhat acute internal questionings. In especial he disliked the fact that Adams was in possession of the Court's side of the case, and as likely as not would give the Head the benefit of it.

" Perhaps we might discuss it all a little more," he said, with a faint air of condescension still lingering about him. " I can—well, go to the Head, because he told me that if I had anything more to tell him, I was to. I might say—I really should be quite glad to—that Crossley and I didn't want to get you into trouble."

" Oh, that's all right," said David cheerfully. " Don't bother about that; you've got us into no trouble at all. I expect we shall come out perfectly right."

" But the Head was awfully sick about it," said Manton. " He laid a good deal of stress on the fact that you did set yourselves up as an authority superior to the prefects."

" I expect I'll make that all square," said David. " I dare say I shall put our case as strongly as you put yours. Adams will have done the same too, I'm pretty sure. Of course we thought we might let you down more easily if you told us what you told the Head, and, after all, we gave you an opportunity of doing so. But you didn't take it, so that's finished."

" Well, I think perhaps I was wrong not to tell you," said Manton.

" I'm sure you were," assented Bags warmly. " Isn't

it an awful pity one doesn't think of that sort of thing sooner ? "

" And so, if you like, I'll tell you now," said Manton, finishing his sentence.

" Oh, we don't care a hang either way," said David. " If you wish you may tell us, but it'll be because you ask us if you may. We don't want to hear it."

" But I thought you asked me to," said this dismal prefect.

" We did, but it's no use to us now. We've made up our minds what to do."

" Well, shall I tell the Head that you did often support the authority of the sixth ? It might make him less sick with you."

" Rubbish ! " said Gregson. " You're proposing these things now simply because you want us not to tell the Head our side of it. Is that the reason, or not ? "

" I think it would——"

" ' Yes ' or ' no,' " said Brother Blaize in a terrible voice.

" Yes."

" Why not have asked for mercy sooner then, instead of giving yourself all these airs ? Get on ! "

It was a very unstuffed Manton who was left at the end of this recital, for though he had not told the Head anything palpably false, yet the picture the Head must have drawn of the whole affair was about as erroneous as it could possibly be. He had let the Head assume that the authority of the prefects over the house was complete and satisfactory until the Court of Appeal set itself up, and he had certainly not said that the Court in most cases endorsed their authority and saw that their orders were obeyed. All this was drawn from him by cool and ruthless questioning.

At the end David gave a long whistle.

" Well, 'pon my word, you are in a mess," he said.
" I'm not at all sure that I shouldn't resign my prefect-
ship if I were you before the Head kicked me out.
You are the deuce of a hand at *suppressio veri*—ain't
that it, Brother Gregson ? Why, there isn't an ounce
of truth that you haven't suppressed. And it's all
as full of *suggestio*—er——"

" *Falsi*," said Bags.

" Yes, *suggestio falsi*, as it can stick. The best thing
you can do is to go and talk it over with Crossley, and
then come back and tell us what you propose to tell
the Head. If you don't make a clean breast of it to
him, and let him see that he's only got a garbled—yes,
I said garbled—version of it at present, you may be
sure we shall. And when you've made up your minds,
come back and tell us. Tap at the door first."

The unstuffed Manton rose.

" Yes, I'll do that," he said. " Er—thanks."

The door closed behind him, and David, who was
growing extremely red in the face with *suppressio risus*,
turned over and buried his face in the sofa-cushions,
kicking wildly in the air. The other learned brethren
stifled themselves lest Manton should hear them, and
for a few minutes the Court of Appeal writhed in the
agonies of silent mirth.

" O Lord," said David at length, " I didn't know
there was such richness in the world ! To think that
half an hour ago that little squirt thought he had us on
toast. Toast's there all right, but 'tisn't we who are
on it. And now he's making up another version which
is ours, and wanting to know if that'll satisfy us for
him to go to the Head with. O Lord ! "

" Too much mercy to let him," said Bags.

" Not a bit of it. It's much more effective if Manton puts our side of it to the Head."

"But what if he doesn't tell the Head all he says he's going to ?" asked Plugs.

"He must. The only way he can save his face is by going to him at once, before Adams can. Oh, there's toast enough ! Besides, when the Head sees us, we can soon tell if Manton's given him the correct version."

David, as President of the Court, was summoned to the Supreme Presence next day.

"I've been into the question of the Court of Appeal," said the Head, "and what Manton told me last night puts a different complexion on it from what I had heard before. Of course the court must be dissolved at once, Blaize, you understand that ?"

"Yes, sir."

A faint smile spread over the Head's face as he looked at the big, jolly boy.

"And tell your—your learned brethren," he said, "what I say. The authorities in your house are Mr. Adams and the prefects, and there are no other authorities. But I believe now that on the whole the court meant well, and I am quite certain it enjoyed itself immensely. That particular enjoyment, I am afraid, must cease ; but I want it—the court, that is —to continue meaning well in a private capacity, and to support the prefects' authority, though it may no longer enforce or reverse their orders. And, Blaize, this is for your private ear alone : I think the Court probably did very useful work. But we mustn't have any more courts. That's all, then. How are you getting on ? Well, I hope, and Mr. Adams seems to think so. Heard anything from your friend Maddox lately ? "

"Gosh, what a brick ! " said David to himself, as he went out. . . .

CHAPTER XV

DAVID was lying on his back under the big eim-tree near the cricket pavilion one Sunday afternoon in mid-June. By him, upright and attentive, sat the faithful Bags, listening and occasionally playing the part of Greek chorus (that is to say, putting in short, appropriate reflections) to a quantity of surprising information. Both boys wore the white tie characteristic of prefects on Sunday, for both had got their promotion into the lower sixth at Easter, and were colleagues of the inefficient Manton and Crossley. Those two young gentlemen, it may be remarked, were vastly relieved to have the burden of authority taken off their somewhat feeble shoulders, and David and Bags (particularly David) ruled the house with genial exuberance, and, when necessary, a rod of iron.

Just now both the iron and the exuberance were relaxed, and David lay there in an abandonment of physical laziness. His straw hat, with cricket eleven oolours, was tilted over the top part of his face, so as to shield his eyes from the speckles and sparkles of sun that filtered through the canopy of leaves above him, and his mouth and chin alone were visible. His long legs were stretched out in front of him, showing a white hiatus between a despondent sock and the end of his trousers, and a persistent fly kept settling there, an attention which he acknowledged by dabbing at it with the other ankle.

" 'Tisn't as if I was a little boy any longer," he said.
" When a fellow is close on seventeen, as you and I
are, it's time he began to realize that he's grown up.
Why, my mother was only seventeen when she married."

" But do you propose to marry at seventeen ? "
asked Bags with sarcastic allusion to the conversation
that had gone before. " Where'll she live ? She can't
very well sleep in dormitory."

David gave a little spurt of laughter, and the sun
shone on his white teeth, and down his red throat.
But he quickly became grave again.

" Is that funny ? " he said. " If so, I suppose I'd
better laugh, though I wish I saw the point. Who
said I was going to marry ? O gosh, what a clipper she
is ! "

" And it's not much more than a fortnight ago that
you thought all girls were rotten," said Bags.

" More fool me, then, and more fool you for still
thinking so.   Lord, I wish I was really grown up, quite
old, I mean, nineteen or twenty. I say, do you think
she looked at me at all in chapel this morning ? "

" I don't think so," said Bags cheerily, " and I was
watching her pretty nearly all the time, as I knew you
would ask. Oh, yes, she did once, when you began to
sing Amen before it was time. But she looked away
again at once."

" Ha, ha," said David in a dry, speaking voice, not
laughing at all. " Well, she's bound to come to the
Old Boys' match, isn't she ? And I don't see how she
can help noticing if I take any wickets."

" Nor if you get constantly hit out of the ground,"
said Bags.

David found he agreed with this.

" You're a jolly sympathetic sort of pal," he said at
length.

Bags had a certain defence.

"Well, it seems so queer of you," he said. "It's rot if you're going to think about and talk about nothing else than a female girl. Besides, she must be frightfully old. I shouldn't wonder if she was twenty. Why, your mother had been married three years when she was as old as that."

"Yes, and had had two children and had also died," said David rather embarrassingly.

"Oh, sorry; I didn't know," said Bags. "But about your girl now," he went on hurriedly. "How do you know she isn't engaged already? She easily might be; she's awfully pretty. I grant you that: at least, I suppose she is, though both you and I used to think that all girls looked exactly alike."

"Idiots! Idiots we were!" said David, kicking wildly in the air.

"And what are you going to do?" continued Bags, who always saw the practical issues. "Are you going to tell her how frightfully keen you are on her?"

"I expect she guesses," said David solemnly. "She came to tea with me twice in my study, and it's rather marked for a fellow to ask a don's daughter to tea twice in the same half, specially if she comes the first time."

"Well, but you didn't say anything sweet and moonlightly to her," said Bags. "You talked about nothing but cricket. Besides, Plugs and I were there the whole time, and so was Mother Gray."

David drew a long breath, and stretched his arms and legs out in the form of one crucified till elbows and knees were taut.

"Violet Gray!" he said, dwelling on the syllables. "Did you ever hear such a jolly name? And it's just like her; it's a slim, honey-coloured-hair name."

Bags groaned slightly. It really was appalling for David to be in this deplorable state.

"Violet Gray," he said, in a business-like manner. "H'm, Violet Gray! I think it sounds better than Violet Blaize."

David sat up.

"Bags, you don't understand one single thing about it," he said. "How can I explain? She's just the most wonderful and beautiful thing that ever happened. I wonder if Frank will understand. I shall tell him, but nobody else. He's coming down end of next week."

"He'll probably cut you out," said Bags, who thought a bracing treatment was best for his idiotic friend.

"Not he: we're pals. Of course he could if he wanted, since any girl would fall in love with Frank straight off, if he held up his little finger. Jove, I'd give anything to see the 'Varsity cricket-match this week. And to think that in final house-match last year I was in at one end, and a Cambridge cricket blue the other."

"Well, that happened to everybody else in the house-eleven," said Bags, "since Maddox went in first and carried his bat!"

David laughed.

"So it did," he said. "I'll back you against any one in the world, Bags, for bald literal prosaicness. You haven't got an ounce of imagination. You see things just exactly as they happen. You've less of romance than—than a horse-roller," he said, looking round for inspiration and seeing that useful article with its shafts in the air.

"Perhaps I have, perhaps I haven't," said Bags. "But it's perfectly true I don't jaw about it. Never mind that. Look here : supposing you might either kiss Violet Gray, twice, we'll say, or see the Oxford and Cambridge match, which would you choose ? "

" Depends on the match," said David. " Of course if Frank was going to make a century, and I were to see him do that, I don't know what else I could choose. O Lord, but fancy kissing her, though ! I wish you wouldn't ask such stumpers. But that's you all over. You want me to be practical, and say which I should like best. But I just can't ! I—I feel like a dog which is being whistled to from opposite directions by two fellows it loves. Doesn't know which way to go."

Bags sniffed scornfully.

" Oh, you've not got it so desperately, if you only feel like that," he said.

David shut his eyes and made his mouth tight with an air of martyr-like determination.

" I should choose kissing her," he said, " because Frank could tell me all about the match afterwards, and besides, it would all be reported in the *Sportsman,* and I could read about it. But I couldn't read about my kissing her in the paper; at least, I don't know in which. Oh Lord, but fancy missing seeing Frank putting perfectly straight balls away to the leg boundary in the 'Varsity match, and then scratching his ear, as he always does when he hits a boundary, as if wondering what on earth has happened to the ball. I don't know which I should choose. I Don't Know."

David looked mournfully round for inspiration and lay down again.

" After all, I wonder whether it's worth while doing anything or getting anything," he said with a sudden lugubrious accent. " I tried to think it would be a damned fine—jolly fine thing to get into the sixth, and yet before a month was out we both got absolutely

accustomed to it. It's been just the same about getting into school-eleven—oh, well, not quite, because I
do enjoy that most awfully still. But I dare say it
won't last. Why, a year ago, if I had been told that I
might have any two things I wanted, I should have
chosen to get into the sixth and the eleven. It didn't
seem that there was anything more to want."

"I should have thought you would have chosen that
Maddox shouldn't leave," remarked Bags.

"No use wishing that : he had to. Besides, if he
hadn't, he wouldn't be in the Cambridge eleven now.
And you can't choose anything that clips your pal's
wings. 'Tisn't my expression; Adams said it the other
day when he was talking to me about Jev."

"Didn't know Jevons had any wings," said Bags.

"Nor did I. But Adams seems to think so. I say,
Adams is rather a wise sort of man, and he sees just
about three times as much as I thought. Oh, and he
told me Hughes had passed into Sandhurst. He must
have become a decent chap again.'!

"They do," said Bags.

"Jolly glad ! About Adams : I always imagined that
as long as he wasn't bothered, he didn't mind much
what happened, short of a public row. But I believe
his funny old eye is on us more than we think."

"And much more than it used to be ! " said Bags.
" You know the bizz about the Court of Appeal woke
him up tremendous. There was a regular Insti- and
Consti-tution going on in the house under his very nose,
and he had never suspected it. Up till then he didn't
bother about what any one did as long as there wasn't
a row. You know, David, the house was a perfect hell
about the time you and I came here, and Adams hadn't
a notion of it.'!

David sat up quickly.

"I dare say," he said, " but Frank kept all that away from me. Anyhow, the house is pretty well all right now. There is nothing to make a row, no smoking, no cribbing, no filth. It's ever so much more cheery to be like that. And just think that less than three years ago, Bags, you and I were just beginning as two dirty little fags. What a bag of tricks has happened since then! What were we talking about? Oh, Jevons. Adams was awfully decent to me about it; made me blush. He said I'd taught Jev to be clean—that's true. When he first used to fag for Frank, I wanted to wash the teacups again when his filthy little paws had touched them—and, oh yes, he said I'd cured him of swearing, which perhaps was true also, though it seemed rather bad luck on him to be whacked by me for swearing, when, as Adams said, he'd picked it up from me. So I had to cure myself as well, which I've almost done. But then I couldn't whack myself when I swore, so Jev got on quicker than I did."

" You're not getting on much now," remarked Bags, patiently listening.

" Yes, I am. Shut up; I'm just coming to the wings. Adams said I was fussing over him too much, and tying a string to his leg, and clipping his wings, when it was time for him to fly about as he dam pleased. (Lord, Jev would have got whacked for that!) But, you see, he's turning out rather a fetching kid—good-looking, you know, and all that, and I'm not going to have him taken up by some brute and spoiled. However, any one who tries will have a nasty time with me first. But I suppose Adams is right: Jev's got to begin looking after himself. I'm rather sorry in a way, though. It's good sport looking after a kid like that, and seeing it doesn't come to any harm. He's an affectionate little beggar, too, and I believe he knows it would make me pretty sick if he got into beastly ways. I say, I'm afraid I'm talking like a missionary."

" On the plains of Timbuctoo," remarked Bags.

" Yes, anywhere. Rum fellow you are, Bags. You let me jaw to any extent without yawning or telling me to shut it. But there are such a lot of frightfully interesting things that you must talk about in order to find out what you really think. Jev, for instance: I had no idea that I was a missionary till I began to jaw. By the way, my father is coming down for the Old Boys' match next week. D'you remember that awful morning when he bowled into the wrong net at Helmsworth and how ashamed I was? Funny how one changes: I should just love it if he did it again now, because it's so jolly sporting of him to try to bowl at all. My sister's coming, too, and of course Frank will be here playing for the Old Boys. What a family! They all love Frank at home; he and my father are tremendous pals: they talk about Norman and Perpendicular and Transitional till all's blue. He stayed with us most of the Christmas holidays, you know, when his mother was abroad."

David sat up again.

" Lord, what a lot of things there are!" he said appreciatively.

" Not to mention Her," said Bags.

" No. Oh, by the way, I saw her coming out of Madden's the photographer's the other day. Do you suppose she'd been done? By Jove, shouldn't I like one?"

" Well, ask her then," said Bags with infinite patience.

David knitted his forehead into a diplomatic frown.

" I couldn't straight off like that," he said. " But I might lead up to it. I might say I thought Madden took jolly good photographs, and see what she said."

"Suppose she said that she thought he didn't," said Bags wearily.

"Well, I could say that—that no one could do justice to some people. Or is that laying it on rather thick ? Oh, by the way, I've been devilish cunning. The Head told me that my last iambics were pretty rotten, and that I'd better have some private tuition, so I asked if I might go to old Gray for it. Jolly smart, that. So I'm going to drop French and have private tu with Gray, beginning to-morrow."

" 'Come into the garden, Maud,' " remarked Bags.

"What's Maud got—oh, I see, you mean Violet. Yes, that's the idea. Going in and out of the house, I'm sure to run across her. See ? Why, it's striking four. Let's go down to house."

David, as is the way of boys rising seventeen, had been growing tremendously these last six months, not in physical ways only, but in stature of the mind. It was impossible to imagine a boy less of a prig than he, or one so unweighted with the sense of duty or responsibility, but with his growth he had taken up his responsibilities quite simply and unconsciously and eagerly, without having any egoism about it. He did not, in fact, do these things and behave in a manner that made him so breezy a treasure to his house-master because he heavily realized that there were things he ought to do, and a manner in which he ought to behave, but because he obeyed unconsciously the bent of his natural instincts, which were those of a very high-spirited and excellent fellow now budding from boyhood into early manhood. He had no private meditations at all on the subject, but merely lived in active and wholesome ways and enjoyed himself immensely, and if by any chance he had come to learn what Adams really thought of him, he would have had no doubt

that his informant was just "pulling his leg." His
genial unconsciousness that he had any influence at all
was exactly that which made his influence so strong.
He had the admirable gift of not thinking about himself, but purely about the large quantity of attractive
affairs that made up life, and the number of "jolly
chaps" with whom he was associated. He had even
been known to admit that Manton and Crossley, to
counteract whose ridiculous ineffectiveness the Court of
Appeal had been founded, were decent enough, though
of course no earthly good as prefects. In the same
way, it was from no sense of conscious duty that he
had educated and still watched over Jevons : "it was
sport looking after a kid," was exactly the true account
of the trouble he had taken. Then, part of his growth,
had come this violent adoration of Violet Gray, as
natural as the strutting of the young male bird, when
first it is conscious of another sex than his. David
had suddenly perceived that though in many things
girls are "rotters," there was something about them
that made it necessary to wear button-holes, and, if
possible, make runs or take wickets for other reasons
than those generally necessary. . . .

The two boys strolled at Sunday pace down over the
hot, sunny field, which wore its air of Sabbatical and
empty leisure. May had been a wet month, and the
grass still retained the varnished freshness of spring
except where in patches it had been worn by pitches or
practice-nets. But for the last fortnight no rain had
fallen, and the light soil, quick to dry, was beginning
to get hard and give bowlers such as David the
crumbling wickets in which his soul delighted. Adams's
house had scraped through the first ties of house-
matches, for though David, on whom they relied to
thwart and discomfit their opponents, had proved on

that occasion to be extremely expensive, and quite useless as a bowler, he had in some weird fashion of his own managed to make fifty of the most awful runs ever scored, chiefly by amazing miss-hits over the heads of point and slips. He had also been badly missed off the first ball he received, which added humour to the performance, and a little later his leg-stump had been smartly hit, though without displacing the bails. (He had hailed this with a shriek of laughter.) But in the second tie played last week he had shown himself in truer colours, and had been bowled fair and square in both innings without scoring at all, but had done things with the ball that really seemed inspired by Satan. He had grown into a bowler of the googliest type, and had discovered, all for himself, that if he let his shirt-sleeve wave in the air instead of rolling it tight up round his elbow it presented a much more puzzling outline to the batsman.* On that day there had been, too, a high cross-wind, and all that most of the batsmen who were favoured with his deliveries knew was that from very far off an immense lanky figure came prancing in a curved run up to the wickets, and that from somewhere at the end of clothes hung up to dry a quavering object that was supposed to be a cricket-ball skidded through the air in such a manner that it was really impossible to tell what it was doing or what it would do. Sometimes when it looked most charged with incalculable waywardness it did nothing but bounce as an innocent and rotund ball should ; at other times (chiefly when it looked almost pathetically guile-less) it played the lowest tricks that the laws of spin permitted. It kicked out like a horse when it pitched, or it leaped nervously aside as if trying to avoid the bat :

* Later in the year, it may be remembered, the M.C.C. legislated on this subject.

in fact, the odds were that it did precisely what you didn't expect. Or, again, the demoniac Blazes would run up to the wickets with less than his usual prance, but in a slow and thoughtful manner as if he had a headache. But if the wary batsman imagined (as he not unfrequently did) that this was the prelude to a slow and thoughtful ball, he occasionally (though not always) found he was quite in error. An extremely fast and straight ball was all that the thoughtful manner meant, whereby we learn the danger of trusting to appearances. And what made all these antics the more flustering and annoying was that David, with guileless sincerity, frankly confessed that he was often by no means clear himself what the ball was going to do.

" I always mean it to do something rum," he said, " but of course it doesn't always come off, and sometimes it does just the opposite. That's such awful fun. It's all silly tosh, my bowling, you know. Comes off in house-matches sometimes, but any school team would hit me over the moon."

This perfectly sincere view of his own performance was not shared by Humphreys, the captain of the school eleven who had twice been one of David's victims, and to whom this opinion was expressed.

" But the one you bowled me with in the first innings," said that much-injured young man, " came round my legs and took the middle-stump, blast you. Didn't you mean that ? "

David put his head on one side, considering.

" Yes, I think I did," he said. " It was rather a good ball for me. I thought it might do something of the sort. Every one gets a good ball in sometimes if they go on long enough."

" Well, I wish you would keep them for school-matches," said Humphreys. " And second innings you had me with a roaring full-pitch, ninety-five miles an hour. I thought it was only eighty-five, and so I missed it by ten miles."

David laughed.

" Sorry. It was rather a fast one," he said. " I thought it had got you in the tummy. Jolly glad it was only your wicket."

" So'm I," remarked Humphreys. " Come and bathe."

Since then, every day had added to the pace of the ground, and this Sunday afternoon, as David strolled down with Bags, he looked at the turf with extreme content.

" Just my luck all over," he said, " that it should be getting into the state that suits me best for Old Boys' match. Lord, what a pity I said that! I shan't be able to send down a decent ball now. But I should love to bowl Frank. Bags, I do think about cricket so tremendously in the summer half. I lie awake making plans."

He took a short run and brought his arm over his shoulder in a complicated fashion.

" Why shouldn't I bring my arm up overhand like that," he said, " and turn my wrist over underhand ? You might say that the ball would simply fly up gently in the air and fall at my feet. But something might be done with it. You can usually do something with anything if you give your mind to it."

" Like you with Jev," remarked Bags.

" Oh, that's only Adams's rot."

He broke off and focused his blue eyes on a group of figures coming up the field towards them.

" Lord, here's Mother Gray and Violet coming," he said. " I say, is my tie straight ? Who's the man with them ? "

" Don't know. Friend of theirs probably."

" Clever fellow ! Hope they'll ask me to tea."

David had been carrying his straw hat in his hand, but put it on, in order to have the joy of taking it off to them.

" Same man who was in chapel this morning with them," said Bags in an undertone.

" Was he ? Didn't see him. Lord, doesn't she look ripping ? "

There is always some slight discomfort attached to a meeting which is seen, while yet a long way off, to be coming, a difficulty in knowing the right moment to cease being absorbed in the landscape or in intelligent conversation with your friend, and to become conscious of it in proper time to apply a suitable smile of recognition to the face. David, with his tingling heart, managed it with wonderful ill-success. He put on a brilliant smile long before it could be seen at all, and, feeling as if his cheeks would crack, took it completely off again. Then he tried to talk to Bags in a natural manner, and pointed to nothing at all away to the right. Then he proceeded to talk to Bags again much too long, and did not look up till the adorable one was but a couple of yards off. On came the smile of recognition again, and he took off his hat and dropped it. And, alas for the hope of being asked to tea, when he had picked up his hat again, the vision had already gone by, and it was only the most instantaneous return of his smile that he reaped from all those muddled manœuvres. So on they went, Bags with face red from suppressed giggles.

" What are you laughing at, you ass ? " asked David in an indignant whisper. " I don't see anything funny."

" No, you wouldn't. You were the funny man."

" What did I do ? " demanded David.

" First you grinned an awful grin miles too soon,"

said Bags. "Then you looked as grave as a judge with indigestion. Then, miles too late, you gave another awful grin and dropped your hat. Sorry you didn't get your tea, but it was too funny for anything."

David was radically incapable of ill-humour for more than a few seconds at a time, and grinned in a less awful manner.

"I never felt such a silly fool," he said. "And I'm not sure I like that man. What do you suppose they were talking about so interestedly?"

"Can't say; run back and ask them," said Bags. "I thought he looked rather a decent chap. Awfully good-looking too; a bit like Maddox."

David gave a snort of disdain.

"Like your grandmother," he observed in a withering manner.

"Which one? I've got two."

David took hold of Bags by the shoulders, and ran him down the bit of steep hill to the gate.

"The ugliest," he said. "And the fattest. And the beastliest. I say, though, it was rather a sell for me."

"Complete suck," said Bags.

There are exactly as many ways of falling in love as there are different natures in the world, and since every one, boy or man or girl or woman, falls in love off the same carpet, so to speak, on which he transacts the other affairs of life, it followed that David's first excursion into the enchanted country was made with enthusiasm and gaiety and innocence, and with that forgetfulness of himself that characterised his other ways and works. That he was in love at all, any grown-up man, who was so unfortunate as to forget what it was like to be a boy, would probably have denied, calling his feelings calf-love at the most, but

no boy, unless he was a shrivelled old man, could doubt
for a moment the genuineness of David's emotion.
It seriously threatened for the next few weeks to de-
throne the dominant passion inspired by cricket, and,
since that absolutely refused to vacate the supreme
throne, love squeezed itself in and sat beside it, so
that if David lay awake on Sunday pondering over
fresh wiles in the matter of his googlies, on Monday
the googlies would not enter his head at all, except as
shadows, and he would devote the whole of his insomnia
(which perhaps lasted half an hour) to the contemplation of the adorable Violet. At such times he would
give vent to a sound between a sigh and a groan, and
Jevons from the next bed would ask if he had tummy-
ache. Then David would say savagely, "No, you
little ass, go to sleep"; and add in a minute or two,
"Thanks for asking, Jev."

At this high level his adoration remained for a whole
month. Occasionally, as during the two days of the
Old Boys' match, he would be more absorbed in cricket
while Violet looked on from the throne of his heart,
even as she looked on from the balcony of the pavilion;
but on the day succeeding the glorious discomfiture of
the Old Boys, cricket, as an active principle in his mind,
lapsed into a state of quiescence, while Violet became
volcanic again. He did not want anything from her
(though the thought of kissing her, a wild flight of impossible fancy, sent his heart into his mouth); he only
wanted that she should be she and he an adorer: he
could have given no further account of it than that.
All his other friends, Frank and his own sister, and
Bags and Plugs, were on a different plane. He loved
Margery, he loved Frank, he esteemed and relied on
Bags, but none gave him any tremor, any sense of
excitement. But for Violet, his boyish heart was full

of a sweet tumult and confusion, whenever the enchantress came within eyeshot.

Meantime the strange young man who had roused David's suspicions on Sunday afternoon continued staying with the Grays, but his presence was accounted for, since, to David's great relief, he proved to be a cousin. He proved also, which was satisfactory, to be a man who played cricket occasionally for his county, and thus had a claim to respect, and took part in a match against the masters, playing for them. On that occasion he proceeded to hit David's bowling to all parts of the compass with the utmost ease and enjoyment, a feat that raised him in the bowler's estimation. Eventually David got him out with a ball about which Mr. Leonard Gray knew absolutely nothing, but he had been treated with wonderful contempt first. And as Gray retired he nodded in a friendly manner.

" Glad you didn't send that ball down sooner, Blaize," he said.

Then, with the suddenness of a thunderbolt, the end came. Bags brought the fateful news, while David was ecstatically employed on a model flying-machine which Frank had given him.

" Did you ever see anything so ripping ? " he shouted. " Frank sent it me this morning. It flew the whole length of hall just now. Wait till I wind it up again."

David picked up the beloved machine and began winding it.

" What's up ? " he said looking at Bags. " Anything beastly happened ? Nothing wrong in the house, is there ? "

" Oh David, I'm so sorry," said Bags.

David let go of the winder and the propeller whirred and pulled as the wheels ran round.

" Well, get on," he said.

" She's engaged to that cousin," said Bags.   " Banns
were given out yesterday at the parish church.   Plugs
told me ; his people were down and he went with them
to church instead of chapel."

David felt the world topple round him. He sat
down and turned very red in the face.

" Oh ! " was all he said.

Then Bags came a step closer.

" I say, David," he said shyly, " if you only knew
how I hate anything that hurts you. I should like to
kill that chap."

And his plain, rather goat-like face glowed with that
which had so long inspired him, namely, his affection for
David, that shy, silent passion of friendship.

David spun the propeller once or twice.

" Well, he's a jolly lucky chap," he said at length.

Then he looked at Bags and saw in his eyes just that
blind devotion that you can see in a dog's eyes, if you
understand dogs.   He got up, and put a hand on Bags's
shoulder.

" It's ripping of you to care, Bags," he said.   " I'm
no end grateful. . . . Hell ! "

CHAPTER XVI

THE school was assembled at evening chapel on the last Sunday of this summer term. To-morrow would be prize-giving, with all its attendant festivities, down to concert in the evening and another house-supper—perhaps—at Adams's in celebration of their again having won the house cricket-cup. On Tuesday the school would break up, to meet again in large numbers on Friday for the match at Lord's.

Just now the hymn after the third collect had been sung, but after that, instead of the chaplain continuing to read the prayers, the Head did so. Next him in his pew was Frank. And before the prayer for all sorts and conditions of men, there was a short pause and the silence became tense, for every one present guessed what was coming. Then the quiet, slow voice began again.

"Your prayers are requested for your friend David Blaize," it said, "who is lying dangerously ill."

Then the three remaining prayers were said, but before the final hymn was given out, there came another pause, and the Head rose. He spoke more intimately now.

"You will all want to know what news I have to give you," he said, "so before we finish the service I will tell you. I saw David Blaize just before chapel. He was quite conscious and not frightened at all. He knew quite well, for his father had told him, that he was in extreme danger. I only saw him for a minute, but I said we were going to pray for him this evening, as we have done. Perhaps you would like to hear what he said to me."

The Head paused a moment, began once, and then mastered his voice better.

"He said, 'Thanks awfully, sir. That'll do me good.'"

A little rustle and stir went round chapel, and all that any one had known of David came and stood quite close to him. Bags, sitting at the end of the seat of the sixth form, leaned forward, putting his head on his hands. Frank, who had come down an hour before, just looked at the Head, waiting.

Then the Head spoke again.

"I have told you this on purpose," he said, "to show you how he faces death, if it is that God wishes him to face. Also to show you that, as he still hopes to live, we must hope it with him in all the power that prayer gives us. But he faces death with all the—the gay courage with which he faced that which has brought him into peril of it. There are many of you who loved him, and I am among them, and we must be level with him in our courage. Now we will sing the hymn, 'Lead us, Heavenly Father, lead us.'"

The whole school, of course, knew what had happened. Two days before a young horse harnessed to a light cart, and frightened by a traction-engine, had bolted straight down the steep High Street at Marchester, full at its lower end with the crowded traffic of market-day, and the driver had been pitched off the box, so that it galloped on, unchecked and mad with fright. At the moment, David, with a bag of macaroons which he had just bought, came out of school-shop; throwing the parcel to Bags, who was with him, he had shouted out, "Catch hold, and don't eat any," and had rushed straight out into the road, taking a header, so to speak, at the horse. He had got hold of a rein, and then, still holding it, had been jerked off his feet, and the wheel of the cart had gone over him. But the horse was checked, and when they picked the boy up they found that the rein was still wrapped round his wrist.

There were severe internal injuries, not necessarily fatal, but, until several days had elapsed, every minute was critical with danger. Up till this morning all had gone well, but a few hours ago there had been disquieting symptoms, with fever and restlessness and signs of exhaustion. He had been conscious all day, and was no longer in great pain, but it was feared that nervous shock consequent on internal injury might overcome the splendid powers of rallying which he had shown at first. His father and Margery had come down the day before, but to-day they had scarcely seen him, since the utmost quiet was necessary. And an hour ago he had been told that he was in great danger. It was to this that the Head had referred.

Adams's house was nearer to where the accident happened than the school sanatorium, and he had been moved there since every extra yard was extra danger, and for two days now a strange silence, as of life in a dream, had lain over it. There had been no need for Adams to tell them not to make any noise or disturbance, for the boys crept about like mice, and no voice was raised. It seemed impossible that this should have happened to anybody, most of all that it should have happened to David. And yet in the room at the end of the passage, just beyond the baize door into Adams's private part of the house, he was lying now, midway between life and death, horribly tired, but not afraid.

Maddox waited for the Head to disrobe after service was over, just outside the chapel. The school and then the masters passed by him, but he only nodded at one and another, and still waited. At last the Head came out into the red twilight after sunset.

" Glad you waited for me, Maddox," he said. " I didn't know you were down till just before chapel."

" Is there anything more to tell than what you told us all, sir ? " he asked.

The Head took his arm.

" No, my dear fellow," he said. " It's not hopeless, you know. They don't say that."

" Would they allow me to see him, sir ? He needn't know I did. I could just look at him without his seeing me."

" You must ask the doctor about that. You got down this afternoon only ? "

" Yes, sir. I only heard this morning."

They walked on in silence a little way as far as the iron gate into the quadrangle. Then Maddox spoke again.

" He's the best chap in the world, sir," he said. " He saved me, you know. Just saved me."

The Head pressed his arm.

" Ah, that's between you and David," he said. " It's not for me to hear. But I know you love him, which is the only point. Please God, you'll have him with you many years yet. And if not, Frank, you mustn't be bitter, or think that it's a cruel ordinance that takes him away. God takes him, and we must give, even as David gave himself when he just jumped at that horse. Do you think he would have withheld himself if he had known what the result would have been ? Not a bit of it; he would have done it just the same; we both know that. His life was his, and, like the brick he is, he chose to risk it."

They walked on in silence half across the quiet quad-rangle.

" Will you come and sup with us ? " asked the Head presently. " I can give you a bed, too, if you like."

" Oh, thanks awfully, sir," said Frank, " but I think I'll go down to the house. Mr. Adams will put me up somehow. Or I shall sit up. I should like to be down there."

The Head nodded.

" I see," he said. " I quite understand. Good night then."

Maddox went out of schoolyard, and down the road to his old house. The afterglow of sunset was fading fast, the road showed grey between black hedgerows, and as he crossed the stream, the reflection of a big star wavered on the quiet, flowing water. The whole place was intensely familiar to him, part of his blood, part of his intimate life; and, passing the fives-court, he re-membered how, on a wet day not yet three years ago, he had given David and Bags elementary instruction in squash, and had walked down this same road after-wards, waiting for David to come in with a parcel for him. Now that friend of his heart lay between life and death in the house of which the lights already shone between the elm-trees. He tried to realize, and again shrank from realizing, what the loss would mean to him. He had a hundred friends alive and well, but he could not measure David by any of them. He was just David. . . .

There was no fresh news when he got to the house : he saw David's father and sister for a minute only, but was not allowed to go in to see him. After that he went into the boys' part of the house, and found that Bags was waiting up also, by permission, in the double prefects' study which he shared with David. Maddox

knew it well: it was the one he had managed to pro-
cure for himself alone the year that David came to the
school and fagged for him.

Bags was full of quiet politeness. He gave Maddox
the sofa, and, since the rest of the house had gone to
bed, suggested that he might smoke if he wished.

"Adams won't mind," he said. "It's jolly of you
to come and keep me company. You know——"

And then Bags could not speak any more at once.

"Thanks, I won't smoke," said Maddox. "You were
with David at his private school too, weren't you?"

"Yes, two years," said Bags.

"And been pals ever since. Same as me. Both of
us David's friends, I mean."

Bags forgot to be shy of this great Cambridge cricket-
blue.

"You should have seen David," he said, jerking out
the words. "He went bang for that horse, like taking a
header. I—I ought to have done it, you know. I got
out of school-shop just in front of him and stood staring."

"Oh, my God, why didn't you?" said Maddox suddenly.

"I know, it was rotten of me," he said. "But David
was so damned quick about it, you know. He just
chucked a bag of macarooms at me, and simply jumped.
And then the wheel went over him, and he was dragged
along with the rein round his wrist."

Bags gave one awful sniff and pointed to a white
paper parcel that protruded from the cupboard where
tea-things were kept.

"There they are," he said. "He told me not to eat
any. Last thing he said. And . . . and I want to
see him again so frightfully—just to see him, you know.
What a ripper! He didn't know how I liked him.
You did too. Same boat, isn't it?"

Bags had no pretence of fortitude left, and mopped his eyes.

"Damn that horse," he said. "Who'd have cared if it had killed the whole High Street, so long as David didn't put his carcase in the light? Silly—silly idiot. But—but a fellow just loves him the more for it. I keep thinking over day after day of these last five years. Do you remember when he was swished?"

Maddox nodded.

"Yes; jolly well deserved it too. And he was so sick with me afterwards when I told him so. But we made it up. David said he was sorry. Silly fool! As if he ever did anything to a pal he could be sorry for."

Bags caught his breath.

"Don't know what there was about him," he said, "but there he was. Just David, you know. And he liked you most awfully. I used to get damned jealous. Sorry if you mind."

The two sat there together while the warm night with many stars wheeled overhead above the sleeping house, talking occasionally, but for the most part in silence. Adams, who also was sitting up, came in from time to time to see them, and they would sit all three together. From the sick-room came no determining news: David was conscious and awake, and they had given him all the morphia that they dared. His temperature had not risen further, but he was very much exhausted; the question was how his strength would hold out unless he got to sleep. This Adams told them, and perhaps they talked for a little of David, recalling some incident of past days. Then Adams would leave them again to go back to David's father and sister.

But not long after midnight he came in again, having only just gone out.

" David has suddenly asked if you were here, Frank,"
he said. " He wants to see you, and the doctor thinks
you had better go to him. He is getting very restless,
and perhaps you may be able to quiet him. That's
what they want you to do. You can trust yourself ? "

Frank got up.

" Yes, sir; I know I can," he said.

The room where he lay was lit by a lamp that was
shaded from the bed, and near the head of it was standing the doctor, who nodded to Frank as he came in,
and beckoned him to the bed, putting a chair for him
by the side of it.

" David, old chap, here I am," he said.

David turned his tired eyes to him.

" Oh, I say, that's ripping," he said faintly. " But
I can't see you very well. Mayn't there be a bit more
light ? "

The doctor quietly tilted the shade round the lamp,
so that the light fell on Frank's face.

" Will that do ? " said Frank.

" Yes, rather. I wanted to see you awfully. I
wondered if you would come. I thought perhaps you
would when you knew. Frank, am I going to die ? "

Frank pulled the chair a little closer, and bent over
him.

" No," he said. " You're going to do nothing of the
sort. We can't get on without you possibly, so you've
got to get well. See ? "

The doctor came close to Frank and whispered to
him.

" Tell him he must go to sleep," he said, and stepped
back again out of sight.

" And to get well," continued Frank, " you've got
to go to sleep and bring your strength back. David,
don't you remember our two beds at the end of dormi-

tory ? Well, think yourself back in yours with me in the one next you, and imagine it's time to go to sleep. It's quite easy, you know. Imagine it's that jolly evening after our house-match last year, when you were so tired you fell asleep without undressing."

" Yes, I remember," said David.

He was silent a little, but his eyes were still wide.

" I say, would it bore you awfully to hold my hand ? " he said. " You're so strong and fit and quiet. I might get some. I don't know. Am I talking rot ? "

" No, not a bit. There ! "

Frank fitted his hand into David's, which lay like a sick child within it.

" Yes, ripping," said he, a little drowsily. " Sure it's not an awful bore ? "

" It's a frightful bore," said Frank.

David smiled.

" You didn't get a rise out of me," he said.

" Shall have another try before long," said Frank. " Comfortable ? "

" Rather."

David lay for some ten minutes still wide-eyed, but quiet. Then his eyelids fluttered, closed and opened again.

" Awfully comfortable," he said. " I wanted just you to tell me what to do. I did so want you to come."

David's eyelids dropped again, and the doctor came round to Maddox's side.

" Sit quite still," he whispered, " and don't speak to him again."

" Sure it doesn't bore you ? " asked David once more.

Again there was silence, and the two, the friend and the doctor, remained absolutely still for some five minutes. Then from the bed came a long sigh. David's head rolled a little sideways on the pillow, and after that came the quiet, regular breathing. Then the doctor whispered once more to Maddox.

" You may have to sit like that with your arm out for hours," he said. " We'll try to make you comfortable presently. Can you manage it ? "

" Why, yes," said he.

The doctor quietly left the room, but came back soon after with pillows, and, as well as he could, propped up Maddox's outstretched arm. Then he spoke to the nurse who was to sit up, and came back to the bed and looked at David a moment, listening to his regular breathing.

" I'm going to get a bit of sleep now," he whispered to Frank, " but I'm afraid you won't. You must stop just as you are. If he lets go of your hand you must still sit there in case he wakes and asks for you. If he says anything, answer him as if he was in his dormitory, and you in the bed next him. You're in charge."

It was a couple of hours before David moved. Then he turned a little in bed.

" Frank," he said.

" Oh, shut up and go to sleep," said Frank. " 'Tisn't morning."

" Right oh ! " said David.

All sensation had gone from Maddox's arm ; it was quite numb up to the shoulder, and it was only with his eyes that, presently after, he knew that David had let his hand slip from his own. Then very gently he withdrew it, and it fell helplessly on to his knees.

David slept on through the hour before dawn when the flame of vitality burns dim and the dying loose their hold on life, until through the curtains the pale light of morning looked in, dimming the lamp-light. Outside the twitter of birds began, and the hushed sounds of life stole about within the house, and the nurse moved quietly to and fro in the room, setting things in order for the day. She brought Frank a cup of tea and some bread and butter, and he ate and drank without moving from the bedside. Before long the doctor paid his promised visit, but there was nothing for him to do, now that sleep had come to David. The immediate necessity was fulfilled, and beyond that there was no need to look at present. Only Hope, the little white flame which had burned so dim and had come so near to being quenched the evening before, shone more bravely.

All that morning Maddox sat by David's bed as he slept. It was he who had brought to him, through the tie of their love and David's instinctive obedience to his suggestion, the sleep that had been so imperative a need, and the sunny morning grew broad and hot as he dozed sometimes, but oftener watched, filled with a huge and humble exultation of happiness that he had been able to help David. And when David woke, as he did, a little after noon, it was the best of all. For even while his eyes were yet scarcely unclosed, he spoke just one word—Frank's name, still sleepily.

" Oh, go to sleep," said Frank, just as he had said it twelve hours before. " No early school."

But this time David reasserted himself a little.

" 'Course not," he said. " But I've slept ages and —and I want something to eat."

The beaming nurse stepped to the bedside.

" I'll bring you some beef-tea in a minute," she said. " Lie quite still."

David turned his head.

" Why, it's quite morning," he said.

" Absolutely," said Frank.

" And I've slept ever since you told me we were in

dormitory together," he said. "How long ago was that?"

"Oh, about twelve hours," said Frank.

"And you've sat here all the time?"

"Think so."

"Oh, I say! And just because you thought I might want you."

David's eyes were bright and untired again: there was life shining behind them, young life that may still be feeble as the snowdrops raising their frail heads above the ground on some sunny morning of February are feeble. But they answer to the beckoning of spring, not, like late autumn blossoms, feeling the chill of the winter that approaches.

Frank leaned over him.

"Yes, I thought you might want me," he said; "but also I couldn't go away. I wanted you."

David smiled at him.

"I was pretty bad yesterday, wasn't I?" he asked.

"Yes, pretty bad."

"I knew I must be, because I didn't care what happened. I do to-day. I'm going to get better."

"Of course you are," said Frank, "and here's your food."

"Lord, it smells good," said David. "Do be quick, nurse."

. . . . .

So there was house-supper at Adams's that night.

E.F. Benson
Paying Guests

New Introduction Stephen Pile

Bolton Spa is infamous for its nauseating brine and parsimonious boarding-houses. Exceptional is the Wentworth. Every summer this luxurious establishment is full of paying guests come to sample the waters and happy family atmosphere. But life in the house is far from a rest-cure. Acrimony and arthritis are the order of the day: battles are fought with pedometer, walking stick and paintbrush, at the bridge table, the town concert and afternoon tea. The trials and tribulations of the Wentworth will be relished in drawing-rooms throughout the land for years to come.

E.F. Benson
Mrs Ames

New Introduction by Stephen Pile

Mrs Ames is Queen of Riseborough society. Sceptre firmly grasped in her podgy little hand, she reigns supreme in a world of strawberry teas, high street gossip, and riotous insurrections by misguided pretenders such as Mrs Altham, Miss Brooks and dear cousin Millie. But her rule is threatened when, to the delight of her subjects, her husband's attentions stray from home and Mrs Ames, feeling all of her fifty-seven autumns, goes on the warpath. The series of restorative treatments – Shakespearian, feminist, but mostly out of a jar – with which she sets out to rewoo her gardening major are exquisitely chronicled in this comic masterpiece of provincial life.

E. F. Benson

Secret Lives

New Introduction by Stephen Pile

Durham Square seems the height of propriety; only the
rumblings of indigestion, the murmur of gossip and
occasional canine consternation threaten its dignity. But
behind the square's genteel façade hide secret lives.
There is Miss Susan Leg at No. 25, for instance: can a
woman who puts caviare on her scones be altogether
respectable? Riddled with curiosity, mordant pen in
hand, E.F. Benson draws aside the plush velvet drapes –
and reveals in this deliciously ironic novel all the hilarious intrigues and intimacies of life upstairs (and downstairs) in one of the stateliest squares in England.

E. F. Benson
The Freaks of Mayfair

New Introduction by Christopher Hawtree

Impaled on the pin of Benson's genius are prime specimens of Edwardian society: inveterate snobs and vicious gossips rolling up to receptions in Belgravia; young men with a taste for embroidery; health-cult devotees playing badminton in parquetted ballrooms; fossilised dowagers off to séances in Chesterfield Square. Here, in a fictional extravaganza, illustrated with the marvellous original line-drawings, are the bizarre, the great and the good E. F. Benson knew so well and all the forerunners of the unforgettable characters in his novels.

E.F. Benson
Dodo – An Omnibus

New Introduction by Prunella Scales

In this bumper edition of three of his most popular
novels, E.F. Benson introduces us to Dorothea 'Dodo'
Vane and the sparkling circle of her eccentric family and
friends. Beautiful, wilful, delightful, Dodo waltzes
through the turn of the century, trumping hearts as easily
as she does cards – but not without paying a price. The
Dodo trilogy is crowded with hilarious portraits of all the
luminous figures Benson mixed with in the salons and
stately homes of almost a hundred years ago; chronicling,
with inimitable wit and poignancy, a way of life, pri-
vileged, frivolous, entrancing, that crumbled under the
bombs of the Kaiser's zeppelins.

E. F. Benson

The Luck of the Vails

New Introduction by Stephen Knight

E. F. Benson is best known for his hilarious novels and
delightful memoirs, but he was also a grand teller of evil
tales. Set amid the rolling Wiltshire dales and the
clattering gaslit streets of London, *The Luck of the Vails*
reveals a long history of corruption and violence amongst
the old aristocracy. It is a vintage crime story.

E.F. Benson
The Blotting Book

New Introduction by Stephen Knight

Darkness falls in Sussex Square, Brighton, and Mrs Assheton's rosewood table gleams in the lamplight. Around it sit her guests; the port is passed, nuts are cracked – could there be a calmer scene? But all is not as it seems – and this tale of covert violence among the sleepy South Downs develops into a cunning criminal escapade, bristling with intriguing clues and gripping courtroom drama, and investigating the darker shadows of Benson's sparkling leisured world.

E. F. Benson
An Autumn Sowing

New Introduction by John Julius Norwich

Thomas Keeling, pillar of Bracebridge society, dwells at 'The Cedars', a spacious residence decorated with an eye for the gothic, and including in its furnishings such treasures as a small stuffed crocodile rampant holding a copper tray. But Keeling stalks unmoved through this opulence, cherishing instead a secret retreat, his book-lined study – and soon a secret passion. For his forceful young secretary, Norah, surprises him with a solitary glimpse of love. Buried feelings clash with the pompous surface of Benson's uniquely comic world in this poignant and extravagant classic.

T. C. Worsley
Flannelled Fool

A Slice of A Life in the Thirties

New Introduction by Alan Ross

This is the story of one young man's rude awakening from the innocence of a prolonged childhood (where hitting a six had been his wildest dream) into the turbulence of contemporary Europe – the rise of fascism in Italy and Germany, the purge of homosexuals, turmoil in Spain, and scandal at home. Like J. R. Ackerley's *My Father and Myself*, *Flannelled Fool* is remarkable for its rueful self-awareness, its hilarious anecdotes, its mirror to a whole generation. Long recognized as a classic portrait of youth in the Thirties – rushing with all its illusions and self-confidence into the crisis ahead – this haunting memoir is frank, funny and unforgettable.